NIGHTMARE BLOOD

Volume Four of *The Fallen*

K.N. Nguyen

ISBN-13 978-1-949322-15-6

To F.N.

You are my world

Thank you for everything

THE REALM OF
CORINTH

NIGHTMARE BLOOD

I

CLEAR SKIES BLANKETED the city of Fa'Tinh as the full moon shone brightly in the inky heavens. A myriad of stars twinkled against the dark backdrop. Crickets chirped as a warm breeze made its way through the empty streets of the capital. No lamps flickered that night. The only light came from the sky. Hroth walked through the city alone.

Fa'Tinh had been decimated in the fight that afternoon. Previously pristine shops were now crumbling, their detritus littering the ground below. Stones and clay lay in heaps while wooden beams jutted out into the sky. Their splintered ends were charred from the fire. In the center of the main square, the majestic fountain was in ruins, having collapsed in on itself. The tinkle of water splashing from the broken piping echoed in the stillness, reminding the Flame of his solitude.

His body ached with every step. Every so often, Hroth stopped to rest as his legs buckled, threatening to give way beneath him. Doubled over, the Flame gasped for breath as pain blossomed in his chest. He'd broken bones before and didn't doubt that he'd done it again. Every breath was agony.

A slender arm wound around his waist, supporting him as he struggled to push himself upright. Next to him, Maen met his gaze with concerned eyes as she tried to help him. Even in the darkness, her deep brown eyes drew him in. With a grunt, he righted himself and continued walking through the darkened streets.

He wanted to get away from the tavern, away from the crowd. Though they weren't celebrating, Hroth still found it hard to join everyone else. He'd failed. The concept was foreign to him. To accept defeat was to die; that was the way of the Myrani. That was what he hoped would happen one day. To die at the hands of a god would free him from all the evil he had done. To save him from the memories. He fought to save others this time, not just earn a few coin. And he had failed. He couldn't even die properly.

The steadily building chatter of the Dancing Wolf spilled out into the otherwise quiet square, her many lamps flooding the darkness with their warm glow. And so he continued on towards the silence. Towards the darkness. Maen supported him with each step.

His inner fire burned low, stoked by his energies as he tried to keep himself conscious. The strength of the gods was truly terrifying. Wyrd had overpowered him, and as the Qu'ari's flames washed over Hroth's flesh, visions of death and destruction threatened to overwhelm him. Countless futures played out in his head, each more gruesome than the last.

"We have to clear out Xan," he rasped. His gravelly voice sounded hoarse in the stillness.

"What?" Maen asked. Hroth felt her body shift his direction a bit as she turned to look at him.

"The gods have shown me something. After all that's happened, we would be foolish to ignore it. We must take everyone somewhere else. Pharn perhaps. The Ras Mountains could provide us with an escape route if we need it."

"But –" Maen's protests died on her lips as she met his steady gaze.

Hroth held her with his eyes, trying to convey the seriousness of what he saw. Words could not describe what possibly lay in store. He knew that if they were going to survive, they needed to act fast. To his relief, Maen did not question him further, her gaze steeling as her resolve formed.

"Let's go back," she suggested. "The Great Heart needs to be made aware of this. Perhaps Wyrd can give us an idea of where we'd be safe. If anyone else understands what you saw, it would be him."

The Flame shuffled from one foot to the other, shifting his weight as he tried to relieve some of the pain in his chest. She was right. He knew it. Hroth just wasn't ready to return to the crowd. There was something about spending time by himself that drew him to the darkness. He let out a non-committal grunt. Suddenly, he realized he was thirsty as his throat felt scratchy. Maybe a nice mug of beer would do the trick. He could also use this as an opportunity to gather more information. There were plenty of known sources he could draw from.

"Or, maybe..."

"No, let's head back," Hroth said. "Just give me a moment in the darkness."

Maen released her hold on Hroth and slipped out from under his arm. He felt himself wobble a bit as he readjusted himself so he could support his weight. Once he felt steady, Hroth took a few steps into the blackness. Closing his eye, he let the night envelope him. It was pleasantly warm that night. It reminded him of his childhood on the coast.

Imaginary wind rustled his hair as he sat on the docks, his feet dangling over the water and catching the spray as the sea waves crashed against the poles supporting him. Gulls cried overhead, breaking the gentle monotony of the sounds of the ocean. Men in small boats dotted the waters as they fished, while the occasional balinger pulled into the harbor.

One of the rugged sailors called out to him, his gruff voice rising over the noise of the gulls. As usual, Hroth ignored him. Old Petre was always hounding him to help unload the fish or get off the docks; he said they didn't have time to watch a kid like him. The local strays liked to join him as he watched all the action, the sun beating down on him, tanning his flesh.

Hroth opened his eyes and found himself surrounded by darkness once more. The sound and smell of the sea still lingered around him, his body hanging onto the residual heat, as he returned to the stillness of Fa'Tinh. The calls of the fishermen were replaced with the growing chatter from the Dancing Wolf. With a sigh, he turned and slowly made his way back to Maen. She slipped her arm back around his waist and helped guide him back to the tavern.

As they left the area, Hroth felt a warm, salty breeze rustle his hair as a gull cried overhead.

A light layer of foam tickled his lips as Hroth took a long draught of beer. He was pleased to feel the calm reassurance that greeted him and his empty stomach. Hroth missed the dizzying effects of stronger drinks, but this worked nicely. He took another drink before reaching over to a nearby plate and pulling it over, digging into the lamb and lentils over rice with enthusiasm.

The lamb's juices created an explosion of flavor in his mouth, making it water despite his vigorous chewing. Rosemary and black pepper mixed together with garlic and cumin beautifully. Though he'd been staying in Fa'Tinh for a while now, he always marveled at the way the seasoning was so strong, yet there was a subtle hint of something delicate underneath. The food was surprisingly still warm. Glancing around, Hroth realized that the barmaids were still rushing around, bringing fresh plates to the tables. They were, however, slowing down as the night dragged on. More and more of them seemed to be refilling tankards and wine glasses.

"What is it?"

Hroth felt his stomach jump into his chest as he turned to face the voice. Years of training with the Myrani taught him how to remain in control despite being startled.

Pram faced him, his wife sitting to his left, as the children now ran around with Len's and Maen's. The general caught his gaze. His brows were knotted in concern. Hroth found himself turning towards Len. He felt Pram's eyes follow him. The Flame allowed himself to look at the Xanan leader for several seconds before breaking away and turning back to face the general.

Now it was Pram's turn to direct Hroth's attention. The two shared a glance at Wyrd. The man was bound tightly, his hands tied behind his back while his legs were secured at the ankle. Another rope connected Wyrd's neck to his ankles, preventing him from escaping. The man, however, seemed uninterested in breaking free. His one orange eye was becoming a dull orange brown, the change in color disconcerting the Flame. He knew Wyrd no longer held the gift of Fyre, but seeing the physical effects bothered him.

Wyrd looked up and caught Pram and Hroth's eye. A feral grin broke out as he held their gaze. The shiny patch of skin around his orange-brown eye did not wrinkle like the other. Instead, both held an intense hunger as he stared at them. As quickly as he flashed the look, it faded away as Wyrd turned to look away from them. However, Hroth got the message clearly: his bloodlust had not been sated. Wyrd had tasted power and wanted more.

"Time is short," Hroth said. "Can you convince him to empty Xan?"

Pram sputtered in surprise, unable to form a cohesive sentence. Hroth waited while the general worked to formulate a response. Taking another bite to fill the silence, the Flame chewed slowly. The fact that the normally composed general struggled to respond unnerved Hroth more than he cared to admit. He forced himself to maintain his usual air of aloofness, using that façade to take in everything. Finally, Pram seemed to find his tongue.

"What do you mean 'empty Xan'?" he whispered, leaning in closely. "Where would we take them? How long would we even need to be gone?"

Resting on his elbow, Hroth mimicked Pram's motions and moved in closer. He tried to keep his appearance casual should anyone glance their way. "Do you remember that thing we encountered outside of Swordbane's mother's home? The thing that made the air around us freezing?"

Pram nodded, taking his cue from the Flame and staring out among the many faces of the crowded tavern. He reached down for a piece of buttered bread with rosemary on it and took a bite, feigning disinterest in their conversation.

"In my battle with Wyrd, I saw things Vahnyre has been trying to fill my head with for years. He tries to seduce those of us with a predisposition towards fyre with the promise of glory and riches. Obviously, most of us resist the temptation. However," Hroth felt his gaze momentarily dart to Wyrd. The man sat with his back to the wall, seemingly unbothered by his captivity. "Not all can ignore his pull. Whatever that *thing* is, it's part of the Darkness."

"What in Freyna's name is the darkness?" Pram muttered.

"*The Darkness*," Hroth said, stressing the importance of the word. "I almost feel as though this is his final objective. There's something the aethren wants that he can't physically do on his own, so he uses other proxies to achieve his desires. Whatever was in the woods that day is still out there, and I doubt it's alone. Xan is not safe. We must leave. Soon."

"Where? Who would take us in?"

Hroth looked over at the table with the Avalanche. He spoke with the chestnut-haired young captain who sat next to the princess. The two men were engaged in conversation, much like Hroth and Pram. No doubt it was important. Out of the corner of his eye, the Flame caught Pram watching them as well.

"We do have an alliance with them," Pram said slowly.

"You told me you would do anything to keep your people safe," Hroth said. "Talk to him. There is no time left."

He felt the general heave a massive sigh that was lost to the sea of voices that filled the tavern. As one, the two moved away from each other and resumed their normal seated position. Hroth took another bite of his meal before washing it down with the last of his drink. He watched Pram talk to his wife briefly before moving over to speak with Swordbane.

His body felt lethargic as the calming effects of the alcohol took a firm hold on him. No doubt he'd feel it in the morning once it all wore off. Hroth knew he'd face it when it came. It wouldn't be the first time.

The Flame's eyes scanned the tavern once more. Barmaids still moved quickly, now clearing the tables instead of bringing things out. The chatter began to die down as exhaustion blanketed the room. Even the pirates that came with Swordbane through the Tempest's portal were remarkably subdued compared to the ones he knew from his childhood. The Bone Coast was not known for its peace and quiet.

Children rested against their mothers, their heads lolling to the side as they slept. Even baby Heru slept soundly in Zaa'ni's arms. Hroth felt an uncharacteristic warmth fill him as he observed Swordbane tenderly stroking his son's chubby cheek. Pride shone in his eyes as he stared at the slumbering infant. Hroth couldn't remember the last time he'd seen his father. The man was a miserable drunk who beat his mother mercilessly before finally abandoning them. He liked to think his father fell off one of the docks late at night.

The soldiers from Pharn were trickling out of the Dancing Wolf in twos and threes. The darkness called to him, pulling him from the light of the tavern and into her embrace. Taking a moment to look for Maen, he found her trapped in her chair, her three children all draped over her, fast asleep. A smile tugged at his lips. With a word to Pram, the Flame pushed himself gingerly out of his chair and shuffled out the door.

Stars sparkled in the heavens, blinking merrily at everyone as they slept safe in their homes. Hroth felt a pang of sorrow as he hobbled into the broken main square. They'd managed to avoid too much unnecessary death during their fighting that afternoon, and for the most part, they succeeded. He couldn't even imagine the carnage that lay in store for them.

Hroth had been so convinced that they needed to go to Pharn for safety. What if he was wrong? He didn't want to think about that.

This is only the beginning, he told himself.

Wincing with each step, Hroth made his way in the darkness to his room on the outskirts of the city. Tapping into his energies, Hroth smirked as he snuffed out the fires in the few street lamps that lined the street. He preferred to walk in complete darkness that night. He wanted to find a way to just disappear.

II

THE NIGHT DRAGGED ON, the conversations never seeming to end in the Dancing Wolf. Alverick felt his eyelids growing heavy and his mind sluggish as the hours slowly passed. Red haze still tinged his vision, but as he got food in his body, it began to gradually recede until it was little more than a faint ring he could ignore. He knew he really shouldn't ignore it, but it was the least of his worries at this time.

To his right, Caitlyn slumped against his shoulder. Her body moved gently as she breathed rhythmically, her eyes closed. He assumed that she was sleeping, but she'd been like that for most of their time at the Wolf. Alverick tried several times to get her to eat something, but Caitlyn refused, moving her head to the side with each proffered bit.

"When will you be able to tell if she's Snapped?" Brody asked, leaning in.

The two spent most of the night going over everything they could remember about the battle. Neither had been around when Caitlyn collapsed on the ground. There had been so much going on, they couldn't even remember when her bolts stopped. Not even the princess could pinpoint the exact moment that Caitlyn fired her last blast.

Alverick glanced at the redhead nervously. When she was brought to them by one of the pirates, she barely appeared to be conscious. Her lips moved rapidly as she mumbled something, but if she spoke, it was too quiet for him to hear. It was the same as when they sat in the tavern: soft mutterings, but nothing he could make out.

"She could just be exhausted, but I highly doubt it." The Avalanche's shoulders slumped as he stroked her hair. A faint murmur escaped her lips, but he still couldn't make it out. It frustrated him so much. "Tomorrow we should know."

"Are you going to be okay?" Brody asked.

The Avalanche shook his head, his eyes closing as if shielding himself from the truth. "I'll be fine." Alverick let the silence stretch between them. "What about you?" he asked suddenly. "I see the tension between you."

It was Brody's turn to close his eyes as he shook his head. Something within him cracked. His normally sparkling eyes appeared shrouded as the corners of his mouth drew down. The young captain busied his hands with a nearby fork as he fought to retain his composure.

"I must do what's best for her," he said simply, his eyes staring down at the spot where his plate had been earlier in the evening. "It was fun pretending that we could have built a life together, but deep down, I knew it wasn't possible. Cie — the princess, she's young. She doesn't understand. But I know better. If I keep this up, I'm just hurting us both in the end."

"There aren't many suitors available to her," Alverick tried to reason. "A few her father's age but not many else."

"Thanks, but we both know that if things with the Oldar don't work out there's a handful of young lords who would jump at the chance to marry a princess. The lines in Corinth are dying out, Al. If things don't turn around, they'll have to start looking to whatever lies beyond the waters."

"Maybe our new friends can help us with that," Alverick replied, nodding towards Ghan and the pirates.

Brody shot his friend a pained look before trying to give him a playful shove. Alverick rolled with the motion, almost forgetting for a moment that Caitlyn slept on him. Unfortunately, it was too late. The redhead toppled over, falling into the princess, who struggled to catch her in her shock.

"What the hell are ya doing?" Caitlyn slurred as she was jolted awake. "You scared me, dammit."

"Cait!" Alverick gasped. He could hear Brody's chair scrape against the aged wooden floor as he moved to face the two of them. "You're fine!"

"I wouldn't say I'm fine," she scowled as she righted herself, Cienna gently guiding her upright. The redhead rubbed her head as though she'd hit it. "I feel like complete shite."

"We thought you Snapped," Brody blurted out.

Alverick felt his stomach knot as he heard the words. Even with her being okay, hearing his fears verbalized was difficult. Caitlyn stared at the two, incredulous. Behind her, Cienna's eyes were wide.

"But we were talking for a bit before she fell asleep," Cienna replied. "We were talking about how exhausted we were after everything."

Caitlyn nodded, sending a wave of relief washing through him. Though he'd been sitting next to her the entire time, Alverick hadn't noticed her engage the princess in conversation. He'd heard Caitlyn talking, but her voice was so soft and easily lost in the din, he thought she was just mumbling. The princess rested her hand on the redhead's arm comfortingly. It pleased him to see that the two had grown so close.

"We should probably find a place for you to rest them," Alverick finally said. "We're both probably a hair's breadth from Snapping and need to recover. Gods know it'd be a hell of a joke if we made it this far and then –" Alverick snapped his fingers. His vision was still a bit hazy, and he wasn't sure how far he was from his limits.

Mercifully, Caitlyn agreed and he too pushed their chairs away from the table before they got up. The tavern had been emptying slowly as the night dragged on, but there were still a considerable number of bodies milling about. Most of the clansmen had already left, leaving mainly the forces from Pharn and the group Swordbane brought through the portal with Dez behind.

Alverick scanned the room, his eyes passing over his men as they began slouching in their chairs. More than a few were draped over the table, either passed out from exhaustion or a night of drinking. The men who accompanied Swordbane, however, appeared as hearty as ever, their group being responsible for the noise. The two women who sat with them spoke to each other, the red-headed woman Alverick recognized as Kayna breaking away to share in a bark of laughter with her crew. Alverick felt his face flush as he thought she locked eyes with him. He almost could've sworn that she flashed him a quick smile before turning back to the woman at her side.

A tight embrace. Kayna's lithe body warm beneath him. The soft moans of ecstasy escaping her lips as sweat beaded on the two of them. Alverick couldn't help it as his mouth twitched upward as he recalled that night.

Hopefully Caitlyn never meets Kayna, Alverick prayed. *The last thing she needs right now is for me to see her. How did Swordbane even convince her to join him?* Alverick struggled for a few moments before finally reaching his decision. *I'll have to find time to speak with her. I hope Brody can keep her busy.*

His eyes finally wandered over to the main table. Swordbane and his general sat with their families, Alverick presumed. The Flame had already left with a young woman, and the two remaining families battled sleep. A slew of children lay passed out at the table, their mothers cradling them as best they could.

Swordbane sat with his arms crossed across his chest, observing the room. His eyes darted from the pirates to Alverick's group, much like Alverick's had moments earlier. Beside him, Pram appeared much more relaxed as he took a draught from his mug. Behind them, Wyrd, the Qu'ari man they'd fought earlier that day, leaned against the wall, asleep.

"We should probably ask Swordbane where we should stay," Brody said.

Alverick turned to face the young captain. "Yes, that's what I was thinking." Returning his attention to Swordbane, Alverick felt a sudden wave of foreboding wash over him. He scanned the table, trying to find what made him uncomfortable. His eyes passed by Wyrd, still sleeping against the wall.

He's listening, Alverick realized. Watching the man closely, the Avalanche realized that his body didn't rise and fall in the rhythmic pattern of sleep. *What's his end game?*

To his left, Alverick saw Brody make his way towards the main table. Taking one last glance at Wyrd, Alverick followed. Eyes tracked the two soldiers as they made their way through the tavern. Alverick felt a swell of relief as he realized he couldn't feel the girls tailing them. They decided to wait at the table with the rest of Pharn's forces.

"Al, you should speak with him," Brody said, keeping his voice down as they passed by a few people. "I think he would respect you better since you fought with both him and his right-hand man."

The Avalanche nodded as the table quickly loomed ahead. Swordbane and his general's eyes locked on the two as they approached. Swordbane's gaze narrowed as Brody positioned himself a step behind Alverick and softly cleared his throat.

Beside Swordbane, Pram pushed his braids, which he wore in a tail, off of his shoulders. His face relaxed into a smile.

"What brings you to Evenhand's table?"

Swordbane laced his hands together, his eyes locked on Alverick. The Avalanche couldn't help but watch the Qu'ari leader. The man was scrutinizing them, taking them in with a hungry gaze. A smirk played on Swordbane's lips as he read their faces.

"We wanted to thank you for your hospitality and offer our condolences to your fallen brothers." Alverick tried to focus on the general, but his eyes kept darting back to Swordbane. "We were hoping that you might be able to provide us with quarters for our men to rest for a night or two to regain our strength. Our magi are exhausted to the point of near Snapping, which could be devastating for everyone. If you could spare a few rooms, it would be greatly appreciated."

Pram sat back, waiting for his leader to respond. Swordbane unlaced his fingers as he motioned for the two to sit. Alverick and Brody cautiously took a seat, their chairs scraping the ground. The Avalanche took a deep breath and placed his hands on the table, his palms flat against the surface, in hopes of displaying his openness. He needed Swordbane to be willing to honor their alliance. Next to him, Brody shifted in his seat.

"I must say, I never thought I would be happy to see you, Avalanche," Swordbane began. "Out of all of my opponents, you've proven to be my most challenging. And yet, I find myself excited to see you once more. If these were different times, nothing would please me more than to settle the score. However, the bones have changed and we must face the new challenges. My people owe you and yours a debt of gratitude, and we do not skip out on our debts. You and your men are welcome to stay here for the two days needed to recover. I will have the owner of the Wolf grant you food and lodging. Tomorrow, we will discuss what comes next."

"Your generosity is much appreciated," Alverick said. He needed to make sure Swordbane felt as though he had the upper hand. Too much rested on how the next couple of days went. "Respectfully, we will be withdrawing for the night. Our men have traveled far, and after the battle this afternoon, I'm sure they're wiped out."

"Until tomorrow then." Swordbane motioned for the two to leave.

As one, Brody and Alverick scraped their chairs on the floor once more as they stood up and made to leave the table. Alverick spared one last look behind him towards Wyrd. The Qu'ari man opened his eyes and smirked at the Avalanche. His grin was the same hungry, feral one from that afternoon. A shiver ran down his spine as he made eye contact with the man. He forced himself to not react as he pulled his eyes away from the man.

"Do you think he will honor the alliance?" Brody asked, his voice could barely be heard over the noise in the tavern. "And did you see his friend?"

Alverick nodded. "I don't trust him," he replied. "But I believe that Swordbane is a man of his word. I don't see him giving any more than he has to. He should keep his friend under control."

"I don't think Swordbane even trusts his friend. The two didn't exactly have an amicable end to their relationship."

A snort escaped Alverick despite himself. "Perhaps the two will deal with each other, so we don't have much to worry about."

"If only it was so simple."

The two made their way to the head of their table and addressed their men. It had been a while since they had something to sleep on. Alverick knew they would have a good night tonight.

III

Dawn arrived, but Alverick felt more tired than he had before falling asleep. His mind swam and the ever-present red haze that tinged his peripherals was becoming more and more common. Its familiar presence no longer worried him like it had. As long as it didn't get much bigger. Warm sunlight streamed in through the curtainless windows, blinding him as it glared into his eyes. With a groan, Alverick rolled over and covered his head with a pillow, a luxury he had not experienced in a while.

Beside him, several soldiers began to stir as the sunlight hit their eyes. Those who were now awake grumbled and swore as they tried to shield themselves from the beautiful day greeting them. Like Alverick, they could only sigh as their grogginess faded and they woke up.

The nearby choir of birds disappeared as Fa'Tinh began bustling. The music quickly became overshadowed by distressed voices trying to figure out how to repair their shop or home. Alverick felt a pang of guilt knowing that he was partially to blame for the damage. More than one voice lamented their loss, while others tried to comfort them.

The road to healing begins now. I wish it wasn't so long. There're too many innocents.

Rubbing his face with the heel of his palm, Alverick tried to clear away some of the cloudiness that muddled his mind before rolling out of bed. Despite sleeping on the floor, he was pleased to find a smooth surface devoid of debris to rest on. The few extra blankets he was given allowed for him to create a small barrier against the ground, not much thinner than his normal barrack cot. He hadn't expected such generous accommodations.

Glancing at his comrades, Alverick saw that many still slept, while those who were rudely woken up somehow managed to fall back asleep. Brody lay curled in a corner by the door; no doubt he'd acted as watch the night before. The Avalanche's eyes scanned the room. The princess lay on an actual mattress, one of the few that had been brought over, surrounded by no less than eight men who now were sleeping deeply.

I hope Brody let them rest, Alverick mused. *Sleeping guards even in one's own home are dangerous. They better not have fallen asleep on duty. They should've woken me.*

Despite his annoyance, Alverick was fairly confident that multiple orders had been given explicitly warning the others to not disturb him or Caitlyn, whom he was pleased to see was still sleeping. Deep down, he was happy for the chance to rest.

The Avalanche made his way through the tavern as quietly as he could. He was surprised to see Kayna coming out of a back room, her arms raised overhead as she stretched. The woman made eye contact with Alverick and picked up her pace. A smile played on her lips. Dread filled his stomach as he motioned for her to stay quiet until they got outside. Dread, and excitement.

"I thought it was you," the pirate said as she shielded her eyes from the bright light outside. "At first, I wasn't sure, but after that look you gave me last night, I knew it was you. Care for another go? We both left quite pleased, if I remember correctly."

Alverick felt his face flush once more. Somehow, the woman always managed to get to him. "No," he said simply.

"Come on," she pouted, touching his arm gently. "I can't be the only one who had a good time."

"No. No, you were... insatiable." It felt wrong admitting their night together. He'd spent so long trying to forget it.

"It's hard to not miss the company of men."

"You're surrounded by men all the time," Alverick said incredulously.

"Yes, but it's not the same," Kayna replied with the wave of her hand. "You were new. Different. Exciting. You satisfied me in a way they don't. Besides, there's that little thing of the Scourge being my father. No one wants to disappoint where the Lord of the Pirates is involved." Her tone took on a wistful quality as she ran her hand through her hair trying to get tangles out. "But you," she said, this time more softly. "You were different."

The pirate met his gaze. There was a tenderness in her eyes that held him captive. In many ways, she was not much different from Caitlyn. Headstrong, capable, determined. Despite what he told himself, he had been intrigued by her. Her forwardness, the way she invited him into her bed. Part of him had wanted to explore the feisty woman.

Kayna bit her lip, a playful smirk pulling at the corners of her mouth as she stared deeply into his eyes. In so many ways, she was someone he desired. His mind flashed back to their night together. There was a frenzied passion between the two of them. Though his mind swam with his newfound Spark powers, he wanted that moment. Alverick then found himself remembering his time with Averna once he'd returned from the outer isles. She had been so young and innocent, yet he gave in to her took her like he took the pirate. Both were clouded by a sea of red. As he stared into her eyes, he realized that only one filled him with regret.

"Kayna, I can't," he said finally, breaking her stare.

"Why not?" The pirate leaned forward, her chest almost touching his. Dropping her voice to a whisper, she added, "It'll be just you and me. No one will know."

Alverick felt himself move closer, his feet almost stepping into the young woman's space as his arms twitched in anticipation of holding her.

"No," he said more forcefully, causing the momentum that was building within him to suddenly halt. "I can't betray her again." Though he didn't mention Caitlyn's name, he was sure Kayna knew who he was talking about. "I am her Anchor, as much as she is mine. If I, if we were to do it again, it would be devastating. She'd Snap."

The pirate took a big step back as she studied him. The Avalanche stood there awkwardly as her eyes went over his entire body. Some of his men trickled out of the Wolf in ones and twos, shooting him an amused look as they walked by. Every time the door opened, he breathed a silent sigh of relief, as it wasn't Caitlyn.

Finally, Kayna broke into a wide grin and punched him on the arm. "Gods, Alverick, I don't know what you've gotten yourself into, but I don't want to be responsible for someone Snapping. Just remember, the offer is still there."

The pirate gently touched his cheek, the tips of her fingers lingering on his flesh as she walked by. A thrill ran through him as he watched her saunter off. Alverick couldn't help but watch her as she disappeared into the slowly growing morning crowd.

As her red hair vanished among the sea of bodies, Alverick took the time to survey the damage done in the square the other day. Bits of rubble and charred buildings stood silently in the bright morning light. Skeletons stood as a monument to the carnage from the day before. On the cobbles under the shadow of one of the ruins, a black stain marred the smooth stones from where the aethren and Wyrd had been.

Alverick found himself walking over to examine the destruction. His fingers trailed along the splintered shards of wood and broken stones. The sound of clashing phantom weapons rang in the air, along with the screams. A woman clutching her baby tightly to her chest flashed in his mind, stumbling around in a daze as she gasped for breath. Behind her, dark pillars of smoke filled the air as the orange flames licked the building. As he watched her tear-streaked face rub her baby's back, he felt the ground beneath his feet roil and buckle once more. His head snapped up as he looked around. The Avalanche's eyes scanned his surroundings, looking to see if anyone else felt the trembling. No one else appeared to have noticed.

"Focus," he told himself.

Closing his eyes, Alverick took a deep breath and forced himself to picture Caitlyn. Her glassed, emerald eyes popped up, devoid of recognition.

"No," he muttered as he shook his head, eyes still closed.

His breathing became ragged as he thought of Bannen. His friend's face filled his mind, Bannen's ghostly eyes darting around.

"Help me, Bannen," Alverick whispered.

"Control yourself, Al," Bannen's voice replied.

Alverick opened his eyes and found himself standing in the dark fields with Bannen. The gnarled branches of nearby trees reached their twisted limbs into the night sky. A sliver of the moon illuminated the darkness around him.

"Bannen?" Alverick was surprised to hear the trembling in his voice. "Are we in…?"

"What are you doing, Al?"

Alverick's eyes popped open. He let out a gasp of surprise as the blinding light of the sun caused his eyes to water. Scanning his surroundings, Alverick found himself next to the burnt ruins in the main square once more. Bannen and the skeletal trees were nowhere to be seen. As his eyes adjusted to the light, he found Brody standing beside him, a look of concern on his face.

"I'm fine," he replied. "Just remembering the day my parents died."

Unbidden, his mind was filled with images of his mother and father, both crushed under the stones of their old home as flames burned the buildings of Loast. The scent of burnt flesh filled his nostrils. It had been years since Alverick thought about his parents. He could hear the screams in the distance once more. A tear welled in the corner of his eye as his lie brought up these visions from his past.

Brody's hand squeezed the Avalanche's shoulder as he moved closer to his friend. Behind the young man, Alverick watched as a few of their comrades stopped to briefly stare at them before moving on. The Xanans paid the two no mind. Alverick observed them going around the square, the women dressed in all black with cloths draped over their heads, picking up the rubble. Every once in a while, a keening wail could be heard as more bodies were pulled from the ruins.

The Avalanche felt his stomach clench as the slight frame of a woman or child, he couldn't tell which, was pulled from a nearby building. Her clothes were charred and torn, with dried blood smeared on her flesh, and rustled in the wind as a Qu'ari man gently held her limp form in his arms. The man spoke to Pram, who was walking through the square providing instructions to his kinfolk as they continued their search efforts.

"Really?" Brody asked, his voice questioning. "You're slipping away, Al. I don't want to lose you."

Alverick's attention was brought back to the young man in front of him. Brody stared at him, his eyes earnest, almost pleading with Alverick to say what he wanted to hear.

"Why haven't I ever thought of you as my Anchor?"

"What?" Brody took a step back, startled by the abrupt question.

"Why haven't I ever thought of you as my Anchor?" Alverick repeated. Brody's brows threatened to disappear into his bangs as he struggled to respond. "You and Bannen have been like family to me. As much as Fren, anyway. He's always guided me when I needed him, but you — I don't know why I never thought of you." Alverick's voice trailed off as his mind began to wander. The Avalanche turned and began to walk away, but Brody's strong grip pulled him back.

"Make me your Anchor." Alverick blinked, surprised by the insistence in the young man's voice as he squeezed the Avalanche's arm. "We need you, Al, and you've been like a brother to me. If I can keep you from Snapping, I will."

"I will."

Brody smiled at his friend before turning to head back. There was a council with the other heads to discuss what was coming next. No doubt, the young man went to find Ronan and Thul to go over plans before addressing the council. Alverick couldn't help but feel his stomach knot in guilt. He would've given anything to have more Anchors. Unfortunately, it didn't work that way.

IV

A TANGLE OF HAIR AND BEDSHEETS greeted the princess as she woke up. Cienna spit out a clump of hair and rubbed her eyes, stretching as she yawned. The Dancing Wolf was relatively empty, only a few soldiers standing watch nearby to make sure she was safe. Even Caitlyn's mop of red hair couldn't be seen as she pushed herself off of the bed and began scanning the room.

I'm glad people thought to wait for me to get up before starting their day, she grumbled to herself. Despite sleeping on a borrowed collection of cushions, Cienna's body ached from her previous exertions.

Cienna moved to get up, but quickly sat back down as her head swam and her legs felt weak. She felt her heart flutter as her body would not support her weight. A groan involuntarily escaped her as the princess worked to regain her composure. She'd used too much energy the day before during their fight with the Pshwani. Cienna wasn't prepared for the toll her exertions took on her body and how feeble it made her feel.

"Gods, I feel like shite." Her voice came out as a whine as she buried her face in her hands. Waves of curly blonde hair spilled over her shoulders, creating a curtain that dangled in front of her.

"Is that any way for a princess to talk?"

Cienna's head shot up, her heart racing in her chest, as her face burned in embarrassment. *How could I be so undignified?* she chastised herself. *I can't believe I —*

"Oh gods, Caitlyn. It's just you." The princess found herself smiling as she stared at the redhead's bemused expression.

"I'm sorry to disappoint you, Waterbug."

Like Cienna, Caitlyn was grinning back at her. The princess found herself awash in relief as she gazed into the archer's emerald eyes. Unlike the night before, they were clear once more. She had feared that after everything they'd been through, Caitlyn had Snapped. Cienna recalled Alverick's glazed look from when he was brought back to Pharn. It'd been a long time since she'd seen the haunted expression of one whose mind had been torn asunder by the power of the gods.

"I'm sorry, Caitlyn. I didn't mean it that way."

"I know you didn't."

The redhead crossed the room and plopped onto the makeshift bed next to the princess. Caitlyn glanced away and stared down at her feet. Cienna watched as the redhead sat uncomfortably, obviously struggling with whatever she was about to say next. Before she knew it, the princess gently grasped Caitlyn's hand and held it lightly against the cushion. Cienna followed the redhead's eyes as she looked up from her feet to their hands.

"Thank you," the redhead finally said. "I heard what you and the others did for me yesterday. I don't really remember much, I blacked out after a while, but from what everyone told me, you were there for me, caring for me. Thank you."

Cienna gave the woman's hand a light squeeze. "I was so worried about you." The princess was surprised to hear her voice come out as a whisper. "I never thought I'd see someone Snap like that. But somehow, you managed to hold onto your Anchor." Cienna paused, unsure of how to ask her question. "Do you... how do you... what do you use for your Anchor?"

Caitlyn's face flushed and her eyes dropped once more. "I used what I always have," she replied softly. "Alverick."

"But you're in this situation because of him."

Caitlyn nodded.

"Why? How?"

"In the beginning, I was so mad. He was all I could think of. Not only did he bed that pirate, but Fren's barmaid as well." The princess' eyes widened at this revelation. "All I could think about was showing him that he was wrong. Well, when I almost Snapped after draughting the man I got drunk, I tried to focus on Al to help me get through. And every time since, whenever the red haze has gotten too strong, I think of him and it goes away. Never completely, but enough that I don't feel like I'm losing myself anymore."

"That's incredible," Cienna breathed. "To be honest, I've never had to worry about that. When I first took the trial to see if I was worthy, I remember the Headmistress telling me to still my heart and remain calm. She said that if my heart is pure, I have nothing to fear. Although, she did mention focusing on something that made me happy."

"It's easier, I'm sure, if you do it with people who know what they're doing." For the briefest of moments, Caitlyn's eyes had a haunted look, as though she suddenly remembered some unseen horror. The expression was fleeting, but the princess caught it. "But enough about that. Come. I believe Brody is looking for you. I saw him talking with Al earlier."

Cienna's face flushed. It had been a few days since she'd managed to find time to talk to Brody. After they kissed on their return to Pharn, she'd hoped he would be more affectionate to her. Instead, her bodyguard dove into his duties with a renewed vigor, most likely because Brody had some big shoes to fill with Alverick and Bannen gone.

Without thinking, Cienna tried to get off her bed once more. Her vision swam and her body wobbled as her legs threatened to give out from under her once more. The princess staggered forward, a gasp escaping her as she began to fall, but a pair of sturdy hands caught her.

"Easy now," Caitlyn said as she slowly helped Cienna upright. "I got ya."

The redhead's hands never left the princess' body as she waited for Cienna to become stable. Cienna noticed that Caitlyn spoke to her in a soft, soothing voice.

"If only you spoke to the horses like this," Cienna said, almost in jest.

A hint of color rushed to the redhead's cheeks as a sheepish grin tugged on the corners of her mouth.

"You do!" Cienna blurted out.

"Forgive me, Waterbug," Caitlyn said. "It's a habit."

"Who would've imagined that daunting Caitlyn is actually a gentle spirit underneath that gruff exterior?" The princess laughed as the redhead gave her a shove, causing Cienna to collapse into the sheets.

"I can't just bark at wild horses. They'd never trust me if I did," Caitlyn finally countered. "I'm allowed to be sensitive and caring. I wasn't always withdrawn."

"I know," Cienna said, sitting back up and grabbing the redhead's hand. "You're a good person, but you've been through so much. I'll never forget it. Zanir will never forget it. I'll make sure that Mother gives you everything you deserve."

Red blossomed on Caitlyn's pale face as she began rubbing the back of her tattooed hand. "That's all right, Waterbug. I don't need any special recognition."

Before the conversation could go any further, a man stuck his head into the room and said something in Qu'arn. The two women stared at him, their eyes widening in confusion as he stared at them. The man raised a brow, his eyes boring into them. When the two didn't respond, he repeated his question, the deep baritone of his voice eliciting the same response as before.

"I'm sorry, but we don't speak Qu'arn," Cienna offered feebly. "Perhaps if you spoke the Common Tongue we could communicate better?"

A scowl crossed his face and he spun around, muttering in rapid Qu'arn to himself. A door shut loudly in another room, causing a different voice to bark out something. Cienna was amused to hear one of the few, less dignified words of the Qu'ari language that she could recognize from her father's lessons.

Cienna couldn't help but share a look with Caitlyn. The princess was relieved to see the same perplexed expression on the redhead's face as her own. After an uncomfortable pause, Caitlyn let out a small bark of laughter, breaking the silence.

"By the gods, I thought that everyone knew Common Tongue. Guess we've just been lucky thus far having everyone know the main language of Corinth."

The princess nodded in agreement. Deep down, she knew she shouldn't be surprised that there were still people who were unfamiliar with the common language. On several occasions, Jaste had hired someone to translate missives to Ayobami or the other mountain tribesmen. Why did that man speaking only his native tongue confuse her so?

"I did too..." Cienna trailed off. Her mind went to her mother. Before they left on this journey, she had been so sure that the queen did not understand the needs of Zanir, and especially Pharn. Seeing her mom managing relationships with the different realms as if it were second nature left Cienna both in awe of her mother and disappointed that she doubted her. The princess felt just as confused then as she did now. "But maybe I am a little short-sighted in how I see the world," she mumbled.

A tear rolled down her cheek as Cienna sat on the makeshift bed. The blankets she'd slept under were now bunched up in her hands, her knuckles turning white as she fought back the urge to cry. Her eyes burned, but she fought down the emotion. Everyone around her seemed to be growing up — everyone but her.

"Waterbug?" Caitlyn asked softly.

Taking a moment to wipe away the moisture that rimmed her eyes and the solitary tear that now dangled off her jawline, the princess turned to look at her friend. Though she knew her eyes would be red, she was thankful for her mother's darker skin to keep her nose from shining as well. She could no longer act like a child. It was time for action.

"I'm fine," Cienna whispered. "I just needed a moment to compose myself." Her voice came out stronger as she spoke. "Now, let's go and find something to eat before we speak with the Great Heart. We need to figure out how we'll be moving forward with everything."

~~~

As Cienna sat outside the Dancing Wolf eating a piece of flatbread with cheese, a peach resting on her lap, she watched as the Great Heart's people struggled to clean up after the fight from the day before. It pained her to see the buildings and homes burnt and crumbling around her. Many of the Qu'ari she saw were wounded, the rest kept their heads down as tears streamed down their faces.

Young families worked together with the elderly to try and sift through the debris, with soldiers and even members of her royal forces rushing in to help lift collapsed beams and large stones. Though the sun had been up for several hours now, the bodies of the fallen were still being discovered. The first one she'd seen caught her off-guard, causing her to almost lose the contents of her stomach — a small elderly woman with blood pouring out of her mouth and nose. The accompanying wailing nearly tore her heart as tears flowed and a heavy stone settled in the pit of her stomach. The dichotomy of the tension inside and her stomach twisting at the sight of the blood left her feeling faint. Watching as the two nations came together during this time of tragedy brought her a measure of comfort amidst the chaos.

The soft cheese atop the herbed flatbread tasted deliciously sharp. With each bite, she could feel her energies returning. Her body still felt weak, but she was no longer in fear of collapsing. The mental fog was slowly clearing as well. She dared to try and conjure up a little water in her hands. The thin
~~~

stream encircled her hands, its movements soothing her frayed nerves. In an instant, it came crashing to the ground, soaking her hand and skirts as she felt herself wobble as she sat.

Cienna forced herself to take another bite of the flatbread. Eyeing the peach on her lap, the princess gripped the fuzzy fruit in her hand, wondering if it was going to be tart or sweet when she bit into it. As her teeth sank into its soft exterior, she was delighted to find that it was sweet and complimented the cheese and bread she'd been eating.

In the distance, she saw Caitlyn and Alverick talking as they helped the people of Fa'Tinh clear rubble. The redhead's eyes sparkled as she spoke to him, a slight smile playing on her lips as he flashed her one of the first smiles Cienna had seen from him. The two worked in perfect harmony, lifting the stones as one and carefully making their way out of the main square to drop the debris off elsewhere. A small sigh escaped the princess as she watched the two disappear into the capital.

Taking another bite of her peach, Cienna let her eyes wander once more, absentmindedly taking in her surroundings. She thought she saw the Flame talking with Pram, the Great Heart's righthand man, his tattooed hand gesturing as he spoke to the Qu'ari general. The Great Heart himself was not in sight. Cienna paused and thought for a moment before realizing that she hadn't seen him since the night before.

"I wonder if he's with the tall man?" she murmured. "Or the beautiful woman."

The silver-haired woman popped into her mind. She couldn't explain why, but the woman seemed so familiar to her.

"I'll have to speak with both her and the tall man. There's an air of mystery around them both. It's troubling. I know that I know them from somewhere." The princess spoke to herself through a mouthful of flatbread.

Brody interrupted her thoughts by walking across the square towards Ronan and a handful of soldiers. Cienna's heart skipped a beat, jumping to her throat, as he went by, and she found herself tucking a strand of wavy hair behind her ear before smoothing down the front of her outfit out of habit. A warmth spread to her cheeks and she noticed she had that same giddy feeling she used to get when she was younger around him.

He hasn't spoken to me in days, the princess reminded herself. *Other than to check on me. I can't leave things between us like this. He's my guard.*

Shoving the remainder of the flatbread into her mouth, Cienna dusted her hands off and took a deep breath before making her way over to her bodyguard. It took her less time than she thought to close the gap between the two. With each step, she felt her stomach clench tighter, but still she pressed on. Ronan noticed her approach and motioned for Brody to turn around. The few soldiers who stood with them wandered off awkwardly to help the Qu'ari clean.

"Your majesty," Ronan said with a nod. "How are you feeling? You had us all worried last night."

"I'm feeling much better, thank you." Cienna was surprised to hear the curt tone in her voice. There wasn't time for pleasantries with her subordinates. "Ronan, would you be so kind as to prepare me an audience with Swordbane? I would have thought he'd want to speak with me by now, but he appears to be stalling. I won't take no for an answer."

"Yes, your majesty," Ronan replied, snapping to attention.

When the princess didn't say anything further, the officer took that as his cue and strode off towards the nearest group. She noted out of the corner of her eye that he stood there awkwardly, not really giving instructions.

Cienna gave a small shake as she blinked her eyes slowly. She wasn't sure why she was focusing on Ronan when the object of her attention stood in front of her, but now that she was alone with Brody, she found that she couldn't look at him. To his credit, her bodyguard stood ready for whatever she had to say. The princess watched as he shifted his weight, but his eyes were locked on her. Cienna felt her face begin to warm as a flush crept onto her cheeks.

Gods this is embarrassing, she lamented.

The silence continued on. With each passing second, Cienna found that she could not bring herself to say anything. Her tongue felt heavy, almost clumsy, in her mouth as she struggled to say something to him.

"How may I help you, Waterdrop?" he finally asked, cutting through the awkward tension that was growing between them. "You seem a bit distracted."

It was as if a large rock had been lifted from her shoulders. Her shoulders relaxed as she exhaled the breath that she didn't know she was holding. His tone was curt, not the normal warm one she was used to, but at least he was talking to her. Finally.

"Walk with me."

It wasn't a question.

With a silent nod, Brody fell in line with her, and the two began meandering through the square. Cienna took the opportunity to gradually move towards the periphery of the square away from the others, Brody following along without a word.

Little by little, the they put distance between the Qu'ari and soldiers as they moved towards what appeared to be a residential area. Small planters with flowers of all colors hung under the windows, while crocuses of deep purple bunched by the doors.

"You know, I don't think I've seen a single pirate this morning help clean up," Brody remarked. His tone was lighter than it had been, but when Cienna glanced his way, she was disappointed to see that he wasn't looking back at her with the mischievous twinkle she adored.

A grunt of agreement escaped her before she realized it.

Damnation! Cienna berated herself. *That was my chance to say something clever, or funny, or... anything really to get him to tell me what's going on. By the gods!*

When she felt comfortable that they were an adequate distance from the closest person, she turned to face Brody. The two stood in a narrow side street surrounded by simple buildings made of clay and stone. As her eyes fell on her bodyguard, Cienna felt something she never had before.

"Why won't you talk to me?" she blurted out. Warm tears prickled at the corners of her eyes as she fought back the urge to cry. All the emotions that she'd been feeling the last few days came bubbling up and threatened to overwhelm her.

Brody's eyes dropped. She saw a wave of sadness wash over his face for the briefest of moments before he caught himself. Or did she imagine it? Everything that she'd been thinking had her second-guessing herself.

"I crossed a line that I shouldn't have. I need to remember my place." It hurt Cienna to hear how flat his tone was.

"I chose you," she implored, her voice cracking. "Your place is with me."

"Your place is on the throne, making and maintaining your alliances. Even if they're with someone you don't want to marry."

The princess balked at his words. He was right, of course. Her father would want her to cultivate and grow Zanir's relationship with Alocar to build a stronger future with Oldar. Her stomach clenched as reality set in.

"You're right," she said softly, her gaze falling. She felt a solitary tear roll out of the corner of her eye, but it managed to get caught in her eyelashes as she blinked. "I'm supposed to be worrying about what's best for my people, but all I can think about is you. I'm just a child. I'm not even capable of taking over for my mother. But..."

Before she knew it, her lips crashed onto his. A tingle coursed through her body, filling her with a warmth that felt right. It was different from their kiss on their way home from the gorge. His lips left her longing for more.

A pair of powerful hands gently gripped her shoulders and pushed the two apart. Cienna's eyes cracked open, and she found him staring back at her. This time there was no denying his pained expression.

"Please," Cienna begged, her voice barely more than a whisper.

"I can't," Brody replied, gently pushing her further away.

Cienna pulled him back close, her fingers digging into his arms. Standing on the tips of her toes, she brought her face so close to him that her lips tickled his neck. "No one will have to know."

She watched as a shiver of excitement coursed through the young man as her hot breath and soft lips played on his flesh. Breaking his gaze from her imploring eyes, Brody scanned the street. A pair of wine barrels outside the houses collecting rainwater obscured them from view. Anyone walking by would be hard-pressed to see them.

As he glanced down at the princess, she felt him leaning into her, their bodies touching. Tracing his jaw lightly with her finger, Cienna pressed herself against him. She was rewarded with him stiffening at her touch. Their lips connected, and she found herself gasping for breath as much as his embrace. Her body tingled as his hand pulled her legs up around his waist as he spun around and rested her against the wall.

His hand slipped under her dress, searching for the source of her tingling. A moan escaped her lips as he found it, his fingers rubbing against her. Brody felt her shudder as his digits slipped deeper into her. Cienna's body pressed closer to him, her teeth lightly biting his lower lip as his fingers alternated between the two actions. His lips moved from hers, settling on her neck just below her jaw. His pants felt tight as his body reacted to hers. Brody let out a breathy sigh before dropping any abandon and letting his animal instincts take over.

V

S UNLIGHT STREAMED through the window despite the thick fabric curtains' attempts to block it out. Len stretched, his arms shooting over the end of his bed and his fingers tickling the wall. Almost instantly, he recoiled with a sharp intake of breath. The wound on Len's arm, though healing, was still causing him pain. Cracking an eye, he groaned as he tried to avoid the blinding light.

He'd left the wound on his bicep unbandaged during the night in an effort to help it heal by airing it out. None of the poultices provided by his shaman worked as well as the salve made from the purple flower that Maya had rubbed on him earlier. No longer warm to the touch, Len was pleased to hear that his healers didn't believe it to be infected. However, they had to reopen it to let out the bad blood before attempting to sew it closed as though his arm were a piece of fabric used by a seamstress.

Despite his exhaustion, Len nearly passed out from the pain as they cut open his arm with one of their sharp daggers. Now, after a good night's sleep thanks to the poppy he'd been given, his arm began throbbing again with a dull pain. Clenching his teeth, Len forced himself to ignore the discomfort for now. There was much to do the repair the damage caused by Wyrd.

Outside his window, he could hear the muffled giggles and shrieks of Bermet playing. They were accompanied by a few other voices, which he assumed were Pram's children. A bundle of blankets lay next to their mat, empty like the other half of his bed. As the effects of the poppy wore off, they were replaced with nausea and a desire for more. Len grunted with the exertion of pushing himself upright on his mat, the blankets falling off his bare torso and bunching in front of him. A wave of dizziness washed over him, but he managed to keep himself composed despite his stomach clenching.

"Why is the window shut?" he muttered, giving himself something to focus on while he waited for the dizziness to go away. "It's too damn hot." His mind went to the calming salt spray of the seas, and he found himself suddenly longing for her warm breezes and cooling mists.

What in the hells? he wondered. Len's stomach was still twisted in knots, making him want to lose what little food he'd had since the fight against Wyrd. *Why would I think of that?*

His vision now clear, Len sat upright on his mat, draped in his blankets. He hated the sea and her bumpy waters. Her rough waters made his stomach wring, just like his poppy withdrawals were doing. But most of all, the pirates — their hierarchy was far too chaotic. It reminded him of the olden days that his mother spoke of. The freedom of the clans before there was a Great Heart, and how each one relied on their own chief and warriors. The brutality of Ghan as he meted out justice reminded Len of himself. He missed the sea and her ruthless existence.

That's not the life for me, he reminded himself. *The bones did not foretell this.*

A light knock on the door pulled him from his thoughts. Ignoring his state of undress, Len stood up, his hand holding the blanket that barely covered his naked flesh, and moved to open the door. Before he could reach it, the door gently opened, revealing his wife. Zaa'ni cradled their son against her breast as the infant fed between the folds of her lavender silks. Her thick hair was pulled up in a high tail, keeping it out of her face.

"Len." Her husky voice washed over him like the gentle waves of the sea. Len didn't say anything to his wife, and she took that as her cue to continue. "I know you need to rest, but Pram is here and insisting that you join him to discuss Wyrd and how you'll handle his actions."

Damn, he cursed, grimacing. *I need to figure out what to do with him. I can't just kill him.* Len paused for a moment before admitting the truth. *I should.*

"Wyrd's caused a lot of damage to Xan, especially Fa'Tinh. I know most won't like it coming from me, but I agree with Pram that something needs to be done."

Zaa'ni's eyes hardened as she spoke about Len's childhood friend. Len couldn't help but smirk at her as he watched her full lips tighten into a thin line and her brows also narrowed. She hated the man, and Len knew it.

"I need to see the shaman first and get something to eat." Len turned and tossed the blanket onto their bed before rummaging through a basket of clothes in the corner of the room. "But I will see Pram as soon as I've found some pants. We have a lot to discuss."

Zaa'ni nodded in agreement, her lips turning up in a tight smile.

"Before I meet with Pram, tell me. Why are the windows all closed and covered? It's damn hot without a nice breeze."

Len did not anticipate the effect his question would have on his wife. Her stony visage quickly melted away and was replaced almost instantly with one of concern and fear. Unconsciously, Zaa'ni pulled their son closer to her chest as her eyes darted to the window.

"I think you'll want to talk to Pram about that as well," she said softly. "While you were gone, Altansari and I saw something, as did Pram, Hroth, and your mother. I think it has something to do with Wyrd's actions. It was something... dark."

Her words troubled him.

"I wish you would tell me, but I will speak with him. With everything that I've seen these last few days, I wouldn't be surprised if some great evil has been unleashed upon Corinth, and maybe even specifically Xan. No doubt Wyrd plays a part in everything that's going on."

Len's refusal to call Wyrd by his true name, like he previously did was not missed by Zaa'ni. Len noted her brows furrowing once more when he said Wyrd's name. It filled him with a small sense of satisfaction that his words had the impact he was hoping for.

"Pram is in the kitchen. I had him join us for breakfast."

~~~

The streets of Fa'Tinh bustled as people worked together to clean up yesterday's mess. Members of the Hanzo, Yshish, and Thurl clans sent men over to help clear up the rubble. The remaining Pshwani darted about in scattered groups, trying to do whatever they could to help out. Their panic brought a smile to Len's lips. The Pshwani's betrayal would be hard to forget. He demanded obeisance from all.

"I received word earlier today that the heads of the remaining clans will be joining us today, Evenhand." Pram's voice brought Len's attention back to his general. The man stared straight ahead, his eyes scanning the busy streets. "They will want justice for Vaardan, most likely."

"Wyrd will have to answer for both the damage he's done here and the death of the head of the Pshwani. The gods are not happy with him."

"Will you act in accordance with the gods?"

At the question, Pram turned his gaze to his leader. Len felt himself retreating inward as he searched within for the answer. The silence didn't last long.

"I am protected by the gods. I am as good as one."

Reaching into his pocket, Len pulled out a few poppy leaves and popped them into his mouth. Chewing on the leaves helped alleviate the pain in his arm. The shaman told him that he wouldn't need to chew them for long, as long as he didn't aggravate the wound. With luck, Wyrd's punishment wouldn't take long to lay out. The effects of the poppy were strong, and Len realized that he could quickly get used to them.
~~~

VI

THE DANCING WOLF was packed. Muted chatter filled the tavern despite all the people crowding her halls. Alverick sat next to the princess, with Brody sitting on her other side, as they waited for Swordbane to arrive. The pair did not talk as they sat next to each other, but Alverick noticed that the air around them didn't seem so heavy. The flush on their cheeks let him know that things were still awkward between them.

Occasionally, the pirates called out for beer and other spirits, but other than that, there wasn't much noise. Kayna had done a good job keeping her crew under control — a stark contrast to when they first met five years earlier. Alverick's eyes were drawn to the back of the room as the blood ran to his face. Kayna's lithe figure wrapping herself around him popped into his mind, and he quickly pushed it out.

Standing against the wall, Dez observed the room. Next to her, the tall man and silver-haired lady leaned casually against the wall, chatting quietly. Alverick made eye contact with Dez, and she gave him a nod, her normally aloof demeanor clearly missing. He noted that instead of her coy smile, the corners of her lips were turned down and her eyes were lost. She also wasn't talking to herself. That disturbed Alverick most of all.

As soon as Dez broke contact, Alverick took the time to take in the tall man and his female companion. The pair arrived in Fa'Tinh under suspicious circumstances. No one saw them arrive, especially the woman.

Why does she seem so familiar? Alverick pondered. *They both radiate great power, like the Grey Man, Thuul. Could they be the same as him?*

He found himself studying the woman first. Her pale skin shone under her long, silver hair. The woman's silver eyes drank in the room greedily, studying everything. Her mouth moved as she said something to the man next to her, but her eyes continued to observe. Next to her, the tall man maintained eye contact with the detained Qu'ari, whom Alverick had come to find out was named Wyrd.

Wyrd sat tied against one of the pillars in the tavern, his hands bound quite securely to the point where only the tips of his fingers stuck out from the knots on his wrist. He appeared to be ignoring everything going on around him, his eyes resting on the tall man. The two locked gazes, and Wyrd let out a feral smile that made his face look lopsided.

The door to the Dancing Wolf opened, and Alverick watched as the Flame, followed by three other people, entered the establishment. Next to the Flame, a slight woman, barely more than a wisp, strode confidently past, taking a seat at a table near the front where Swordbane would no doubt be seated. To the Flame's left, the now pale skin of the hammer maiden seemed to glow in the firelight. On her other side, a Qu'ari man walked with her, his fingers clasped around hers.

As the group made their way to the table, Alverick noticed that Wyrd's eyes finally left the tall man's and settled hungrily on the pale-skinned woman. The Avalanche couldn't figure out where she was from; her dark hair marked her as one of Xan. Wyrd, however, was enraptured with her.

"He knows something about her," Brody said, leaning over towards Alverick. "We need to keep the two of them apart."

A grunt of agreement left Alverick's lips as he kept his eyes on the pair.

"See how that tall man in the back is watching them as well?" Brody asked.

Alverick's eyes darted over to the tall man next to the silver-haired woman and saw that he readjusted himself. Instead of casually leaning against the wall, he now stood upright, ready to move at a moment's notice. The man's eyes narrowed as he observed Wyrd with an unwavering eye.

"I don't think this will be a quick meeting," Alverick replied. "Whatever happens to Wyrd will not be an easy decision."

As if on cue, the door to the Dancing Wolf opened, and Len and his general's shadow filled the room. The already hushed room fell quiet as the leader of Xan made his way to a table at the back of the tavern. Alverick watched as the young Qu'ari general took a seat next to his wife and an older woman. A sudden movement behind the general as he took his seat caught Alverick's attention. The Flame who had been fighting Wyrd, whom Alverick believed to be named Hroth, adjusted his position, putting himself between Wyrd and Swordbane.

He doesn't have his fyre anymore, Alverick noted, recalling a conversation he overheard Swordbane having with the tall man and silver-haired lady. *But that Flame still sees him as a threat. I'll have to keep the princess close by while he's still alive.* The Avalanche narrowed his eyes as he turned his gaze back to Wyrd once more.

The bound Qu'ari man sat comfortably on the floor, ignoring the ropes that restrained him. His eyes continued to stare at the hammer maiden. Wyrd didn't seem to be paying anyone attention other than her, not even his leader and kinsman. Behind him, the Flame shifted once more. The two locked gazes and Alverick felt a shiver run down his spine.

When did he move? He was seated not a moment before. I don't know if I can trust him either. Damn, there are too many unknowns right now.

A sharp nudge to his side startled Alverick. A moment later, it was accompanied by a slight hiss as Brody tried to get his attention.

"Al, look."

Alverick followed where Brody had motioned with his head and saw that the door to the Dancing Wolf opened once more. Light spilled into the already lit room, causing him to throw up his arm in an effort to keep the sun from blinding him. Four figures stood in the doorway, blocking the light and giving Alverick time for his eyes to adjust.

"We have come for the sentencing of Wyr-raji," a voice rang out from one of the newcomers. "Where shall we sit?"

"As my Eyes, Ears, Mouth, and Feet, you deserve a seat at my table," Swordbane said. "However, I do not have an empty seat, so please sit here." The young general motioned to the nearest table. As the four men approached the table, the people occupying it got up and quickly found new seats.

"If we have no more people coming, I believe we can now start." Alverick watched as Pram stood up and approached the side of Swordbane's table. "Before we begin, Honorable Mother, would you be so kind as to lead us in prayer to the mighty Windstrider?"

The frail-looking woman sitting at the table nodded her head. The room was so quiet that the sound of her chair legs scraping on the worn wooden floors was amplified in the large tavern. The Honorable Mother gave Swordbane a pat on the arm before interlacing her fingers and closing her eyes. With a voice as brittle as aged parchment, she began speaking quickly in Qu'ari. Murmurs occasionally joined her as the clansmen lent their voices to her plea. With an inflection of her sing-song monologue, the room was filled with a final chorus, ending their prayer.

The Honorable Mother bowed her head in thanks to the gods before lowering herself into her chair. Alverick noted that Swordbane helped guide the woman into the chair with his hand by placing his hand on her back. The Avalanche couldn't help but flash the briefest of smiles as he observed the young leader's gentle concern for the elderly woman.

"Thank you, Honorable Mother," Pram said, breaking the silence and drawing Alverick's attention back to himself. "Before Evenhand speaks, I would like to take a moment to thank each of our brothers for joining us."

A rumble from the Xanans filled the room once more.

"Tuk-kan, leader of Yshan, our Ears. Pak, leader of Thurl, our Mouth. Yettan, leader of Hanzo, and our Feet. And Viir, representing Pshwan, our Eyes. Thank you, Viir, for taking up Vaarden's mantle. It is with a heavy heart that his time has ended."

As the head of each clan was announced, the leader stood up and received a growl of approval from the attending Xanans. At the mention of Vaarden's demise, Alverick watched as a wave of anger washed over the faces of those in attendance.

"This can't be good," the Avalanche mumbled.

Brody grunted in agreement, leaning forward to better observe the proceedings. "I smell blood about to be spilt."

The rumblings died down as Swordbane stood up. Alverick's eyes narrowed as he studied the young general. A cloth was tied around his bicep, the bulge of the wrapping showing clearly underneath his mustard-colored tunic. He surveyed the full tavern with hard eyes before his face relaxed. Alverick and Swordbane met gazes briefly, a smile playing on the young general's lips, before the Qu'ari returned his attentions to the room.

"My brothers." Swordbane's voice filled the room, echoing off the walls. "It is an honor to have our people together like this. I am disappointed that we must meet under such circumstances, but seeing the might of the brothers of Xan brings me great joy.

"As you may know, your Great Heart has been betrayed by one of our own. His actions led to the death of Liir, the death of Vaarden, and an attempt to return our people to the old ways of barbarity and chaos."

Swordbane surveyed his people. Alverick took the opportunity to glance around the room as well. The tall man and silver-haired woman stood silently against the back wall; the tall man's arms were crossed and his face unreadable. Dez had moved from her spot by the door, having opted to sit next to Kayna and the woman seated at her righthand side. The Tempest leaned over to the redheaded pirate and whispered something in her ear, causing Kayna to nod in agreement.

Forcing himself to look away from the outsiders, Alverick turned to observe the Qu'ari and their fellow Xanans. The Qu'ari and Pshwani all glared daggers at Wyrd, some muttering under their breath as they stared through the bound Qu'ari's soul. The four leaders representing the various tribes remained stoic, their faces more controlled. Alverick was surprised to see how composed Viir was. After speaking with Pram briefly the night before, Alverick expected the current head of the Pshwani clan to be apoplectic.

Tuk-kan, an elderly man, but younger than the Honorable Mother, solemnly stood up, his hands flat against the table's surface. All eyes turned to the head of the Yshan clan. Swordbane remained standing, but nodded to the older man in respect.

So, he does offer deference to those he deems equal, Alverick noted. *There has to be a way to earn that same veneration.*

"Great Heart, if I may, with all due respect, word has reached my ears that all of Wyr-raji's actions were done on your command." The man, though aged, spoke with a strong, clear voice. "As such, his actions are your own."

"By the gods," Alverick swore. He could hear Brody's sharp intake of breath beside him.

Swordbane's lips were pulled into a tight line, but his eyes were a mystery. Giving the head of the Yshan tribe a chance to finish his thoughts, Swordbane nodded his head in understanding before speaking:

"Tuk-kan, you are right. The laws state that if a champion cannot control his men, he must atone for their actions. However, when one acts in defiance or against their orders, I believe that the fault no longer lies with the leader, but falls on the shoulders of the individual."

Swordbane's words came out evenly despite the anger building within. Alverick could see that the young general's shoulders were tense, as were the muscles in his face.

They must be speaking of the old ways. Alverick's brow furrowed as he watched the exchange closely. *This is a pivotal moment. Will they be honored, or will Swordbane's new laws reign?*

The sudden sound of a fist pounding the table captured the attention of the room. The Avalanche's eyes narrowed as he saw the younger head of another tribe, not Thurl by the looks of their hair, jump up in anger. Next to him, Tuk-kan observed the new speaker out of the corner of his eyes. Len remained calm, but alert, waiting to see what this man had to say.

Neither trust this one.

"Don't try and deflect the blame for your friend's actions!" the man cried. "By the Mighty Windstrider, you have failed us in a way the Great Heart has not, Len."

A hush fell over the room. Alverick could feel a blanket settle over the room. Calling Swordbane out of his title was the ultimate sign of disrespect. His eyes darted over to see how Len reacted. The young general stood calmly in front of the group. A vein twitched in his jaw, and his eyes bore into the man. Alverick watched as a cloud passed behind Swordbane's eyes, darkening as his anger built inside.

"Yettan," he said slowly, ice freezing his words. "I do not take disrespect like that. I will let it pass this one time, but know that I will not broach that again."

Yettan glared at his leader, grinding his teeth, but did not protest.

"I understand your anger, believe me. But it is misguided. Wyrd has double-crossed me in almost every step of my journey. Despite his treachery, I have still managed to bring Xan forward. Everything Wyrd has done has been to the detriment of our home and to only further his gain." Len's shoulders tightened, but he maintained control of himself and kept his gaze on the man in front of him. "I have never ordered the deaths of my brothers. Wyrd cannot say the same."

Yettan opened his mouth to protest, but a third man stood up, silencing the head of the Hanzo. The man looked familiar to Alverick, but he couldn't place him.

"If I may speak," the man cut in. "I know I do not hold the same level of respect that Vaarden did, but I would like to speak on behalf of my people." He motioned to the few Pshwani that remained in the room from the night before.

"Speak, Viir," Tuk-kan said, motioning for Yettan to mimic him and sit down.

"Thank you, Brother Tuk-kan," Viir said with a nod of the head. "Great Heart did everything he could to keep the peace between my brothers and his own, despite my own efforts." The man smiled sheepishly, unsure of himself as he stood with the heads of his country. "When the Great Heart's campaign returned after their siege, I blamed him for my brother's death. I still do, truth be told. But he did everything he could to maintain balance despite my attempts at intimidation. I hope I can be forgiven, Great Heart."

Viir dipped his head in obeisance. Alverick noted that the corner of Swordbane's lips curled up in a smirk, but he did not say anything.

"Stop kissing the Great Heart's ass. You obviously are trying to save your hide, but we are here to discuss more serious matters. Why, you don't understand the intricacies of leadership. Leave this discussion to the men and sit down with the rest of the children." Yettan spat out his words quickly, the tone cutting through the tension that had once again settled over the room.

Viir stiffened at the tirade, but did not dare reproach the Hanzo leader. Behind the standing Xanan clansmen, Alverick watched as Wyrd sat calmly against the wooden pillar. His eyes followed the exchanges with amused interest, darting between each party as they spoke. The Avalanche glanced over at Swordbane. The young general clenched his jaw; his hands were surprisingly relaxed as they lay flat against the table.

A soft shuffle drew Alverick's attention back to the arguing clan heads. Thurl's leader, one of two women, moved delicately forward until she stood near Tuk-kan. Her half-shaven head contrasted with her long, grey hair, braided and hanging over her shoulder. Wrinkles lined the corners of her eyes and mouth, but her body was strong.

"Thurl has long been a land of peace," Pak began. Her voice rang out in the Wolf. "We travel the realm selling our spices and teaching Corinth about the beauty of Xan. The actions of the last month have severely harmed our kin. Corinth sees us as bloodthirsty monsters, much like the days before Ras. Too many people don't know our histories or our ways; they just judge us."

"And who is to blame?" Yettan cried out as his hand slammed the table.

Pak gave the man a withering look, ignoring the outburst. "And it is because we can't manage our own. Great Heart, it appears to be tied on how to handle the traitor — two for him taking the blame and two for you bearing the burden of his guilt. Tell me, if Thurl were to back you, will you swear to return Xan to her former glory under Ras?"

The young general's face twitched in annoyance, caught off-guard by the question. Behind him, Pram's eyes widened as he took a sharp breath. The general's eyes darted toward his leader in an attempt to read the man's body. Seated at the table, the Honorable Mother bowed her head and began mouthing something rapidly, possibly a prayer.

Alverick felt a squeeze on his arm before Brody's warm breath tickled his ear.

"Hells bells, Al," Brody whispered. "This is it."

The Avalanche nodded, not daring to make a sound. Taking a quick scan of the room, he saw both Kayna and Swordbane watching intently, as well as the trio leaning against the back wall. The tall man in particular seemed to be taking a keen interest in the outcome of this meeting.

"You have my word, Pak," Swordbane's voice sounded strangely hollow in the silent room.

"Then it is done," she replied. "His fate is his own, only for you to decide."

Yettan gawped at Pak as she shuffled back to her seat. A bemused Tukkan followed, leaving the Hanzo chief by himself. Throwing one last contemptuous glare at the young general, Yettan finally acquiesced and joined the other three clan heads at their table.

VII

T HE CRISP MORNING AIR sent a shiver down the young king's back. Pulling his legs closer to his body, Oldar tried in vain to keep what little warmth he had in his body from escaping. The night had been long, filled with blood-curdling shrieks and the occasional scream from some unfortunate soul that happened to encounter whatever monstrosity Alastaire unleashed on Madden.

A soft knock on the door caught his attention. Unrolling from his little ball, Oldar rubbed the aches from his limbs as he shuffled towards the wine cellar door. A yawn escaped his lips as he tried to massage his sore muscles.

"What information do you have for me, Pru?" he mumbled.

Taking a moment to touch the ancient rune carved over the door, Oldar took a deep breath before opening the door a crack. His body was tense, praying that he hadn't been deceived and that one of the Faceless stood on the other side. To his immense relief, it was indeed his matronly childhood caretaker waiting for him.

"Come in, Pru. Quick."

The young king opened the door just wide enough that she could squeeze through it before quickly shutting the door and locking it once more. Pruvencia moved deep into the wine cellar, rubbing her arms in an effort to get warm. A thick shawl lay draped over her shoulders, while mittens covered her hands.

"Blessed Aria, it's as cold as death out there." The old woman's teeth chattered as she struggled to find warmth. "Thank the gods this cellar isn't. Must be Blessed Zemé's mark upon the door."

"Is it that bad out there, Pru?" Oldar asked.

The elderly woman nodded her head. "Ice covers the walls, and the pyres struggle to stay lit. I've moved all of the castle staff to the kitchens, and we've been huddling there all night next to the fires. There've been so many shrieks moving down the hallway. I don't even know how Lord Alastaire and Lady Constance can stand it. Even the soldiers stay out of the castle proper now."

Oldar's brows drew together as he bit the skin around his thumb. "Damn," he murmured. "What of Ingmar?"

"He's managed to sneak in a few times to check on us, but we daren't have him stay long. If he got caught, we'd all be in trouble."

The king paced in a small circle, his mind racing as he tried to digest everything. Faceless running rampant, the castle under siege, and not even the guard was safe. Alastaire must be mad. Everything swirled around in his head, bumping off of each other, leaving him more confused than he was before Pru brought him the news.

Oldar couldn't think of anything to say, but the silence that was stretching on between the two of them was making him uncomfortable. Pruvencia didn't seem to be bothered by the quiet; she was too busy trying to rub some life back into her fingers, but the young king didn't seem to notice her distraction. Instead of focusing on what he was going to do to move forward, Oldar found himself asking the first question that popped into his head.

"Has Schaed been laid to rest?"

The matronly woman stopped rubbing her hands together and met her lord's gaze with baleful eyes. That was all the answer he needed.

"They haven't been able to find all of him," her tired voice whispered. "When Ingmar went back to look for him, bits were missing. What has been recovered has been moved to the dungeons so the undertaker can prepare the body for burial. I'm so sorry, my love."

A lump formed in Oldar's throat and his eyes began to burn. All he wanted was to spend one last evening with his friend, drinking and talking about the old days. Now, he'd never be able to do it again.

"Oh shite," the king muttered. "I'll never be able to get justice for the Queen."

"Pardon, my lord?"

Oldar turned to face his caretaker, his face a mask of anguish. "Before I left the last time, I was nearly thrown in the dungeon like a common criminal because Schaed poisoned the Queen and almost got Cienna. Damn, how am I going to explain this to her?"

Subconsciously, the young king's fingers found themselves wound through his auburn hair, gripping tightly as he struggled to process everything. His mind moved sluggishly, unwilling to accept all that had happened.

"I would never have punished him, but I would've at least made a public display to appease Cienna."

A soft clucking sound startled the young king. His eyes darted up, searching for his caretaker.

"My lord, do you really think it honorable to mete out punishment only in name? I know he was your best friend, but justice still must be met. It pains me to say this, but perhaps Schaed's passing was a blessing in disguise. Now, you can enact strict discipline without damaging your friendship."

Pruvencia's fragile voice hit him with a strength he didn't think she had anymore. After everything she'd been through, Oldar thought that she would be tired, ready to end it all. Instead, she was as vibrant as when she raised him.

"Assuming my uncle lets me," he pouted. "And that's seeming less likely as the days go on."

"By the gods, Oldar," she responded, her voice rising to a harsh whisper, cracking as her emotions threatened to overwhelm her. "Stop your self-pitying at once! This is most unbecoming. Right now, you need to focus on how to stop your uncle and save your people. The whole palace is praying for a miracle. To be honest, without the Guard, we're almost guaranteed to be dominated by your uncle and his monsters from the seven hells. You need to dust yourself off and come up with a plan to stop him."

The young king recoiled at her words as though he'd been slapped. His hand rose, almost touching his cheek, and he took a step back, eyes wide in confusion.

"You're right, Pru," he said at last. "I've been so overwhelmed, so full of questions and self-doubt, that I did not stop and think of how to best protect Alocar."

Oldar began pacing once more, his wanderings having a somewhat calming effect on his caretaker as she began rubbing her hands. This time, he wasn't sure if it was for warmth or comfort. His mind raced as he ran over the scenarios in his head. Teachings from his tutors and talks with his father played through his mind in quick succession.

Pruvencia walked over to the corner of the room and perched herself on one of the wine barrels, removing the shawl around her shoulders. Oldar stopped, turning his attention to the elderly woman. As she rested her feet, he saw all of Alocar. Through her, he saw his castle staff and all they did to keep the palace functioning; he saw the royal guard and soldiers of his kingdom; he saw the guild members and their staff like Rez'maré; but above all, he saw the hope of his people.

The answer was easy for him. Oldar couldn't believe it had taken him this long to come up with it. Closing his eyes, he said a prayer to every deity in Corinth that he could think of before grabbing Pru's hand and pulling her out of the cellar door.

VIII

The queen sat delicately on a rock as she waited for their scout to return. Despite the heat that already built as the sun continued on its journey in the sky, she warmed her hands by the smoke of the dying embers. The smoldering flames and gently wafting smoke relaxed her. Her husband and a few of his men stood off to the side, discussing their plan of attack. It was all so tedious.

"And once they've returned, we can decide if we should focus more on coming from the side or taking them from the north." The soldier spoke to his lord in a quick, clipped tone.

"Excellent," Dzvorth replied. His fingers traced the lines of his chin as he studied the map laid out in front of him. "Mmm... yes. That will do nicely. They'll never see it coming."

"How long do you plan on this taking?" Dzvareliah drawled. She was pleased to see her husband turn towards her in annoyance.

"What do you mean?" His voice held back the snarl she saw in his face. Barely.

"Well, you're talking about sending some of our men all the way to the northern part of Xan only to come back down and trap their people between our forces. It's a good plan, but I didn't think you were planning for something that would take that long. It'll probably take a couple extra days to get everyone in place and coordinate the attack. Don't you want to be home in time for the blood moon so we can do the Choosing ceremony? It's only a few days away, and Her Holiness' blood, the little I have left, will be at its most potent."

Dzvareliah felt her anger boiling in her stomach as she thought about how little holy blood she had left. That damned daughter of hers had taken most of what she had, leaving her with precious little to use to find more magi. This was their most sacred of events, and it happened to fall on a once in a century event. She needed that blood back.

She found herself returning to the conversation. Surprisingly, no one was talking. Dzvareliah found her eyes moving from person to person, studying their expressions one by one. They all told the same story — everyone but her husband. When she looked at him, all she saw was rage. Dzvorth's eyes blazed, a vein twitching in his jaw as she tried not to meet his wife's gaze. Dzvareliah felt pride as she watched him struggle to not gnash his teeth. It quickly replaced the anger she'd felt a moment ago.

"We'll confirm with Dzeon when he returns, but we will sneak around to the back and push them towards the gorge. We won't create a double phalanx and trap them." To his credit, Dzvorth kept his voice steady and kept the anger out. Almost.

"You won't regret this," Dzvareliah said. "Once the blood moon is over, we'll be able to come back and take over. Then we can visit little Dzvaresh."

Without waiting for another word from either monarch, the Scrymmen soldiers dispersed. Dzvareliah's lips curled up as her husband stood frozen in front of her, a snarl on his face, as the others worked to prepare the camp for their eventual departure. The king stared holes through her as Dzvareliah went back to nonchalantly warming her hands in the dying embers.

When the king didn't move, Dzvareliah looked up at him from under her heavily lidded eyes. A bemused smirk played on her lips once more as the pair locked gazes. Despite the thin tendrils of smoke wafting heavenward, she found that the last bits of heat were enough to warm her fingers.

"What do you want?" she asked. Dzvareliah tried to keep the question unaccusatory, but unfortunately, her distaste towards the man seeped through enough for him to notice.

Within moments, Dzvorth closed the distance between the two, his hands resting tightly around the queen's slender neck. Dzvareliah's eyes flew open at the uncharacteristic action. Her husband usually tried to restrain himself around her to keep up appearances.

Fire blazed in the Scyrmmen king's eyes as he squeezed his queen's neck. Dzvareliah's fingers dug into his hands and scratched his arms in an attempt to break free of his grip, but her resistance only angered him.

"Dammit woman!" he spat, his face inches from hers. "You undermine me again, and I will kill you. I am your king and will not be mocked. Do you understand?"

Dzvareliah tried to nod, her mouth parted open as she struggled for air. Her vision began to swim, but he did not let go. If she hadn't been sitting on the rock, she most likely would've dropped to her knees. Her hands fell to her sides one by one. As darkness crept into the corners of her vision, he suddenly let go. With a gasp, Dzvareliah's hands flew to her throat, and she slipped off the rock and onto the ground. She barely managed to catch herself with one hand on the ground as she drank in the air, clearing her vision.

"Don't think I won't do it," Dzvorth's voice threatened from above her. "There are plenty of young girls for me to take in your place."

The crunching of sticks and gravel let her know that her husband had left. Her vision now clear, Dzvareliah gently lifted her trembling body back onto the rock. Tears pricked at the corners of her eyes, and she wiped them away hastily with the heel of her palm. A soldier standing nearby caught her eye. The man watched her, his expression frightened, as she worked to regain her composure.

"I- I'm sorry, your highness," he muttered apologetically.

Dzvareliah raised her hand, silencing the soldier instantly.

"Let me know when Dzeon arrives. I want to be present to hear his report."

"Yes, your highness."

The queen watched as the man went about his business. She wondered for a brief moment if he would say anything, but quickly pushed it out of her mind. No one would willingly get involved in a dispute involving her or her husband. Dzvareliah chided herself for the thought. No, it would be better to focus on how she was going to handle this act of disrespect. Dzvareliah Ari was not known for being merciful. Dzvorth would've been wise to remember that.

IX

Tʜᴇ ʜᴏᴛ Xᴀɴᴀɴ sᴜɴ beat down on the main square of Fa'Tinh in the late afternoon. Now devoid of buildings to provide a bit of respite, those who left the Dancing Wolf scrambled to find someplace to keep them cool. Alverick left the tavern more confused than before the meeting started. What he thought was going to be a simple discussion between him and Swordbane nearly turned into a civil war. The Avalanche had managed to speak with the young Qu'ari general once everything had been settled regarding Wyrd, but he never realized how tenuous the hold on Xan was.

"Well, that was exciting, now, wasn't it?" Kayna's voice popped up right at his elbow. Before he could respond, the pirate snaked her arm around his, so the two were walking arm in arm through the square. "Who would've thought that Len's people were frothing at the mouth to steal his position? I thought he had a tight grip on them."

"Kayna, what are you doing?" Alverick's voice came out in an exasperated sigh. "I thought I said that we shouldn't do this."

"This?" Kayna asked, raising their linked arms with the question. "Surely two people can talk military gossip together." Unhooking her arm from his, the pirate slipped out in front of him. Pressing her finger lightly against his chest, Kayna stood up on her toes, her lips almost touching his, and said softly: "Especially two people with a connection like ours."

Alverick felt his face flush, causing Kayna to wink as she returned to her previous position. Her arm slid comfortably around his, and her hand rested lightly on the back of his.

"What in the seven hells?"

Alverick felt his blood freeze. The quick stomping of footsteps approaching announced the fiery redhead archer. Still wrapped up with Alverick, Kayna rested her head on his arm as Caitlyn rounded in front of them. Her emerald eyes were icy cold as she stared daggers at the pirate. Alverick could almost feel the anger radiating off of her.

"Oh, darling, what's wrong?" Kayna asked as she peered around at the redhead.

Caitlyn stammered out an incoherent response as she glared at the pirate. Her emerald eyes were frozen over as she seethed.

"Come now," the pirate chided. "Surely it's okay for Alverick to take a walk with an old friend?"

In an instant, Caitlyn whipped out a dagger from her thigh and closed the distance between her and Kayna. Alverick found himself quickly detangling himself from the pirate's grip as he grabbed Caitlyn by the arms and held her away from Kayna. Behind him, he could hear Kayna's amused chuckle and the sound of metal leaving a sheath.

"Cait, please," Alverick whispered. "We were just talking about the meeting, I promise."

"You have no reason to distrust Al," Kayna added. "Me, on the other hand... well, let's just say there's a reason why I don't work well with women."

Alverick could feel Kayna's presence right behind him. He thought he caught the glint of steel out of the corner of his eye, but he didn't want to take his eyes off of Caitlyn. He felt her body tense, causing the Avalanche to tighten his grip on her.

"What makes you think that you can come into our lives again and act like nothing's happened?" Caitlyn spat. "Do you even realize the damage you've caused?"

"My darling girl, do you think that I care about *your* troubles?" Kayna's voice, though aloof, carried a steely undertone. "There's something unprecedented going on, and you're letting a spat of jealousy cloud your judgement?"

Alverick felt Caitlyn tense once more, but she made no effort to move towards the pirate. To his dismay, Kayna rounded him and put herself within striking range of the redheaded archer. He noticed that her weapon was no longer in her hand, having re-sheathed it at some point during their discussion. Caitlyn suddenly relaxed in his arms, surprising the Avalanche. Her eyes, however, remained stony.

"Do you not think that perhaps I have a method for garnering information?" Kayna continued. "Surely, you have your own methods to best gain an advantage? When you live in my world, you use whatever means necessary."

With a smooth motion, Caitlyn returned her dagger to its sheath and dropped her arms at her side. She stared death at the pirate, but the fire that had previously burned behind her icy eyes had burnt out.

"I'm joining this discussion," Caitlyn said flatly. "But know this: if I catch you trying to lure him to your bed, I will not back down."

A smirk flashed across Kayna's face. "Suit yourself. Shall we find somewhere and find a drink while we talk? I know we just left a tavern, but I really could use a strong ale right now, and there's too much going on in there." The pirate motioned to the Dancing Wolf by jutting her head once behind her.

"I could use a drink," Alverick admitted.

Caitlyn remained silent and did not protest.

"I think I heard one of the Qu'ari talking about there being a smaller tavern, not as prominent, somewhere on the outskirts of Fa'Tinh. We can probably find something to eat there too." Alverick hoped that by getting food and something strong to drink, the girls would be able to remain calm.

To his dismay, Kayna wrapped her arm around his once more, forcing Caitlyn to move to his other side, and took the lead by directing the group where to walk. The difference between the two women was staggering. Kayna held onto him lightly, her body following him loosely, except when she wanted the trio to take a turn. On the other hand, Caitlyn walked stiffly, her hand gripping his with a vice-like grip. Alverick rubbed her thumb with his in an effort to try and get the redhead to relax. If he was successful, he didn't know.

The afternoon sun beat down on the group, causing beads of sweat to form on the Avalanche's brow and causing his tunic to stick to his back. As they tried to find the tavern, he felt Caitlyn finally ease up, and her grip on him diminished. Alverick enjoyed his time walking with her hand-in-hand down the streets. He almost didn't even realize that they'd been walking for longer than they probably should have been.

"Do you know where we're going?" he asked.

Kayna shrugged her shoulders in a nonchalant manner. "Not really," she replied. "I figured we'd find it eventually."

"The clans are huge and blend into each other. How could you lead us so blindly?" Alverick asked.

"Calm down. We'll find our way. That's always been our mindset on the seas. No use fretting over something you can't control."

The Avalanche let out a sigh of exasperation as he disentangled himself from the pirate. "I doubt you let yourself wander aimlessly on the seas," he muttered. He looked around, taking in their surroundings, and noticed a young couple walking around.

"Wait here," he told the girls.

Rushing over to the couple, Alverick struggled to get directions to the tavern, but eventually they offered to help walk him and his group over to the Amber Rose.

~~~

Inside of the Amber Rose was vastly different from the Dancing Wolf. A few worn tables, chips visible on their surfaces even from the front door, dotted the floor of the small building. The chairs were thin but covered with burgundy cushions. On top of every table, a narghile with a rubber hose rested, the cerulean glass shining in the dim light. Thick smoke filled the room, choking Alverick with its pungent scent.

"Gods, I haven't seen a narghile since I was out east in Maya's land," Kayna breathed. "I thought smoking was too refined for you mainlanders."

Caitlyn let out a small cough, her tattooed hand covering her nose in an effort to discreetly prevent herself from inhaling the smoke. Alverick nodded. He didn't even know where they found the materials to make the device. He couldn't believe Xan had something so impressive.

"You've seen this before," Alverick said to Kayna. "What is that black stuff connecting the glass to those little silver tips?"

"It's rubber. It grows on trees out in the east, and they found a way to harvest it to make these narghiles."

"But what do they do?" Alverick asked.

"They smell," Caitlyn groused.

Ignoring the archer's annoyance, the pirate continued. "You put a little herb in there and you smoke it. It's not incense you're smelling." A small smile played on Kayna's lips. "If you put the right stuff in, it leaves you feeling really good."

Alverick just eyed the contraption in wonder. Zanir didn't have anything made with rubber. He'd have to remember this and talk to Vashe about it when everything was over.
~~~

The three tried to make eye contact with the barkeep as they shuffled awkwardly near the entrance, but he paid them no heed, so they made their way to one of the few empty tables towards the back. Kayna wasted no time in waving down a young woman in a revealing dancer's outfit and ordering something for the narghile. The woman took the request with a smile and quickly brought over the pirate's order. Kayna took a long puff on the narghile and exhaled a cloud of smoke. A sigh of contentment escaped her as she leaned back in her chair.

"Not bad," the pirate said. "I might have to come back here again. Care to try?"

Kayna held out the pipe for Alverick and Caitlyn. When neither moved to take it from her, she took another puff and closed her eyes. The three sat in silence for a while, Kayna enjoying her smoke and Alverick and Caitlyn sharing a dish together. One of the women serving the patrons began dancing between the tables, the coins on her hip sash clinking in time with her movements.

Alverick glanced over at Caitlyn. The redhead sat quietly in her chair, her arms crossed against her chest. Though her stare didn't have the same intensity as earlier, her jaw was still clenched. He slipped his hand out and gently touched hers with the tips of his fingers. Caitlyn's eyes flashed his way for the briefest of seconds before returning to the dancing woman. A small smile crinkled the corners of her eyes, however. Taking his chance, the Avalanche pulled at her hand and interlaced his fingers with hers. Alverick felt a wave of relief when she didn't tense up.

He almost didn't notice the young wisp of a woman sidle up next to Kayna and begin whispering in the pirate's ear. She looked familiar.

X

The Flame's agitated pacing distracted Len as he tried to concentrate. The sentencing of Wyrd and discussions of how to move forward and rebuild Xan left the young Qu'ari feeling overwhelmed. Alliances needed to be renegotiated, Fa'Tinh was left in shambles, and a new choosing of the champions needed to take place. Vaarden's death was unexpected and left the clans unbalanced. Viir was maintaining a decent grasp on the Pshwani for now, his brother's good name helping to lend credence to his rule, but the Pshwani were fighters, and Viir was not. It was only a matter of time before they began fighting amongst themselves.

And then there was Pak. Her support was instrumental to his success. However, his stomach churned at the thought of returning Xan to the state it was under Ras' rule. Ras united them, sure, but he held Xan back from reaching her true potential. Trading rights and diplomacy were all well and good, but Xan's strength lay in her warriors. No, balancing between his promise to Pak and his vision for the future would be more difficult than he anticipated.

Hroth continued to stalk the perimeter of the Wolf. Len found himself following the Flame's movements out of the corner of his eye. Brow furrowed, Hroth chewed his bottom lip, an uncharacteristic sign of agitation as he paced. Occasionally, the Flame would summon a small ball of fire in his hand. Every time that happened, he quickly extinguished it, surprised that the magic manifested subconsciously.

Sitting quietly to the side, Pram kept a watchful eye on his leader. Several times during his musings, Len noticed the general observing him intently, expressionless. Pram had lived and served in both regiments. Undoubtedly, he would have thoughts about how everything was turning out.

"I won't kill him yet," Len finally said, breaking the silence and cutting through the tension.

He was pleased to see Pram straighten up in his chair and Hroth stop pacing. The general focused on Len much like a predator would on its prey, waiting to see what his next move would be.

"Wyrd is useful to me," the young Qu'ari continued. "He will atone for his sins. Only once he's paid will he be forgiven and released to the seven hells."

"How is he useful, Evenhand?" Pram asked.

Len choked back the annoyance that filled him at his general's question. He didn't like being questioned, but he knew it was Pram's duty to do so.

"Yesterday's battle was a precursor for something bigger. Unless Vahnyre is driven from Corinth, I'm sure he'll look for another way to strike." Len paused for a moment, trying to remember something. The two sat in silence as he wracked his brain. Finally, it hit him. "And, if I recall correctly, you mentioned some horrible monster outside my mother's home a little while ago. Perhaps the incidents are related."

"I am almost certain of it," Hroth replied.

"The fact that Wyrd was able to channel the aethren's strength is unprecedented. Who knows if there's a way for others to do the same? If there is, I will command the strength of the Windstrider. Wyrd could be key in defeating this and gaining the power of the gods." A hungry spark flashed in the young general's eye as he thought of the power he could wield.

Both Pram and Len turned to face the Flame. Len's face reflected the amusement he felt; he didn't expect Hroth to be the one to speak.

"The fires have been speaking to me," Hroth continued. "They warn me of a darkness blanketing Corinth. I believe they brought both the forces of Zanir as well as the gods to us for a reason. We should not ignore it."

"Damn," Len muttered, the spark returning once more. "The gods are becoming more of a nuisance than I expected."

Now it was Len's turn to lose himself in his thoughts. Sitting down at the table, the young Qu'ari leaned back in his chair and crossed his arms. To his side, Pram mimicked his movements in silence. The Flame sat down next to Pram and rested his elbows on the worn surface of the table. The young general went over everything that had happened in the last month. With every setback he'd experienced, one of the gods could be found close by.

The bones have been disrupted by the gods, he thought. *My future is no longer in my control. I need to stack the odds in my favor once more and bring fate back into my hands.*

Len closed his eyes and leaned back in his chair until only two legs rested on the floor. He rocked back and forth on the two legs, the front two hovering in the air as he bounced his legs with an exaggerated slowness.

"It's time to use all of our options to our advantage," the young general finally said, opening his eyes. "Gather all of our brothers and sisters. We leave tomorrow before midday for Pharn. If they want to maintain an alliance, they can shield our people and suffer any damages."

"Will we be able to round up all of Xan in such a short time?" Hroth asked.

"People are coming over to help rebuild after yesterday's battle," Pram replied. "The leaders can send word and quickly get our remaining brothers to Fa'Tinh."

"We will give Zanir's men Xan's best tonight before leaving," Len said. "They should have the best means to transport Wyrd. He'll need to be tied up and surrounded by guards at all times."

Pram nodded in agreement.

"We should also have guards to keep my mother and family safe," Len added. "Zanir has a soft spot for keeping their women sequestered amongst their soldiers. There's no reason we shouldn't use this resource as well. I'm sure they'll see it as noble."

"Evenhand, if I may. Would it also be possible to keep my family and Hroth's protégé under protection? His ward can add an extra layer of protection, or at least eyes, on our families and alert others to any potential threats."

The young general glanced over at the Flame, looking for any reaction. When Hroth didn't respond, Len waited a moment longer before nodding in agreement. As he announced his decision, he was pleased to see the Flame's face relax as his shoulders dropped as if he sighed in relief. His word still held weight in Xan, and it wouldn't be long before things were as they should be; he would make sure of it.

"If what Zaa'ni and Altansari experienced while I was gone is true, I would not want to put them in harm's way. If your apprentice is as observant as you say, her services will be most useful. Who knows, she might even find some weaknesses in Zanir's defenses."

"And what of Wyr-raji?" Pram asked bluntly.

"He'll face punishment on the battlefield. I'm sure there's more than one person who'd love to put a blade in his back."

Pram and Hroth nodded in understanding, neither one betraying their emotion. The young general let the front legs of his chair drop to the floor with a *thud*, his arms still crossed as he stared up at the ceiling. Without warning, Pram and the Flame got up as one and made their way out of the Dancing Wolf, leaving Len alone with his thoughts.

The young general closed his eyes, his head still facing the ceiling. In his mind, visions of goat knuckles and chicken bones being thrown into a small fire came into focus. The smell of sandalwood hung heavily in the air as a lamp with red glass bathed the room in an ominous glow. In front of him, an ancient woman, her features sunken into the wrinkles on her leathery face, stared intently at the bones. A sheet of stark white hair hung down in front of her face, obscuring one of her already hidden eyes.

Her lips moved as she read the message within. Len sat across from her with a confident smirk on his face. There was no doubt what the bones would tell him. All he needed was confirmation from the seer. The witch.

"Your life is filled with conflict, but Freyna has blessed you with victory. You will see much turmoil, but everything you seek, you will achieve." Her voice cracked as she croaked out his fortune. Her knobby fingers delicately traced the formation of the bones as they sat in the fire, the flames licking their smooth surfaces, having already claimed the fat and tissue years ago. "However, there is a spot of blackness upon your life where you stand to lose it all. As long as you keep Freyna's favor, you shall come out victorious."

The young Qu'ari rested his hands on his knees. He watched the bones sitting in the fire, the red light and sandalwood causing the bones inside the flames to cast long shadows in the darkened room. Everything was going according to plan.

XI

WANING CANDLELIGHT FLICKERED in the otherwise darkened library of Caer Grey. Heavy maroon cloths were swathed over the few windows in the tower, blocking out the sunlight and casting eerie shadows against the stone walls in the light of the flame. Queen Hera sat at an oaken table next to the drapes. Across from her, a spindly old man with wild white hair and long, gnarled fingers poured over a pile of parchment, scrolls, and a few leather tomes that rested on the floor next to the table. Away from the pair, a bowl with crushed lavender filled the room with a delicate fragrance, contrasting with the unnerving atmosphere of the dark curtains and flickering light.

Hera fingered the thin leather strap holding her holy periwinkle petals inside a worn leather pouch around her neck. On her lap rested her effigy of Freyna, the young girl's hair splaying across the queen's thigh. Despite her growing curiosity, Hera tapped her foot anxiously as she waited for the dream reader to finish his research. It had been three long days since she first told the ancient man about her dream while she was recovering from her poisoning. Three long days with no answers.

The elderly man rustled through a few papers before checking a chart in one of the scrolls on the floor. The queen's eyes glazed over as she looked at the positions of the stars, with lines and annotations written off to the side. She'd seen these images for what felt like a thousand times in the last few days. None of it made a bit of sense.

"It appears you may have had a true vision," his feeble voice croaked out.

Hera was caught off-guard, her eyes darting up to the old man's face. Instead of facing her, he was scribbling notes on a spare piece of parchment. He rustled the pages he'd taken notes on earlier in between his thoughts and the queen's recounting. Splotches of black ink dotted the parchment from his hasty attempt to document everything.

"The mighty Freyna, goddess of the central realms of Corinth, has deemed you worthy of bestowing such a gift." His hand trembled as he wrote. "Though Zanir's protectors are the Siblings of Water, it seems as though you have been chosen by the goddess herself as a worthy vessel. Interesting," he paused, scratching his chin with ink-stained fingers, "since you are from the Western Isles and have no ties to the central realms." The elderly man closed his eyes as a faint smile tugged on the corner of his mouth as he mused over the implications of his statement.

Hera gripped the folds of her dress in anticipation, her doll to the goddess shifting as the fabric bunched in her hands. What does it all mean? She wanted to cry out. Instead, the queen held her tongue and hoped he'd provide an explanation soon.

"As such," he finally continued, "we must heed her warning lest there be dire consequences. The gods do not contact Man lightly."

"Please, Kusmir," Hera entreated. The suspense was proving to be too much for her. "What does this mean for Zanir?"

The elderly scholar did not seem bothered by her interruption. Instead, he finally put his quill down and smoothed an imaginary wrinkle on the sheet of parchment. Hera was impressed that he didn't smudge the ink as he did so.

"We need to pull the important details from the dream elements. First, we have the blessed Freyna contacting you at great risk to herself. We know this because there was darkness in the shadow of the tree. Next, we notice the twelve monoliths arranged in a circle. In the center of the circle, there is a single golden flower. The twelve stones could stand for several things, but

I believe they represent the great deities: three of Water, three of Ayr, one of Fyre, one of Earth, and the four great ones. The ones they call Ancients.

"I can only speculate what the flower signifies. Part of me thinks that it is humanity, while another thinks it is the delicate balance of the world. I am unfortunately unable to give you a definitive answer, your majesty. I apologize. I fear that without knowing what it means, we are missing a key piece of the vision."

Kusmir wiped his brow with a shaking hand, streaks of black smudging his thin, wrinkled skin.

"We can try and surmise the location based on the images shown to you, but we cannot be sure completely of our accuracy. You stood on a knoll over-looking a grassy field. The tree, gnarled and ancient, kept watch over the stone circle. As you mentioned, you said you believed you stood on the out-skirts of Alocar. I, too, think it is our sister nation.

"If you trust my reading of your vision and the motions of the stars, go to the field on the border of Zanir and Alocar. There is a large oak with white bark, her leaves thick and of the deepest green. The tree overlooks a lake, crystal clear and ringed with small stones. They're nothing like you saw in your vision — just a collection of smooth stones encircling the waters. I wish I knew what you'd find there, but that is where I believe your answers lie."

Hera leaned back in her chair and rubbed her hand over the dress of the effigy on her lap. She was familiar with this lake, having gone there several times when she and Jaste were first wed. It always felt special to her, as if it were somehow alive, but she just attributed it to the fact that she and her husband were being less than discreet under the shade of the surrounding trees. Hera remembered how the sun delicately warmed her flesh as the sweet smell of honeysuckle floated around her. She never would've imagined it was a place for the gods.

"How much time do I have?" she asked.

Kusmir stopped slipping his papers into the books and shuffling his scrolls. He scratched his head as he read one of the scribbles in his notes. "The Blood Moon is coming in two days," he murmured. "I think that is important. The stars are showing something coming around then."

Hera clutched the leather pouch around her neck. Despite the trepidation she felt rising within her, the petals inside brought her a measure of comfort. "I thought as much. Kusmir, thank you for your help. I must leave immediately. Forgive my rashness. I will properly thank you upon my return."

Without waiting for a response, the queen rose and quickly made her way out of the darkened room. Behind her, she could hear the rustling of parchment as Kusmir resumed gathering his documents.

XII

A COOL BREEZE RUSTLED Oldar's hair in the crisp afternoon. Though the sun hung high in the air, it was uncharacteristically chilly that day. The young king pulled the hood of his cloak up over his head, shielding his eyes and subconsciously wrapping it around himself like a blanket, as he stood in front of Castle Storm. The once-welcoming portcullis now stared at him, its angry maw ready to swallow him whole. A shiver ran down Oldar's spine. Whether it was involuntary or not, he couldn't be sure.

Two haggard guards stood off to the side. Oldar considered walking over to speak with them, but he decided against it. He wasn't supposed to be in Alocar. It wouldn't do for him to alert others to his presence. Before he slipped in through the entrance, he took one last look at the pair. Dark bags gave their eyes a sunken, almost dead appearance. Adding to the scruff covering their chins, the duo looked like a pale version of their former selves. Taking a deep breath, Oldar ducked into the portcullis and disappeared into the darkness.

The entrance to the keep proper was darker than the young king expected. Though the sun shone brightly outside, whatever seemed to filter through the windows appeared dull, a mere shadow of what it should be. The sound of boots hitting the worn stones echoed in the empty hallway, leaving Oldar feeling exposed. Where there was usually chatter and bustle, all that remained were the carved sentinels lining the path. Statues and suits of armor provided watch where humans should.

Oldar's hands moved to his mouth and he blew into them, trying to warm them. His efforts were in vain. As soon as he felt a modicum of relief, the pervasive chill that surrounded him would seep into him once more, reaching down to his bones.

"I should've grabbed a warmer cloak from Schaed's," Oldar muttered to himself as he blew onto his hands once more. "It's damn near freezing here." Rounding a corner, Oldar was hit with a chill that stopped him in his tracks. "It's colder than freezing," he gasped, his breath coming out as a puff of smoke.

The frigid air pulled at his chest, making it difficult to breathe. Each breath came out in a cloud of smoke, leeching what little heat he had left from his body. With a conscious effort, the young king willed himself to continue moving.

"I'll die of frost if I stay in one place," he told himself. "I need to move forward."

He wasn't exactly sure what he was looking for, but he knew that whatever it was, his uncle would have the answers. It took almost an eternity for Oldar to find the throne room. By the time he walked up to the chambers, he noted that a thin sheen of ice covered the stones, making his footing a bit slippery.

Ahead, he was surprised to see that there were no guards stationed at the throne room doors. Alastaire must be confident if he didn't even have attendants or protection nearby. The lack of normal safety protocols unnerved the young king. His thumb went to his mouth for the briefest of instances before he yanked it away. He wouldn't bite his nails again. Summoning what little courage he had within, Oldar strode up to the throne room doors.

As his hand touched the knocker, he recoiled as though he were bit. The metal handle felt colder than ice, and his hland began prickling. By the time he released the knob, it had already begun going numb.

Maybe I should turn around and head to Ånchal with Pru as planned, he thought. *Nothing good can come from this meeting. I don't even know if I'll make it out alive.*

Oldar stood in front of the doors for several long minutes. His mind raced as he tried to decide what to do. There was nothing for him in Alocar right now. He needed help, and Zanir could provide that aid. However, a small voice in the back of his mind nagged at him, telling him that he needed to stay and protect his people.

What good am I to them dead?

He knew the answer. But he also knew what he needed to do if he was going to succeed. With a deep breath, he bypassed the knocker and placed his hands on the door. The age-worn wood had been smoothed by hand oils over the decades, leaving the grain as smooth as cobblestone. Relieved that it was warmer than the metal, Oldar pushed the doors open and entered the throne room.

~~~

A roaring fire burned in the hearth, providing the room with a welcome warmth but also casting eerie shadows upon the walls. They elongated and undulated against the stone as though they were alive. In front of the fire, Oldar's uncle sat in his father's throne, his Aunt Constance sitting comfortably by her husband's side.

Alastaire's eyes widened in surprise for the briefest of moments before being replaced with an almost greedy expression. His mouth twitched up into a menacing grin, and his fingers wrapped the ends of the throne's armrests tightly. Constance, ever the epitome of grace, shuffled ever so slightly in her seat. Her face did not betray the emotion she felt. Watching the two as he moved to the center of the room, Oldar couldn't decide who unnerved him more. His uncle looked mad, but his aunt was more calculating.
~~~

When he'd finally reached a spot in front of the hearth that provided him with an abundance of heat, Oldar inclined his head in respect to his aunt before addressing the two.

"Good morning, Aunt Constance. Uncle Alastaire." Oldar's eyes darted to each of them as he stood before them. "I can't say that I'm exactly pleased to see you here after our last encounter."

Alastaire leaned forward in his seat, his knuckles turning white as he still gripped the finely carved armrests. Instead of letting him answer, Constance decided to speak.

"My dear, Oldar," she said with a purr. "When we heard you'd been accused of murder, why, we couldn't leave your people to flounder once more. Mighty Zemé has tasked our family with keeping Alocar safe. We knew you would be fine," she added, almost as an afterthought. "There's no way our nephew would be capable of something like murder."

Oldar could feel his chest tighten as anger welled within. Constance's smirk only fueled his irritation. Instead of taking her bait, he forced himself to calm down and wait. He wanted to give his uncle time to speak, like he knew Alastaire wanted to do. Oldar's patience was rewarded when Alastaire spoke.

"I'm sure you can appreciate our generosity by taking time out of our lives to rescue you in your time of need. You should be thanking us on bended knee." Alastaire's eyes flashed as he leaned forward.

"Thank you? For what? For constantly trying to usurp my throne?" Oldar felt his frustrations rising and fought hard with himself to keep his voice level.

"No, you fool," Alastaire hissed. "For doing you the favor of showing you your weaknesses. All your life you've been a damned idiot pissing around Alocar like some fucking ass. I had been waiting for your father to straighten you out, but he was too soft on you. Too much of a philosopher to see what needed to be done."

"And you know what Alocar needs?" Oldar found himself blurting out.

As soon as the words left his lips, he regretted his rashness. His uncle clearly was unwell, and anything he said would only incite the man. Even as the young king's statement hit Alastaire's ears, the man's face twisted into something dark and unnatural. Rage flashed behind his eyes as the corners of his lips curled up in a snarl. Next to him, Constance gave her husband an uneasy sidelong glance. Oldar watched as she scooted her tiny frame as far as she could from Alastaire in her ornate throne, leaning away to put even more distance between the two of them.

The air in the room gradually became heavy and cold. Oldar noted the chill and quickly looked at the hearth. The flames still roared inside, the logs cracking and popping merrily. However, all around him, the same deathly freeze he'd felt earlier in the castle seeped in, as did the darkness.

"You know, Gwyn was as dimwitted as you," Alastaire replied. "And look where that got her. Beheaded after Snapping."

Oldar felt his blood boil at the insult to his mother. His hands were clenched at his sides, the left hand gripping a bit of his trouser fabric as well.

"I had a plan to deal with her though," Alastaire continued, ignoring his nephew's emotion. "A way for us normal people to counteract the unnatural curse given to those supposedly chosen by the gods."

Alastaire's hand unconsciously went to his hip as he stared hungrily at the young king. As he touched whatever was there, the shadows in the room deepened, elongating towards Oldar as he stood in the light of the fire. The man's fingers gently grazed what appeared to be a sheath, the muted glow emanating from it now growing in strength as his flesh touched the sheath. Oldar felt an icy breeze rustle his clothing, and the flames in the hearth flickered, threatening to go out.

"Knock it off!" Alastaire roared, his head snapping to his right.

Oldar tried to lock gazes with his uncle to see who he was talking to, but the man's eyes darted feverishly around the room. Next to him, Constance gawked at her husband, abject horror on her face.

"Calm yourself, dear," her voice cracked out. "No need to get them into a frenzy."

In another part of the castle, a shriek rang out. The sound sent chills down Oldar's spine that he wouldn't have imagined considering how cold he was. In response to the cry, the shadows in the room danced wildly. The glow at Alastaire's hip wavered for a moment before being covered by his hand as he let out a low growl.

Taking this as his cue, Oldar began backing up slowly towards the open doors leading out into the hallway. His eyes darted from the hearth, where flames waved valiantly while threatening to go out, to his uncle, who appeared preoccupied with something else in the room. They finally landed on his aunt, Constance. The woman, normally imposing with her regal nature, looked small and fragile in the chaotic shadows, and frightened. Her usually smug countenance faltered, and her eyes betrayed the terror within. Her hands gripped the ends of the armrest as her body struggled to get as far away as she could from her husband. Oldar felt a pang of pity for his aunt.

A wave of bone-chilling freeze washed over the young king once more, and without waiting to see what was going on, Oldar turned and ran out of the throne room. He worked to pull the heavy wooden doors shut behind him as another one of the shrieks filled the room he'd just escaped. Cold sweat beaded on his body as he gasped for breath, his frozen hands not wanting to cooperate.

He felt something pulling against the door, his body lurching forward as it cracked open once more. Inside the room, Oldar's uncle shouted out, having risen from his throne. A pair of hands grabbed the knocker and yanked it, startling the young king. Swiveling his head, Oldar saw Ingmar, covered in thick clothing, struggling to help him shut the door. The two men grunted in exertion as they pulled the door closed. Their efforts were rewarded as the door finally closed with a merciful thud.

A cry rang out in the throne room once more, only to be answered somewhere nearby. Ingmar grabbed the young king's hand and began running. Oldar didn't question him; he just let the soldier lead him to what he hoped would be safety.

XIII

T HE EMPTY HALLWAYS PASSED in a blur as Ingmar and Oldar raced through them. Shrieks rang out in the distance, occasionally sounding uncomfortably close to the young king, but he didn't falter. In what felt like ages, the two arrived at a simple door that led to the kitchens. The two darted inside and quickly slammed the door.

A wave of warmth washed over the young king as the multiple fires worked their magic to keep the room heated. Oldar let out a sigh of relief as he felt the blessed heat reach his very core. The chill and terror he'd just experienced slowly began to melt away, making way for the myriad of questions that had been kept at bay.

A mug of warm cider was shoved into Oldar's hands, startling him. He looked around to see who had given it to him and realized that the entirety of the castle staff, and even a few of the guards, were crammed tightly into the small kitchen. Children huddled closest to the fires under a pile of coats, blankets, and rags, while the adults and their eldest children worked to keep the fires stoked and food cooking. An elderly woman proffered Ingmar a mug of cider as well as steamy towels to treat his frostbitten hands. The soldier took both with a wan yet grateful smile.

"What are you doing here, my lord?" an elderly steward asked. "It is not safe for you here."

Several others nodded in agreement, their heads barely moving as if they dare not speak. A multitude of eyes peeked out from the lump of clothes as the young ones stared at their king in awe. Oldar felt a knot form in his stomach. Seeing his people suffer like this made his next steps more difficult.

"I came to talk to my uncle," he replied lamely. "I need to know why he came here and what he's after."

"With all due respect, your majesty," Ingmar interjected. "We all know what he's after. We've started piecing together the why, and I think you might have the last piece we need to put the story together." The grizzled soldier eyed his king from behind his mug of hot cider. His eyes bore into Oldar in a way that reminded the young king of his old bodyguard. And his father. "What did he say to you, your majesty?"

Oldar racked his brain, trying to remember everything that had occurred. It all happened so quickly that his mind only had time to process one thing. He needed help. Closing his eyes, the young king forced himself to calm down and replay everything Alastaire said.

"He mentioned taking the throne, obviously. And that he thought both me and my mom were fools." Oldar's eyes fluttered open as the true weight of what his uncle said finally hit him. "And that he'd found a way to deal with my mom."

Ingmar's face blanched.

"What is the cause of those howls I've been hearing?" Oldar pressed. "They're also the reason the castle is so frigid, right?"

"Yes," the soldier replied.

"You must leave, your highness," the elderly woman who gave Oldar the cider added. "It's not safe for you here."

"It's not safe for you either," Oldar countered.

"We'll manage," the elderly steward said. "Your uncle hasn't noticed that we're not attending to the castle's needs any longer."

"As long as we drop off food for him in the throne room, he leaves us be." The elderly woman's voice cracked. The weight of keeping everyone safe while maintaining the castle was taking its toll on her weathered body. "And we daren't let the children out of the kitchens."

"Sometimes the soldiers drop by to check on us. We feed them and make sure they're warm during their rounds. Well, as warm as they can be." The steward glanced over towards Ingmar. "Sir Ingmar here has been here almost daily. He's the one who usually accompanies us while we make our food deliveries to keep us safe."

Oldar felt the knot lessen as he admired the unity of the palace staff. He hoped that one day, when he regained the throne, he would be able to properly thank them for all their hard work. He took another sip of his cider and felt the now warm liquid slide down his throat, bringing him relief once more.

"Your majesty," Ingmar said, breaking his train of thought. "I must insist on escorting you out of the castle immediately. The danger has passed, for now, but I fear that it will be back with deadly consequences should you stay here a moment longer. Shall I take you back to your special place?"

The inflection in his tone let Oldar know that the soldier spoke of Schaed's wine cellar, where they'd met a few days prior. A wave of grief washed over him, the ever-changing emotions leaving him feeling drained of all energy at the thought of his friend. It was quickly replaced by despair. All Oldar wanted to do was sink into a chair and rest.

What would Pru think if she saw me acting like this? he lamented.

The matronly woman's face filled his mind. He knew he couldn't give up. Her wrinkled smile and wispy white hair tied back brought him something he'd always treasured when he was younger: hope.

"Send someone to pick up Pru," the king said to Ingmar. "I'll need you to take me to the tunnels and have someone meet us there with her." Oldar took a deep breath. "I'm going to Zanir for help. They're mostly likely in Xan, but it'll be safer for me to seek aid than wait here."

The idea of running across the Myrani once more terrified the young king, especially with his old caretaker in tow, but he knew that he needed to find Cienna and beg her to send her forces to Madden. Oldar looked over at the venerable, old guard and saw him finishing off the last of his mug of cider before throwing on his coat.

Time was running out.

XIV

THE HURRIED CLATTER of boots on stone echoed in the hallway. In the adjacent room, Zanirian soldiers bustled about, preparing to move. Voices called out in a cacophony as they competed to be heard against the sound of armor clanking. Among it all, Hera strode through the chaos.

Dressed in riding pants, a tan colored tunic and cape, the queen cut an imposing figure with her already short-cropped hair. At her hip, a small silver dagger lay strapped and ready. Her brown riding boots never seemed to stop as she moved from station to station inspecting her soldiers and speaking with the few remaining commanders.

They were split into two groups: one to accompany her to Alocar, and another, smaller force to remain at Pharn until her brother-in-law and his men arrived. She'd left directions with her handmaiden, Aeliana, to keep Pharn running as smoothly as possible so as not to arouse suspicions. Hera did not want anyone to know that she was leaving her people essentially unprotected.

"Your majesty," a man with long hair tied back in a low-hanging tail called out as he quickly approached her.

Hera stopped and turned to face the voice, her cape swishing as she spun. Anxiety plucked at her nerves, her stomach already in a twisted knot, leaving her feeling more unsure than she already felt. Jaste had always been the one to handle any military affairs; Hera never bothered herself with that.

Now, she lamented her inexperience, praying to Freyna and the Siblings that she wouldn't let her people down.

Composing herself, the queen addressed the soldier: "Talk to me."

Her blunt tone caught the man off-guard and he faltered slightly.

"Forgive me, your majesty," he said. "I wanted to let you know that everything is in place and we are ready to leave. If you would please, a few of my cohorts and I would like for you to look over our forces once more, just to make sure we've got enough men to meet our needs."

Hera's eyes swept over the room. The bustling bodies and constant movement made it difficult to get an accurate count of everyone there. However, the queen thought she could get a rough estimate of her remaining soldiers. Fewer people rushed up from the armory with their arms full of weapons, and the sound of pounding boots died down. The general chatter in the room also lessened as men positioned themselves in accordance with their superior's instructions.

"It's probably a good idea to do one final sweep," Hera replied. "We're taking a big gamble, and I don't want to come back to any surprises."

The man nodded his head curtly and motioned for the queen to follow. Group by group, the pair walked over and inspected the ranks. Her escort explained each section's specialty and introduced her to the commanding officer.

As they moved deeper into the preparation room, Hera felt the tingles of doubt begin to creep in. Many of the small squadrons she'd met were specialty ones that she planned on bringing with her. It seemed as though the majority that she was leaving behind were not as experienced, and regret seeped in. There wasn't enough time for her to stop and take stock of her forces; too much time had been wasted after speaking with the dream reader, and there wasn't much left.

Nearing the next bunch of soldiers, Hera was relieved to see a somewhat familiar face: the young boy who had stood outside her door while she was recovering from her poisoning. She remembered hearing his name a handful of times among the soldiers, and for some reason, it seemed to stick in her mind.

"And this lot here is comprised of some of our best bowmen. Master Thol has worked with each one of them personally, ensuring their proficiency."

The man's voice droned on as he listed off the achievements of certain members of the group. Hera found herself watching the young soldier, Cody, as he listened to the accolades of his peers. Despite his young age, the boy stood confident, his right hand gripping the staff lightly but still ready to wield it at a moment's notice.

"Lastly," the man's voice continued. Hera found herself jolted out of her thoughts and returned her attentions to the soldier. "We have Cody. He's one of our newest recruits, but he's already proven himself against Swordbane. He also was assigned guard duty for you while you were recovering. This group here will be staying behind to help protect Caer Grey." Motioning for the queen to move forward, the man began, "Now, if we move right along, we'll get to one of our remaining squads."

Hera, however, did not take his lead and begin walking. Instead, she glanced from Cody to the preparation room and back. Her mind whirled as she attempted to process everything she'd been told during the last half hour.

"Your majesty?" the man asked tentatively, seeing as she had not moved. "Is everything all right?"

The queen's eyes continued to bore into Cody, causing the young man to turn a brilliant shade of red. The leather pouch hidden under her blouse began to grow hotter against her breast. There was something about this boy.

"How many groups are there left to see?" she asked.

"Four," the man replied.

"And are they to stay here or accompany me?"

"Remain."

The queen's fingers went to her chin, stroking it gently as her brain worked nonstop to finalize her plan. It sounded crazy, even in her head, but something inside told her that she was making the right decision.

"I want you to add one more soldier to the list of officers who are remaining to watch over the capital," Hera ordered. "He'll also be in charge of gathering information and preparing it for my return."

"Of course, your majesty," the man said, clicking his heels to attention. "And who would you like to handle this position?"

Hera's head swiveled towards the squad of bowmen, the soldier following her gaze.

"I'd like Cody to handle this duty," the queen stated. "He's proven his worth to the kingdom on several occasions for someone with such a short military career," Hera explained at the quizzical glance from the veteran soldier. "I sense great promise in him and would like to afford him the opportunity to prove himself."

"Your majesty," the man began.

"Of course, he will have someone he reports to for making any big decisions," Hera added. "I'm not ready to grant him free reign over the country. Once Jaste's brother Jaes arrives with aid, we can leave word that his senior officers are to take over along with our senior-most officer. Cody will then be relegated to informant."

The soldier signaled his understanding with a curt nod. "Then, with your leave, your majesty, I believe we should be heading out before the barracks ring the dinner bell. After all, time is of the essence."

The queen voiced her agreement before waving the man away. There were a few loose ends she wanted to tie up before they left, and the sun was already nearing the horizon.

XV

Dawn broke with a riot of colors as birds flew across the sky, their chatter mixing with the myriad of voices down below. Despite the early hour, the people of Xan, along with the forces of Pharn headed towards Zanir. Kayna and her crew left the night before, stating that their part of the deal was done. Both Kayna and Maya left with the offer for Alverick and Len, promising that there would always be a spot for them among their ranks.

Len found himself seriously considering Maya's words. He couldn't explain why, but the sea called out to him, pulling him back towards the Bone Coast. However, he knew he needed to stay. Alverick, on the other hand, thanked Kayna for her offer, but let her know that his place was in Pharn. For now.

It was a bit of a surprise, however, when Ghan decided to stay with his sister and accompany Xan on her journey to Zanir. The pair actually went with the heads of the clans to gather their people and bring them all down to Fa'Tinh. Now, the entirety of the clans have congregated at the capital. Such an event hadn't occurred in a great many years.

A massive, tear-producing yawn ripped from Alverick, causing his body to shudder as he felt himself stretching with it. The night proved to be longer than he'd anticipated. He and Swordbane sat up until the late hours of the night discussing their next steps. The Flame was adamant that they leave Xan no later than the next morning, but what was to follow, neither knew.

Another yawn escaped him as he lightly bounced atop Styx's back. Brody rode next to him, the two trailing at the end of the convoy. Brody gave his friend a nudge with his leg as the Avalanche swayed in the saddle, his eyes drooping dangerously. As his eyes snapped open, Alverick saw the boyish grin the young man was known for greeting him.

"Can't have you passing out on your horse now, can we?" Brody's eyes twinkled.

"You're in good spirits," Alverick replied, rubbing his hands over his face in an effort to wake himself up. "I take it you two finally talked?"

Brody's gaze shifted over to the princess as she rode a dun stallion surrounded by a thick circle of Zanirian guards. Her curly hair was tied loosely in a tail that hung down the middle of her back. Beside her, Caitlyn walked amongst her guard, and the two spoke animatedly. Cienna's eyes radiated joy, the smile on her face evident as the corners of her eyes turned up as the two talked. The young man let out a soft sigh as he watched her.

"We did," he finally said. "We decided it was best to not pursue our relationship. For Zanir," he clarified.

Alverick could see that his friend was disappointed. He knew that Brody and Cienna were doing what was best for their people, but deep down, he hoped that the young man would find happiness with her.

"I'm sorry," Alverick said softly. "I know she meant the world to you."

"It was to be expected; after all, she is a princess."

Alverick couldn't help but notice how the corners of Brody's mouth drooped and the twinkle left his eyes. It was only for a moment, but the pain was still there. The young man worked hard to conceal it, however, as his smile returned. The Avalanche noted how it did not reach his friend's eyes.

The two rode in silence for a while, the horse's hooves clopping on the worn dirt road and kicking up dust. Clouds of the red powder pocketed the group as they traveled, marking the steps of the other horses. Soon, everyone had a fine layer of soil covering them, tinging their clothes a faint red hue.

General chatter filled the air, despite the early hour. Children, the younger ones draped over their mother's shoulders, wove between people as they marched. Giggles and occasionally a shriek of mirth erupted over the regular conversations. The warriors of Xan moved with solemnity, their silence contrasting with the jovial talk from the forces of Zanir.

"What do you think the Flame was worried about?" Brody asked.

His sudden question caught Alverick off guard, causing him to jump in his saddle. Styx nickered at the unexpected movement, her ears twitching. The Avalanche turned and stared his friend in the eye. Leaning over, Alverick spoke quietly, hoping that no one else would hear them.

"He said that Vahnyre showed him something during the battle with Wyrd." Alverick's gaze darted about to see if anyone had overheard. "Destruction. Chaos. Xan in complete ruin."

"Sounds a little like what you were talking about when we brought you back from Aramaine," Brody whispered. When Alverick didn't respond, he continued. "You were talking about a Darkness and some crazy stuff, Al. What if it's all linked?"

A knot formed in the pit of the Avalanche's stomach. He hadn't told anyone yet about his time in Themba for fear they would think he was mad. One simply did not travel to the land of the dead and traverse the Halls of the Fallen, let alone battle a god amongst the greatest warriors and kings in history. If anyone had told him that, Alverick would've assumed he'd Snapped. And yet, he'd been there on several occasions. He feared he was mad. Bannen had told him as much on one visit.

However, the desire to see his friends once more pulled at him. Alverick wanted nothing more than to see Bannen and Jaste again and to visit those sacred halls. To see Vialle. The dead still called to him. If he wasn't careful, he could see the twisted tree in his mind's eye. It took a great deal of his energy to keep the tree at bay. He found the red tinge at his periphery seeping into his normal vision more often whenever Themba appeared to him.

"I think it is," Alverick mumbled, distracted.

The Avalanche felt the knot within him tighten as Brody's eyes widened. The young man didn't want to believe it. Brody's head rapidly shook with small little no's, as though he could convince himself that it wasn't true.

"Al, no. It can't." Brody stared at Alverick, his gaze imploring the man to say he was just joking. "What does it mean for us?"

The agony in Brody's voice pulled at Alverick's heart. He felt the fear and the pain that the young man must be feeling. The Avalanche wished he could alleviate his friend's anguish, but he knew that he must be forthcoming.

"Brody, there's something I must tell you." Alverick noted how a grimace flashed on his friend's face for the briefest of moments. "I've been to the Halls and seen the dead. I've seen..." The Avalanche's voice caught in his throat as he tried not to cry. He felt his face grow warm as tears pricked the corners of his eyes. "I've talked with Bannen and Jaste. Your brother's proud of you," he finished quickly.

Brody's face became a mask at the mention of his brother. His hands gripped the reins tighter than usual, his knuckles turning white.

"Brody, I don't say this to you to upset you," Alverick said. "I think there's something big going on. Clearly there is. The gods have been showing us the future in pieces, hoping we can figure it out. We need to be prepared for something — "

"Nothing is going on, Al," Brody said through clenched teeth. The young man's sudden outburst startled the Avalanche. "Obviously, you and the Flame are both Snapped, or at least he might be touched, but clearly you spout nonsense."

Brody's words cut Alverick deeply. He knew his friend was grieving the loss of his brother, but it seemed foolish for Brody to dismiss all the signs so quickly.

"You don't mean that," Alverick said softly.

"Al, you've been Snapped, or on the verge of for quite some time. You've been talking to my brother ever since his death. Don't you think that you're allowing yourself to believe what you want and creating Bannen's image in your mind?"

"It's not like that. Yes, I have struggled since his death, but I tell you, I've been to Themba."

"Please," Brody implored. "It can't be true."

His eyes bore into the Avalanche, begging him to affirm his thoughts. Alverick couldn't help but feel a twinge of regret at stirring up so many emotions within his friend. Neither one had properly grieved yet, and now the consequences were catching up to them.

"I wish I could say I was lying, but with everything we've experienced and from so many different people, I think it would be foolhardy to ignore the signs. Something big is coming, and we must be prepared."

With a sigh, Brody nodded. "It doesn't help that we have two literal gods walking just in front of us," he said, motioning to Ghan and Aria. "I suppose to deny it would be like putting your head in the sand."

The two traveled in silence for a little while. Despite their mounts, the convoy moved slowly through the streets of Fa'Tinh. Soldiers and young men helped support the elderly, while the women kept the children in check. Most of the women also ushered the livestock along and carried baskets and jars filled with supplies and water since the wains were filled with arms, spice, and ore. The sole exception was one which Pram had insisted was to be for the infirm, wounded, and those who couldn't walk. Wyrd followed that wagon, bound to it by a rope and surrounded by armed men.

"You know," Brody said, breaking the silence. "I would love to see Bannen again, even if it is just in a dream."

Alverick caught the wistful look on his friend's face as the boy reminisced about his fallen brother. He couldn't help but feel a twinge of guilt knowing he'd spoken with Bannen when Brody could not. A solitary tear rolled down Brody's cheek as the twinkle returned to his eyes. The corner of the young man's mouth turned up in a fond smile as he remembered some precious memory.

A shout from ahead startled the two men. Nearby, cries rang out as word traveled down the line. Women and children moved closer together, the smiles now gone from the young ones' eyes as they clung to the closest adult.

"What's going on?" Alverick called out.

"Scrymme!" someone called back.

XVI

IN A QUICK MOTION, Alverick slid off the saddle, handing Styx's reins to the nearest Zanirian soldier. The man took them with a bewildered expression but did not protest. Weaving his way through the group, the Avalanche thought he heard someone arguing behind him. He didn't stop to look, but he thought he heard the sound of heavy footsteps following him.

It took a few minutes, but Alverick found himself at the head of the throng next to Swordbane and his general, Pram. The Flame and his consort stood off to the side, observing. Moments later, a second set of footsteps could be heard. Alverick caught Brody rushing over to them, weaving between the startled citizens of Xan, and realized that the young man must have shoved his reins into the man with Styx's hands, earning him the shout of reproach he'd heard earlier.

"What's going on?" Alverick asked the two as Brody approached. "I heard someone say Scrymme?"

The Avalanche's eyes scanned the horizon ahead, looking for sign of the unexpected visitors. Off in the distance, not too far from where they stood, Alverick caught a glimpse of the dark-haired, statuesque isolationists under the sparse tree line on the outskirts of Fa'Tinh. Their mounts were tied up and munched on a few tufts of grass that grew out of the red clay that surrounded the clans.

"Our Flame caught sight of their forces a moment ago. They were securing their horses and strapping their weapons to their bodies," Pram said.

"There's a woman among them," Swordbane added. "Probably an elite."

"It's possible," Alverick replied. "Their magi are quite skilled, and their assassins are a mix of men and women."

"No," Hroth said. "That's not an assassin. That's Dzvareliah, the queen."

Alverick and the others spun to face the Flame, Brody's jaw dropping at the news. The man was pulling off his cloak, revealing the bandages underneath, as he spoke. His gaze hardened as he scanned the now approaching Scrymmen warriors, his eyes narrowing.

"Looks like Dzvorth is there too," he added.

"Shit," Alverick muttered. "The king and queen."

"This must've been something big they've planned," Pram said. "I don't think I've ever heard of a member of Scrymme leaving their homeland."

Alverick didn't say anything, but he could think of one or two. As he anticipated the royals' approach, his mind wandered to Vashe. He hadn't seen her since the night before the siege on Pharn. He wondered how she was doing and if she knew anything about this. With a mental shake of the head, Alverick almost laughed at himself. Why would she know anything about some Scrymmen attack? She hadn't been home in almost a decade, and she only used her scrying pool to delve into other dimensions. There would be no reason for her to watch her people.

"I wonder if Vashe knows about this?" Brody asked, mimicking his friend's thoughts.

"Why would she?" Alverick asked.

"No time," Brody replied quickly. "Another time. I promise."

"Well, if the king and queen have decided to come, it must be important," Pram said. "We should probably have our brothers move up front to protect the others."

"Brody," Alverick commanded. "Go and gather both Xanan and Zanirian men. Also bring that axe maiden and Caitlyn. They will be useful against Scrymme. Make sure Dez is with them. She'll be able to combat their magic with her own."

Glancing over at Swordbane and Pram and seeing them make no response, Brody gave a quick acknowledgement and darted back into the crowd. The young officer quickly disappeared into the throng, the general populace moving aside as he wove through.

Alverick's gaze wandered back over to Swordbane and his men. The young general watched the approaching Scrymmen forces with a keen eye. The invaders made their way towards the fleeing people of Xan at an almost leisurely pace, as if they didn't feel the need to rush an attack.

"Smug bastards," Swordbane spat. "They think their numbers will intimidate us. Well, they've been hiding in Scrymme for far too long."

Alverick's brows almost disappeared as they flew up. Surely, he knew about their superior numbers when it came to magi.

"Are you not worried about them all being god-blessed?" Alverick asked incredulously. "We may be strong, but our numbers are no match for Shadows and Liches."

"You underestimate me, Avalanche," Swordbane replied. "Xan has almost no god-blessed. We rely on our own strengths and natural abilities and have flourished for ages. A few magi will not deter us. Besides, we have our own ultimate weapon."

The statement baffled Alverick. He looked from Swordbane to Pram to the Flame, but none seemed the least bit bothered by a team from Scrymme. In fact, the Flame almost seemed bored as he stood with his arms crossed, his tattooed arm exposed.

What could our secret weapon be? he wondered. *Surely, he doesn't mean...*

Alverick's attention turned back to the young general. Swordbane stood casually with his hand resting lightly on his hip and touching the hilt of his battle axe. Behind him, he heard the sound of approaching men and the startled cries of civilians as a collection of soldiers broke through the crowd to join them.

⌐⌐⌐

Dzvareliah hung back and watched as more and more soldiers pushed their way to the front of the group. The green livery of Zanir mixing with the red of Xan surprised her. She hadn't expected there to be other nations involved with the heathen tribes. Most likely, her dear husband hadn't thought of this possibility either. A cruel smile played on her lips as she watched Dzvorth make his way towards the marching armies.

Her knowledge of the clans was minimal: they did not worship Aria, and they were bloodthirsty. So much so that they frequently fought amongst themselves. Dzvareliah acknowledged, however, that her information was outdated at best. The people in front of her appeared to be a cohesive nation. This miscalculation could prove to be very interesting.

A gentle breeze tickled her face; her long, dark hair was tied in a low tail and hanging down her back. Taking that as her cue, the queen of Scrymme tied up her sleeves with the ribbons around her wrists and joined her husband.

XVII

A GIDDY SMILE PLAYED on the lips of Dzvorth Ari, but he quickly masked it, making it one of confidence and power. Flexing his fingers, he felt the dormant energy within, waiting for him to tap into it and release it — power that most would only dream of. But his excitement wasn't only because he was about to commence his slaughter of these heathens, no. It was because there was a veritable trove of wealth to be found in the ore mines, and more resources meant more conquest.

His soldiers flanked him, keeping the sides tight in case of an archer attack. Dzvorth, however, maintained his position in the center, his cape fluttering behind him as he strode forward. The sun beat down on the king, blinding his silver eyes, but he did not squint. He couldn't show any weakness. Once the head of the column was in earshot, Dzvorth stopped and held up a hand for his men to do the same.

"Greetings, heathens of Xan!" Dzvorth's voice carried as he spoke. "Today is your lucky day. On this day, two days before the Blood Moon, we, the chosen people of Her Holiness Aria herself, have come to deliver you from yourselves."

The barbaric leader shifted his weight, but Dzvorth pretended not to see the man's discomfort. Clearly, he already knew the outcome of this engagement. The Scrymmen king licked his lips hungrily before continuing.

"Her Holiness Aria has tasked Scrymme with maintaining the purity of Corinth and her holy lineage. We are not here to fight, but we will if you force our hand. It is better for everyone involved if you come willingly with us. We don't want needless bloodshed."

The young leader removed his hand from his hip and crossed his arms. No one else said anything, though some of the warriors in green and red livery shuffled in silence, their hands unconsciously gripping their weapons. The king's eyes shifted back to the leader once more. Dzvorth's breath caught in his throat as he saw the young man grinning, and the king's eyes narrowed in confusion.

"Will you be coming?" the king asked.

"The Brothers of Xan will not be beholden to any man. We would rather die."

The man's response did not surprise Dzvorth. He'd been hoping for such. Raising his hand, the king motioned for his men to begin their attack. A smile tugged on the corners of Dzvorth's lips once more as he looked inside himself and tugged on the magical reserves within. Once he felt their familiar power, he reached out to the young heathen and touched his shadow. Once he felt the man was under his control, Dzvorth knew the end was near.

Pockets of cries broke out as men began to realize that they could no longer move. The king nearly growled in delight; his soldiers had all latched onto one of the Xanans or Zanirians. Dzvorth swiveled his head, looking for Dzvareliah. He saw his wife standing off to the side, watching him intently.

Damned woman! Dzvorth fumed. *Smug as always, the bitch.*

Snapping his attention back to his prey, the king felt a wave of pride as he saw the concern on the young leader's face. He watched as the man's muscles tensed in a futile attempt to move. Useless. The heathen wouldn't even be able to turn his head.

"Release me and fight like a man," the Xanan leader seethed.

"Now, now," Dzvorth replied. "There's no reason to draw this out. I told you, I don't want bloodshed."

"That's complete shit," a dark-haired man spat.

The king's attention was drawn to the new speaker. His hair was dark, like the clansmen, yet his skin was pale — a strange combination. Then he saw it. The man's arm was covered in tattoos marking him as a Flame.

"So, you heathens do have power amongst your ranks," Dzvorth chided. "You've kept secrets from me."

Dzvorth was pleased to see that the Flame was one of the people immobilized by his Shadows. However, if there was one mage, there could be more. Taking his time, Dzvorth scanned the crowd carefully, looking for the telltale signs of holy blood. To the side, away from the main group of warriors, he saw two young women with markings: one redhead and a wavy-haired blonde.

Motioning to the two women, the Scrymmen king pointed to two of his men to take care of them. Startled gasps broke out from the women as they realized they could no longer move either. A young man in green livery with short, chestnut hair called out, demanding they be released. The man beside him quickly silenced him.

"I give you one last chance," Dzvorth said. He not only grew bored, but he also noticed that more men and women were moving forward, weapons in hand. Just because they were not wearing the colors of Xan didn't mean they could not fight. The longer this went on, the more dangerous it became for Scrymme. "Accept your liberation, and I will spare you." Waving his hand, the king pushed his soldiers forward, their swords and daggers drawn. "Give yourself to Her Holiness, and we will save you."

The Scrymmen warriors advanced on their immobilized foe. Steel gleamed in the hot Xanan sun as the Scrymmen fighters neared. Dzvorth crossed his arms and watched the spectacle with satisfaction. His legs trembled with anticipation, as did his soldiers'.

Cries of alarm rang out as the ground began to shake. Men from every nation toppled to the ground as the rumbling grew. The horses screamed in fear, dancing around to maintain their balance. Behind him, Dzvorth heard his wife trying to soothe the startled beasts. His eyes rapidly scanned the bodies in front of him once more. Surely, he had missed something earlier.

The roiling continued to grow in intensity as the seconds passed. Scrymmen warriors quickly sheathed their weapons and ran back towards their mounts, releasing their captives in the process. People from Xan and Zanir were flung to the ground as they suddenly found themselves no longer held by some unseen force.

It felt like an eternity, but Dzvorth found the problem: an Avalanche dressed in the green livery of Zanir stood by the young leader of Xan. The Avalanche's eyes were closed as he tugged at the earth, building up the strength of his quake.

"The Avalanche!" Dzvorth shouted, pointing to the mage.

Battle cries rang out from the Scrymmen warriors as they stopped their retreat and turned to obey their king. By the time they started their attack, men from Xan and Zanir had regained their balance enough to raise their weapons in response. The young Xanan leader and those closest to him pulled their weapons and made their way to the forefront, battle lust gleaming in their eyes.

Steel met steel, and shouts of pain rent the air as flesh was pierced. The Scrymmen warriors attempted to immobilize their opponents using their Shadow skills, but the rumbling of the earth prevented them from getting a strong hold. Those in the middle and back of the Xanan army rushed to grab a weapon, hoping to overwhelm their attackers. Dzvorth reached out with his Shadow magic to grab onto those in red and green livery. From his vantage point, he managed to freeze his opponents one by one, enabling his men to cut them down.

As blood stained the red clay earth, the shrieks of the dying became mixed with the cries of the children. Women called out, begging for mercy, as they urged their elders to flee with the young. More warriors of Xan streamed towards the battle. Chaos reigned.

The young warlord wove through the bodies, his battleaxe and warhammer whirling in deadly arcs. With a sickening crunch, his axe landed in the neck of a Scrymmen warrior with a spray of red. This was quickly followed up with a swift smash to the temple by the hammer. By the time the blade of the battleaxe was pulled out of the flesh, the Xanan leader's enemy was already on the ground in a crumpled heap.

Dzvorth struggled to control as many of his opponents as possible, but he watched in horror as a second and third Scrymmen warrior fell to their deaths. Minutes dragged by like an eternity when suddenly a booming voice rang out. The chaos subsided as men from both sides turned to find the source of the voice. Xanans parted, allowing for two statuesque people to pass by. The damned sun continued to blind the Scrymmen king. He tried following their movements as they made their way to the front of the throng.

⌒⌒

Dzvareliah's mouth dropped as two massive people stepped out from the crowd. The sun shone off their silver hair, causing it to sparkle. She was too far away to see, but the queen thought their eyes were also silver. The male had black streaks in his hair, and his muscles could be seen under his cream-colored tunic. His tanned skin wasn't what she expected to see on him. Next to the man, a slender woman with alabaster skin stood. Her hair and loose-fitting riding clothes rustled in the slight breeze. Dzvareliah felt her heart jump to her throat as she beheld the beautiful woman. The woman was a picture of Scrymmen beauty, one that every woman tried to emulate.

"Why are you stopping?" Dzvorth shouted at his men. "Charge!"

The queen couldn't help but smirk as she watched her husband flounder. She knew his soldiers' hesitation would only make him angrier. The horses stood calmly now that the ground was no longer shaking. Their tails swished languidly, and their ears gave an occasional flick, shaking off the rogue fly that may have landed on them. More than one knickered as they turned to graze.

Dzvareliah couldn't help but be impressed by their laidback demeanor. It filled her with confidence that the pair standing before her husband were no threat. At least, not to them at the moment.

Uneasy chatter from the Scrymmen warriors elicited a growl of rage from her husband, drawing her attention from the horses to him. Dzvorth's rigid form stood, imposing on his people. Though she could not see his face, she knew her dear husband well enough to know that he was struggling to keep his composure.

"You," the intimidating, silver-eyed man called out. "What is your purpose? You speak of maintaining the holy lineage and of not wanting bloodshed, yet here you are, pushing your men to their deaths. What do you hope to gain?"

"I have no duty to answer you," Dzvorth spat. "I answer to Her Holiness."

A smirk flashed on the man's face, and he turned to the woman next to him.

"You hear that, Sister?" Dzvareliah couldn't help but note the amusement in his voice. "He only answers to you. Perhaps you can speak reason to him."

The woman's eyes sparkled. With a serene smile on her face, Her Holiness Aria glided towards the king of Scrymme. Dzvareliah noted that his body twitched, but the man stood his ground. As if a gust of wind blew by, the goddess' hair fanned out, engulfing her in an ethereal aura.

"Tell me, my son," Aria's melodic voice rang out, although she did not raise it. "What do you hope to gain from this? There is no glory in unnecessary violence."

The king's body trembled, though Dzvareliah could not tell if it was because of anger or fear. When he spoke, he fought to keep it steady. How she wished she could see his face right now. His attempts to maintain composure were commendable, although futile.

"Our people have worked for centuries to uphold the sanctity of Her Holiness' teachings," Dzvorth said, ignoring who he spoke to. "While the rest of Corinth forgot your ways and began worshipping other deities, we have held steadfast. It is through her blood that we are pure. It is our duty to bring all of Corinth under Her Holiness' rule."

Such lofty ideals for one who blasphemes, Dzvareliah smirked. *If she truly is Her Holiness, it will not end well for him.*

The queen continued to attend to the horses as she stood in the background, her back to the beasts. Several of their wounded soldiers hobbled their way over to their mounts in search of anything to treat their injuries in their saddle bags. She noted that Dzvorath, the young Scrymmen guard and her husband's illegitimate son, attempted to subtly make his way over to the horses along with the wounded. The young boy's face was pale and his eyes wide, having never experienced the true terrors of battle. It wouldn't do to punish the boy. He would be of much better use alive.

Dzvareliah turned her attentions back to her husband. Her Holiness stood patiently in front of him, a despondent expression on her face. A moment of understanding flickered across her face before the expression turned to resignation. Lifting her hands, she held them out for the Scrymmen king to see. Gasps broke out from the crowd. Those that hadn't already staggered back to where the queen stood did so, sharing uncomfortable glances with those around them.

"I wish you hadn't done that," Aria sighed.

The goddess turned to her brother. Next to him, an olive-skinned woman with chocolate hair watched the entire exchange. Pity filled her silver eyes. The queen started, noting that the woman's eyes were indeed silver and not a trick of the light. As the goddess returned to her husband, Dzvareliah couldn't help but linger on the olive-skinned woman. There was something familiar about her, though she couldn't place it.

A blinding flash of silver startled her, ripping a cry from her lips as she threw her arms up. Her scream was drowned out by the myriad of shouts that erupted around her. It lasted but an instant, but by the time her vision cleared, Her Holiness remained where she stood. The king lay on the ground in a crumpled heap.

Deafening silence permeated the area. Only the whistling of the wind could be heard. Minutes passed without a soul rustling. Dzvareliah gawked at the fallen form of her husband, waiting for him to get back up. He never did.

"The bloodshed is over," Aria's voice rang out through the stillness. "Go home. I have seen his desires, and you will not move forward with them. Not as long as I am here."

Warriors from Scrymme shuffled, unsure of whether to follow their liege's orders and face the wrath of their patron goddess or retreat. Awkward glances turned to their queen, who struggled to calm the horses once more.

Dzvareliah's mind raced as she tried to process everything that had just occurred. All options appeared to point to the same conclusion. The queen took her time soothing the horses as her soldiers one-by-one made their way back to her. As the last mount returned to staring out over the field, Dzvareliah finally turned to address the group.

"Our time here is done," the queen announced. "As we have seen, there is nothing to be gained by displeasing Her Holiness. Load him onto his horse," she instructed a pair of nearby men. "We must prepare for his burial." Turning to the goddess and, what must be her brother, Dzvareliah Ari curtseyed deeply, dropping her eyes. "I beseech Her Holiness and Venerable Brother to forgive us. Dzvorth has shown that he is foolhardy and disrespectful, but please understand that the people of Scrymme are reverent to your teachings. I hope his actions do not cause you to think poorly of the rest of us. We cherish your teachings and hope to still spread the word of your greatness."

As she spoke, Dzvareliah's people dropped to their knees, their hands clenched in a fist and placed over their hearts. They too dropped their gaze as they awaited their goddess' response. Though she couldn't see them, she could feel the tension around her grow as the silence stretched on. The queen maintained her subservient posture, waiting for Her Holiness to speak.

Time dragged on, and Dzvareliah began to grow uneasy. Several times, her eyes wanted to flick upwards, but she fought the urge. She didn't want to further upset her goddess. After what felt like an eternity, she was rewarded with a judgement from Aria.

"Please rise," Aria said.

The voice sounded close to the queen. Lifting her gaze, Dzvareliah gasped as the goddess stood in front of her. Her Holiness' silver eyes bored into the queen, unblinking. Dzvareliah did everything she could to not blink or avert her gaze. She couldn't explain why, but if she did, she believed she would meet the same fate as her husband. Again, time dripped by excruciatingly slowly. The queen's eyes watered, but she held steady.

"You may leave," Aria said at last. "Leave your vendetta against Dzvaresh." The goddess' voice dropped to a dangerous tone, only the queen able to hear her. "She is under my direct protection."

Dzvareliah managed to keep her displeasure to herself as the goddess hissed at her. All the queen could do was nod her head, her eyes finally managing to drop in submission. As if a cloud had passed, Dzvareliah felt a warm radiance shining down on her. To her surprise, Aria beamed at her. She'd received the goddess' approval.

Without a word, the queen of Scrymme gathered her men and beat a hasty retreat. As the goddess disappeared into the horizon, Dzvareliah found herself re-examining her next steps. Her daughter's death was out of the question, for now. Glancing to her left, she saw her husband's illegitimate son flanking her. A smile played on her lips as she observed the youth. Perhaps she could still enact her vengeance. Not only was she still young and her body fertile, but her son still roamed Corinth.

XVIII

S TALE AIR FILLED the wine cellar. Despite the heady aroma of barrels of wine sitting on the loamy earth, the room lost its freshness. Or perhaps, the young king no longer found the smell of wine as appealing as he once had. Either way, the change disturbed him; made him feel uneasy. In the corner, Pruvencia still slept, her weathered form curled up under one of Schaed's quilts. A simple sheet separated the elderly matron from the dirt floor. Oldar's makeshift bed lay undisturbed in his corner between the barrels, witness to his long night awake.

His mind kept replaying the conversation he'd had with his uncle, while flashes of the entire servant population huddled in the kitchen as haunting shrieks echoed through the castle sent chills down his spine. And as if this wasn't enough to distract him, images of his Aunt Constance's uncharacteristically concerned body language decided to join the mix as if to further impress upon him the seriousness of the situation.

Schaed's dead. Rez is unwilling to admit there's a problem. Ingmar and the staff are trapped. If none of these were indicative of a problem, my conversation with Uncle certainly is.

Snippets of the king's last words with the head of Alocar's military played through his mind: *"You must leave. Find help for Alocar, but for the love of the gods, you must not be caught. If you are, news of our plight will never leave."* The grizzled veteran's face shone with concern as he spoke to his lord outside the castle proper. The two hid in an alley out of direct sight from any of the keep's windows. The sun, though shining right on them, did nothing to warm the deep chill which permeated their bones.

Everything combined kept the young king from much needed rest, but still, he pushed on.

When Pru wakes up, he told himself, *we'll prepare to leave. If we're lucky, we can still catch up with Cienna in Xan. Gods willing.*

Oldar shook his head. It all seemed so daunting. Ever since his parents were killed, he'd found himself struggling to keep his head above water. And yet, his problems were not going to go away. Oldar knew he needed to take decisive action to save his people. Glancing at his still slumbering caretaker, the king decided to get a start on some of his packing preparations. He would talk to Pru when she woke up. It was hard to tell, but he didn't think the sun had fully risen yet since he couldn't see any light seeping under the heavy oaken door. Tracing the ancient rune at the top of the door for protection, the young king spared one last glance towards his sleeping caretaker before taking to the streets.

He was right. The sun hadn't fully risen and the deep oranges of dawn blended in with the purples and blues of night. An eerie quiet gripped the streets, causing the young king's body to tense as he went on high alert. Oldar's ears strained to pick up the slightest sound, while his eyes worked to take in his surroundings. The streets lamps, normally flickering in the early morning light, all appeared to be blown out. This only added to his discomfort. It reminded him of the castle.

The young king regretted not bringing something to help him see better, but he knew that if anyone saw him, it would be disastrous. No, it was best for him to draw as little attention to himself. His feet echoed on the cobblestones, the sound amplified in the dead quiet. Oldar craned his head from side to side, looking for any sign of life on the empty streets. Not even a cat prowled about.

A chill wind blew through Oldar, freezing him like the inside of the castle. His body tensed, waiting for the ear-splitting shriek he knew would follow, his body frozen in place out in the open. Seconds dragged by with agonizing slowness as his eyes darted around, straining to see or hear something. From what he remembered, the creatures he'd heard in the castle were soundless, except for their screams.

When the area around him did not become darker, he dared to have hope. The king found he'd been holding his breath, and exhaled slowly. As he did so, he felt some of the tension in his body melt away and the knot in his stomach loosen. The sun had risen further, pushing away the darkness of night and sending her beams of warmth onto the streets of Madden. Window shutters began opening and faint chatter could be heard as the capital's inhabitants started their day. However, he wasn't out of danger yet.

〜〜〜

Oldar's attempts to dodge people as he traveled through Madden became harder as more people took to the streets. He found himself darting through alleyways and racing across the open roads when he had no other option like a madman. Oldar cursed himself on more than one occasion for not grabbing one of Schaed's cloaks to help conceal himself. It would have made everything a lot easier if he could just pull a hood over his head.

A pang of grief hit Oldar so fast and so unexpectedly that he stopped dead in his tracks. His breath became rapid and shallow, causing him to hyperventilate in the middle of the street. Images of his parents, his friend, and even Grymme, his old bodyguard, flashed through his mind in quick succession. As soon as the bloody form of his old guard disappeared, Pru popped up. The matronly woman's body lay splayed out on the cobblestones, her limbs broken. Blood spilled out of her chest from the deep gashes that ripped her open; her mouth was parted in a silent scream.

His vision swam as he tried to catch his breath. Cold sweat ran down his back as adrenaline made his limbs tremble. The few homes nearby that had movement inside startled him back to the present. Closing his eyes, he allowed himself to take a few deep breaths. He forced himself to push all the images out of his mind. Instead, he pictured his destination. It wasn't much further. If he could at least get there, Oldar could give himself a moment to let it all out.

"Focus," Oldar whispered. "Almost there."

His leg felt leaden as he pushed himself to take the next step. His body still shook as his adrenaline dissipated. Dawn appeared in all of her glory, the sun shining brightly and the sky a clear cerulean by the time he stood in front of a rundown home. A herd of children ran about, the younger ones chasing each other while the older ones tended to the vegetable boxes in front of the house. An old woman, her hair a stark white and with wrinkles etched into her paper-thin skin, leaned against one of the older children as she fed the chickens.

"What can I do you for?" a teenaged boy asked. His eyes narrowed, giving his freckled face a scrunched appearance.

"Is Rez'maré in?" Oldar's voice came out as a hoarse croak.

With a flick of his head toward the aged house, the youth returned to the goats he had been milking. His gaze followed the young king as Oldar thanked the boy and made his way into the home. The elderly woman standing near the door greeted him with milky eyes and a wide smile as the girl she leaned against turned to face the king. More than one tooth was missing from the smile. Oldar smiled back, unsure if the girl would return his gesture, as he wove his way into the building.

Oldar's boots echoed on the ancient wooden floors, their wood grain run smooth from the hundreds of feet that ran upon it over time. The early morning light streamed through the windows, a couple of them covered by tattered curtains. The king stopped to look out one of the windows at the children. Many were at work, gathering vegetables, milk, and eggs as the young ones played.

"What are you doing here?" a feminine voice asked. A hard edge tinged her question, catching the king off-guard.

Oldar spun around to face Rez'maré. The scowl on her face melted away in an instant as she saw his face and was quickly replaced with surprise. A small gasp escaped her parted lips, as she crossed the room in an instant as she threw arms around his shoulders.

"What are you doing here?" she whispered. Emotion hung heavy in her voice as she choked out the question. "You should leave."

Gently grabbing her, Oldar broke free of her embrace and held her gaze. With his thumb, he delicately wiped the tear that rolled down her cheek.

"Maré, I need your help."

Rez'maré nodded, waiting for him to continue.

"Schaed is dead," he began, ignoring the choked back sob that almost broke free from her lips. "I need to get help, but I need supplies. I'd be forever in your debt if you could buy me some food, herbs, and prepare a few flasks of ale, along with a waterskin."

A hiccup was all she would give him by way of answer. He took that as consent.

"I would love it if you came with me." Oldar was surprised by the earnestness of the request. He knew he needed to get Pru out, but after hearing from Schaed that she chose to stay, he didn't expect to ask her once more.

"I can't," she whispered. Pointing to the children and elderly woman, she bit back a sob. "I can't leave them."

"Who are they?"

"Mama Ethyl has taken in as many of us as she could from all over Alocar. The hungry, the homeless. Those without families." Rez'maré glanced towards the woman, now sitting on a chair that had been brought outside. Her rounded shoulders rocked side-to-side as a couple of the younger girls sang while braiding her white hair. "She took me in long ago." Rez'maré's voice was wistful as she remembered her savior all those years ago. "She watches my little ones while I work."

Oldar followed her gaze. Two young children no more than five, a little girl and her younger brother. He felt his breath catch in his throat. They resembled Rez'maré so much.

"I will get you what you need, but I need to keep them safe," Rez'maré said as she stared at her children.

Oldar's mind raced. "I have someplace I can hide you all while I'm gone. It'll keep you safe, but you'll still need to be careful if you go out."

Rez'maré gazed into Oldar's eyes, a glimmer of hope flashing in hers.

~~~

By the time Oldar returned to Schaed's shop, the sun was hanging comfortably above. A few wisps of cloud dotted the sky, but they were too thin and too few to provide any relief from the heat. The further he moved from the center of the capital, the warmer it got. Despite the sun, Rez'maré's street felt cooler, but now that he was further out, he found himself pleasantly warm.

Pruvencia waited for Oldar inside Schaed's shop. She'd prepared breakfast for the two of them with the few remaining ingredients in his kitchen upstairs and laid them out on one of the tables downstairs. The matronly caretaker greeted her king with a relieved smile as she pushed a plate of egg and sausage towards him.

"Morning Pru. Did you sleep well?"

"I did, thank you. I don't mean to rush, but I think it's best if we eat quickly and return to the cellar to plan our day. Normally I would've brought the food inside already, but it's just so beautiful out that I couldn't help myself." Pruvencia glanced toward the front door nervously, but plastered on a smile for Oldar.

"Thank you," Oldar grabbed a fork and began eating.

The eggs were a little cold, but he found himself savoring them. She'd managed to find some herbs and black pepper to season them with instead
~~~

of just salt. The sausages were a special treat too. Oldar realized he hadn't had any since he was last home before leaving for Pharn. It felt like a lifetime ago, but it was only less than two weeks since he'd last eaten at his table.

"What I'd give for a fresh loaf of hot bread," he said, his cheeks bulging.

"I'm sorry, your majesty," Pruvencia replied. "I didn't have time to go to the shops."

"No, it's better that you didn't. We can't risk being seen."

Oldar's heart dropped. He expected Rez'maré to be there by now. Disappointment tried to seep in, but he pushed it away. He didn't have time to despair.

"Pru," he said earnestly. "Once we finish eating, we need to leave Madden."

He watched as the matronly woman's jaw dropped. Fear washed over Pruvencia, her eyes betraying her. Oldar's heart ached as he saw the emotion flood the elderly woman. It had been years since she'd left Madden, let alone Alocar. He wasn't even sure if she could handle the arduous journey ahead. They needed to push on.

"We need to get help," Oldar continued. "The Greys. Our alliance may not be what it was, but I've talked to Cienna and she will not abandon us. Zanir will fight with Alocar."

"Oh, my dear, are you sure? This is wonderful news. But I can't come with you." Pruvencia's gaze dropped and her voice shook. "I am too old to travel. I'll only slow you down."

Oldar held up his hand to silence the woman. "I will not leave you behind. Ingmar will take care of everyone in the castle, and I will protect you. Please, Pru. Don't leave me."

Oldar found himself tearing up at the thought of his caretaker staying behind, cowering in the castle kitchens. He forced himself to finish his food as the two sat together not saying a word. All too soon, the sound of utensils scraping against plates signaled to the pair that they were done. Oldar could not make eye contact with Pruvencia, choosing to glance towards the door once more. He'd have to make do without any supplies.

Plates clinked together as Pruvencia cleared the table. Her feet could be heard climbing the stairs and moving around in Schaed's living quarters. Instead of offering to help, Oldar sat back down and buried his face in his hands. The sun was up and the streets would be busy now. His chance for escaping was dwindling with each minute.

"Oldar?" Pru's feeble voice tore at his heart. "I just don't want to slow you down. I'm an old woman, a liability. If you got in trouble because of me, I don't know what I would do."

"I *want* you to come, Pru." His voice shook as much as hers as his gaze begged the woman to say yes.

"How will we escape?"

A wave of relief washed over the young king. The emotion was short-lived, however, as the door creaked open. Pushing the matronly woman towards the wine cellar, hoping to at least get her to safety before one of the monsters could come in.

"Oldar? Are you still here?"

Oldar's body melted as he heard Rez'maré's voice call out softly to him. Her head peaked through the cracked door, her eyes darting about nervously as she scanned the empty room. As soon as she spotted him, her face relaxed and she opened the door all the way. Oldar rushed over to help her as she ushered her two children into Schaed's shop. Behind them, Mama Ethyl and a gaggle of children stood in a tight group. Apprehension clouded the older ones' faces, while the younger children looked around, excited to be in the business district of Madden.

"How, how many are there?" Oldar asked as he motioned for them to hurry inside.

The king surveyed the streets, making sure no one saw them as they entered, before shutting the door tight behind them. Young children began exploring the shop floor as Pruvencia lead Mama Ethyl to a nearby chair. The caretaker darted upstairs for a few moments, only to return with a cup of tea for the blind woman. Mama reached out with a shaking hand and took the warm drink with both hands, Pru's wrinkled ones encompassing Mama's. Rez'maré was busy pulling down the shawls from her children's heads, directing the older children to place a pocket, the dual pouched bag bursting at the seams with supplies, on the table. The worn straps didn't look like they'd hold so much, but Oldar hoped he was wrong.

"Including me and my little ones, there's twenty of us," Rez'maré finally answered. "I hope you don't mind." Straightening up, Rez'maré took a moment to take in Schaed's empty shop. "He's really gone?" Her voice became soft and fragile. "You know, he told me that we should leave. I just assumed he was drunk or on the poppy, he looked so crazed. I can't believe he was right."

Oldar could only nod. "Thank you," he said, motioning to the supplies. "I really appreciate it."

"Just make sure you come back," Rez'maré said with a forced smile. "That was my dad's pocket."

"I'll keep it safe," he promised. "Maré, how busy is it out there?"

"There are not too many people in this area. You should be able to get out unseen. You're leaving by the main gates, right?"

"The tunnels."

"Oh," her face dropped. "I don't know about over there. I'm sorry."

"Don't be." Oldar grabbed her hand, hoping to reassure her. "I'm really grateful for everything you've done." His eyes glanced around trying to find Pruvencia. His caretaker stood by the blind woman, speaking to her while watching the younger ones as they explored the shop. "We need to go," he said loudly.

Pruvencia gave Mama Ethyl a kiss on the head. The blind woman returned her kindness with a toothy grin, the wrinkles around her milky eyes deepening. Some of the children discovered the door to the wine cellar and raced inside, the door held ajar. The older children attempted to corral the younger ones, but curiosity got the better of them.

"Stay in that room as much as possible," Oldar told Rez'maré. "It seems to be the only safe space in Madden. There's old magic or something in there."

~~~

Pulling the hood of Schaed's cloak tighter over his head. Sweat beaded on his brow, but he couldn't risk removing it lest he was recognized. Behind him, Pruvencia huffed behind him in the heat. Together they maneuvered their way through the streets towards the entrance to the tunnels leading to Ånchal. He was surprised at how empty they were. Usually, the streets would be full, happy chatter filling the air as everyone walked around checking out the shops at their leisure.

As the tunnels loomed into view, Oldar couldn't believe to see the posts abandoned. No soldiers manned the gates, giving the tower sitting over the tunnels a haunted appearance. The air around the darkened tower chilled the young king. Shadows danced across the weather-worn stones and Oldar found himself on edge.

"Maybe we should turn back?" Pruvencia whispered, her hushed voice sounding like a shout in the stillness. "I don't like the looks of this."

"We're almost there, Pru," he mumbled back. "We'll be safe once we get out of here."

Images of the Myrani came to the young king's mind unbidden. The threat the group imposed caught Oldar by surprise. He hadn't thought of them since he'd returned to Madden. Shaking his head, he forced the mercenary magi group out of his mind, along with the sentient shadows that patrolled his home, and pushed open the smooth wooden door.

The door shut with a soft thump, echoing in the empty chamber. Oldar's unease built as he walked deeper into the empty room. It didn't make sense
~~~

that the entrance to the capital was abandoned. Sunlight streamed through filthy glass windows. Removing his hood, the king made his way to the underground staircase. With each thundering step, his hopes of running into one of the city guard diminished. Pru's soft shuffle behind him was the only thing keeping Oldar from breaking into a full panic. Cold sweat beaded on his brow and his heart thudded in his chest. A gentle weight fell on his shoulder. Pruvencia's warm hand helped calm his nerves. The chills he was feeling in the empty room had nothing to do with the Faceless. He didn't think they were there with the two of them.

"Do we go down there?" she whispered, her shaking voice barely audible.

"Yea- "

A muffled howl rang out from the streets of Madden, accompanied by a chorus of chaos. Screams rent the air, only to be followed by wails of grief. The cold dread that had barely left him moments before returned in earnest, causing the king's knees to nearly buckle. Without sparing a look back, Oldar grabbed Pruvencia by the hand, threw open the door to the tunnels, and raced down the stairs. He prayed that neither he, nor Pru slipped. Pruvencia's hand clamped on his, her breath coming out fast and panicked.

In what felt like no time, the two found level ground and took off at a sprint. A lone guard at the bottom of the stairwell called out, startled by their sudden appearance. Oldar ignored his shouts, taking a risk and letting the man know he challenged the king of Alocar, sparing but a glance back in the darkened halls hoping that the soldier wouldn't question him further. A clinking on the stones behind them, in conjunction with Oldar's proclamation seemed to satisfy the lone guard as he no longer appeared to be pursuing them.

Despite not hearing anything following them, the duo did not slow down. Oldar's breath came out in ragged gasps as he raced through the tunnels of Ånchal. His hand gripped Pru's so tightly he was afraid he would break it. Unfortunately, he didn't have time to slow down or readjust his grip. He needed to reach the outpost and find the princess.

XIX

THE SUN HUNG HIGH in the midday sky. As the people of Xan moved through the sparse trees toward the Rydash Gorge, Cienna couldn't help but wonder if what happened that morning was a warning of things to come. An ambush from a powerful nation, one very familiar with the gifts of the gods, after their narrow defeat against one who was god-blessed could not be a coincidence. Then there was the Flame's urgent insistence that an entire nation evacuate their homes before the Blood Moon. The princess had seen the Flame a few times, and he did not strike her as one prone to fits of mania. Coupled with Oldar's sudden disappearance and complete silence after, not even a messenger sought them out with an update of his whereabouts. Everything left the princess feeling uncomfortable.

She found herself glancing towards Brody, hoping he would give her an idea of what they were in for. Unfortunately, his training allowed him to keep a neutral expression as he spoke with Alverick. Even as the pair issued instructions to the others, they did not betray any emotion. Cienna found herself wishing he would catch his eye. She knew she shouldn't dwell on their last encounter, however...

They approached the gorge quicker than they expected. The red clay earth became looser and more dirt-like as they neared, and the trees all but vanished. Instead, stones covered in moss and sand lizards were all that could be seen. The reptiles sunned themselves on the rocks, scurrying away as the column of people got closer.

We're not too far from home, the princess told herself. *Just a few more days. Perhaps I can go to Alocar with a few people to check on Oldar.*

Though she hadn't admitted it to herself, Cienna worried about the young king. Their time together marching to Xan had shown her that he was just as awkward and unsure of himself as she was. He unfortunately had the added bonus of being thrown in charge of an entire nation instead of having the luxury of leaving the tough decisions to a parent.

I've been a real fool lately. Even Oldar has shown that he's more capable than me. Once this is all over, I owe both him and Mom an apology.

As she slid off her mount to climb down the steep ledge of the gorge, Cienna found herself wishing for a breeze to break up the heat. Her hair was beginning to mat onto her head as sweat built on her forehead and rolled down her neck. Feeling a twinge of guilt, Cienna cupped her hands together and conjured up some water. The cool liquid went down her throat and cleared away the dust that had been building up since they first left Fa'Tinh.

"Looks like there's more than one benefit to being a Stream," a feminine voice teased.

Cienna glanced over and saw Caitlyn behind her, preparing to go down into the gorge with her. Her face flushed, and she held out her hand, offering the redhead a drink as well. Caitlyn shook her head, the smirk still sitting comfortably on her lips.

"No need to feel self-conscious," Caitlyn said. "If I had your gift, I'd never go thirsty again. Probably would never be as dirty as I am now, either," she added.

Cienna spared a quick look down at her clothes and repressed a shudder. If it was possible, she looked worse than she did the first time she visited the gorge. Taking a cloth she'd shoved into her saddlebag when they first left, Cienna drenched it in water and began wiping down her face and neck. The cold water refreshed her, leaving her feeling both clean and more alert.

"How have I never thought of this before?" Cienna mused. Shoving the cloth back into her saddlebag, the princess took the reins and began leading her mount down the steep cliff and into the gorge. "You'd think that I would look for every opportunity to cleanse myself."

"I think it shows that you're aware of what's important right now. To be honest, if I saw you taking a bath every time you got a speck of dirt on you, I'd probably have to have Brody talk some sense into you." Seeing the princess' wistful expression, Caitlyn asked, "How are things between you two? I know you wanted to talk to him." The redhead trailed off, unsure of what else to say.

"We did talk, and he helped me see how childish I've been." Cienna's voice took on a soft, airy tone as she focused on each step in front of her. "We've decided that it's for the best if I take my role as princess a little more seriously, instead of living in a fantasy world."

A soldier walked over to the two, offering the princess a water skin and something to eat. She waved the man away, both irritated and grateful that she didn't have her handmaiden shadowing her every move.

"Oh, I'm sorry, Waterbug. I know how much he means to you."

"It's okay. Really. What about you and Alverick? Have you two had much time to talk?" Cienna was surprised to find herself changing the subject. Talking about Brody hurt more than she expected.

"He's doing well. I think he's found his Anchor once more. He seems... more stable."

Though she didn't dare turn around, she could hear the hope in the redhead's voice. It brought a smile to her lips.

"I hope he has," Cienna replied. "He's been through so much. More than I could ever imagine."

The two continued on in silence down the side of the ravine. Despite having someone to help guide her every step, Cienna couldn't help but imagine that each one brought her one step closer to her death. Every pebble that was kicked over the side represented her, screaming as she plummeted to the red sand below.

It felt like an eternity, but Cienna's feet finally touched down on level ground once more. She let out a sigh of relief, nearly collapsing in the sand as her legs threatened to give out from beneath her. The princess' heart pounded in her ears, her ribcage thumping as it raced in her chest. Cienna almost yelped when a hand rested on her shoulder.

"Sorry," the princess apologized. "Every time I go down, I panic. I thought it wouldn't be a problem considering I walk the towers at home all the time."

"Don't you have a rope to help guide you down?" Caitlyn asked, trying to be sympathetic.

Cienna nodded, finding it difficult to talk still.

"What did you think of this morning?" Caitlyn pressed. "I really want to talk to Al when he gets down here."

The princess took a moment to collect herself. Her legs trembled but no longer threatened to give out beneath her, and her pounding heart was slowing. She'd been wanting to do the same thing but couldn't push herself to bring it up to him or Brody.

Cienna tried putting herself in her father's position to analyze as many possibilities as she could think of. They could continue on to Pharn, but something was pulling her to Alocar, to Oldar. His departure had left her feeling uneasy, but his continued silence concerned her. There were so many things that were still unexplained, so many questions left unanswered, that Cienna feared she was making the wrong decision. Having Alverick and Brody there to give her the benefit of their experience and insight would be a greater boon than they could ever know.

So much of their current travels remained a mystery to the young princess. Though she would never admit it, her mind wandered during the meeting late the night prior discussing the next steps. Exhaustion plagued her, both in mind and body. All Cienna had wanted was to crawl into the makeshift bed they'd fashioned for her, curl up, and sleep.

"I've missed so much," the princess muttered. "How do I explain this?"

"What do you mean?" Caitlyn asked.

"I know we're to travel to Pharn, but I feel a pull tugging at me to meet Oldar in Madden. Ever since he went off on his own, something has been telling me that we're needed there. At the same time, I've been so preoccupied with how I've let Mother down that I don't even remember why we are heading home. It's all become a muddled mess, and I can't seem to sort it out."

The redhead pulled the fraught young woman into a tight embrace, burying the princess' head into her shoulder. Cienna let herself be held, tears welling in her eyes, and allowed herself a moment to let the emotions wash over her.

The last time, Cienna told herself. *This is the last time I give in. It's time I grow.*

The princess took a deep, shuddering breath and pushed herself away from the redhead. The time had come for her to accept her role as next in line for the throne, and if she was going to be ready for the responsibilities, she needed to grow up.

"Find Alverick and Brody," Cienna told Caitlyn. "Have Ronan take charge and lead the people of Xan home. When the time comes, I will go to Alocar, and I will need them to accompany me."

"What about me?" the redhead asked.

"You'll come with me. Between Ronan, the others, and those still at home, Mother should be fine. I need to fix the mess I made."

"And you're comfortable leaving Swordbane alone without any real resistance?" Caitlyn dropped her voice as they spoke. There were still Xanans all around. "Vashe may not be back either. What happens if he decides to strike while our forces are weak?"

The princess didn't hesitate, her resolve staying firm.

"I plan on taking him, his right-hand man, and the Flame with me. He can either leave the traitor in our dungeons, or bring the man with us. If Dez and the Siblings need to, I'll have them take care of Wyrd themselves."

Seeing the redhead glow with pride told the princess she made the right decision. It felt good to feel like she was finally on the right track. She wondered if Oldar felt this way before he discovered that someone close to him attempted to poison her mother. Or even after, when he all but surrendered himself to her judgement. He must have. And now it was her time to do what she knew must be done.

As more people trickled down the side of the ravine and those who were already in the gorge rested, Cienna took the opportunity to search for Swordbane. She left her mount with one of her soldiers before setting off on foot. Most of the people she saw took the chance to grab a bite to eat, resulting in a collection of small fires popping up in various spots. Waterskins were being passed around; some, she was sure, were filled with something other than water. As the general volume of conversation increased, Cienna found herself losing some of her apprehension.

It reminded her of the markets in Pharn. She pictured herself walking among the different pavilions, their colorful clothes providing shade over the vendors and their wares. Cienna passed a couple of Thurlish people sitting on some rocks in a small circle around a fire. Unbidden, the taste of the meat buns she'd bought from the Thurlish couple before this whole ordeal started made her mouth water. The marvelous explosion of cumin and turmeric-soaked pieces of lamb hit her so strongly that she could almost believe that she was eating them once more.

The flood of memories that hit her, reminding her of a time lost long ago, brought her an inner peace that she wasn't sure she'd ever experience again. The thought pained her, but she pushed it away, instead allowing herself to enjoy the simplicity.

Len and his entourage lounged around a fire, enjoying a bite while they waited for the rest to make their way down the ravine and into the gorge. Cienna couldn't help but pause as she saw a rare smile grace the lips of the young warlord's face as he watched a young girl run by, spinning in circles as she beamed at him. What could only be the girl's mother wasn't far behind — a babe strapped to her chest with a swath of orange fabric. The little girl was followed by three other children and their mother a moment later. Cienna wasn't sure she had seen the women and their children earlier in their travels. Most of the general populace packed into the middle of the march for safety, surrounded by soldiers.

Of course he'd have a family, Cienna chided herself. *Someone as powerful as himself would have multiple wives. Though... I don't think I've seen anyone other than her. Maybe he's more like us than I thought.*

She tried to recall her training about the clans. Ever since the Great Heart had first emerged, everything about the warlord nation had been shrouded in mystery. How a man advocating peace among the tribes rose to power, Cienna still didn't quite understand. But now was not the time to focus on her questions.

"Excuse me," the princess said, hoping her voice didn't quiver as she addressed the imposing leader.

Swordbane and his company turned from their discussion toward Cienna. At least the young general had the decency to look nonplussed at the princess' sudden interruption. Cienna felt her breath catch in her throat, but continued. He was not a man to expose your fears to. Next to Swordbane, the other general, Pram, she thought his name was, watched her curiously. Cienna almost thought she saw a twinkle of amusement in his eye for some reason.

"Yes?" Swordbane's simple reply caught her off-guard.

"I... I want to go to Madden in Alocar." Cienna cursed herself for her hesitancy. If her plan was going to work, she needed to impress the warlord leader.

"There's nothing stopping you."

"I need men," she began.

"You have plenty traveling with us," Swordbane replied, cutting her off. "I'm sure you'll be able to find a suitable number amongst your own ranks."

"No." Cienna surprised herself at the force of her statement. Even Swordbane seemed caught off guard. "I mean, I have a few who I plan to take, but I need Xan. I need you."

Swordbane handed his snack to the little girl who was spinning around his council moments earlier. The young child grabbed the piece of meat with a smile and greedily tore into it. The young general placed his now empty hands on his lap and arched an eyebrow at the princess. He made no effort to hide his amusement at her attempts at being imposing, much to her consternation.

He's playing with me, she thought. *The bastard.*

Taking a moment to calm down internally, Cienna forced herself to adopt an authoritative expression. Or what she thought it would look like. She'd seen her father go from jovial to stern in the blink of an eye and hoped that she could pull off the same look of power.

"Xan holds an alliance with Zanir," she said finally. "As Zanir does with Alocar. I require your help and the help of those in your council."

Cienna gestured to Pram and the Flame sitting around the fire. The young woman sitting next to the Flame looked at him questioningly, but the Flame ignored her gaze. Instead, his focus was on the princess and Pram

"I will be taking some of my men as well, but the rest of my forces shall accompany Xan to the gates of Pharn and help the queen find accommodations for your people." When Swordbane did not respond, Cienna took the opportunity to push forward. "I fear that House Storm needs our help and plan to provide it."

Keeping her demands concise, she now stood in front of the group, staring straight into Swordbane's dark eyes. They remained locked in this battle of wills for what felt like an eternity. Neither dared to drop their gaze. As time went on, Cienna found herself struggling to maintain her focus. The more she stared into his eyes, the deeper into those dark orbs she sank.

A life of ruthless calculation pulled at her, threatening to envelop her. A lifetime in Xan, training for combat from a young age, enduring the strains and fatigue that came from those long hours, surrounded by countless men and their schemes to achieve the title of Great Heart. Years of conniving, of plotting, and of decisive action taken against those who conspired against the head of Xan. Despite the multitude of failures, he was the one who succeeded, the one who seduced those closest to their now fallen leader and turned them into his strongest allies.

Inside Swordbane, a monster hid, waiting to strike.

"And what does Xan get in exchange for our blood?"

Swordbane's unexpected question startled Cienna. His gaze had been solid and unwavering, and she expected to be the first one to break. She gave herself a moment to think about the question. She knew she couldn't be hasty in her answer; he'd hold her to whatever she promised. Cienna also knew that she had to think about how her mother and father would handle the situation.

What would Mother say? she wondered.

After several long seconds, she realized she had no idea. Cienna hated to admit it, but she never took the time to observe her mother's rule, even after her father's death. Instead, the princess had spent more time trying to undermine her own mother in her attempts to be more like her father. Her heart ached, but she pushed the emotion away. Now was not the time.

What would Father say? Something kind but absolute.

As she gathered her thoughts, Cienna noted Swordbane's smirk creeping up on the corners of his mouth. He was interested in what she had to say.

I need to use this to my advantage.

"My guard told me that you answer to no king," Cienna said. She was rewarded with a flash of intrigue crossing his face. "Though I think we can be great allies to each other, and Zanir has no desire for war with the mighty brothers of Xan, I will release you from your oath to Zanir made in this very gorge not two months ago. Help me save House Storm, and you will serve no king once more."

Cienna knew it was a huge gamble. One she hoped her mother wouldn't criticize her for later. The seconds ticked by as Swordbane weighed her offer carefully. Next to him, Pram and the Flame watched intently.

"Agreed," Swordbane replied simply.

Cienna felt a wave of relief wash over her as she tried not to show any emotion. The first part of her plan was falling into place, and now she needed to speak with Alverick and Brody.

"Thank you," she said with a curtsey. As she turned to leave, Cienna was struck with one final thought. "I would also like the shield maiden to join us."

Cienna couldn't help the ear-to-ear grin that filled her face as she walked away from the encounter. Though she'd probably cost her nation a valuable asset, the princess was pleased with how her second attempt at negotiation turned out.

How did things turn out so badly with Oldar?

XX

"I'M SURPRISED you accepted her offer so easily," Pram remarked. "Had it been her father, or even that young guard you made the deal with, I doubt they would've gotten away so easily."

Len stopped watching the young princess as she retreated and turned to face Pram. The general watched him with a keen eye, concern hiding behind his mask of decorum. Next to his general, Hroth sat quietly, his hands pressed flat against his thighs. The normally aloof Flame's face betrayed him, and Len knew he made the right decision.

In the background, Zaa'ni, Altansari, and Maen stood quietly, the children playing in the red-brown dirt. For some reason, their chatter was muffled as everything around him was preternaturally amplified. Len could feel his wife's eyes boring into him even though she whispered to Altansari. Even his mother, whom he didn't realize had joined them and kept a close eye on the kids, stood out unusually clearly.

"Her gift of autonomy is a great boon to our people," Len replied. "I had plans to use Zanir, and specifically Pharn, to our advantage, but the offer was too good to pass up. Xan is not meant to be in an alliance with any nation. We are strong enough on our own. We've managed for centuries without their help. Besides, their notion of equity will still play out to our advantage. Zanir will not forget her relationship with Xan so quickly."

Intan turned ever so slightly, her ears straining to hear her son's words. The movement wasn't lost on Len, and his eyes locked onto his mother.

Though she didn't say anything, Len could see that her body was tense, waiting for something. Intan began speaking softly to herself, but in his heightened state, Len could hear that she chanted an ancient prayer of protection. His stomach clenched; it was an unfamiliar sensation to the young warlord, but he pushed the sensation away.

On the stone, Pram reached over and handed Len a new strip of meat. The fire crackled as the last of the kindling burned away, smoke rising up in black tendrils. Len chewed his food in thoughtful silence, his eyes panning around the camp. No one else appeared to be on guard like Len and his group. The gorge was filling up quickly as more of Pharn's forces continued to trickle down the ravine. Those remaining at the top were few.

Turning his attention to the west, Len felt his heart drop once more. Though it was still early afternoon, a dark cloud crept over the horizon. The rainy season was not due for another few moon cycles, so something like this was quite out of the ordinary. What bothered Len more was that this wasn't the first time he'd seen the darkness. As the dust calmed down after the battle at Fa'Tinh, he thought he'd seen a hint of the blackness, which he attributed it to a combination of exhaustion and stress. Now, seeing the phenomenon clearly left his blood running cold.

"You see it too?"

Len started at the sound of Hroth's gravelly voice. The Flame watched the young warlord intently, his knuckles whitening as the pressure against his palms intensified. The two shared a glance, ignoring the questioning gaze of those nearby. Len nodded, turning his attention back to the encroaching blackness.

"It's been growing since Vahnyre's appearance two days ago," Hroth said. "I've been watching it. Your friend, Wyrd, can see it too."

"What does it mean?" Len asked.

Hroth shook his head. "I can't say. I don't know of any Aethren associated with the darkness. I think that the princess is right to be worried, however. If I've gauged the direction correctly, it appears to be coming from Alocar."

"Then sending our brothers and sisters to Pharn is the best option," Pram said. "Though all our brothers are strong and our sisters can hold their own, this is something that I would not want to leave them to handle. It is better for them to seek shelter."

"Is it related to the shadow you told me about?" Len asked. He raised a skeptical brow at the two.

"I wouldn't doubt that they're related," Hroth replied. "There is something going on that is beyond our comprehension. We shouldn't wait any longer to leave. The sooner the better."

Len took in the campsite once more. Those who had been resting for a while joked around, pleased with the long respite from their earlier march. The few who had fought with Scrymme earlier in the day reapplied the poultices the healers had placed on them and rewrapped their wounds. Several twisted their bodies or rotated their arms, checking their mobility. They had been lucky to not lose too many during the fighting.

The bones had cracked and were no longer in his favor. The arrival of the gods proved to be his undoing, and now, darkness was creeping into Corinth. It was only a matter of time before it settled over Xan, bringing who knows what trouble to his home.

"Bring the Avalanche and the princess to me as soon as possible," Len instructed. "And bring Wyr-raji. He's coming with us."

Pram and Hroth left to fulfill his request. As their forms retreated into the distance, Len shoved the remainder of his strip of meat into his mouth, chewing slowly as his mind raced. He hadn't been given any indication that Freyna was watching over him anymore. Perhaps he'd used up all his luck. Behind him, he could still hear his mother muttering a prayer in the old tongue.

It appears the bones have been thrown once more. I can't see how they've landed. All I can do is hope they're in my favor once again.

XXI

Her body ached as she bounced in the saddle. The sun, which had once hung brightly in the sky, was now hidden behind a wall of darkness. Thick clouds threatening rain filled the heavens, their presence making the air hot and sticky. Sweat rolled down Hera's back, her riding blouse sticking uncomfortably to her flesh. The sound of clopping hooves surrounded her, accompanied by snorts and heavier breathing from the horses.

One of the soldiers next to Hera called out for a break. Hera slipped out of her saddle and stretched her arms over her head. Her mount quickly looked for tufts of grass or clover to snack on. Patting the beast on the neck, the queen was surprised at how much sweat her hand picked up from the light contact. She proffered a handful of travel pellets, a mixture of grains tightly compressed to provide the horses with a high energy snack after a long day of work. Her mount took the offering with a grateful nicker, the horse's lips tickling the queen's palm.

The two shared another moment of affection before Hera left in search of her own food, handing her reins to the nearest man. Saddlebags were opened and waterskins were passed around as the camp took a much-needed break. A hand held out a chunk of bread and an apple to the queen, which she took with a kind smile. A second man offered her a waterskin, having removed it from her mount's saddle.

"How are we doing?" Hera asked one of the soldiers. She bit into her apple with a satisfying crunch and waited for his response.

"We're making good time," he replied. "We haven't pushed the horses because we don't want to exhaust them before we reach the border, but we should pick up the pace if we want to find the spot before the Blood Moon."

"There's not much time yet," Hera muttered. "How hard can we push them? I want to give us time to rest once we get there, and to make sure I can find the right spot."

She held her breath as she waited for the man's answer. The queen's body ached from the long hours sitting on her horse. Hera was unsure if she could continue going at this pace, let alone switch to a faster one.

"I wouldn't push them too much more since we've been walking them all day, but I will need to ask someone with a little more experience with them. To be honest, I've spent more time as a foot soldier, so I don't feel comfortable saying exactly how much we can push them. We also need to worry about you, your majesty. Our men have trained for a march like this, but we should make sure we don't push your body too hard."

Though she didn't want to admit it, Hera knew that she posed a liability to her cause if she kept on pushing herself. The queen thanked the man and asked that he report back to her once he'd discussed the matter with the horses with his colleague.

The heavy skies concerned Hera. It was unusual this time of year to see anything other than the occasional pillowy cloud, white and brilliant against the azure heavens, with sunlight peeking out from behind them, bathing everything around it with a pleasant warmth, and bringing out the symphony of animal chatter. Instead, there was darkness. The birds remained silent in the trees, deer and rabbits hid in the shadows, and even the bugs did not hum. It did not feel like the foreshadowing of rain. The air didn't smell musky. Everything just felt heavy.

The queen leaned against a tree, her back resting comfortably against the trunk, as she observed her camp and surroundings. The men moved efficiently as they took advantage of their break. Rations and waterskins were passed around. Arrow fletching was double checked, bindings were tightened, and sheath straps were cinched. They moved with an ease that only came with years of practice.

Officers moved through the ranks, checking on their men and sharing an occasional laugh. Smiles could be seen all around as they stretched, massaging their shoulders or lower backs from the long ride, in between sips of water and bites of food. No one seemed concerned about the darkness looming overhead. A passing soldier offered the queen a drink, which she took absentmindedly.

"What do you think of the clouds overhead?" Hera asked.

The man blinked, taken aback. "Clouds, your majesty?"

"Yes, those blocking the sun." The queen gestured to the blackened sky.

"It's naught more than normal clouds, your majesty." His apologetic tone left her feeling nonplussed. "However, it's been mentioned more than once how strange it is that there's no wildlife about. One of the men, used to go boar hunting with the late king, may he rest in the Halls of the Fallen, remarked how unsettling it is to not see any animals. Not even a tit."

Hera reached up to touch her sacred petals hidden in an old leather pouch around her neck. Could this all be related to the visions she'd been having about Freyna? They all seemed so vivid, but surely they had only been dreams?

The man leaned forward and whispered conspiratorially. "I don't mean to be rude and encroach on your royal personage, but if you're going to stay here, I can bring Kellian over. I heard him mention the dark clouds earlier as we marched, but I just thought it'd been a while since he'd seen the sun, you know? Training the new recruits and all keeping us busy."

The queen dismissed the man with a wave to bring back his comrade. As he retreated, she leaned her head back against the trunk and closed her eyes. A faint wind rustled her hair. It proved to be a welcome relief as it broke up the stale air around her.

Why can only I see the darkness? she wondered. *Something is not right. But... the dream reader did not mention anything about this. Could he not see it either? I thought he saw it when we discussed my dream, my vision.*

A gentle pressure on her hand startled the queen. Hera's eyes popped open to a small girl standing in front of her. Her pale skin, periwinkle hair, and cream-colored dress blew in an invisible wind. Strands of blue hair flew around the girl's bruised face. The queen felt a twinge of regret as she saw the now-healed cut on her pale skin turning a rich purple, as well as the healing split lip.

"Dear Freyna," Hera murmured, the queen's hand raising and touching the goddess' cheek with the back of Freyna's own. "How can I thank you for protecting me?"

Freyna shook her head, her eyes pained. Raising a bruised hand, the goddess reached out to touch the queen's neck. The two locked eyes, and Hera felt her stomach lurch as she was pulled into darkness. A dark figure, tall and lithe, loomed in the background. In front of this figure, something moving caught her attention. At first, it waved, with long tendrils of what looked like smoke rising up and disappearing into the blackness. With each passing second, the undulating mass became more distinct.

It was not a single form, but rather multiple figures. Slight of frame, with wisps of what appeared to be smoke rising off from them, they stared at her with white eyes. Hera averted her gaze once their eyes came into focus. A shiver ran down her spine, warning her to not make contact with whatever those monsters were. Keeping a downward gaze, she tried to see what they were doing. The distance between her and the shadow creatures closed. Tears welled in the corners of her eyes, her body trembling. An ear-piercing shriek split the darkness, nearly deafening her. Hera's hands flew to cover her ears, and she squeezed her eyes shut.

"Your majesty?" a tentative voice cut through the shrill cry.

Hera's eyes fluttered open. A confused pikeman stood in front of her, the man who'd offered her the waterskin moments earlier by his side. Both men hesitated, seeing their queen disoriented. Hera looked for Freyna, but she did not see the goddess anymore.

"Your majesty?" the soldier asked "Shall we come back later?"

"No." Hera rubbed her face, trying to clear her head. The shadow creatures' cry still echoed in her ears, their white eyes burned into her mind. "Please, leave us. I would like to speak to him."

The man backed off, leaving his queen and Kellian.

"I hear you see the darkness," Hera said without preamble.

"Yes, your majesty."

"What do you know of this? Have you seen the gods?"

Kellian shuffled his foot uncomfortably. "I know not of why the darkness comes; my apologies, your majesty. Of the gods, it has been many years since I have seen them. I was but a boy when I thought I saw her. I grew up on the outskirts of Pharn on a farm. One day, my foot slipped, and I fell into the pond and hit my head. When I woke up, I was underwater, and darkness was encroaching. My lungs burned for air, but I couldn't break the surface. Before everything went black, a hand reached into the water and pulled me out. I didn't get a good look, but her green hair made me think it was Zemé, the patron goddess of the harvest."

Hera tapped her chin, deep in thought. "And you've never seen her again?"

"No, your majesty."

"Thank you, Kellian, is it?" She was rewarded with a nod. "Please find whoever is tending to the horses and bring them to me. I would like to leave while it is still day."

Hera took another bite of her almost forgotten apple as Kellian rushed away. Her thoughts swirled in an endless miasma of questions and speculation as she tried to make sense of everything. Freyna's appearance once more only resulted in more confusion, muddling the answers she thought she'd received from the dream reader.

I see Freyna and the darkness. Is it her petals that show me these things? No. Kellian sees the darkness too. Is our tie to the gods? They've come to both of us. A warning for me and saving his life. She comes to me still. Is it that simple? The gods showing themselves to us? The other soldier doesn't see the darkness, but he sees clouds. It seems everyone has noticed the lack of wildlife. Perhaps they can't see everything because they haven't been... chosen?

But what was that last vision? The last two were death and destruction. The tall man is always around, watching. Leading? There's death to Zanir, Alocar, and Xan. No one is singled out or safe. But what were those shadow monsters? The scream. An involuntary shiver broke the queen from her thoughts. *Could they be the source of the darkness? Or is it that tall man?*

Gods! The stones in the vision. Mighty, yet... crumbling? Like Corinth. Like the... gods? But what are the remaining four? What is more powerful than the gods?

Hera heaved a mighty sigh as she tried to make sense of it all. She only guessed that the stones represented the gods. The vision had twelve, and eight could easily represent them. The dream reader had alluded to that earlier. But who did the other four belong to?

"Gods, I wish Vashe were here."

XXII

As the darkness rolled in over the horizon, Alverick watched on with mounting unease. He and Brody had finally reached the bottom of the ravine and were looking for a spot to rest at the basin of the Rydash Gorge when they ran into Dez. The Avalanche was surprised to see her away from Ghan and Aria. Ever since she'd split from the goddess, the Tempest hadn't left her side. Much had changed about Dez. Most notably was her formerly unbothered nature. Where before she would talk to herself and had no problem confusing others with her mysterious ways, she now kept to herself, barely talking to even the goddess who shared a body with her for countless years.

"You see it coming, don't you?" Her blunt question surprised the two.

"See what?" Brody asked.

"Yes." Alverick's answer drew both their eyes.

"The winds have been speaking to me. It's not good."

Brody's eyes darted between the two, confusion evident by how wide they were. The young man's mouth parted as though he wanted to speak, but words failed him, and he ended up flapping his mouth in silent question. Alverick caught his friend's gaze and felt a deep twinge of pity. The young man spent so much time trying to understand everything Alverick had been through, to be there for him regardless of whether he understood the Avalanche's dilemmas, yet Alverick always seemed to baffle him. Throw Dez into the mix, and it was a recipe for chaos.

He caught the approach of the two aethren and nodded to Brody and Dez. Brody, still lost in the conversation, missed Alverick's cue. Dez didn't. Her eyes darkened, but she didn't say anything else until the two arrived. Taking advantage of the opportunity, Alverick tapped into his Avalanche energies and sent out tendrils into the earth, trying to see if he could sense anything.

Reaching into the sandy ground instead of the usual thickly packed dirt left him amazed at how quickly he was able to go through the layers of earth. In what felt like no time, he was checking their surroundings for great distances all around their camp in the gorge. He almost thought he could feel the retreating forces of Scrymme, but Alverick was sure he was just imagining it. They should be long gone by now.

To the west, he did note a small band heading their way. The group moved at a casual pace, unbothered and seemingly at ease. Most likely, it was nothing more than a caravan passing by. Other than that, there was nothing else he could discern outside the camp. Absolutely nothing. It reminded him of his first time in Themba when he couldn't even feel the mice scurrying across the earth.

This time, he felt a few people approaching his group of three, but for the most part, the movement in the gorge was dying down as the sun began to work its way towards the horizon. Or, at least, he assumed that was accurate. With the thick black clouds obscuring the sun, the Avalanche wasn't exactly sure what time it was.

"What do you think?" Ghan's deep voice greeted the group with somberness. "You can see it, yes?"

As the god gestured to the sky, Alverick found himself staring at the blackness that stretched toward them. He knew Brody could not see it, but how many others would be just as confused as the young guard? Would they even take him seriously after all he'd been through when he barely could do so himself?

"I've heard things."

The classically ambiguous response from Dez sent a small butterfly of happiness fluttering in Alverick's chest. He couldn't help but shoot her a glance. As quickly as the butterfly came, it left. Dez, a former shell of herself, did not have the glint of mystery in her eye as she spoke to the gods. Alverick thought he heard the tiniest tinkling of a sigh from Aria, but when he turned toward her, all he could see was her pitying stare.

"Dez," Aria began. "You really shouldn't listen to the winds. Not all it tells you is true."

"It's all I have," Dez replied. "And to be honest, I've spent so much of my life listening to voices in my head that I'm not sure what's real or not anymore."

Dez flashed a weak smile, but Alverick could see her pain. The Avalanche was really interested to hear what the gods had to say about everything going on. He waited for what they would say to help determine how serious it was. He felt a small nudge on his arm. Brody shot him a curious glance, asking so many questions with just one look.

"What does it all mean?" Alverick asked. "I don't think I've noticed it before, but it may have been because we've all been so focused on Vahnyre."

"I agree," Ghan said. "I know that I was strictly focused on Vahnyre. But this, I don't know if it's related to him or something else. It seems a little out of his realm."

"I don't remember him being associated with the darkness either," Aria joined in. "But the Ancients might have that power. Dez and I were talking about them, and I think that she may have a point with what the wind says."

"It was right about Zemé," Dez mused, a glimmer of her coy smile playing on her lips.

"That they were," Aria agreed.

"If the Ancients are involved, this is bigger than us," Ghan interjected, breaking up the moment shared between the two women. "I can only think of two people who would bring the Darkness, and one has been sealed away long ago."

"Maeyu'dana would never actively bring Darkness," Aria countered. "She sacrificed herself to keep Apophmet's influence from spreading past Enlil." Aria's expression darkened. "It's a shame Enlil fell with her."

The goddess and Dez both shared the same look of grief at the fallen realm. Alverick didn't know much about the land, but he knew that it was a place that captivated Vashe for as long as he knew her. A secret land where no one went and nothing was supposed to survive. Ghan's attention was on the approaching clouds.

"Apophmet?" Brody asked, finally speaking. "Is he the same as Apophos? I've heard the shieldmaiden, Jytte, talk about the mark of Apophos, or something like that."

"They are the same," Ghan answered. "As are Re'nukhtet and Re'nukh. In the Northern wilds, their people have adapted the names to fit their language over the centuries. At the core, though, they still refer to the Ancients."

"One thing that I always found interesting," Dez added, "is that they are the only people who strictly revere the two Ancients instead of the rest of the aethren. I didn't know who they were at the time, having never connected the Ancients to Apophmet and Re'nukhtet, and assumed that they worshipped foreign gods. Maybe even some dead religion like the people of Enlil. It all makes sense."

Alverick stepped away from the group while Brody asked the three a few more questions. His mind raced. Beings more powerful than the gods. The concept both terrified and intrigued him. He'd only just learned that there were gods outside of the Siblings, and now a whole pantheon presented itself to him.

"Everything has changed so quickly since you've died, Bannen," Alverick whispered to himself.

A gentle breeze rustled his hair, and heaviness settled beside him. Glancing over his shoulder, the Avalanche half expected to see his friend standing next to him. Instead, he saw Brody and the others still talking. Deflated, Alverick turned back to the west.

"I shouldn't be surprised," he told himself. "You said it's all in my head. Still, I wish you were here." A wistful smile played on the Avalanche's lips as he watched the sun move lower into the horizon. "You know, I don't see as much red right now." He chuckled. "Normally, when I see red, it means I'm close to Snapping. I never wanted to admit it, but I also never did anything to stop it. I think I wanted to Snap. To forget everything. You were right," he turned to his left, where he felt the heaviness. "I am a shell. But I need to stay strong."

The princess' approach caught his eye. Alverick stopped talking and observed her arrival. Next to Cienna, Caitlyn matched her stride for stride. He admired the princess' determined countenance. Something had boosted her confidence, finally pushing her from young child to young woman and heir to the throne. She would be ready to lead sooner than she imagined.

Caitlyn, on the other hand, carried herself with a poise that belied her. She too helped mold the princess into the woman she was becoming. The redhead's guarded demeanor she'd held when they first reconnected melted away, revealing the woman he knew years ago, the one he remembered. Both her hands were bare as she embraced her Tainted Spark status, the jagged tattoos covering her hand but stopping at the wrist, large breaks in the markings evident.

He thanked the gods that she'd managed to pull through after their battle at Fa'Tinh. Unused to wielding her magic, Alverick was afraid he'd lost her to the Taint that should have consumed her years ago. But they'd both survived.

"I have my Anchor, Bannen," Alverick whispered as he watched the redhead.

The heaviness to his left lifted, but did not disappear completely. The change in energy around him caused the Avalanche to pause. The moment was bittersweet.

"I guess this is good-bye, Bannen." Alverick turned to his left, facing where his friend would have been. "I'll see you in the Halls, old friend."

A tear rolled down his cheek as the heaviness completely disappeared. Throughout the conversation, his vision did not turn red.

<center>~~~</center>

"We will have more than enough forces to send back," Cienna was saying as Alverick returned to the group. "But I need you all to join me on my trip back to Madden. Swordbane has agreed to join us and bring who I've asked for. His remaining forces will protect Pharn alongside our own."

The princess' eyes burned as she pleaded her case. She didn't need to ask Brody or himself to join her campaign, but the other three were not hers to command. No one could command the gods, and Alverick wasn't too sure who Dez served. He almost suspected she swore fealty to no nation thanks to her mysterious background. Next to the princess stood Caitlyn, her arms crossed in front of her chest. Their eyes met, and a coy smile played on her lips.

"It is time to act," Cienna continued. "Clearly, something sinister has befallen Corinth, and I would rather meet it head-on than be caught off-guard."

As no one moved to speak, Alverick noted how the princess' confidence waned. Her gaze darted to each member of the group, imploring someone to say something. The Siblings loomed over the gathering, their visages an unreadable mask. Aria's silver hair sparkled in the sun as she pulled it over one of her shoulders. The kind eyes Alverick had been used to seeing now matched her more ruthless brother's. Dez was even more of an enigma, her silver eyes reflecting the rapid thoughts flitting through her head.

He didn't trust Swordbane, but if the man was willing to give Cienna whatever she asked for, he must have seen something troubling as well. The young Qu'ari wouldn't do anything unless it benefited himself; that much Alverick knew, and that alone swayed the Avalanche's decision.

"Zanir has been surprised too many times since all of this started," Alverick said. "Ever since the attacks on the spice mines, we've faced high losses because we've not been prepared. At the same time, Swordbane has also struggled, and he's been the one who's been making all the plays. If he's concerned enough to grant us everything we've asked for without asking for much in return –"

Alverick paused to confirm his assumption. Cienna's nod encouraged him to proceed.

"He's not a man who will give up anything easily," the Avalanche continued. "I believe Swordbane is troubled, just as we are. I don't have a say in the matter; I will follow my lord's direction, but I believe it is the best course. If you trust my judgement," he addressed the Siblings and Dez, "I hope you will join us in meeting this threat directly. I don't know what exactly it is, but we have at least a hint of what it could be. Without you, I believe we will fail."

Silence from the group greeted Alverick and the princess. Around them, the general chatter of the camp muted, as though a bubble had fallen over them. All other sound in the nearby area appeared amplified. Alverick was aware of his heart pounding in his ears. The impending Darkness concerned him, and he knew that if the gods did not join them, Corinth was doomed. He quietly prayed to the gods who stood before him that there would be a favorable resolution.

"I am not ready to die," Brody spoke up, startling the Avalanche. "And I agree with Al's assessment. Swordbane is a selfish man whose only concern is furthering his own goals. He is driven by his ego and the power over his people."

"Right now, he's shaken," Alverick added. "At the meeting after the fight, he did not have the same surety that I saw when he put a blade through our king. All of the setbacks he's faced have been difficult for him. But he is still cunning."

Dez crossed her arms across her chest. The movement caught the Avalanche's attention, and he paused to give her time to speak. She stood for a moment in silence as she processed her thoughts. He could see that she was close to making a decision, whatever it may be. To Alverick's surprise, Dez didn't say anything as the time passed. Both he and the princess waited patiently, but instead of offering her advice, the Tempest chewed her lip, biting back her response.

"I think we should go," Aria said, breaking the awkward quiet that settled over the group. "From what I saw during my time with Dez and after speaking with my brother, I feel it would be unwise to ignore this threat. I will go with you."

Alverick noted Cienna's sigh of relief. He knew that she still hoped that the other two would accompany them, but convincing Aria was a start. Personally, Alverick felt that if Aria went, the other two would follow, but Dez had been so unpredictable lately. He almost didn't feel like he knew her anymore, or what little he thought he had known prior. To his relief, both she and Ghan nodded in agreement, though the Tempest seemed to do so grudgingly.

What holds her back? Alverick wondered. *I would almost think she is in mourning the way she is so subdued. Perhaps her separation from Aria?*

The Avalanche tried not to think about it too much and focus on the task at hand. Now that the group had reached a consensus, he knew he must speak with Swordbane, or at least Pram, to get a better understanding of what they knew.

The sun was nearing the horizon and preparing to set. Instead of pushing the armies further, it seemed that Swordbane preferred to settle down for the night. Campfires were no longer cropping up in small circles. Instead, large fires took over, providing warmth for the cold night that was to come. Alverick hoped that the walls of the gorge would shield them from the elements, or at least the winds.

He found himself wandering off while Cienna spoke with the others in their small group. He could hear Ghan's deep voice at last and wondered what took so long for the god to join the conversation. His mind, however, kept returning to Dez. The more Alverick thought about it, the more he was certain that she mourned her separation from Aria. It all came in such an unexpected manner, much like Bannen's death, that he believed she hadn't processed everything.

It was a feeling Alverick was intimately familiar with.

"Do you think we do the right thing trusting Swordbane?"

Alverick turned to find Caitlyn trailing behind him. He didn't realize she'd followed him so far through the camps without him noticing. The Avalanche scolded himself for being so distracted that he allowed someone to sneak up on him, even if it was Caitlyn. Turning his attentions to the saddle bags attached to Styx, he busied himself with pulling out his sleeping bag and any other essentials he may need for the night.

"His pride gives us a good method to gauge the situation," he finally replied.

"Al?"

The Avalanche flinched as her hand touched the small of his back. Her delicate touch sent an electric shock through his body that had nothing to do with either of their Spark skills. He pretended to be busy with Styx, hoping she would continue her question.

"Al." More insistent. "There's a good chance we're all going to die, isn't there?"

The Avalanche's breath caught in his throat. Hearing her fears laid out in such a blunt manner, knowing that their failure would most likely result in the destruction of Corinth, left him terrified. Tapping into his energy reserves, Alverick found himself searching for signs of life as far as he could reach. Bodies in the valley pulsed on the ground, their movements beating into the earth. A wave of relief swept through the Avalanche. The emotion was short-lived, however, as he kept pushing. Tendrils of energy strained, pushing further into the gorge, up the walls, and onto the exterior of the ravine.

What once filled him with hope was replaced with dread. No lizards, snakes, or other animals could be found in the sand or climbing on the rocks. At the limits of his reach, no rabbits, foxes, or other fauna finished their daily hunt for food or laid curled in their holes to sleep. The air remained eerily quiet, the symphony of birdsong absent as the day dragged on. Tempted to test his limits, Alverick pushed onward. The periphery of his vision bled red as he reached out further than he'd ever done before.

Nothing.

Withdrawing his energies, Alverick felt exhausted, the red fading from his line of sight. He needed to eat, or there could be ramifications from overexerting himself. Silence greeted the Avalanche once his senses returned. Caitlyn still waited.

"We can't worry about that," he answered. "But to put it simply, yes. I would love to have Vashe with us; Dez's melancholy concerns me. I don't know if I can trust her to do what needs to be done, whatever it may be."

Caitlyn's hand landed on his shoulder, gently turning him around to face her. Her emerald eyes stared deeply into his dark ones, searching. He knew what she sought and despaired at not being able to provide it: hope.

Her eyes sucked him in, their clear green depths laying bare her soul. She was beautiful. Before he knew it, his lips met hers, his hand cupping the delicate curve of her face. Alverick felt Caitlyn melt into him, her hand resting on his as he held her cheek. The redhead's body pressed into his, sending a shiver of excitement coursing through him. Time stopped for the Avalanche, and nothing mattered at that moment.

XXIII

OLDAR STRODE towards the end of the tunnel. Behind him, a trio of guards he'd encountered as he raced through earlier kept a close pace, their boots striking loudly on the stone floor. His heart beat wildly in his chest as he began climbing the stairs that would lead him to Ånchal. Sweat slicked the king's palms, his hands becoming clammy. Oldar's breath caught in his chest as he realized the air around him was cooler than the tunnel had been.

"What's going on?" one of the men behind him whispered. "Ghan's mercy, it feels wrong."

"Blessed Aria," another muttered.

Light filtered into the darkness as they reached the entrance of the outpost city. Heavy footsteps on the wooden steps raced down towards Oldar and his tiny entourage. The king steeled himself for the newcomer, his hand moving to his hip as a pair of hands pulled him backwards from behind.

"Who's down there?" the voice ahead called out. "Stay where you are!"
"Make way for the king!" one of Oldar's guards called back.

A flurry of confused voices broke out from above. The harried steps from moments before stopped on the worn wooden steps. The flicker of light from a nearby sconce cast long shadows on the walls, giving the stairway an eerie feeling with the chill that hung in the air. Oldar pushed forward, earning himself a startled exclamation from his guards as he passed their protective barrier. They quickly moved to catch up and put themselves between the young king and those above.

It wasn't long until the afternoon sun broke through the dim light of tunnel. Oldar swore as he almost ran into a group of four still standing on the wooden steps, talking quietly amongst themselves. A bark of surprise ripped from the lips of the man Oldar nearly hit. The man staggered back and stumbled into his comrades, who swore as they almost fell down in their haste not to fall over each other.

"Your majesty!" one of the men in the back exclaimed, managing to keep his balance as he danced out of the way of his companion's clumsy feet.

Oldar waved his hand, having regained his composure seconds before. "I don't have time for formalities," he said simply. "I am in a hurry. I need to find the fastest way to clear people out of Madden, possibly Alocar." Glancing behind him, Pruvencia's face flashed in his mind. She needed to be the first to safety. "Please."

The men on the steps in front of him shared a glance before the one closest to the king motioned for him to follow. With a grateful smile, Oldar and his small group of soldiers followed the outpost guards into the city proper.

Fresh air wafted through the last bits of the tunnel, clearing the stale air and providing much needed relief after their long journey. They had stopped multiple times throughout their escape so his elderly caretaker could rest. He didn't realize how fragile Pru was. She'd always seemed so full of life as she took care of the castle and staff — and him. Pushing his concerns to the back of his mind, Oldar forced himself to focus on getting them to safety. As long as she was safe, that's all that mattered to him.

～～～

The air was warm as the sun hung in the afternoon sky. Wisps of white clouds floated lazily overhead, and birdsong punctuated the surrounding sounds with trills and melodic warbles. A trio of butterflies flew by, their golden wings glinting against the rich azure. The heady scent of the nearby pines provided a subtle fragrance to the outpost city.

As Oldar stepped out from the tunnel connecting Madden to Ånchal, he raised his arm to block the brilliant rays from hurting his eyes. The air around him was pleasantly warm, contrasting starkly with the unnatural chill he'd felt earlier in the tunnels. Blinking rapidly to try and keep his eyes from watering, the young king took a moment to acclimate to his surroundings.

Soldiers raced around the city, some calling out to their comrades as they rushed to complete the task at hand. Gradually, the pain from the sun disappeared and was replaced with confusion. In the middle of the outpost, a circle of soldiers hovered over something on the ground while the others moved chaotically. The men who accompanied him through the tunnel stood frozen by his side. Motioning to the king, the men who met up with him on the stairs made their way towards the circle.

Oldar glanced around the city. The frenetic movements made him uneasy. A sudden splash of red on the packed dirt ground made his stomach twist. As he neared the circle, the splashes became more frequent until large swaths of the earth were covered in them. Nearer to the group, Oldar noticed a foul odor. His stomach lurched, and what little he'd eaten while hidden in Schaed's wine cellar threatened to come back up.

"Be forewarned, my king. It isn't pretty."

Pushing back the urge to retch, Oldar turned to face the man who'd spoken to him. Without so much as a word, the king felt his stomach clench once more as he stood on the outskirts of the circle. Inside the ring of soldiers, four blood-stained sheets covered what could only be bodies in the middle of the city.

Pools of blood seeped from under the sheets, coalescing around the fallen as it seeped into the dirt. Flies hovered around the bodies like predators watching fresh carrion. The day's heat did not help. In fact, it seemed to exacerbate the stench of decomposition.

"We found them early this morning," one of the soldiers said to Oldar. "The last couple days, we've seen some of our supplies go missing, but we couldn't figure out how. Til now."

Oldar felt his stomach wring itself as he took a step closer to the bodies. He crouched down and reached out for the edge of the cloth that covered the nearest body.

"I wouldn't do that if I were you, sire," the soldier from before warned. "It's not a pleasant sight. Haven't seen anything this bad since the wolves tore up an escaped goat."

"I can handle it," Oldar replied. "But thank you for your concern."

The man grunted in response. Oldar's fingers trembled as they brushed one of the few white spots remaining on the sheet. He found the soft fabric surprising; he didn't think they had such luxuries out in the outpost. His amazement was short-lived, however, as he steeled himself and quickly lifted the sheet, throwing it in a high arc as he exposed the body.

A soft cry escaped his lips. Below, the mangled corpse of a small woman stared back at him. Claw marks raked through her body, creating deep gouges into her soft flesh. Her clothes hung in tatters on her slim frame. The curving tattoos of a Stream along with the jagged lines of a Spark, all shrouded in the hazy markings of a Shadow, ran up her dark flesh. As his eyes traveled over her ravaged body, Oldar struggled to keep himself from voiding his stomach.

"Lift the other sheets," the king instructed the nearby soldiers.

His gaze lingered on the fallen mage, studying her face. He remembered that face: Ka'lev. The *whoosh* of sheets fluttering as they were flung off the remaining bodies sounded preternaturally loud in Oldar's ears as he locked stares with the leader of the Myrani. Somewhere far away, the birds' symphony sang, their beautiful melodies muted as a bubble of silence enveloped the young king.

Voices spoke to him, their gruff words muffled by the bubble surrounding him. Sensing them more than hearing them, Oldar turned to look at the remaining bodies. The bodies of the small man from the mountain tribe and the larger Xanan man lay beside their leader. Like Ka'lev, large slashes marred their flesh, ripping chunks and exposing the muscle and bone. As his eyes moved to Bikal, the smaller man, Oldar felt his stomach lurch once more as he noticed the man's right arm was torn cleanly off.

"What happened to them?" he whispered.

He wasn't sure if anyone could hear him through the bubble of silence that engulfed him and was pleasantly surprised when the man responded.

"We're not really sure." The soldier hesitated, catching Oldar's attention. Tearing his gaze from the mutilated corpses, the king looked up at the grizzled man. "The night became unseasonably cold. We've been sheltering inside more, the men on shift seeking shelter in the alcoves of the wall-walks. They didn't see anything."

The soldier stopped once more, his eye dropping as he remembered something. Oldar glanced around at the others in the ring surrounding the bodies. He could see men racing in the background, but he was drawn to those nearby. Many averted their eyes, shifting uncomfortably in the silence. The king found himself growing anxious as the pause stretched on.

"What next?" he prompted.

The man who had been speaking earlier locked gazes with Oldar. His eyes begged the king for forgiveness. For understanding.

"Then came the howls," the soldier replied, his voice dropping. "They were like nothing I've ever heard. No wolf or rabbit sounds like that."

Oldar felt his stomach drop. The Faceless were already on the outskirts of Alocar. The king found himself putting everything together. It all made sense. The slight chill at the entrance of the tunnel. The chaos in the normally boring Ånchal teeming with excitement. The dead Myrani. Oldar found himself looking down at the fallen mercenaries once more. He couldn't believe they were killed, and so viciously.

So they were following me after all, he mused. *I can't believe I led them here. They could have snuck into the capital and no one would've noticed. I doubt anyone would've noticed until it was too late.*

Chewing on the inside of his cheek, Oldar studied the corpses with morbid curiosity. His eyes were drawn to the wounds. The claw marks primarily covered the torsos, but something caught his interest. On their arms, or anywhere else where they had tattoos, there were thin, deep lines carved into their flesh, breaking up their tattoos and exposing the tendons just beneath. Oldar's eyebrow twitched as he noticed they were on each of the Myrani.

Why are there small scratches on their arms? They weren't meant to kill. They almost seem like an afterthought.

"We tried collecting their blood for our soldier to draught," a nearby soldier said as he watched the young king examine the bodies. A second man walked up carrying a pewter tankard. "But –"

The second soldier offered the tankard to the king. Oldar grabbed the mug and stared at its contents. Instead of red blood, he saw swirls of black defiling its purity. Oldar felt his eyes widen in surprise, his brows disappearing into his hair as he saw the strange phenomenon. Glancing back to the bodies, he noticed that in the smudges on the ground and in the puddles still seeping into the earth, thin tendrils of inky blackness marred the spilt life essence.

"Fascinating," the king murmured. "And they all are like this? Why? Does it have to do with... where is the other one?"

"Other one?" inquired one of the guards. "We only found three bodies."

"Three," Oldar repeated. "Three," he said under his breath.

Turning from the grisly spectacle, Oldar walked away from the circle surrounding the corpses and wandered away, his hands behind his back. The commotion at the outpost calmed down as the afternoon wore on. As the king roamed the dirt path, he thought he caught sight of Pruvencia away from the tumult, sipping something from a clay mug in a small patch of dandelions. The sun's rays kissed her wrinkled face, shining brightly as she closed her eyes, savoring the heat. The king felt the corners of his lips turn up for the briefest of moments before he returned his attentions back to his musings.

"Where is the pale one? Where is Dzerik? Did he ambush his own people? No. This seems like the Faceless. They look just like Schaed. But what happened to their blood?" Oldar turned, heading back towards the gathering in the middle of the outpost. "And why break the tattoos?" Oldar stopped in his tracks, his head bent down as he chewed on his thumb. Slowly, he lifted his head, his hand falling to his side.

"Break the tattoos," he muttered. Taking a moment to recall the tankard of collected blood, he remembered how tainted it looked with the black swirls. It was almost as though it were defiled of its magical purity. "I wonder," he said softly.

Miming with one hand that he was slicing his other arm, the king made his way over to the tunnels once more. Oldar kept his eyes peeled for any disturbances in the stone or on the ground. He was no hunter, but a patch of bent grass or scratches on the walls of the tunnel would surely be something.

With his arms clasped behind his back, Oldar combed over the area, pacing back and forth as he searched for any sign of a struggle. Every turn brought him more disappointment and confusion. After his fifth pass, he gave up and decided to return to the main group once more. There was absolutely nothing to suggest that Ka'lev and the Myrani put up any kind of fight. No stones were marked, no grass disturbed. Even the dirt under his feet was still smooth.

A gauged track off to his side caught his attention out of the corner of his eye. Following the break in the dirt, Oldar noticed a set of footprints lightly pressed into the ground. They were suddenly, almost violently, broken as they were replaced with deeper tracks leading backwards before new prints appeared nearby. A splash of blood darkened the dirt nearby. As Oldar approached the splatter, he noticed a bit of cloth that appeared to have been ripped from its owner.

They had fought. They just didn't stand a chance.

Squatting over the discarded piece of fabric, Oldar tried to figure out the Myrani's last moments. All he could see was Schaed's frightened face, staring death in the eye. The king closed his eyes and shook his head.

I can't dwell on that. I have to figure out what's going on. Forcing himself to focus, Oldar tried to figure out what breaking tattoos would mean for magi. *Those wounds really seemed like an afterthought. The rips to their bodies would've killed them.* Shaking his head once more, the king pushed himself up and began walking towards the bodies once more. *I need to see Alverick. He might know something about this.*

"What are you going to do with the bodies?" Oldar asked as he approached the group once more. "I would love to preserve them for the headmistress of the Mageri to study, but I feel these three probably suffered enough and deserve at least a simple burial. Maybe somewhere outside the city walls?"

"A simple burial is the least they deserve," the captain said. "The gods would smile on us for that small act of kindness."

At the mention of the gods, Oldar felt his blood run cold. So much had happened, and yet so few were aware of all that was truly going on. The king opened his mouth to reply when a cry rang through the outpost. Soldiers and Oldar all spun towards the sound, many running towards the source inside a red stone building.

A man staggered out the door, barely managing to stay upright as he looked around, his face frantic. Several soldiers race over, trying to calm the deranged man. As they neared, the man swung his arms at them, shouting incoherent curses as he tried to hit anyone who dared approach. With each passing second, his eyes became vacant as he stared into the unknown. Behind the man, a couple soldiers stood in the doorway, disbelief etched on their faces as they watched their comrade flail about.

"What's going on?" the captain shouted. "Somebody restrain him!"

The soldiers who stood at arms' length from the violent man, tentatively closed the distance. As they worked to corral him, one of the soldiers standing in the doorway held up a tankard and shook his head. Next to him, the other soldier held up a small dagger. Blood stained the tip.

With a primal shout, Oldar watched as the soldiers finally managed to pin the man to the ground. Wriggling against his captors, the man spat curses all around him as he tried to break free. On more than one occasion, he tried to bite one of the soldiers holding him down. His eyes were wild and completely unfocused as he raved on the dirt. Small clouds of dust were kicked up from his exertions. The soldiers in the doorway slipped out, managing to avoid being kicked by their violent comrade, and quickly made their way to their captain and king.

"What is the meaning of this?" the captain asked, gesturing to the scene before him.

"I've never seen anything like it," the first replied.

"Thom just wanted to draught the blood, but minutes after he did, he began screaming about the gods and other nonsense." The second soldier's face was ashen. He was clearly shaken at Thom's sudden change in demeanor.

"What do you mean?" the captain asked.

Oldar glanced over at Thom once more and noticed for the first time that the dark markings of tattoos covered his hand and forearm. The more he looked, the more something seemed off to the king. Oldar watched the man for several long moments, ignoring the conversation going on behind him between the captain and other soldiers.

The group managed to lift Thom to his feet, with one soldier dusting the raving man off. Their faces were troubled, their jaws tense, and their eyes heavy as they struggled to maintain control over their friend. One of the soldiers looked away as they began ushering Thom inside, unable to look at his former brother-in-arms.

As Thom turned, something caught Oldar's eye.

"Breaks in the tattoo," he muttered. "Captain."

The captain and the two soldiers he'd been speaking with turned to face their king. By this time, Pruvencia had hobbled over to the group, her concern causing her wrinkles to sink even deeper into her face. The elderly woman reached out for Oldar's arm, her hand gently gripping him for security.

"Yes, your majesty?"

"Is the Myrani blood in that tankard?" the king asked.

The captain blanched before turning to look at the mug in the other soldier's hand once more. "Yes. Yes, it is, sire." His voice lacked the brusqueness it'd previously had as the man struggled to understand where his king was going.

The soldier proffered the tankard filled with inky blood to the king. Oldar took the mug and stared absent-mindedly at its contents.

"And the man, Thom, is he a Tempest or a Spark?" Oldar asked.

"No, your majesty," the soldier replied. "He's a Stream, actually."

Oldar paused. This was surprising news. "But... he's Tainted."

"What do you mean, your majesty?" the soldier asked.

"Streams aren't one of the styles that become Tainted," the captain added.

The king rubbed his chin as he stared into the tankard. Instead of staring past its contents, Oldar took the time to further examine them. The blackness mixing with the blood slowly spider-webbed out, small tendrils of the impurities creeping across, overpowering the magical essence. Something was wrong. Jutting his chin, Oldar tried to figure out what bothered him.

Birds began chirping once more as the screams disappeared into one of the buildings. Every once in a while, a shriek would startle him, pulling the young king from his reverie. Around him, the group stood in silence. In hushed tones, the captain instructed his men to remove the corpses. Quickly and efficiently, the bodies were removed from the center of the city and prepared for disposal. A large fire burst into life on the outskirts of Ånchal.

Glancing away from the tankard, Oldar watched as the dead were placed near the pyre. A lone soldier stood in front of the bonfire, singing in a rich baritone as those nearby began anointing the bodies with oil before lifting them up and placing them within the dancing flames. The lone soldier's voice carried in the wind, singing praises of the gods and asking that they welcome the newly dead to their final resting place.

A lump formed in the young king's throat and his face flushed. He'd missed out on his parents' funeral and remembrance ceremony. It pained him to know that he wasn't able to wish them a safe journey to the Halls of the Fallen. A solitary tear rolled down his cheek as he watched the last body get hoisted into the fire.

The soft touch of someone brushing his cheek startled Oldar. His eyes darted over to see who it was, and he felt a warmth fill him as Pruvencia's wrinkled hand rested gently on his flesh. Her tired eyes brimmed with moisture as she cupped the young man's face. She was all he had left in the world. His hand grasped her own, and he closed his eyes as he pulled her hand closer to him.

"I wish we had a service for your parents," she said, her voice coming out as a hoarse whisper. "It's the least they deserve."

"When this is over, I want to give them one." Oldar opened his eyes and stared at the flames as they curled around the smoldering flesh, tendrils of smoke rising up to the sky in dark plumes. "And I think I'll invite the Greys. They should be honored for what they did to my parents when I could not be there."

Pruvencia's hand trailed down the side of his cheek, her fingers tickling his flesh. Her gentle squeeze on his arm filled him with reassurance. They just had to get through this. To survive.

Oldar forced himself to look back at the tankard in his hand. He almost dropped the cup in surprise as he stared at the contents. What had previously been the deep red of blood tinged with inky black was now almost all dark. The thin spiderwebs of whatever the blackness was had now overpowered the blood, turning it into something unnatural.

"It's the blood," he gasped as his head snapped up. "Captain, don't let anyone else draught the blood. The Faceless, or whatever killed the Myrani, poisoned their blood. They made it so we can't save the magic."

The grizzled captain's face blanched as the news set in. One of the other soldiers standing nearby took off towards the barracks to warn the others of the king's discovery. Oldar sank to the ground as the implications of his words hit him. He knew the Faceless were horrible creatures, but if he was right, Oldar's uncle had unleashed fell monsters upon Corinth. His uncle found a way to negate the strength of the magi.

XXIV

THE FORESTS OF RO'THRE covered the ground with cooling shadows, providing a welcome break from the stifling air. Leading her mount by foot, Vashe closed her eyes, taking a moment to enjoy the tranquility. Fallen pine needles blanketed the earth, making it nearly impossible for a trail to be worn into the dirt and moss. She'd traveled a considerable distance from Enlil in the last few days, and her body ached from the constant movement and lack of food.

Her journey was at least bearable thanks to Dseti, the Ancient she'd met in the Forgotten Land of Enlil. He'd disappear for lengthy periods at a time, leaving her struggling to find her way, only to return with her saddlebags filled with mushrooms, berries, and small game. Other times, he'd spend the entire day with her, keeping her mind from wandering back to the things she'd seen at the Temple of Maeyu'dana.

Ever since she bathed and draughted the vials of holy blood in the temple, Vashe felt her mind drawn to Enlil even further. What secrets did she uncover during her short stay there? What did she miss in the shadows? The questions threatened to consume her, tugging at her subconscious. Vashe didn't think she was in danger of Snapping; it had been long enough that she would've expected there to be the beginnings of madness by now. Dseti also didn't seem concerned.

"What do you know of bindings?"

The unexpected question popped Vashe's eyes open. The pair didn't usually speak to each other while they traveled for fear of attracting attention. She wasn't sure what kept her quiet, but word of Ro'thre's inhospitality was enough to keep her from trying to find out.

"Are they similar to twinning?" she asked.

The Ancient shook his head. "It's a way for entities to either attach to another or remove the soul of a being and replace it with part of their own. Think of the birth of Alazi."

The explanation caught Vashe off-guard. It had been commonly discussed over the ages, she noticed as she poured over her tomes, that Alazi had long been thought to be a demon of fyre from the Abyss. Czand's disappearance was assumed to have been because he was consumed by Fyre, his mind and essence completely replaced by the other aethren. There had been no consideration given to the possibility that they'd shared consciousness or anything like that. The new information provided her with a myriad of questions.

"No," Dseti cut in before she could reply. "You probably won't find any information about it. You could be the one to document it, though. Assuming we come out of this all alive."

Silence filled the forest at the last statement. Vashe had inklings that things were bad, but she never dreamed it was this dire. The air around her felt heavy. She hoped it was just in her mind.

"Is bonding the only way to save us?" Vashe whispered. "Is there something you're not telling me? What do you know?"

She held her breath, the trepidation making her heart beat wildly in her chest. The two hadn't known each other very long, but Vashe felt she could trust him. Everything he'd done appeared to benefit her, and he'd been forthcoming thus far with any information she wanted from him. She hoped he wasn't misleading her.

"Yes."

His answer was as quiet as her question, sending chills down her spine. The heaviness she'd been experiencing moments before intensified. It reminded her of the unease she felt as they fled Enlil; it was as though someone was watching her, following her as she traveled. Vashe began questioning whether the oppression was in her mind.

"What is needed for a binding?"

Vashe feared the ritual would be extensive. Most of her research taught her that things like twinning or scrying into the Abyss required time, energy, and quiet. They were not things that could be rushed. Twinning the necklace she'd given Brody and Caitlyn to her ring left her feeling exhausted, unable to do much for half a day. In battle, if it came to that, she wouldn't be able to protect herself if it drained her like twinning did.

The pair walked into silence, covering a good distance before she realized that Dseti hadn't responded. Turning to look over her shoulder, she saw the Ancient walking behind her, keeping pace as he had earlier. His presence afforded her a measure of relief, knowing he hadn't walked away.

"Why don't we look for a spot to set up camp?" the Ancient suggested. "The sun is getting ready to set, and I don't want to be caught unaware out here. Let's get off the main path. Follow me."

Vashe couldn't help but be perplexed. How would he know where the main path was in the needle-strewn forest? Without questioning him, the Scrymmen woman led her mount down the route Dseti took. The further they got from the trail they'd been following earlier, the more the oppressive energy she'd been feeling lifted, much the same way the sensation of being watched had when they traveled out in the open.

Many thoughts swirled around in her mind, leaving many questions unanswered. Vashe knew she would need to press the Ancient if she wanted anything. His unusually unforthcoming responses let her know she'd have to tread carefully. A branch cracked in the distance. Her heart jumped into her throat. There was a reason he wasn't answering her right now.

XXV

Fires crackled as the sparse kindling snapped and dripping fat made the flames hiss. Len eyed the multitude of campfires that dotted the floor of the ravine with distrust. He'd had too many encounters with the unpredictable element to last him a lifetime. A light wind encircled him, filling him with a sense of calm. Though he couldn't see her, he knew the Windstrider was there, watching him once more. The sun dipped lower on the horizon, the inky blackness of night blending in with the ever-approaching darkness that moved in from the west.

It had been a while since Pram and Hroth went off to bring Wyrd and the Princess of Zanir to him. The Flame's companion, the young woman with dark hair, had wandered off closer to sunset and hadn't returned. Her absence raised questions. The woman had not strayed far from his sight since she and the Flame began working together.

The children played close to his fire, their smiles illuminating in the firelight as they ran by. Bermet's eyes sparkled as she twirled, her dress fanning out with the momentum of her spin. Zaa'ni plopped down on a nearby stone, a sleeping Heru snuggled against her chest, his shock of dark hair sticking out from the blanket he lay wrapped in. His wife's eyes dropped, the flight of the flames casting shadows that deepened the bags under them. The children's laughter didn't seem to faze her as she rocked in her seat.

Altansari swopped over and placed a comforting arm around Zaa'ni's shoulders, steadying her as she struggled to remain awake. His wife's head rested on Altansari's shoulder, her eyes closing. Pram's wife brought up another hand, pulling Heru's tiny body from his exhausted mother to her own. Len's mother strode over, a kabob in her hand. A chunk of meat was missing from the stick as the elderly woman snacked.

At a word from Honorable Mother, the children quieted and slowed down whenever they neared the fire. Only Bermet appeared unfazed by her mother's fatigue as she continued to spin around in graceful circles around the women. Intan sat down on the stone next to the other two, rubbing her little legs in between bites. Altansari said something softly to the Honorable Mother, but Len couldn't catch what she said.

Another draft rustled Len's hair. He thought he heard the soft chatter of voices on the wind. The young general's eyes darted around, searching for those closest to him. No one was near.

Follow the Darkness, it seemed to say. Anything else that may have been said was drowned out in the collection of voices. Len hoped he didn't miss anything important.

Maen sauntered over to the fire, a stack of kabobs and flatbread resting on a tin plate in her hand. Next to her, the foreign shieldmaiden kept pace. In the waning light, Len was surprised to see that the mixture of coffee and cocoa powder she'd used to rub onto her body to camouflage her pale skin had been completely washed off.

He eyed the women's approach, vaguely remembering that the Zanirian princess had asked for the barbarian woman to join them. Len didn't pay them much mind, however. His mind struggled to piece together his next plan of action despite his exhaustion. Ever since they'd made it to the gorge, he felt an unusual lethargy, as though his energy had been drained from his body. He knew that he couldn't rest. Not until he'd reinforced his position within Corinth and as the greatest leader of Xan. The young general took a bite from one of the kabobs that Maen offered him without saying a word. Len waited for Pram to return with Wyrd and the princess.

Len fought back a groan as he thought about his childhood friend. Since the meeting at the Dancing Wolf, he hadn't given much thought to how to deal with Wyrd and his traitorous actions, apart from having the man cut down during battle. The young general knew he needed to make a decision soon, lest he lose the support of the clans. Even his hold on his own people felt tenuous, despite their reverence for his mother. The thought left him seething. He would need to do something big to get Xan back under his control.

"I couldn't find the Avalanche," Pram's voice called out, startling the young general from his thoughts.

Surprised that his general could sneak up on him like that, Len felt himself fuming. The anger and exhaustion he felt were quickly replaced by an emptiness that consumed him in a way he'd never imagined. Behind the general, the Flame, the princess, and Wyrd took seats on nearby stumps, rocks, or the ground in front of Len. The men grabbed a kabob from the tin plate while the princess smoothed her imaginary skirts after sitting out of habit.

"What news do you have, Princess?" Len asked.

He noted the hesitancy in her face as she faltered for the briefest of moments. The emotion was fleeting as his exhaustion swallowed it. Maybe things weren't as bad as he thought.

"I have spoken to my chosen few, and we are ready to leave first thing in the morning."

"And what of your gods?" he asked, cutting to the point.

The princess stumbled once more, her confidence from earlier that day now melting away. She dropped her eyes, unable to meet his gaze temporarily as she cleared her throat.

"Our divine companions have graciously agreed to join us to Alocar. I am also pleased –"

"Then we must –"

"Excuse me," Cienna cut in. "I have not finished speaking. You will hold your tongue and let me finish."

A fire burned in her eyes as she glared at Len, giving him a small flash of amusement at her lack of control. Her words were still diplomatic and composed, but he could see her simmering under the surface. Len motioned for her to continue, hiding a smirk. Only his eyes betrayed him, but the dancing flames hid them in the encroaching darkness.

"Thank you."

Her curt reply only deepened his amusement.

"Our holy guests have agreed to join our cause. We are also most fortunate that Dez has agreed to join us as well. We now have four magi joining our quest on top of your Flame and considerable skill."

Well played, Len mused. *Catering to my sensibilities and complimenting my forces. She's doing better than I thought. Let's see if she has any more surprises.*

"I think that our group, though small, will be formidable. Having two of the Qu'ari elite, one of whom happens to be *the* Swordbane, fighting at our side should be enough to make any enemy reconsider their actions. Alocar has been a staunch ally to Zanir, and if we show a united front, especially with the blessing of the gods, we should be successful and hopefully suffer no casualties."

"Who are the god-blessed?" Len asked.

"We have our Avalanche, Dez is our Tempest, a Spark, and myself as a Stream. Our group is balanced and should complement each other, filling in any weaknesses or gaps in our power."

It was back now. That confidence he'd seen earlier that day had returned. Perhaps all it took was a bit of fire to pull it out of her. She would be most beneficial to his plans.

"You are right, princess," Len replied. "Ours will be a force to be reckoned with. I believe whoever holds the King of Alocar hostage will doubt the wisdom of their actions."

The princess appeared pleased and excused herself with a curtsey. As the night carried on, Len and his little group ate and prepared for the next day.

Wyrd even contributed like he used to, albeit infrequently due to the stares he received. Len tried not to focus too much on the tension. The Flame never got along with Wyrd, and Pram never trusted him. But the glares from the barbarian caught him by surprise. No matter; he needed to take in all sides before formulating his plan.

If things go well, we could be owed a boon from Alocar. Their king and his people would be indebted to us in a way Zanir couldn't even imagine. The bones are shifting, but they favor Xan once more.

XXVI

NIGHT'S VEIL BROUGHT with it a darkness Hera couldn't imagine. What had been darkening the skies during the day now blocked out the moon and the stars, leaving her in an eerie blackness. Only the light of the fires provided any reprieve. Her men lay quiet in the camp, the soft clatter of tin plates and cups ringing out in the emptiness. The queen lay in her sleeping roll surrounded by a ring of armed soldiers. Her eyes and ears strained for any sign of life but were greeted with silence. It unnerved her like nothing she'd ever experienced before.

Her eyes could not pierce the blackness despite their best efforts. The fires did not attract any other life, as no eyes stared back at her from the shadows. She struggled to find anything, but not even a twig snapped. The lack of life nearby blanketed her camp in a tension that was palpable to more than just herself.

Her soldiers seemed disturbed, too.

A lone guard cleared his throat, startling the queen in her roll. The man apologized to his queen, unaware of how much his noise had set her heart racing. Unaware that Hera was still awake, the man began a whispered conversation with one of his nearby guards. The discussion proved to be a welcome relief, the muffled sound providing the background noise she missed while in their surroundings. Hera touched her pouch with petals. Once again, they afforded her a bit of comfort and filled her with the security she needed to begin drifting off to sleep. It wasn't the same sensation she'd felt in the past, but it was enough to push away her fears. For now.

~~~

The unnaturally dark night disturbed Cody. He scanned the blackened streets, hoping to see anything despite the starless heavens. The torches and lanterns dotting the capital provided the only source of light, casting their surroundings in an eerie glow. Shadows danced on the building walls, their forms elongated against the stone.

"Strange night, eh?" a nearby guard remarked.

The sudden question startled Cody so badly that he jumped. He had been thinking the same thing.

"I've never seen a night with no moon or stars. At least not when it wasn't raining."

Cody couldn't pull his gaze away from the blackness. He trained his eye on the heavens, hoping that the darkness was only a thick patch of clouds obscuring nature's light. Seconds passed with agonizing slowness. Whatever was blocking out the moon was not a cloud.

His partner's voice droned on, but Cody paid it no mind. The youth's own thoughts wandered as he struggled to explain why the lack of moonlight frightened him. Safe in the caer, there were enough soldiers to provide a decent resistance against any attack. Not to mention that word had reached Pharn earlier that day that the late king's brother, Jaes, was within a day's ride from the capital. Scouts had been hunting in the King's Forest, searching for any enemy that may attempt a sneak attack, but they had discovered nothing.

There was no reason for Cody to be afraid. And yet, the darkness unnerved him the same way a thunderstorm terrified him as a small child. Cody wished his mother was still alive. He wanted nothing more right now than to have her pull him close to her, her arms squeezing him tightly as she whispered into his ears like she did in the past. But she was gone.

"Do you think we should tell the captain about this?"
~~~

The silence after the question pulled Cody from his thoughts. His partner watched him, his head tilted in a comical fashion like a dog begging for a scrap. The absurd visual in combination with the seriousness of the situation nearly brought a smile to Cody's lips.

"I would guess that they're somewhat aware of the situation already," Cody replied, unsure if he had answered the question.

When the man didn't press further, Cody turned back to the window and the darkness engulfing them. Pharn's scouts were highly skilled. He didn't doubt that they would be sending frequent reports to their captain. Cody didn't want to admit it, but he'd kept himself in the shadows to avoid receiving any messages. The youth didn't know if he could handle any bad news.

He prayed they would make it until morning. Something within Cody told him that things would change once the sun rose. Until then, he just needed to keep the fear at bay. He was Pharn's last line of defense.

⌐⌐⌐

The fire smoldered in the makeshift pit Dseti created. The Ancient used moss to keep the flames from getting too big and attracting attention. Ever since they'd gone off the trail, he'd been on the lookout for something, his body tense as his senses were on high alert. A couple rabbits cooled on sticks, their pink flesh tempting him and Vashe for another bite. Though she'd managed to eat her fill that night, the Scrymmen woman couldn't help but eye it occasionally. And every time she did, she would scold herself.

Much of their evening had been spent trying to figure out the secrets of binding. By the waning firelight, she poured over her ancient texts. Nothing came remotely close to mentioning it. The stories of Czand, the youngest Sibling, all alluded to his death upon Fyre's victory and not the possibility of his survival. But her conversation with Dseti earlier that day hinted that the gods could not truly die; at some point Czand would be reborn.

Frustrated, Vashe turned back to the pages she'd earmarked about twinning. Despite the Ancient telling her the two bits of magic were unrelated, part of her felt that there was something she was missing. The whole point of twinning was to put a part of herself, whether blood or some other part of her essence, into two objects, linking them together so she could track their movements. It worked, and she was able to keep an eye on Caitlyn and Brody while they were in Aramaine, drawing her to them in their hour of need.

How was it different from binding?

"To properly bind, you must find a part of your intended that has been weakened. It could be a physical wound or a mental one. Once you find your target, you must strike quickly and precisely before they have time to bring their guard up," Dseti had told her.

Sparing a glance at the Ancient, Vashe watched with a keen eye as he sat stiffly against a redwood tree trunk, his eyes staring into the darkness. His fingers drummed on his thighs as he kept a silent vigil. The man's preoccupation worried the Scrymmen woman. Normally, they would share the night watch, but he had been insistent on doing it all today.

I'll let him rest while we ride tomorrow, Vashe told herself. *For now, I need him to stay alert while I figure this out.*

The age-worn pages crinkled loudly in the quiet forest as she turned a page. Every time that happened, she cringed, worried that someone would hear her. Her heart would thump in her chest as the seconds passed in silence. She needed to avoid detection.

"Do I need blood for bindings?" Vashe asked Dseti.

The Ancient remained frozen, his gaze staring deep into the forest. Vashe wondered if he'd fallen asleep in that position. His answer caught her off-guard.

"No," he replied simply. "You need a way to project yourself onto your target."

The answer baffled Vashe. What in the hells did that mean? She opened her mouth to seek clarification but was cut off as Dseti continued.

"Much the same way you attempted a binding with Maeyu'dana at her temple. I don't know if you succeeded, but that's the closest I've seen in a long time. I'm hoping it worked."

"I what?"

"When you bathed the vials of Aria's blood in the pond at Maeyu'dana's temple, you performed the binding ritual. My only concern is that she is no longer in your world, so it may not have worked. Regardless, you achieved a draughting without Snapping, so something good came from it."

At the last half of his response, Dseti finally turned to face her. The Ancient was drained. He gazed through her, his eyes almost vacant. She couldn't tell if he was sleep-deprived or if he used up his energy shielding them from something. The heaviness and sense of being watched had disappeared, leaving her feeling relaxed for the first time since she left Enlil. Vashe couldn't help but wonder if it was his doing.

He turned away to stare out into the darkness once more, leaving Vashe to her research. She studied the Ancient for a bit longer before returning to her tome. The dying light of the fire cast dark shadows on the text, making it difficult to read, but Vashe wasn't focused on reading. Her mind wandered as she tried to remember her time in the Temple of Maeyu'dana.

There had been a calm that consumed her, as well as a sense of purpose. Despite the apprehension she had previously been feeling, everything melted away as she focused on strengthening the vials. Could it have been that simple? The bigger question was whether she could replicate that tranquility in the midst of battle, for she knew she would surely be fighting at the rate things were going.

Questions came, but the answers did not. With a sigh, Vashe closed her tome and slid it back into her leather pouch that she kept tied to her saddle.

Sleep seemed to be the only answer at this point. Vashe hoped her dreams would guide her in the right direction.

There were only two days left.

XXVII

WEAK RAYS OF SUNLIGHT struggled valiantly to break through the hazy morning clouds. In the distance, the sounds of the cooks making breakfast could be heard amid the slumbering camp. Alverick rolled over. His tattooed arm snaked around Caitlyn's bare shoulder as she slept beside him. The light dusting of freckles on her flesh drew him in much the same way the scars on his chest did to her. Alverick planted a tender kiss on the base of her neck, tickling her with his lips and causing her to stir.

The redhead rolled over onto her back, her emerald eyes staring deeply into his for a moment before the two shared a passionate kiss. Caitlyn's slender fingers pushed back a lock of Alverick's hair while the two held each other. He didn't want the moment to end.

"The camp will be waking up soon," he whispered, stroking her cheek. "We probably should get dressed before anyone says anything."

"Why?" Caitlyn teased. "Afraid someone will see you so vulnerable?"

The comment elicited a snort from the Avalanche. He knew she had no idea of the struggles he'd had since they'd rescued him from Aramaine. The willpower it took to keep those around him from seeing his mental breaks was just as draining as the experiences themselves. Alverick knew she must never know.

"I'm sure the only person who would be surprised by what they see would be either the children or the princess, and I suppose it wouldn't be proper to subject Cienna to my sword when she's only seen my Avalanche skills. It might frighten her."

The two shared a laugh and disappeared into the bedroll for a while before slithering into the early morning light. Alverick lurched forward as he nearly fell while putting his pants on while standing, drawing a snort of amusement from the redhead as she pulled her blouse over her head while sitting on the ground. Her lithe figure tempted him once more, but Alverick scolded himself, promising another fiery evening once everything ended.

Finally dressed, the two cleared up their camp spot, with Caitlyn taking the bedrolls and anything else they'd brought with them to their mounts to prepare for departure. Alverick snagged a bite to eat from one of the cooks while he continued to look for Brody or the princess. In the distance, he saw Dez tying her bedroll to a horse she borrowed from someone. The Avalanche couldn't remember ever seeing her on a horse before; he wondered if the Tempest wanted some time to herself.

To his surprise, Alverick found himself making his way to Dez instead of his intended. The Tempest's visage remained stoic, almost stone-like, as she moved about. Alverick knew that expression — he'd worn it on many occasions, the most recent being after Bannen died. It pained the Avalanche to see someone who usually went through life in such a carefree manner suddenly become lost and without purpose.

"Are you ready?" Dez asked, not facing the Avalanche. "I apologize, but the winds carried your concerns over to me last night."

Alverick blanched. He didn't realize Tempests could listen in on conversations like Flames could through nearby fires. The thought unnerved him a bit.

"No," he replied honestly. "You know as well as I that this is a fool's mission, but if we don't go, many will die."

Dez's silver eyes greeted Alverick, her long lashes framing them in dark chocolate. They stared deeply into his, searching for something hidden within. Her mouth parted as she mouthed words only she could hear.

"Her Holiness has the same reservations," Dez said finally. "Divine Ghan is hesitant, but he agrees with your princess that this is a matter that needs to be addressed urgently. He is the only one I would say is confident in our abilities."

Her eyes found his once more, diving into them and probing his soul. They flitted side-to-side as she searched for whatever she was looking for. Discomfort at feeling as though she were laying him bare caused the Avalanche's stomach to knot.

"You've seen Death," she exclaimed. "No mortal has traveled to the Halls in Themba before."

Her abrupt question caught Alverick off-guard. He hadn't planned on telling anyone of his experience there for fear that he would be dismissed as having Snapped once more and breaking Zemé's gift. The revelation that she even knew about the land of the dead surprised him. Then again, she was Vashe's master and ageless. It wasn't outside the realm of possibility that she knew more than she let on.

"How do you know?" he whispered.

"Your soul has been touched by those before you." Her eyes flickered back to his once more. "And you've been touched by more than one god. The winds tell me you've seen the middle brother of Ayr. They're all speaking, almost incoherent in their fervent exclamations, that you have been through much. You've been touched in some form by all of the elementals, though not all in their family. You're a threat to the Ancients and have already been influenced by their Darkness."

"Wha- what?" Alverick sputtered. "That makes no sense. Families and influences? It's madness. Yes, I've been to the land of the dead, but that shouldn't expose me to anything above others."

Dez's slim fingers caressed his jaw, her silver eyes full of despair. Her reaction was almost a motherly one, leaving Alverick feeling both frightened and protected.

"My dear boy," she began. "You have fought both Fyre and Ayr. Through Fyre, you have also fought young Czand of Water. And you've been healed by blessed Zemé, mother of the aethren. You've been places no other mortal has. Not even me. Themba has wrapped you in her arms and seeks to pull you back, back to Apophmet and his Darkness. There's a reason you have managed to avoid Snapping for so long. You're special, like my little Dzvaresh, and I will do whatever I can to protect you."

A tingling warmth spread through Alverick's body. It pushed away his uncertainties and fears while filling him with a sense of serenity. He hadn't felt something like it in a long time and couldn't quite explain what it was. It had been too long since he'd had a mother figure to watch over him.

The skies were brightening and more people stirred in the camp. A queue formed for breakfast and quickly spilled into a shapeless gathering as children and their families rushed to join the line. Chatter picked up in the ravine, waking others and adding to the clamor. Alverick noticed Brody and Ronan wandering through the throng, no doubt discussing their duties once Brody and Alverick broke off from the main group.

Ronan's expression forced Alverick to stifle a chuckle. The poor man always struggled to contain his emotions whenever he wasn't on the battlefield. At least he managed to keep a straight face when in front of an opponent. The arrival of Dez and the aethren didn't help. A messenger raced through the camp, shouting for people to wake up and clear out. The camp would be continuing on before the sun fully crested the horizon.

"I guess we should go," Dez said, her voice soft. "Get to your horse, and I will come for you once it's time to break off from the rest of the group. Get some food and rest. Make sure your Spark does as well."

The Tempest's switch from despondent to motherly baffled the Avalanche, but he didn't object to her coddling. It was a welcome relief, almost therapeutic, and he craved more.

<div align="center">~~~</div>

Despite the sun's vibrant rays stretching across the heavens, the air was cool. Not even a breeze stirred the air, and as the hot season was almost upon them, the chill was unusual. It reminded Solveig of her home during that time. Bright sun, long days, but mild temperatures. Tyr walked beside her, his tongue lolling out as he panted from the continuous walking. They'd covered much ground in the few days they'd been traveling.

The surrounding greenery both fascinated the chieftainess and confused her. It had been at least a century since their people ventured from their frozen wastes, and their maps were rudimentary at best. Much had changed since their last cartographer had left Grimmrheimr. She blessed the mighty Re'nukh that at least the general layout of the land hadn't changed too much. They'd been able to follow the maps thanks to the major landmarks identified.

Cursing under her breath, Solveig couldn't believe that one of her predecessors had closed the borders of Grimmrheimr so long ago, cutting out all contact with the lower realms. Henrik and the elders occasionally spoke of the period of great darkness: a time when the spirit of Apophos threatened to overwhelm Corinth, and so to protect the land of Re'nukh, Kongurr Sverre decreed that Grimmrheimr remain isolated from the rest of Corinth.

His plan had worked. Most did not want to travel up to the frigid north to trade for furs or their sweet pine anyway, so many credited him with keeping the land safe. But not Solveig, and not her mother. Both women sought to push past their boundaries and send out more than just spies. Her mother's death had been a tremendous blow to Solveig as a young child. She suspected it was not accidental.

But for now, she trekked with her small band of warriors towards the heathen land of Xan, home of the warlords.

To her left, Hegvaldr and Tormund kept guard, with Eivind trailing behind. The large man, always eating something, was polishing off strips of dried deer meat. She almost thought that Eivind was keeping an eye on her mate, but Hegvaldr was her mate for a reason. Solveig wondered if there was something going on and considered speaking to Eivind, but thought it was better to just keep both in her sights.

To her right, Tyr began growling, his pace slowing to almost a crawl as he leaned back onto his haunches. The dire wolf barred his teeth as his yellow eyes flashed. In Solveig's mind, wolves always more than earned their keep.

"Kongurr," Fenris' voice called out. "Einer's sent word that there is a large company heading this way. He can't see the end of the party."

Solveig's body tensed as her hand dropped to her battleaxe on her hip. They weren't expecting any armies to be making any moves and were unprepared to engage in any kind of major skirmish. The rest of her group began closing ranks, trying to determine the best course of action before they stumbled upon the large group. With a whistle, Solveig slapped her thigh, signaling to Tyr to stay close.

"Kongurr," Fenris said as he retreated to help shore up their defense. Behind him, Einer raced to join their group, his own battleaxe gripped tightly in his hand. "We should move off the path. We can assess the situation from the periphery and figure out our next move from there."

"Have we determined who they are?" Solveig asked. "Did we miss any intelligence of an impending attack by one of the nations?"

Solveig didn't want to admit that she'd been working with some of Xan to further expand her own kingdom. Had they decided to betray her and move to attack after Hegvaldr's return? Word had made it to Grimmrheimr that Alocar and Zanir were feuding, so perhaps that was it.

"Nothing," Fenris apologized.

"No banners are flown, but I could make out what looked like green livery. But there's no reason Zanir would be out here unless they had a grievance." Einer scanned the nearby tree line, searching for cover.

Was it Alocar? Had they passed the border without realizing it? Solveig couldn't be sure, but there was a good possibility they had.

"We should get off the road," Einer continued. "You know as well as I that we are at a huge disadvantage as it stands. Better to at least increase our odds of taking a few down or fleeing should things go bad."

The chieftainess weighed her options, motioning for the group to move off the main road to find cover. Tyr darted off the path, seeking cover in the tall grasses as the others quickly joined him. Solveig signaled to the others to close in.

"If they are merchants, we strike from the back," she whispered. "Soldiers, we'll see if we can surround them and trap them. It's not likely we can take them out, but if we can diminish their numbers, we can hopefully escape during the chaos. Keep guard and wait for my word."

<center>~~~</center>

Alverick napped in his saddle, his body swaying lightly as he fought to keep from drifting off into deep sleep. Caitlyn led Styx and her own mount, keeping an eye on him as he rested. After their conversation that morning, Alverick expected Dez to be more present as they made their way to Alocar, but she'd kept her distance during their travels. The Avalanche made sure to be alert so he could be ready to leave as soon as word was sounded. He didn't know when they'd break off, but he thought it would be sometime soon.

Soft voices spoke nearby, their conversation soothing him into a deeper sleep. Alverick shook himself awake to keep from falling fully asleep. To his shock, Dez and Caitlyn huddled together as they discussed whatever Dez needed to say. Their backs remained to him, ignoring the Avalanche. After several minutes, Dez glanced over her shoulder, a coy smile playing on her lips.

"The winds told me that we may have some bandits ahead," the Tempest said. "I wanted to warn her since you were still out."

"I'm fine," Alverick said as he slipped out of the saddle.

His legs wobbled as he worked to wake up and recover from the sudden dismount. Reaching out with his Avalanche energies, he sent out tendrils into the earth in hopes of finding the people Dez spoke of. It took a while, but he finally found a small party hiding off the main road not far from them. He couldn't help but notice that there was no life other than theirs and his own traveling party. The discovery still unnerved him. He'd hoped they would eventually run into some animals, even a rabbit or quail, on their travels.

"I see them," he said. "Should we tell Swordbane?"

He didn't really want to speak to the young general, but he didn't trust the man to not engage the small party. Alverick would prefer to keep things peaceful. He had too much on his mind to worry about expending any energy on a pointless fight.

"It would be smart to warn him," Dez conceded. "If not to make him aware so he can prepare an intimidating front. I don't doubt that he can handle the matter, but I'd like to avoid unnecessary conflict."

"As would I," Alverick agreed.

<p style="text-align:center">~~~</p>

Soft growls emanated infrequently from the dire wolf. On more than one occasion, Solveig swatted at Tyr to quiet him. Each time, the wolf would back away, but his hair remained raised on his haunches. Her hand rested on the handle of her battleaxe, ready to unsheathe it when the time was right. To her side, Hegvaldr bounced on the balls of his feet, ready to leap out at Solveig's signal. Time inched by, the anticipation making the usually composed chieftainess antsy. The thrill of bloodlust coursed through her.

In the distance, the sound of voices and wagon wheels announced the approaching caravan. It was difficult to tell how many were in the group, but their disregard for keeping their conversations quiet led Solveig to believe they were just a group of merchants or travelers. As they neared, the awaiting ambushers tensed.

Moments later, a wain filled with children, chickens, and rations rounded the bend. Women carried clay pots filled with water, with infants strapped to their bodies in brightly colored clothes. Dogs danced at their feet as the older children ran about. Men, both young and elderly, circled the perimeter of their caravan, providing a small measure of security for the traveling group.

Blood pounded in Solveig's ears as she prepared to give the signal. The shaved half heads marked these people as Thurlish. Of Xan. The perfect people to spring their attack on before moving deeper into Corinth and Xan proper. As pacifists, they were less likely to put up resistance. Anything that would be a threat to Solveig and her men, at least.

Raising her hand, the chieftainess motioned for her men to move closer to the edge of the brush. Making sure they remained hidden, Solveig pulled her battleaxe from her waist and carefully cradled it in both hands. She thought it best to strike with aggression at these people to reduce their chances of responding with force.

Tyr's low, rumbling growl pierced through her bloodlust. Her hand flew back to swat the wolf on the snout. Her breath caught in her throat as fingers caught her wrist, squeezing it in a tight grip. Spinning around, Solveig found herself staring into a pair of dark eyes. In her periphery, she noted that her companions were standing in front of the band behind them, their hands half-raised and weapons held limply in their hands. Her dire wolf glared at the group, teeth barred, as it stood surrounded by a ring of fyre, a Flame keeping a close eye on the beast.

"I wouldn't move, if I were you," the man holding her warned.

XXVIII

Held at bladepoint, Solveig and her group marched out from their cover and onto the main road. Her eyes flashed back to their hiding spot and she watched as the Flame stoked his fyre so Tyr could not jump out to escape. The wolf paced back and forth within the circle, growling in distress as the flames danced around him. Her battleaxe hung loosely in one of her captors' hands. The man eyed her hungrily but did not say a word.

Rage filled the chieftainess as she found herself encircled by a group of Qu'ari elite. Men in the green livery of Zanir dotted in the sea of colorful Xanan-dyed cotton and silks. Apart from the Flame, Solveig noticed a handful of people with the mark of Apophos, tattoos earned by the unholy blood of the false gods the people in lower Corinth believed in. To her dismay, a pale-skinned woman with dark hair wound her way to the front of the group, the Thurlish decoys blending in with the rest of the caravan.

"Almighty Re'nukh," Solveig swore under her breath. To her side, she heard several gasps from her warriors. Raising her voice, the chieftainess called out in her native tongue: "Jytte, is that you?"

Jytte pushed her way to the front and dropped in a bow to her leader. Solveig marveled at Jytte's darkened hair. What once was a golden-blonde shieldmaiden now stood a woman with dark hair and the colorful garments of a Qu'ari woman, her clothes modified to fit her preferred battle aesthetic of hugging her body tightly to prevent her blade from being caught in their folds.

"What brings you down from the mountains?" Jytte asked, speaking in the Common Tongue. "Surely there is nothing here for you."

Holding her tongue, Solveig read between the lines of what her spy said. It wouldn't do for her to reveal their plan, putting them all in harm's way. But her rage pushed her to test the boundaries of her captors.

"I come with my guards in hopes of establishing a trade route," Solveig replied vaguely. "I have grown weary of the isolation of our people from the rest of the land and welcome the opportunity to grow Grimmrheimr's wealth through the blessings of the Almighty Re'nukh."

"With a dire wolf and a group of elite soldiers?" the man at the head of the caravan asked.

His dark eyes and hardened face bore through her. He carried himself with the air of supreme confidence that only a leader could muster. The man must be the leader of the Qu'ari clan. What he was doing with the rest of the clans of Xan put her on edge. None of her information hinted at the tribes of Xan working in consortium before.

"I am but a frail woman," Solveig replied, trying to play to the low-land's notion that she could not be a threat for the mere fact that she was a woman. "My life and virtue would be nearly forfeit if I were to travel on my own. It's best to bring protection."

A snort of derision escaped the Qu'ari leader as he narrowed his eyes in amusement. Solveig saw how he measured her up against her own men. Perhaps she miscalculated. The women of Xan were known to be fierce warriors, afforded the opportunity to train alongside the men should they choose to do so, much like her own sisters in Grimmrheimr. Would he not believe her?

"You come seeking trade, yet I don't see any wares to offer," the Qu'ari leader pressed, ignoring her previous statement. "And you seem to know this barbarian who has been hiding amongst our own for some time now. You are not being truthful."

The Qu'ari's ability to see through her left her unnerved yet excited. Her rage receded, giving way to the thrill of the challenge. It had been a while since she'd matched wits with another. Widening her eyes in shock, Solveig allowed for her lips to part slightly in feigned helplessness. The man watched her with intense scrutiny, not betraying any emotion. It wouldn't be an easy exchange.

"I speak the truth when I say I come looking for a trade partner," she said. "Grimmrheimr's isolation has proven to be more of a detriment than a blessing. Though we have been able to follow the Silver Wolf and the Almighty Re'nukh's teachings, we have missed out on much of what Corinth has to offer. We've missed out on the advancements and changes that come with the natural passage of time. It was our hope to forge an alliance, preferably with someone whose values align closely with our own, in hopes of returning to relevancy.

"As such, we've had to send some of our own out to do reconnaissance in order to learn what we can bring to such a union. Jytte was sent to report back on what we could best offer you in exchange for your support. I apologize for our deceit, but it was the only way."

Solveig waited to see the Qu'ari's reaction. He watched her with the keenness of a hawk, his expression never changing. To her side, Fenris shifted, the pebbles under his feet giving way to his anxiety. His muscles tensed, ready to strike out and fight to the death for his freedom, as was the way of the Silver Wolf. Solveig hoped he wouldn't ruin their chance with his impatience.

"And what would you offer Xan in exchange for such a boon?" the Qu'ari asked after a lengthy pause. "Our bounty and detailed knowledge of Corinth would be a princely gift. Can you even hope to match our generosity?"

From the crowd, a familiar face broke free. One eye orange and the other brown, the man watched the chieftainess with a hungry, almost feral eye. To his left, Jytte laid her hand on her weapon, glaring at the newcomer with a seething hatred Could this be her initial contact with Xan? Behind her, Hegvaldr cursed in their native tongue, confirming her suspicions.

A knot formed in her stomach as she watched the newcomer, Wyrd, as she believed his name was, cross his arms and take in the exchange. He glanced over at Jytte and licked his lips, the hunger in his eyes intensifying. Solveig cursed to herself. The damned man could ruin everything if he wanted to.

"I offer you my two strongest warriors on your travels," the chieftainess blurted out.

She thought she would regret the words, but despite her haste, she knew she needed to keep a close watch on Wyrd and Jytte. The Qu'ari raised an eyebrow, intrigued by the offer.

"Hegvaldr and Eivind are my strongest and most favored warriors. I would trust them with my life."

Behind her, she thought she heard a soft moan from one of the men. Solveig knew that Hegvaldr had no love for Xan, but he knew that he had yet to be punished for withholding information from her earlier. This would be both an act of penance and a great service. With three spies, one of whom was an unimposing oaf, she could gather great knowledge.

"They will not stay with you indefinitely," she quickly added. "Just long enough to accompany you on your current quest."

"And?" the Qu'ari prompted. "What else do you offer?"

The corner of his lips turned up in an amused grin. He knew how to play the game and did so perfectly. The Xanan leader had the advantage, and he knew it. Solveig forced herself to remain calm and keep her expression earnest, hoping he wouldn't kill them all or worse.

"We have sweet pine that can be used as incense, for cooking, or for carving into a decorative piece. I would offer our furs, but I'm not sure if that would entice you. It is much warmer down here than back in Grimmrheimr."

"What about gold or silver?" His smile deepened.

The chieftainess felt her jaw tighten as she struggled to keep a scowl from her face. Solveig knew she'd lost control of the negotiations and needed to figure out a way to turn things back in her favor quickly.

"We do have gold," she began. Behind her, she heard Tormund curse under his breath. "But it is still in the stone. We do harvest the stones and shape them around the gold lines, but we haven't found thick chunks of ore to mine and turn into coin."

Struck by an idea, Solveig pulled out a small necklace she'd worn since she was a little girl. On a simple chain, a piece of white quartz was carved into a white wolf. Delicate veins of gold branched through the stone, but the largest chunk was right at the heart. It had been a gift from her mother, and Solveig treasured it.

Intrigued by her explanation, the chieftainess noted that the Qu'ari's brows had lifted. It seemed as though down in the low-lands the gold veins were not as common and could be a strong bartering chip. Solveig would never hand any over, obviously, but she hoped that her gamble would pay off.

"I can give you five percent of all gold line harvesting once Hegvaldr, Eivind, and Jytte return at the end of your venture," the chieftainess continued. "And anything gathered thereafter. The extra time will give us the opportunity to extract more from the mines."

The Qu'ari leader mulled over the offer as she put away her necklace. Solveig was sure it would be too tempting to pass up. Exclusive rights to their white stone gold to carve into statues or craft into jewelry would be unique to the rest of Corinth. Her previous intelligence indicated that some of the wealthier nations loved to decorate themselves with ornate jewelry and fancy clothing. Xan could sell them at a premium.

Of course, she'd never hand anything over. Most likely, the young leader would have her people killed and still demand the gold. When they came to collect, she'd be ready.

"A quarter," he finally said. "We want a quarter of all gold stone produced."

Solveig sucked in her breath, widening her eyes in mock dismay.

"That's quite a lot," she said softly.

"Information and loyalty come at a price," he replied.

Behind her, Solveig heard a general hiss of dissent from her men. With every ounce of strength she could muster, the chieftainess kept her expression concerned, forcing the smile that pulled at her mouth away. Tormund could be heard in their native language growling out curses towards their captors. It was all too perfect. Dropping her eyes, Solveig feigned resignation as she nodded her head.

"A quarter," she replied softly.

"Excellent," the Qu'ari said.

Motioning to her warriors, he whistled, beckoning Hegvaldr and Eivind to join his ranks. Keeping her gaze downward, Solveig could hear the pair shuffle towards the young Qu'ari. Hegvaldr could be heard grumbling curses in a mixture of their native tongue and the common tongue. Even Eivind spat out the occasional curse in the common tongue. The chieftainess was taken aback at the usually laidback man's vitriol that he spewed, even though it was infrequent.

Once the trade was made, Solveig was able to see the Qu'ari motion for his men to release her and her remaining group. The fyre around Tyr dissipated, releasing the wolf, who came bounding over to his master's side, where he resumed his growling at their attackers.

"Thank you," she muttered. "Your generosity towards my people is greatly appreciated."

Turning, Solveig began walking back the way they had come, towards Grimmrheimr. A few calls of dismay broke out, but she did not respond. Reluctantly, the remainder of the group fell in step behind their leader and began their return home. They didn't get very far before the Qu'ari's voice rang out once more.

"Remember, you will be supplying the gold whether your people survive this mission or not."

The chieftainess stopped in place, her back remaining turned to the Qu'ari leader. She counted to ten before letting out a deep breath, causing her shoulders to sag dramatically, before she continued walking without a word. Several exclamations broke free from her warriors' lips, but they followed her without further dissent.

Solveig traveled in silence for a decent period of time. The sun had just peaked, reaching its midday zenith, before she decided to stop and rest. Tyr dropped to the ground, panting. Despite the brilliance of the sun, the chieftainess noticed once again that the temperature was cooler than she'd anticipated. Her remaining warriors sat down next to her, with water and wine skins being passed around.

"Kongurr," Fenris began.

Meeting the man's gaze, Solveig's crazed expression cut off the rest of his complaint before it could be uttered. Her eyes flashed as a smile, which had been threatening to creep onto her face during her exchange with the Qu'ari, emerged.

"Kill any that come to collect the stone," she said. "No one receives the bounty of Re'nukh but us. These low-landers think they can force us into submission. They will feel the wrath of Grimmrheimr."

"But what about Hegvaldr and the others?" Tormund asked.

"Assume they're dead," she spat. "I highly doubt he'll leave anyone alive after all this."

Pulling out the chain around her neck, Solveig admired the pendant her mother had given her, the smile still on her face. She couldn't believe she'd managed to pull that off. Now, she could focus on picking off the Qu'ari's numbers bit by bit while still gathering much-needed information to help her better integrate with the rest of Corinth. The Silver Wolf always rewarded those who followed the Almighty Re'nukh's teachings.

XXIX

MEDICS STATIONED IN THE OUTPOST of Ånchal raced to the barracks to treat the newly Tainted Stream. Thom's outburst had subsided thanks to a concoction that had been heavily infused with poppy, and now he rested. Those in the barracks with him paced about, their unease at the previous events evident on their faces. In the short time from him draughting the tainted Myrani blood to his now fitful slumber, Oldar and the other soldiers watched in horror as the tattoos on Thom's arm began fading in places, breaking the thick lines marking him as a Stream.

The young king couldn't believe what he saw. There was nothing in the annals documenting the Tainting of a Stream. There was always a risk, but the water element style usually was associated with no risks after the initial blood ceremony, especially if the mage draughted from another Stream or safe style, like an Avalanche.

"We can't keep him here," one of the healers explained. "His mind is too fragile, and he poses a risk to the rest of the outpost. He needs to return to Madden for treatment."

"What can our healers do?" Oldar asked. "There is no cure or treatment for someone who's Snapped."

"We can begin the transition to his new life and help him adjust. The late King Storm had set up homes to house those who'd fallen to the Taint, where they could live out the remainder of their lives under a collective of caretakers to keep them off the streets. We should be able to get him in with no problem."

Oldar found himself chewing on his thumb as he sought to process everything. Dead Myrani. Monsters that could nullify the powers of the god-blessed. An uncle who somehow managed to control these beasts. It all unsettled him. Alastaire found a way to upturn the balance of the world as Corinth knew it.

Without a response, the king made his way outside into the sunlight. The cool air contrasted with the bright midday sun, and the chill helped him sort through his thoughts. Buildings and soldiers blended into the background in a colorful blur, their features disappearing. His mind returned to his conversation with his uncle back in the throne room. Alastaire hinted that he was responsible for creating whatever monsters he'd brought with him.

His uncle wanted to give the impression that he was in control, but something nagged at Oldar, leading him to believe that Alastaire couldn't completely overpower them like he wanted the others to believe. His uncle seemed distracted. Whether it was from madness or exhaustion, Oldar couldn't be sure. More telling was his aunt's reaction to whatever monstrosities they'd introduced into Alocar as she sat in the throne room.

Constance had always been dignified and poised, ever the definition of a classic lady. But in the throne room, her body sat stiff in the chair, and her eyes darted around, uncomfortable, searching for something. Oldar didn't think it was necessarily related to the cold, but because of what brought the cold.

The realization hit the young king hard. Stopping in his tracks, Oldar nearly bumped into one of the hitching posts. The horses tied to the post pawed the ground nervously, their agitation evident as they were almost run into by the oblivious king. A familiar nicker caught Oldar's attention, pulling him from his thoughts. A dun stallion greeted the king with bright eyes and a swish of his tail.

"Aelthur," Oldar whispered, reaching out to pat the horse on the nose. "I hope they've been treating you well. I thought they would've brought you into the capital to rest in the stables after our ordeal. I'm glad to see you."

The king knew the horse couldn't understand him, but he'd grown quite attached to the beast after their ordeal with the Myrani. Being one of Cienna's horses also brought him hope that someone would be coming to help him. His leaving Bells with the princess now didn't seem like such a bad idea. At the time, Oldar wished he didn't leave her, but the thought of her having to live through what he and Aelthur went through left him feeling heavy.

Slipping the knotted rope from around the post, Oldar freed Aelthur from the group. The two walked through the outpost, ignoring the curious glances from the other soldiers. Everyone was still busy and scrambling around. Thom's outburst proved to be quite the distraction from the discovery of three dead Myrani torn asunder on the grass. No one would admit it, but the fact that they were able to sneak in had left many on edge.

If they only knew that one was still missing.

"I'm sorry, but we must leave," Oldar told Aelthur.

With the stamp of a foot, Aelthur shook his head, his beige mane whipping around. Oldar knew the beast did not want to leave, and he didn't want to bring the horse back to the capital when there was little chance of either making it out alive, but he needed answers. He needed to find Pruvencia.

It didn't take long before he found his caretaker sitting on another hitching post, this one devoid of horses, in the midday sun. Her eyes were closed, and her grey hair fell down her back as she tilted her head up towards the light. Despite everything she'd been through, the elderly woman's visage appeared serene. A small smile played on her lips, her wrinkles deepening around her mouth, and a sigh of contentment escaped her. It pained him to disturb her, but Oldar needed to break her peaceful respite.

Leaving Aelthur to graze on the grass, mostly stubble sticking out of the ground thanks to the constant trampling by the soldiers and horses, the young king made his way towards his relaxing caretaker. A frosty breeze rustled her hair, sending shivers down the young king's spine. It reminded him of the bone-chilling freeze in Castle Storm. He prayed that nothing followed them through the tunnels.

"Isn't it nice to be out of the capital?" Pruvencia's soft voice cut through the strange quiet amongst the bustle of the outpost. Her unexpected question started Oldar. "It's been too long since I had time to myself away from the noise of Madden."

"It is lovely out here," Oldar replied.

The crisp air around the outpost, mixed with the scent of pine and heady earth, was intoxicating after years of life in the city. Apart from the fresh bread baked daily, the mixed aroma of fabrics being dyed, the smoke from hearths, wood lacquers, and horse excrement, he could see how the light scents of nature would be appealing.

"You know, when I was a girl, I lived outside the capital," Pru continued. "We'd pick daisies and honeysuckles, braiding them into my or my sisters' hair. We felt like little princesses." A short, soft laugh punctuated her statement as she remembered her youth. "I didn't think I'd find time to leave the city again."

"Pru," Oldar broached. "I need to go back to Madden." The tender quality of his voice caused his caretaker to turn and look at him, concern in her eyes.

"No." Her simple response startled him. "I cannot let you do that. You must find help."

"I have to." More insistent. "If I don't face my uncle, I won't be able to figure out how to stop him."

Pru's eyes watered, tears rolling gently down her cheeks. It broke his heart to see her so upset.

"I'm so close to solving this," he continued. "If I can figure it out, we stand a chance of having a smooth transition. No one else needs to die."

"It's too dangerous. I promised your parents I would look after you." Her voice cracked as she spoke. "Don't make me break my vow."

Oldar gripped Pruvencia's wrinkled hand delicately and gave her a squeeze. With his other hand, he wiped away the tears that trailed down her cheeks. The elderly woman brought up her hand and placed it over his, her eyes staring deeply into his. Resting his head on his childhood caretaker's forehead, Oldar closed his eyes and breathed slowly and deliberately. The two remained in this position for several minutes, savoring the physical contact.

"I need you to stay here," the young king whispered. "I couldn't live with myself if anything happened to you." He opened his eyes and saw she'd done the same. The two held each other's gaze. "You'll be safe here, and if anything does happen, you can take a horse and ride to Pharn. I'll leave word that a few soldiers provide you with protection until I come back for you."

Moisture stained the king's cheeks. With a trembling hand, he reached up and rubbed his face. To his surprise, he found himself crying as he held Pru. She was the closest person he had to a grandmother, and his bond with her was unbreakable.

"If... if I should not come back, tell the Greys that Alastaire has found a way to negate the magical abilities of the god-blessed. I'm not completely sure how, but he's created monsters, the ones you've heard them in the castle halls, that can poison the magical blood, making draughting without Snapping impossible. He almost all but admitted it when I spoke with him the other day. They need to know."

Oldar felt his voice catch in his throat several times as he told her what he'd discovered. A fear so palpable that it choked him engulfed him as he finally verbalized everything he knew. It blanketed him so heavily that it threatened to break him.

"Don't talk that way," Pru said. "I will see you when you get back. Promise me."

An undignified sniffle escaped the king as he worked to maintain his composure. A gentle squeeze on his hand from Pruvencia brought a little bit of hope, cracking the fear enough to let a ray of light shine through. The gesture was small, but he was grateful for it all the same.

"Good-bye, Pru." The king's voice shook as he spoke.

"Good-bye, my dear. May the gods bless you and protect you."'

The two broke away, tears still falling from their eyes. Giving the elderly woman's hand one final squeeze, Oldar retrieved Aelthur once more and made his way towards the tunnels once more. He spoke to the nearest soldier, providing instructions on what to do in his absence, before making his way down the weather-worn stone steps and entering the darkened tunnels once again.

XXX

THE DARKNESS COVERED the skies, blocking out the sun completely. Hera stared into the heavens, watching as flocks of birds that had somehow remained hidden flew away, towards the western coast. Towards Zanir. A frigid wind blew, causing the queen to pull her blanket tightly around her in hopes of receiving a small respite from the unusual chill.

All around her, soldiers raced about setting up camp and trying to find kindling for a large fire. The cloudy sky and unnatural winds led to a general panic in their little clearing. Those who had seen the darkness the day before were uncharacteristically quiet, while the others shouted out orders to establish a secure perimeter or complete some other task. The camp was on the brink of chaos.

Even as she touched the petals that were usually stored in the leather pouch around her neck, Hera was distressed. The expected feeling of warmth and calmness that usually accompanied their touch wasn't enough to dispel her worries. She waited until things settled down, eager to begin her search for the ring of stones and golden flower she'd seen in her dream. However, she wasn't sure she'd ever get that opportunity.

A soldier rushed past her with an armload of dried brush to stoke the fire. Before he got too far away, Hera called out to him. Torn between feeding the flames and answering his queen, the man teetered back and forth for a brief moment before dropping everything in his arms and approaching his lord.

"How can I serve my queen?" he asked.

Battle-hardened eyes, used to seeing the atrocities of war, stared back at Hera, widening in fear. Despite her own nerves, Hera couldn't help but feel pity for the man. He looked exactly like she felt. She could only imagine how she presented herself to her soldiers. Hera felt like a complete wreck and hoped that it didn't translate to her physical appearance.

"I need to find a specific landmark in the area and would like a small group for additional protection. There's something about this place that has me on edge."

Hera held her breath, praying her request wouldn't be denied.

"Do you need to do this now?" he asked, his voice trailing off in hopes of not offending his queen.

"I do," she said, her voice firm.

The soldier glanced back to the center of the camp and his kindling on the ground. Hera noted how his shoulders drooped in resignation as he prepared his answer.

"Of course, your majesty. As you wish. If you could wait a few minutes, I can run the brush over to those handling the fire and bring a few men with me. Would a group of five suffice?"

"That sounds perfect." Hera couldn't help but smile in relief. "I will see you shortly."

The man darted off, snatching the kindling off of the ground and disappearing into the camp. Using the opportunity to prepare herself for the trek, Hera pulled down one of her saddlebags and rummaged through it. Inside, she found a small knife that belonged to her mother, sheathed in tarnished silver, a few pieces of dried meat, and an apple. Taking the waterskin from her other bag, she squeezed it in and waited for the soldiers to return.

True to his word, the man came back with a few others in tow sooner than she expected. Behind them, Hera could see their campfire raging. Pillars of black smoke rose into the air, tapering off from the dancing flames beneath. Blasts from the wind carried the smoke in all directions while at the same time chilling her to the bone. The camp proper had condensed itself to conserve body heat, with everyone practically sleeping on top of each other, but the queen noticed something else concerning. Her men weren't even trying to conceal their whereabouts now.

"Where to, your majesty?" the kindling-carrying soldier asked.

Motioning to the saddlebag on the ground, Hera took off. Scrambling to follow her, the soldiers grabbed her bag and rushed to join their queen. Though she didn't know where she was going, Hera felt a pull that guided her into the middle of a field not too far from their camp. Here, the knee-high blades of grass were buffeted by the winds, flailing every which way and slapping the small group's legs as they walked through the meadow.

Without any trees to shield her, Hera quickly found herself shivering as the wind gusts slammed into her. She wished she had brought her blanket or coat for a little protection against the chill. She could only imagine how her soldiers felt. Then again, most of them wore leathers over their tunics. An eerie howl carried through the field. Whatever part of her body hadn't been taken over by goose flesh from the cold temperatures definitely was whenever the cry sounded.

As if on cue, one of her soldiers could be heard over the wind speaking to another.

"It's just the wind, you feckin' arse! There's nothing out here, not even a damned hare for supper."

"Oh, shut yer yap!" a second voice snapped. "Don't you think I know that? But that's not the wind. I lived on the coast, and I've heard the wind howl before. There's something out there."

The two went on for a while, bickering back and forth while the other three plodded quietly along. The way their voices were almost lost on the wind felt strange to the queen. She too was no stranger to strong gusts, but there was something about this that set her hackles on edge. The wind ripped at her clothes, digging deep into her body and scraping her bones in a frenzy. Then there were the cries. They carried through the air in a way no sound she'd ever heard before had. Hera couldn't help but agree with the nervous soldier that something was not right.

Their journey across the field took forever. Exposed to the elements, they inched their way through the tall grasses as the blasts of wind tried to push them back. The bickering soldiers had fallen silent long ago; their only focus was guiding their queen to wherever she wanted to go. Hera could tell by their stiff bodies that they questioned the rationale behind her motives, but she was grateful that they followed her, the tallest men leading the way to break through the strength of the wind even just a little.

The black clouds hanging overhead made it difficult to tell how much time had passed. Finally, they came upon a small pond filled with crystal-clear water. On one side of the bank, a small collection of rocks ringed the pond. Their smooth surfaces beckoned Hera for a moment's rest. The group made their way to the pond and were surprised to find that, as they exited the field of tall grasses and walked through the shorter blades nearer to the pond, the air around them had stilled. The surface of the water was still and peaceful.

Free from the wind's onslaught, Hera and her soldiers slumped to the ground, exhausted. Although the sun still remained hidden, the sudden lack of wind biting and tearing at them gave them a chance to finally warm up. One of the soldiers took the opportunity to replenish the waterskins while Hera found her way to one of the rocks, pulling herself onto it to sit.

The queen found herself breathing a prayer of relief to Freyna, hoping that the goddess was the one responsible for their respite. Reaching into her blouse, Hera pulled out the leather pouch and dumped the periwinkle petals into her hand. The familiar warmth she felt from touching the holy petals returned, bringing her a sense of tranquility that she hadn't felt since she left Pharn.

"Your majesty?" one of the soldiers called out, breaking her reverie. "Will we be needing to push forward? It is getting late, and we should probably start heading back soon."

Hera noted the hesitation in his voice. He didn't want to leave the safety of their little haven any more than she did. Taking a moment to look around, Hera marveled at the beauty of her surroundings. The grass shone emerald even without the light from the sun. Her hand moved over the surface of the stone. She couldn't describe how smooth it was, but it reminded her of the rare blown glass she'd seen back home on the Isles when she was a girl. A singular fuchsia tulip stood near the edge of the pond, surrounded by small pebbles.

Slipping off her seat, Hera kneeled in front of the flower and dipped her hand in the pebbles, letting them fall from her fingers with a gentle *clink*. They were as smooth as the stone she had been sitting on earlier. The tulip's petals were soft as velvet. She'd never seen anything like this place.

Ignoring the soldiers as they pressed her for an answer, Hera watched as a butterfly fluttered down and landed on the tulip. Its golden wings flapped as its probiscis dipped into the flower to drink some of the sweet nectar. There was something about the butterfly that felt familiar. She almost felt as though she'd seen it before.

"Your majesty?" one of the men prodded.

With a gasp, Hera clenched her hand around the periwinkle petals. The butterfly darted up, circling the pond for a bit before settling back down on the flower. She had seen the butterfly before; there was no denying it. It visited her in her library before she had her first encounter with Freyna. She had never seen a golden butterfly like this one, and its look shone brightly wherever it went. Hera was positive.

Everything was falling into place, and hope welled in her breast. With the serenity she was feeling in conjunction with the collection of stones and golden butterfly, though it wasn't a golden flower like in her dream, she was willing to stake her royal claim on the fact that they'd found the spot Freyna took her too.

XXXI

CREAKING GEARS SCREECHED into the air as the gate lowered at the portcullis of Pharn. High prince Jaes and his men waited patiently to enter the capital of Zanir. In addition to his impressive collection of soldiers, a large gathering of people from the surrounding villages and cities stood amongst the green livery of Zanir. Scared children clung to their families, little hands grasping onto skirts or anything else they could grab onto. Behind them, a wall of darkness chased them into the capital.

From his vantage point, Cody felt his legs tremble as he gripped the stone ledge on the walkway. His knuckles shone white against his already pale skin, and a cold sweat ran down his back. With every beat of his heart, he grew more anxious whenever he caught a glimpse of the black skies. A cheer broke out from those on the wall-walk around him, welcoming Jaes and his followers. Cody opened his mouth to join in the revelry, but found he couldn't make a sound. His eyes kept getting drawn to the clouds obscuring the sun.

With a heavy *thud*, the wooden gate slammed into the ground. Several men muttered an exclamation of relief as the damaged wood did not further splinter after the destruction it received when Swordbane attacked. Instead, it held firmly. The sea of people below rushed into Pharn, Jaes' soldiers ushering in the others before following them inside.

Shouts rang out along the wall-walk, calling all men who were not positioned along the ledge for duty to return to the throne room and await further instruction from the high prince. Cody felt his body moving on its own as he made his way down the stairs towards the throne room. Inside the stone tower, Cody realized how cold he'd been standing on the wall. Overhead, the whistling of wind echoed in the tower as it blew outside.

"Damn, it's nice getting out of the cold," someone behind Cody said. "I didn't realize it was so windy outside until just now."

"Strange weather," another agreed.

A spark of relief flickered inside Cody as he realized he wasn't alone in his feelings. Too many times he'd felt alone as he worked to support his mom with her mind sickness. On more than one occasion, he wondered if he suffered from the same ailment as she did. He hated the self-doubt but kept it to himself, striving to overcome every obstacle he encountered.

Inside the throne room, the late king Jaste's younger brother stood in front of a roaring hearth, warming his hands next to the flames. His long, auburn hair was tied in a low tail behind his back. The high prince's broad shoulders and tall stature reminded Cody so much of his late lord. They were almost mirror images of each other from behind. A page announced the arrival of the final soldier to his lord and closed the doors for privacy.

"I am impressed by your efficiency and hospitality," Jaes began. "I heard that the more seasoned men left to accompany my dear brother's wife and my beloved niece. On my way up here, I came to the realization that we should prepare for a long siege, and so I brought as many of our people with me as I could. Our numbers are tired and hungry, but we are ready to secure the caer.

"When we left, the sun shone and birds sang. Deer and rabbits were plentiful for hunting, and I regret not taking advantage of the land's bounty. The closer we got to Pharn, the fewer signs of life were to be seen. And the darkness spread. There is something unholy about this, and I fear we are to be beleaguered for a long time. I urge you all to eat your fill now while you still can. I have ordered for the gates to be locked and only open upon my command. Word has gone around Pharn to bring her people into the caer for shelter and protection. Once you've finished eating, you will split into groups based on your skill, and we will position you around the city. Now go."

The doors to the room creaked open, and the soldiers shuffled out in silence. Cody followed the others, his mind spinning as he went over Jaes' words. The high prince acted so decisively, not sparing a moment for question, as a leader should. Cody wished he could be that efficient.

Bodies rushed through the hallway, doing everything they could to avoid crashing into him. Cody passed through them in a daze, oblivious to their efforts to move around him. All he could think about was the impending sense of dread he felt whenever he looked into the sky and how helpless he truly was. There was only one thing to do. Bypassing the food station in the barracks, Cody grabbed his spear and climbed up the winding stairs to the wall-walk. If he couldn't eat and calm his mind, the least he could do was make sure another person had that opportunity. One way or another, he would be useful in this war.

XXXII

THE ROAD TO ÅNCHAL proved difficult to follow. There was no distinct path to take, leaving Cienna and her small band of warriors to guess which direction to go. Hroth thought he could make out a path in the worn grass, the blades bent from the infrequent trampling of boots and hooves, that they ended up following. The princess trusted the Flame's guidance since he'd spent much time traveling through Corinth during his time as a mercenary with the Myrani.

Ever since they split from the main group, with Ronan and Thol taking charge of leading the rest of Xan back to Pharn, Cienna had been struck with how quiet everything around her was. Birds did not chirp, frogs and insects didn't buzz, and the absence of wolves howling in the distance left her on edge. The world felt empty when it was devoid of sound. All she could hear was the muted clopping of their horses' hooves on the thick grass.

Icy blasts of wind hit the group, infrequent but bone-chilling when they struck. The princess wished the sun would peek out from behind the clouds and warm her a bit, but it had remained hidden so far. Cienna found herself huddling close to Caitlyn whenever the winds hit her, wanting to maintain a level of decorum as befitting her station but instead clutching the redhead's arm for a little bit of warmth. On occasion, she caught Swordbane glancing her way, a smirk playing on his lips. Every time he saw her, she felt her face flush in shame.

The Qu'ari leader took everything in stride. The wind did not seem to affect him, even though he wore a light, short-sleeved tunic that exposed his arms above the elbow. He spoke to his right-hand man in length, no doubt coordinating some plan of attack with his general. Cienna was surprised, however, to see the man who caused all the chaos in Fa'Tinh walking freely next to Swordbane. She thought he would've been kept under close watch, or at the very least, definitely not allowed to join in on what would most likely end in a fight.

Seeing the man walk without guards, other than Swordbane and his general, left the princess feeling uncomfortable. Not for the first time, Cienna scanned the group to see how they were doing and if they were as concerned as she was about the traitorous Qu'ari walking among them.

Dez sat in her saddle with the grace and poise of a queen. The Tempest stared forward, her eyes unblinking as she lost herself to her thoughts. Cienna wished Dez would mutter something to herself, maybe engage in a disjointed conversation that left the princess with more questions than answers, like she was familiar with. Unlike the others, the winds did not seem to bother Dez. Cienna wondered if Tempests could manipulate the air around them, preventing gusts and gales from inconveniencing them. She liked to imagine that Dez would be one such Tempest who could do so.

Between Dez and Swordbane, Alverick also traveled in silence. The Avalanche gazed at the clouds, transfixed by something, with a blank stare. She wasn't sure if he was doing all right because Alverick seemed to be distancing himself from both Brody and Caitlyn. She hoped he was. The thought of him Snapping scared her. Cienna counted on Alverick serving as a counterbalance in case anything went wrong with Swordbane or his people.

Their newest companions, the barbarians, also left her worried. The two men spoke in their native tongue in hushed tones. They shot furtive glances towards her and the shieldmaiden while also glowering at Swordbane and his two Qu'ari companions. The barbarians glanced worriedly at the Flame, muttering Apophos whenever they laid eyes on him. Both men were massive, towering over even Swordbane, and the loose tunics covering them hinted at their muscles, if the men's broad shoulders were any indication. Cienna hoped Alverick's skills wouldn't need to be used on either group.

Strangely enough, the shieldmaiden appeared to be unbothered by everything going on. She and Caitlyn had been speaking earlier in the day, and the maiden seemed to pleasantly surprise Caitlyn enough for the two to share deep conversations. Cienna hoped to have a chance to speak with the woman on her own before everything was over.

With a furtive glance, Cienna looked over at the two gods. Their imposing figures stuck out amongst the rest of the party as they towered over even the barbarians. Even though the clouds blocked out the sun, the pair's hair sparkled brilliantly, the pure silver of Aria and the silver streaks from Ghan shining as a beacon of hope in the darkness.

A shiver ran down the princess' spine as she gazed upon her gods. She had not been particularly religious growing up after her Blood Ceremony when she was twelve, only observing alongside her parents as was proper. Cienna had never figured out why, clearly, she'd been graced with their blessings when she'd received her Stream gift, but for some reason, the idea of the gods being something more than a myth seemed foreign to her. Yet here they were. Breathing, bleeding beings who she'd not only heard speaking, but people who fought to protect those around them from other gods. Every time she beheld them, Cienna felt like an imposter.

The Siblings traveled close together, speaking softly to one another. Occasionally, they would glance up at the sky, but they'd quickly return to their conversation. Aria's tinkling voice could be heard faintly, the words getting lost amongst the sounds of the party as they trekked to Ånchal.

Cienna also longed to speak with them, but insteadresigned herself to use Dez as an intermediary for any questions she had.

"We should be nearing Ånchal by the morn," Alverick's voice called out. "If we press through the night, we can make it before sunrise."

"Let's set up camp and establish a perimeter," Ghan replied.

Cienna wondered why they shouldn't move forward and arrive as early as possible at Madden. A nagging feeling pulled at her, urging her towards the capital of Alocar like an undine called to sailors.

"It makes more sense to carry on through the night," the slimmer of the two northmen said in his deep baritone. "The darkness will protect us, and I would rather we reach our destination sooner than later."

"It is safer to travel during the light," Ghan said, steel tinging his voice. "There is an evil out here that threatens to consume us. It would be prudent to not leave ourselves open to attack by settling down for camp. This way, we also get a chance to rest."

"*We*," the barbarian spat as he pointed to his companion and the shield-maiden, "are protected by the Almighty Re'nukh. Whatever fate befalls you will be of your own doing."

"If we fall, you will too," Swordbane said. "Whatever is going on will affect everyone."

"The problems of some king are none of our concern," the man said.

"Quiet, Hegvaldr," the shieldmaiden hissed. "This is bigger than you can possibly hope to understand. Kongurr can't even fathom how deep of shite we're in. If you want to stand any chance of survival, I suggest you listen to what those two say."

Jytte pointed to the two Siblings as she glared daggers at her countryman. Beneath her withering gaze, Hegvaldr relented. To his right, the larger barbarian smirked behind his companion's back before reaching into his hip pouch and pulling out a strip of dried meat. The man had an unlimited store of food with him, much to Cienna's amusement.

"I agree that we should settle down," Cienna said. She hoped that she wasn't too late in asserting herself into the conversation. "Although I do admit that I'm having the hardest time figuring out how long until sunset. Perhaps we should begin looking for a secluded spot that will afford us a modicum of protection."

Several people in the group, including Alverick, nodded in agreement. Their affirmation sent a wave of relief washing over her. There was still a chance that she could effectively lead her people after all.

~~~

Night crept onto the streets of Madden, the inky blackness blanketing the capital city in her all-encompassing embrace. Without the moon or stars, everything felt more alone. The light of the flames from the street lamps danced feebly, barely illuminating the surrounding area. No one wanted to be out at this hour, despite it being barely past sunset. A heavy chill hung in the air, freezing everyone unfortunate enough to be outside to the bone.

Oldar wished he'd brought something thicker than his cloak with him as he tugged at the thin fabric, seeking a little relief from the icy temperatures. Not even the shelter from nearby buildings provided much of a respite. The biting cold almost appeared to be searching for warm bodies to freeze. Numbness set in, making his trek unbearable.

And then the howling began.

The screeching cries that echoed in his mind carried on the winds, only to be answered by more. Oldar still hadn't seen what made such a bone-chilling noise, but anything that did, that could rip people to shreds, was nothing short of nightmare fuel. And the young king had been plagued by them since his visit with his uncle in Castle Storm.

Shadows flickering out of the corner of his eyes caused Oldar to jump every time. His body tensed and his heart raced as he kept a look out for the monsters. On more than one occasion, the flames of the street lamps threatened to blow out as a particular frigid breath of wind blew through the streets of Madden, and Oldar's body waited for a death blow every time.

Aelthur's hooves clopped loudly on the worn cobblestones, only adding to the young king's anxiety. If they were not the only two souls walking the streets, he would not have been so wary. However, he couldn't even get that
~~~

small bit of peace of mind. The horse's ears lay flat on his head, and his uncomfortable snorts sent puffs of steam into the frozen air. Oldar found himself patting Aelthur to pacify the beast as much as to calm himself. Neither felt reassured.

His travels led him to a familiar place. Schaed's. Standing outside the wine shop, Oldar couldn't help but feel a flicker of hope fill him. Here, he knew he'd be able to at least get a good night's sleep. Afraid to leave his equine companion outside, Oldar brought Aelthur into the shop.

Inside, things appeared undisturbed. No bottles of wine had been consumed, and no glass had been broken. Oldar worried that Rez'maré and her family fled the shop after he left. An eerie quiet filled the building. He called out to her, his whisper echoing loudly in the empty shop. Each call came back unanswered. Each time, he became more desperate.

Minutes dragged by with what little hope he had at finding Rez'maré quickly disappearing. He gave up as exhaustion consumed him. With a tentative knock, he held out hope that Rez'maré and her family would open the door to the wine cellar. His breath caught in his throat in anticipation. Tears welled in his eyes as he heard the soft voice of a child behind the door almost immediately get shushed. A lump formed in his throat, and he felt his voice quiver as he tried to speak.

"Maré?" he said in barely more than a whisper. "It's me."

The lock inside the cellar clicked, and the door opened a crack, revealing the hazel eye of his only remaining friend in the city. A gasp escaped her, and the door was flung open, Rez'maré's arms smothering Oldar as she embraced him tightly.

"By the gods!" she breathed. "I can't believe you're back, Oldar."

Breaking her hug, Rez'maré studied the king, her eyes sweeping over his body as she held his arms. Behind her, Oldar saw all of the children packed snugly in the cellar with barely any room to move. Most lay curled in a ball asleep, their bodies pressing against each other in an effort to remain warm.

One of the older kids spoke to the elderly caretaker, explaining what was going on.

"Why did you come back?" Rez'maré asked. "You were supposed to bring help. Where's your caretaker?"

Rez'maré searched the main floor of the wine shop, trying to find Pruvencia, but seeing only Aelthur. A tear rolled down her cheek as her hand flew to her mouth.

"Oh gods, Oldar. I'm so sorry. Did... did one of those things get her?"

"No, no," he replied gently, pushing a strand of hair behind her ear. "Pru's fine. I have her safe outside Madden."

Her relief was palpable, calming the young king by extension. Locking the door behind her king, Rez'maré motioned for one of the children to bring him a bite to eat. Oldar hated to leave Aelthur in the shop, but there was barely any room for the group of twenty, let alone adding him and a horse. He hoped his friend would be safe wandering around the shop. He took the crust of bread offered to him and ripped off a bite.

Curious eyes watched his every move as more of the children woke up. Finding a small spot along the wall, Oldar curled up with his back against the sweet-smelling wood. The grains of the planks were surprisingly smooth as he rested his head against the wall. Rez'maré and the rest of the group settled down in the cramped cellar for the night.

Oldar's mind raced as he tried to figure out his next plan. As his eyelids drooped and his head slipped until it rested on his chest, the young king's plan for the next day drifted out of his mind and instead was replaced with images of creatures hiding in the darkness, their shrieks causing his blood to run cold. But with each passing minute, they grew weaker. Forming in the background, a giant tree with gnarled roots sticking out of the soil appeared. At the trunk, the roots began to take shape. They twisted and knotted together until they formed a rune of protection, just like the one carved into the door frame of Schaed's wine cellar.

As the rune came into focus, Oldar felt a sense of tranquility wash over him, stilling his anxious mind. The images of the nightmare-ish creatures began to fade, their cries fading into silence until all that remained was peace. Oldar fell into a deep sleep, free from any bad dreams, for the first time since he left for Pharn to ask for Cienna's hand in marriage. His head lolled to one side as he slumbered, finally finding the respite he so desperately needed.

XXXIII

SOFT SNORES AND HEAVY BREATHING filled the wine cellar as the children slept. Their tiny bodies lay in a tangle on the earthen floor, arms and legs entwining as they tossed and turned in their sleep. Oldar woke up before any of the others, feeling refreshed. A sense of contentment and tranquility filled him with hope for his upcoming mission. The king dug his fingers through the dirt floor, making little trenches in the rich soil. He relished the calm that washed over him. A good night's sleep hadn't been had in a long time.

Not wanting to wake anyone up, Oldar delicately maneuvered his way through the slumbering bodies, being careful not to step on any little bodies, and made his way to the door. He wasn't sure what time it was, but something inside the king told him that now was the time to make his plea with his uncle. Pausing in front of the door frame one final time, Oldar reached up and rested his hand on the rune of protection that was carved into the wood. Energy coursed through him, filling him with determination.

I'm glad I came back, he thought to himself. *This is the right thing to do.*

As quietly as he could, Oldar opened the wooden door to Schaed's wine cellar one last time and slipped into the shop. Aelthur waited for him, his tail swishing as he saw the king once more. As if he sensed Oldar's urgency, he kept quiet, allowing the king to prepare his lead. Oldar spoke in quiet tones to the horse, patting the beast on the neck as he left to face his destiny.

A dense fog blanketed the streets of Madden in the early morning, or what appeared to be the early morning. Oldar couldn't tell what time it was thanks to the swath of blackness that completely devoured the heavens. No light managed to peek through the darkness. Oldar was also discouraged to note that the flames of the street lamps had also blown out at some point in the night. Whether by accident or from something else, the effects were the same — Madden was hidden by the gloom.

Despite his wishful thinking, the fog did not afford him any modicum of warmth as he rode Aelthur through the streets towards Castle Storm. Still covered by his think cloak, Oldar's hands quickly went numb as the bone-chilling freeze seeped into his body. His breath came out in thick puffs of smoke, his chest tightening as he struggled to breathe in the cold. Aelthur snorted heavily, his breath coming out in a steady stream of smoke.

Throwing all caution to the wind, Oldar rode Aelthur in the middle of the street, not bothering to stick to the shadows or attempt anything to silence the sound of hoofbeats against the stone. His body remained tense as he traveled towards home, but he hoped the horse could outrun anything that may have pursued them.

The calm he'd been feeling earlier in the morning hadn't dissipated, much to his delight. The night in the cellars and his last moments touching the rune over Schaed's cellar door still lingered, as if providing him with a layer of protection. He was anxious, but he didn't fear a death blow as much as he did the night before.

The imposing silhouette of Castle Storm, now no longer the familiar home he once knew, came into focus quicker than he expected. As he stood in front of his home, he saw that the stone walls were slicked with ice. An unbelievable freeze emanated from the open portcullis. The lack of castle guards unnerved the king. He hoped nothing bad had happened to them.

"Okay, Aelthur," he whispered into the horse's ear as he slipped off his mount. "Please stay safe out here. I may need you for a fast escape."

The king patted the horse on the neck once more, earning him a nuzzle against his arm and a snort of appreciation. The dun stallion's dark eyes somehow managed to sparkle in the non-existent light, and Oldar saw the beast's intelligence. A shuddering gasp escaped him as he wished the horse well.

"I'm ready for you, Alastaire," he muttered as he crossed the threshold.

Inside the castle, Oldar found himself shivering as his body went numb. He rubbed his hands together constantly, blowing into them in a vain attempt to warm them up. He may as well have been holding a block of ice. A column of steam poured from him as moved through the icy castle. But all of this did not disturb him as much as the deathly silence that surrounded him.

His last visit to Castle Storm had been fraught with blood-curdling screams and a sense of absolute dread. At the time, he couldn't explain what terrified him, but now he knew: the fear of knowing that there were creatures lurking in the shadows, waiting to deal a death blow. He didn't know if he managed to avoid them the last time or if they let him pass, but this time, Oldar didn't think he would be so lucky.

As he expected, the halls were empty once more. No servants could be seen maintaining the needs of the ruler or performing general upkeep. Soldiers did not roam around, checking in with the castle staff between their shifts. The halls of Castle Storm were dead.

Like the exterior, the walls were slicked with ice. Sculptures and tapestries were coated in a thin layer that shone with a reflective sheen in the wavering hall lights. Oldar noted his family's tapestries covered in frost, despair rising as he pictured the delicate embroideries ruined once they finally thawed. The silken threads, which managed to maintain their brilliantly dyed colors of deep crimson, verdant, azure, and gold, among others, had survived for centuries, and he prayed that his uncle's greed didn't destroy them.

The flames in the castle struggled to survive in the stifling, frozen air, with little balls of fire flickering dangerously in their sconces. The darkness outside contrasted with the wan light inside the halls, casting shadows on the walls and intensifying the eerie atmosphere. Oldar could only hope that there would be a roaring fire in the hearth in the throne room like before.

Oldar stopped in his tracks as he heard one of the shrieks reverberating throughout the castle walls. It was answered in short order by two others in different directions. The king's blood ran cold, impressing him since he didn't think he could shiver any more than he already was. He found himself saying a prayer to any of the gods that came to mind, going through almost the entire pantheon as he asked each god individually for protection.

He ended his entreaties by drawing the rune of protection on his chest. Oldar didn't know why he did that, but once he completed the symbol, he felt the familiar calm he'd experienced that morning wash over him once more. Not only that, but some of the chill dissipated from his body. The king wondered if the rune had any ability to counteract the effects of his uncle's monsters or if it just protected him from the side effects of their being nearby.

Outside the door of the throne room, Oldar found himself hesitating. His hand, raised in a knock, couldn't strike the worn wooden door separating him from his uncle. His mind ran in circles as he weighed his options for what he was about to do. Would his uncle listen to him, or was he so gone into madness that any attempt at compromise would be futile? With a sigh, Oldar knew he needed to do something. Saying a quick prayer and drawing the symbol of protection once more, he was astonished at the peace it still brought him. The king placed his hand on the door and pushed.

Once inside the throne room, Oldar was greeted by a blazing fire in the hearth. The sight of the dancing flames raging as they hungrily devoured the logs fed to them made the young king want to race over and warm himself in front of them. Oldar stepped into the room, hoping for a respite from the freezing temperatures out in the halls. It took a moment, but to his horror,

Oldar realized that the heat from the hearth did not fill the room. Instead, it only appeared to serve as a light source in the otherwise dark room.

Shadows played on the walls, waving in the bright light. Oldar wasn't sure, but he thought he saw humanoid forms flitting from shadow to shadow. Feeling exposed, Oldar pushed away the knot forming in his stomach and took a quivering step forward. Sitting on the thrones, Alastaire and his wife, Constance, watched their nephew's advance, their eyes shining eerily in the darkened room.

Giving his eyes a moment to adjust to the light, Oldar tried to read the expressions on his aunt and uncle's faces. Constance sat stiffly in her seat, her lips pursed. Her usually well-put-together exterior betrayed her discomfort. A face once beautifully painted was now smudged, with dark bags forming under her eyes. Glossy hair, so radiant and styled in the most popular fashions of Corinth, now lay limply on around her face, its usual luster now lost. To his dismay, Constance's face appeared gaunt, as though she'd lost a lot of weight in a short period of time.

Alastaire, on the other hand, sat proudly in his chair, his fingers alternating between drumming on the armrest and moving toward his hip. The man's eyes stared straight at Oldar, wide and crazed. His hair was unkempt, and the normally well-manicured beard he prized was now a scraggly mess.

Oldar couldn't help but pity them both for different reasons. His eyes kept darting back to his aunt. The woman, typically a pillar of grace and composure, was now a shell of her former self. Oldar surprised himself with how much compassion he felt for her right now.

"Good morning, Oldar," Alastaire said, breaking the awkward silence.

"Good morning, Uncle," Oldar replied curtly.

"Happy Blood Moon." Alastaire's eyes flickered from his nephew to the door for a brief moment. "What brings my dear nephew back to my chambers?"

Constance tensed but did not say a word. Tracing the rune of protection on his thigh and savoring the strength it seemed to bring him, Oldar pushed forward. It was now or never.

"I've come for information, Uncle."

The man arched his brow, his interest piqued. "Information is costly, dear nephew. What price are you willing to pay?"

"I have an offer I think you'll find most palatable."

Alastaire leaned forward on his elbows, his eyes gleaming hungrily. Taking his uncle's actions as permission to continue, Oldar took a deep breath and continued.

"As you know, my father was a man of his word. Whatever he promised, he delivered. As his son, I share the same beliefs. But you are a smart man and know that such information cannot be given for free. And so, I request answers first."

His uncle's brow creased in displeasure, but he didn't speak.

"Why have you attacked Alocar, specifically Madden, and what monsters have you brought with you?"

"Are these your only questions?" Alastaire asked, a smile playing on his lips.

Oldar thought for a moment before adding, "And how did you come by these creatures?"

"If I answer these questions, you will provide your payment after?"

Oldar nodded, his fists clenched in resignation. He hoped his uncle couldn't see his emotion.

"Very well. I have come to lay claim to your throne; I'm sure you knew that. You are an unfit ruler, and under my leadership, Alocar will only grow in strength and fortune. I told you last time when you threw me out of your home that you could not handle the duties of a king. I have now proven myself correct. You are merely a boy playing king. A charlatan.

"And so, in order to bring Alocar into stability while you chase foolish dreams, I brought with me an army trained to handle any situation and took your kingdom from you without so much as a whimper. My forces are unlike anything ever seen. Even those with the blood of god are no match for them."

The shadows on the walls quivered at this statement, and the fire in the hearth shuddered as it almost went out. A shiver went down Oldar's spine as he saw such a mighty fire almost completely extinguished without so much as a whisper of wind. The tiny bit of tranquility he'd been feeling thanks to the runes of protection he'd drawn on himself were snuffed out as the fire flickered.

Alastaire's eyes widened as his head snapped behind him. When he faced Oldar once more, there was fear mixed in with his apoplectic anger that the young king didn't miss.

"Knock it off," Alastaire seethed as the shadows danced higher, the fire in the hearth flickering once more.

Oldar did not say anything as he waited for his uncle to continue. When no additional information was forthcoming, Oldar gently prompted the man for answers.

"How did you come by this army?" Oldar kept his voice soft so as not to further enrage his uncle.

"My dear boy," Alastaire replied with a laugh. "I did what any good ruler should do. I made one. Do you think I could find such a skilled group competent in nullifying the gifts of the gods? No. Your dear aunt happened to find a book that mentioned creatures called the Faceless. It was in some heathen script, but Constance managed to translate it thanks to her knowledge of the various languages of Corinth. And I must say, it's turned out far better than I imagined. I now have an army of superhuman beings at my beck and call, and there's nothing anyone can do to stop them."

The shadows on the walls shivered once more. Humanoid figures began to take shape, the tops of their heads trailing off in wispy tendrils. With each second, they came into sharper focus. Oldar nearly jumped as a pair of white eyes stared back at him from the shadows. More popped up after the first pair. On his uncle's hip, the glow Oldar had seen during his last visit dimmed.

"All I needed were the hosts bodies," Alastaire continued. "And the gods have provided. I managed to convince young men with foolish ideals and disgruntled soldiers to join me at my home. There, I began the process of unleashing their true potential."

Oldar staggered back a step. "These were people?" he stuttered.

In response, one of the creatures let out a shriek that had frozen him to the core of his being on more than one occasion. Stepping out of the shadows, the figure exposed itself as a very real creature with long claws and thin, sharp teeth. Its mouth turned up in a grimace as it stared at the king.

"Alastaire," Constance said, her voice quivering. "Leave the boy alone. Let him pay you for the information and leave."

Another cry erupted, the room filling with an unholy chorus of screams as more of the Faceless emerged from the shadows. Teeth flashed and claws flexed as they inched closer to Oldar. Jumping up from her seat, Constance shouted at the creatures to leave Oldar alone, but they ignored her command.

"Alastaire, control your army, and I will deliver on my word," Oldar called out, stepping backwards towards the door.

Reaching for the dagger on his hip, the silver stone shining in the darkened room, Alastaire pulled it from its sheath, revealing a brilliant blade that looked as though it were made from the stars. The Faceless shrieked at the light, but they did not withdraw. Instead, they continued to move forward towards the young king.

"Alastaire!" Constance's voice trembled.

In an instant, the fire in the hearth went out, plunging the room into darkness. Constance let out a primal shriek of fear. The quick patter of feet on the cobblestones caused his body to tense as he tried to turn his body and flee the room. Constance's terrified face flew past him as she tore out of the throne room, her hair flying behind her. Howls in the hallway echoed, drawing ever closer. Oldar's mind screamed at him to run, but his body wouldn't obey.

"Run!" Oldar commanded himself.

Hearing his voice ring out in the darkness broke whatever spell held him rooted to the spot. Adrenaline coursing through his body, the king managed to scramble towards the worn oaken door. Behind him, he heard a scream of pure terror rip from his uncle as the shrieks of the Faceless filled the room. Alastaire's pleading lasted for seconds before the room was filled with complete silence. The only sound was a metallic clinking on the stone floor.

As Oldar struggled to close the heavy door, he saw the light from his uncle's dagger shining on the floor. The shadowy figures of the Faceless huddled around the dagger momentarily, unwilling and unable to pick it up, as each time their hand went near it, they recoiled with a hiss. The cries echoing in the halls were quickly approaching, and Oldar still struggled to close the throne room door. In the light of the dagger, he saw several pairs of white eyes turn in his direction, the fangs of the Faceless gleaming in the light of the dagger's stone.

"Come on!" he begged, throwing his weight against the door.

Like the last time, it closed slowly, only to be pushed open once more by a hoard of Faceless clawing at him. Adrenaline flowing through him, Oldar let out a primal scream as he pushed with all his might. A second pair of hands landed on the door, helping him slam it shut, enraging the trapped Faceless.

"Run," Ingmar's voice said from behind Oldar. "They won't be stopped for long, and more are on the way. I'll meet you at your safe spot. Go!"

Backing away from the door, Oldar couldn't believe his eyes as the soldier held the door closed against the group of raging Faceless on his own. Sweat beaded on the veteran's brow despite the frigid temperatures from the strain of his efforts, but he held his own. Growing ever nearer, the cries of the remaining Faceless became louder.

"Go!" Ingmar shouted.

As if struck with the urgency of the situation, Oldar dashed down the hall, slipping on small patches of ice that had formed on the stone floor. He managed to put distance between himself and the Faceless as he sped towards the castle entrance. With each pump of his leg, his chest burned from the frozen air he gulped in, but he did not slow down. As the entrance neared, the king began whistling feverishly, hoping Aelthur was alive and close.

A whinny greeted him as he rounded another corner, and Oldar flung himself onto the horse. Behind him, a nightmare chorus of blood-curdling shrieks resounded throughout the castle. Without urging, Aelthur turned and fled the castle, heading almost blindly into the streets of Madden. As the castle disappeared, an explosion of black shadows filtered out through the windows and into the capital. Oldar couldn't help but worry about Ingmar, hoping against hope that the soldier who had saved his life so many times managed to escape.

XXXIV

Anchal stood in front of the group of tired travelers, an unimposing wooden structure with a thick tree trunk fence lining the perimeter. The tips of the trees had been sharpened into a point, allowing any soldiers who may be on the wall-walks to peek through and fire an arrow or drop hot oil on an attacker. The few red-roofed buildings hidden behind the wall barely snuck past the tips of the trees, most of them invisible below the fence line.

Alverick and the rest of his party gazed up at where the wall-walk would be, hoping to find a soldier who would let them in. Despite their efforts, the previous night did not afford them any rest. Instead, most, if not all, slept fitfully as images of their unknown enemy plagued their dreams. Alverick personally had dreamt he was back in Themba with Bannen. He knew this time that the dream was only that, but being able to talk to his friend once more still comforted the Avalanche. Few woke up feeling refreshed, Alverick guessed. Even Swordbane moved with less purpose than usual.

A hot meal and a nap would do Alverick wonders. He didn't fear Snapping, there was no red that tinged the periphery of his vision like when he was struggling. Instead, he just wanted a chance to relax and recover. As if on cue, the Avalanche thought he smelt the tantalizing aroma of army stew and found himself cracking a smile. When did military food become so appealing? For what it was, Alverick found Ånchal to be a quaint base and thought to himself that it would be a nice change of pace from the Royal Guard.

On the wall-walk, a tuft of dark brown hair bobbed between the pointed ends of the trees lining the perimeter of the outpost. Next to him, Brody called out to the soldier, waving at the man to get his attention. The head of hair heard Brody's call, and a thin face peeked through the fence, distrust heavy on his face. The suspicion quickly turned to surprise when he saw the green livery of Zanir and the red of Xan, along with the leathers and furs from the northern realm.

"Ho there!" the man called out. "What brings you out to Ånchal?"

"We come to speak to your king," Brody replied. "Please let us in."

"King Storm is not in Ånchal anymore."

"We need to find him immediately," Cienna called out, startling Alverick. "Please help us."

The man watched the group with a keen eye. It didn't take long before the brown-haired man disappeared and the gate opened. Alverick and his group scrambled through the entrance, thanking the soldier as they made it in.

"The king was here yesterday," the man said as a crowd began to form. "But he left shortly after his arrival back to Madden."

"We need to get back to Madden as quickly as possible," Alverick explained. "King Storm was traveling with us before he returned to Alocar without much explanation. The princess," he said, motioning to Cienna, "has an urgent matter she needs to discuss with him. We've brought our best soldiers with us because, in his haste, he left the impression that there was an emergency in Alocar."

The brown-haired soldier shot a worried glance towards one of his approaching comrades and waved the man over. The two put their heads together as the brown-haired man whispered fervently into his brother-in-arms' ear. The newcomer's eyes shot open, his attention turning to the small band in front of them. Replying in hushed tones, the second man hurriedly whispered something in the first man's ear. After several tense minutes, the two turned to face Alverick and his group.

"I think you should come with me," the second man said as the first returned to his post. "You can grab a bite while we talk."

"Thank you," Cienna replied before the others could. "Your hospitality is greatly appreciated."

The second man barked out an order to a nearby soldier, asking for something called "proo", as he led the small party towards one of the wooden buildings. It was a single story barrack that reminded Alverick of his early days in the king's army.

"I'm Jennson, by the way."

Jennson did not turn when he addressed them, his attention focused on getting inside the building. As soon as they sat at a table, worn and chipped from constant use, bowls of stew were placed in front of the group. The small chunks of meat, which smelled like rabbit, mixed with carrots and onions, steamed in front of him and made Alverick's mouth water.

"Soldier?" Jennson asked, seeing Alverick's reaction. "Can always tell when a man's had a taste of the stew. It's been a while, eh?"

Alverick cracked a smile and nodded. "Yes. It's been a long time since I've had such familiar food. I didn't realize I missed it so."

Digging into his meal, the Avalanche found himself closing his eyes as he savored the stew. Despite being a simple meal, the combination of delicate lamb with carrots and some herb he could not name exploded with flavor on his tongue. He eagerly spooned more into his mouth. The others ate with as much enthusiasm as Alverick, although Swordbane and Pram ate more reservedly. The northerners appeared to enjoy the food as well, with the larger one digging in with a vigor that rivaled a hungry wolf tearing at a deer.

As their meal quickly disappeared, an elderly woman walked over and joined the group, a burly soldier leading her by the arm and depositing her own bowl of stew in front of her with a gentle "Here you go." The woman thanked him and delicately began eating.

"How can I help you, Jennson?" The elderly woman's voice rang out strong despite her frail figure. "Have you heard anything from my Oldar?"

"I'm sorry, Pru," Jennson replied. "We haven't received word from Madden since his majesty left. I do have a convoy from Zanir who would like to get some information from you before they leave for the capital."

Jennson's raised inflection partway through his statement, asking Alverick for clarification as much as offering hope to the elderly woman. The two caught each other's eyes and shared a look that spoke volumes. He was concerned about Oldar as well.

"Thank you, Jennson," Pru said. Taking a look at her company, she let out a small gasp. "To what do I owe the pleasure of being in the presence of the Princess? Please excuse my manners. It's been getting harder to stand and pay my respects the older I get."

"Please," Cienna said, a tinge of color staining her tanned cheeks. "Don't feel obligated to inconvenience yourself. I appreciate your efforts. If you could, we would like information about Oldar. Have you seen him?"

Pruvencia's expression fell. "Up until yesterday, I did. He secreted me out of the capital and left me here while he went back to confront his uncle."

Alverick couldn't help but notice the venom that tainted her voice. He wasn't sure he'd ever heard about the Storm's extended family, but he wasn't sure if he wanted to at this rate.

"Can you tell us about his uncle?" Alverick asked.

The elderly woman's knuckles turned white as she gripped her spoon. "He's a greedy man whose only desire is to be king. He tried usurping the throne after dear King Storm passed, may he rest in the Halls of the Fallen. He then came in with an army of some hellish creatures right after Oldar left for Pharn after your majesties left Madden after some discussions turned sour." Pruvencia nodded to the princess in respect.

"His wife, on the other hand, is calculating but understands that the throne isn't hers to take. Honestly, I believe she fears her husband and his instability. I pity the poor woman. She's our beloved lady Gwyn's older sister, did you know?"

A small gasp escaped Cienna at the information as her hand flew to her mouth. Her mouth hung agape as she tried to formulate a response, but no sound came out.

"Is he mad?" Swordbane asked. "Or just deluded? Both types of men are dangerous, but one is easier to handle than the other. If he's deluded, at least your king stands a chance of still being alive."

"I can only hope he is," Pruvencia replied. "But I couldn't answer your question. I've had thoughts that he's a bit of both."

"Then we have no choice but to head to Madden as soon as possible," Alverick said, pushing himself out of his chair. The legs of the chair scraped against the ancient wooden floor, catching on the cracks in its grain. "There is no time to rest. Thank you, Lady Pru, for your help. I hope to bring you good news when all is said and done."

One by one, the others slipped out of their seats and joined Alverick as he prepared to leave. The elderly woman moved to get up, but the Avalanche motioned for her to sit down and mention her meal. He saw her wipe a tear from her eye before he disappeared out the door, looking for the nearest soldier.

It didn't take long for them to run into someone. After requesting their mounts, Alverick spoke to Brody and Swordbane before asking for some additional horses so the others could have their own instead of having to share with another. As the group took their seats, Alverick noticed that the northerners sat uncomfortably atop their mounts, but they did not complain. The slimmer one, Hegvaldr, grumbled something to the larger Eivind, causing Jytte to break out in laughter.

A few of the soldiers in the outpost helped lead Alverick and his party to the entrance of the underground tunnels before wishing them luck. More than one offered to accompany them as protection for the princess, but to Alverick's amazement, Cienna turned down the offer. The drastic changes that had occurred since the battle at Fa'Tinh filled the Avalanche with pride. He couldn't help but admire how much she had grown and take note of the leader she was becoming.

The horses' hooves clopped on the stone steps as they descended into the tunnels. Soon, the echoing cacophony carried all around them as they reached the tunnel proper and began their journey to Madden. A slight chill filled the passage, but the winds above had been harsher. Lights flickered in the sconces, providing a bright pathway towards the capital, warm and welcoming when the cloud-laden skies had not.

Periodically, guards from Alocar could be found standing against the wall of the tunnels, keeping watch as the small group passed through. They nodded in acknowledgement, some saying a word of respect for the princess, but never more than that. Alverick noticed one similarity amongst them all: no one looked comfortable. They all had the same expression of keeping a secret from his party, although they desperately wanted to tell.

A damned bunch of professionals, Alverick groused. *They know something is going on, but they don't want to create problems. This is more than just the uncle and his vain attempts to usurp the throne.*

The Avalanche's eyes darted over to Swordbane. The young general sat lightly in his saddle, his back rigid, creating the impression that the Qu'ari knew how to ride a horse. However, he stared straight ahead, not sparing a glance towards any of the soldiers standing guard on the side of the tunnels. Alverick couldn't help but wonder if Swordbane knew how to ride, but he remembered that when the general first attacked Pharn, he would've needed a way to get there and retreat quickly.

What is he thinking about? the Avalanche asked himself. *There's something going on that he's not telling me. I wish I knew his take on the situation.*

As the horses found their breath after the last stretch of cantering, Alverick took the chance and sidled over to Swordbane's general, Pram. It was a rare moment where the man was not speaking with his leader or the Flame, and Alverick intended to use it to his advantage.

"There seems to be more going on than anyone wants to admit," Alverick said as his horse walked beside Pram's. The general glanced at him, a question on his face, but he was unwilling to say anything just yet. "I'm sure you've heard it in their voices and seen it on the faces of the guards down in these tunnels," he pressed. "I don't know if we made the right choice bringing so few men. The only one who's given me a straight answer is that older woman."

Alverick knew that Xan valued their elderly, especially their matrons. He hoped he didn't insult the general. To his relief, Pram shot a furtive look at his leader before answering in a deep voice:

"I've been wondering the same."

The simple answer disappointed the Avalanche. Did he say too much just now, validating the general's own thoughts, or did the man not want to discuss anything with Alverick since they were from different nations? He'd heard from Brody that Pram was a man of few words, but Alverick had attributed it to the battlefield not being a good place for conversation. Perhaps he misjudged the man? He almost pulled on Styx's reins so he could fall back and talk to Brody or Dez, but he decided to hold his pace and not give the Qu'ari the satisfaction of knowing that he'd bested Alverick.

"Before you arrived," Pram continued in a low voice, catching the Avalanche off-guard. "I experienced something that left me filled with questions. Hroth, the Honorable Mother, Evenhand's own wife, and mine as well, all shared the same experience. Since he was not in Fa'Tinh at the time, Evenhand did not have the same encounter, but it is my hope that he believes me, his mother, and his wife."

Alverick held silent, hoping Pram would continue. Hearing that something strange had happened only reinforced his beliefs that they were in for something much bigger than them, and he didn't have to wait long.

"We have a myth in our land, more of a child's tale really, but what I always believed to be just a story nonetheless. Our people believed in a creature called the Faceless. They were used as a way to keep children from staying outside late and to remind them to listen to their parents. After hearing our combined experiences and listening to the Honorable Mother, I believe we may have almost run into one. I don't know how it got out there, but the tales always spoke of them bringing with them the Darkness. I assume you can see it as well?

"Well, this Darkness is what I think awaits us at the other end of the tunnels. I never would've thought that it would be something affecting Alocar. When we ran into the Faceless, the air grew cold, and we heard these cries that chilled us to our very core. I don't think I've ever experienced anything like it, even when Alazi roamed free. Be on your guard, Avalanche. The end of whatever trials we've been chosen to endure will happen once we step foot in Alocar."

The general shared a meaningful look with Alverick before nodding to the Avalanche to signal that he was done talking. True to the rumors, Pram indeed was a man of few words. Powerful, but few. Alverick chose that moment to fall back a bit, but he did not drop back to where Brody or Dez were in line. He needed a few moments to think to himself about all he learned. Having been to Themba, he didn't discount the possibility of the existence of something otherworldly and beyond anything he could comprehend.

Bannen, I could really use you for this one. I'm glad you're safe in the Halls though. You're a lucky bastard.

XXXV

For the first time since they left Xan, there was no wind. No gusts to pull at their clothes, no breezes to cool them off and tickle their hair. The air was still. Unnaturally still. Birds did not sing, bees did not flit from flower to flower, pulling nectar from them to turn into honey. There was only silence. Though the air was still, it carried a chill that bit Ronan and the traveling caravan to the bone.

Women pulled at the shawls on their shoulders, trying to keep the freezing temperatures from seeping further into their bodies. Children no longer ran about, preferring to be carried by their parents for additional warmth or snuggling together in the wain under blankets. Men wrapped their arms around their loved ones' shoulders while soldiers marched in disciplined silence, struggling to ignore the debilitating cold. Among the animals, huddled together in a wagon, the chickens and dogs were lethargic, while the cattle marched without a complaint.

Ronan looked around for a blanket, but he gave up when he admitted to himself that it would not be fair to the children and the elderly. A cough of annoyance broke free, and he felt a twinge of guilt at his lack of composure. Ronan knew he was chosen over Thol to help lead the caravan back to Pharn because of his leadership skills. Though he was quick to scoff at Dez and call her a conjurer, his conscience always led him to the right decision in the end.

Swordbane had left five people in charge on his behalf, one for each of the tribes. The four representatives of the other clans were their leaders. Ronan vaguely remembered them from the council after the battle in Fa'Tinh.

The fifth representative, the Qu'ari one, was his wife. Ronan couldn't help but wonder if he also set up his mother to act through his wife to keep the two in a position of power. Almost everyone who encountered the two women, especially the elderly one whom they referred to as Honorable Mother, revered them.

He didn't blame Swordbane. If Ronan had any family, he would want to do everything he could to keep them safe as well. Unfortunately, his family lived far from Pharn, so he never saw them. Ronan had no wife either, preferring his free lifestyle where he could enjoy the local women without any true commitment. He found himself wishing he'd taken the time to properly court someone.

Off in the distance, Ronan's attention snapped back to the present as he heard the voice of Swordbane's daughter speaking to her mother and grandmother. The young girl spoke loudly, her voice carrying in the silence around them.

"Why is it so cold, Mommy?"

Why, indeed? Ronan wondered.

Swordbane's wife answered quietly, her voice still carrying despite her attempts to keep their conversation private. The frail voice of the Honorable Mother joined their conversation, her voice cracking as she spoke. The two women managed to muffle their responses enough that, though Ronan could hear them, he couldn't make out their responses.

"But what about the darkness?" Bermet asked in the innocent way only children can. "It's been so dark. Those clouds have blocked the sun for days."

More soft responses, primarily from the Honorable Mother, with a few encouraging words from Swordbane's wife. Ronan found himself straining to hear their answers. He wondered what they knew about the departure of Swordbane and others.

I wish Alverick said something about it all, Ronan groused. *It would be nice to have an idea about what we're up against. Him and the conjurer leaving means it's nothing good.*

"The blue-haired girl hasn't been back for a while."

Bermet's voice did nothing to hide the disappointment she was clearly feeling. Ronan's ears perked up once more, curious as to who the blue-haired girl could be.

Obviously, someone important if she's spending time with Swordbane's daughter. Is this a family member? Some other warrior like the shieldmaiden?

Ronan's mind spun with possibilities as he tried to figure out who this mysterious blue-haired person was. He hoped she would be someone who could help them, but the more he thought about it, the less likely it seemed. Swordbane's wife's answer after a pregnant pause caught Ronan by surprise.

"Freyna is watching over your father. She's always keeping him safe and will make sure to bring him back to us."

Jaw dropping, Ronan couldn't believe it. If the women were talking about *the* Freyna, one of the goddesses he actually knew from the foreign nations, then they were in danger. Clenching his fist and bringing it to his mouth, Ronan found himself uttering a prayer his mother taught him when he was a child. Always a superstitious man, the captain couldn't shake the feeling that he would not get out of this situation alive.

They see a darkness that I cannot. Thol and I have talked about clouds with Brody, but I can't believe there is something more happening here. The fact that even more gods are here... gods... we are in trouble. I can't do this. I'm not ready.

"Ronan!" a voice called out to him. "Hold on!"

Thol hastened his pace so he could join his brother-in-arms. The spearman huffed, rubbing a stitch in his side. Taking the opportunity to force himself to focus, Ronan regained his composure, plastering on a curious expression that he hoped didn't make him appear too unsure of himself. He didn't have much time, as Thol found his breath quickly.

"Ronan," Thol hissed, his voice low so no one could hear.

Ronan feared it would carry like Swordbane's family's did, but to his surprise, no one seemed to be paying attention to the two captains from Pharn. In fact, no one appeared to notice the conversation between Swordbane's daughter and her elders. It was almost as though it had been carried to him on the wind.

"We have to pick up our pace," Thol continued, pulling Ronan from his distractions. "The back of our convoy is experiencing extreme cold. People are scared. The quiet is so unnatural, but now they're starting to hear things. Screams carrying on the wind or something like that."

Ronan gazed back at the man, perplexed. "There's not been even the faintest breath of wind today, Thol. All I've heard in the reports is that the skies have been dark, black even, thanks to the damned clouds." He didn't dare tell Thol what he'd overheard from Swordbane's family. "Surely a bit of cloudy and stormy weather isn't enough to frighten the warlord clans?"

As if on cue, Yettan and Pak approached the two. The Thurlish woman's finely braided hair on the left side of her head was tied up in a high tail, with small clasps of gold encircling some of the braids just like the golden band she wore on her arm. A petite woman, she adorned herself with orange silks that complemented her dark skin.

The leader of the Hanzo clan, clad in fine travel silks of cream, scowled as he approached. Ever since the counsel, he snapped at everyone he encountered, even Swordbane's general. He made no effort to hide his anger at Wyrd not being put to death in the main square of Fa'Tinh or to mask his frustrations with his leader.

Taking the opportunity to avoid any preamble, Pak nodded her head in respect to the two Zanirian captains. Ronan and Thol returned the act, grateful that she was the more level-headed of the two. Ronan hoped that she would be the one to speak for the two.

"Greetings, friend," Pak said. "It is under most unfortunate circumstances that I come to you today."

"Good day, Lady Pak," Ronan replied. "How can I be of service?"

"We need to find shelter immediately," Yettan cut in.

His straightforward demeanor left Ronan taken aback. Compared to the composed Thurlish woman, the Hanzo leader displayed his rash disposition openly. The Hanzo were not known for being so abrasive, so Yettan's actions appeared most unusual.

"I have spoken with the other leaders," Pak continued, talking over the agitated Yettan. "And they believe that our current situation requires us to seek shelter. I know the Great Heart and your princess wanted us to make our way to Pharn, but we Brothers and Sisters of Xan do not believe we have enough time. We have been watching the darkening heavens, and with the arrival of your gods, we do not want to discount their warnings."

His spirit dropping, Ronan couldn't stop his face from betraying his emotions. He tried to arrange his face in a neutral expression, but the damage had been done, and both Pak and Yettan saw his dismay.

"I'm sorry, my lady," Ronan said with a slight dip of his head. "But I'm not familiar with the area. I don't know if we'll find anything to house us all."

"We've sent out scouts and found a small farm with an attached building nearby," Yettanreplied bluntly. "It'll be tight, but it looks big enough to house us."

The thought of a shelter to provide them with warmth from the cold and a break from their never-ending trekking appealed to Ronan. He knew that he was supposed to get them all to Pharn and within the strong stone walls for protection, but he couldn't pass up the temptation the two offered. He was spared coming up with a response when Thol interjected.

"Please forgive me, Lady Pak, but is there something more we should be concerned with? I don't mean to be rude, but we are under orders to get you and your people to safety."

"You don't believe, do you?" The incredulity dripped from Pak's voice as she stared at the spearman with a bewildered expression. "You have to have seen the darkness. It has only been growing since we left Xan. Does the arrival of two gods, ones your people worship, mean nothing to you? If I were in your place, I would be listening to every word spoken by them. That should be reason enough for you. There is no time. We must go now."

The two captains shared a glance, and Thol gave a slight shake of the head. The spearman did not believe like Ronan and the others did. Unlike his companion, Ronan did. Growing up, his mother would warn him about the dangers of not listening to the signs of the gods, even if they seemed like coincidences.

"The weather is getting too inhospitable for us to travel," Ronan said, more to Thol, in hopes of convincing his partner. "We need to think of the children and the elderly. We do not serve our princess if they die on the way. Let us take a day and rest at the farm. The home and barn will be enough to keep everyone safe and allow the animals time to eat."

He hoped he spoke to Thol's logical side. The spearman's stubbornness was unusual. Ronan wondered if this was his friend's way of dealing with his nerves. Perhaps Thol did believe, but he fought the truth. Pak stood off to the side with an approving look. Yettan, on the other hand, maintained his glower toward the Zanirian pair. With a sigh, Thol nodded.

"You're right," he muttered. "The death of children and the elderly would be exactly what the princess wanted to avoid. Send word that we will be seeking cover and taking the day to rest."

A small smile spread over Pak's face, and she left to spread the word and redirect the caravan, while Yettan stalked off. Ronan couldn't tell if he was pleased with the results or not, but he decided not to worry about it, although he did make a mental note to keep an eye on the man. He couldn't shake the feeling that the man would kill him if he had the chance.

"Thank you," Ronan said to Thol.

It was as if a mask dropped from his friend's face. Exhaustion seeped into his entire body, and his body sagged. Dark circles seemed to appear under his eyes in an instant, and his cheeks suddenly looked hollower, giving him a haunted, gaunt appearance. Without a response, Thol heaved another sigh before walking away in silence.

<p style="text-align:center">~~~</p>

Following the lead of the scouts, Pak and Ronan walked side-by-side at the head of the convoy. Word quickly spread throughout the caravan that they would be finding a place to rest, and the mood lightened noticeably. The children, though still huddled under the blankets or latched on to their mothers, could be heard talking, and even a bit of laughter broke through. The heavy, overcast clouds following their every move did not bother them as much. However, the adults and elderly remained apprehensive, their eyes still darting to the heavens every few steps.

Off the main road, the scenery was much different. Tall, green grasses waved in a non-existent breeze, the little white flowers peeking through the tops of the blades reminding the group of the stars they hadn't seen in a few days. White maple trees lined the edges of the meadow the tall grasses were housed in. Under the trees, lilacs grew, their brilliant purple contrasting with the verdant. Ronan was pleased to see that the darkness overhead could not hide the beauty nearby. All that was missing was birdsong, bees, and butterflies.

It didn't take long for the farm to come into view. A small home with a thatched room, more like a cottage, sat alone in a clearing. Flowers decorated the yard, a riot of colors against the white maple wood. Boxes hung from the windows, holding orchids and small orange dandelions. The orchids hung limply from the side, the cold having damaged them beyond saving. Not too far from the home, a large wooden barn sat next to a pile of firewood that appeared to be freshly chopped.

Relief flooded Ronan as he saw the little sanctuary. His hands were numb, and he struggled to breathe, the freeze causing his chest to constrict. He glanced over at Pak and couldn't imagine the discomfort the Thurlish woman was feeling. The change in temperature from Xan's dry heat must be unbearable to her in her delicate silks.

Cries of thanks rang out behind him. Bodies surged past Ronan and Pak as children and young families raced towards the shelter. Dogs streaked ahead, their tails wagging in excitement. Xanan warriors helped carry the elderly on their backs into the farm home while the hale men made their way into the barn. Longhorn cattle let out low calls and began grazing on the tall grasses just on the outskirts of the home.

The heavy thud of a hand clapping Ronan on the back caught his attention. Thol's face, the exhaustion hidden once more, appeared next to his. The spearman was beaming as he quickly made his way to the barn. Ronan couldn't help but share in his friend's excitement at finding a place to keep them safe. For now.

~~~

A steady stream of bodies filed into Caer Grey. Thick fog blanketed the capital of Zanir, trapping the freezing air underneath. Thick streams of hot air poured from the mouths of the people of Pharn as they continued their slow trek into the castle. Families huddled together, heavy blankets thrown over their shoulders, in a vain attempt to keep themselves warm. Mothers attempted to comfort their babies, but not even their breasts could soothe the freezing infants.

Cody paced the queue, constantly rubbing his hands, in an effort to both keep everyone calm as well as keep himself warm. His feet dragged against the cobblestones, his body too cold to properly lift them as he moved. A handful of other soldiers also patrolled the lines, rounding up stragglers who
~~~

sought shelter in their homes or shops. Others worked at gathering supplies to bring to Caer Grey. Baskets of fruits and vegetables and trays of bread from the bakeries trickled into the castle. There were many mouths to feed and not enough supplies.

The fog was so thick, the blacked skies couldn't even be seen. Cody tried to find comfort in his inability to see the source of his discomfort, but it didn't work. Instead, not being able to see the darkness only heightened his unease. Nightmares had plagued him since the arrival of whatever was causing the phenomenon.

Shadowed figures darted around him, slicing at him with invisible blades, incapacitating him. All around him, pairs of gleaming eyes appeared from the unknown. With each cut to his flesh, Cody's body shook, the shallow strikes sending a wave of pain burning through him. As their number increased, his body was aflame, the final death strike causing him to wake up screaming, his entire being trembling as he gasped for air, covered in cold sweat.

Even when he blinked, all he saw were the eyes.

And so, Cody forced himself to stay awake, not even allowing himself a moment to rest his heavy eyes. His body ached from standing for almost a whole day. He didn't even take breaks, instead offering to cover his brothers-in-arms shifts under the guise of just starting his own. No one noticed his exhaustion.

The arrival of Jaes and his soldiers helped keep the city from devolving into complete chaos. His men sprang into action, despite not having much time to recover from their week-long journey to Pharn, and set to work organizing the soldiers of Pharn into groups to help with securing the capital. Jaes himself, a living reminder of the late King Jaste, stood at the forefront, barking orders and making sure he was seen by both the soldiers and the people of Pharn.

With the influx of people brought into the capitol with Jaes and his men, the city reached its maximum capacity. Her resources were unable to keep up with the demand. Those who had arrived the day before had already managed to find shelter inside the caer, with the healers from the Magericium tending to the injured and ailing. Cody had been surprised to hear that more than one woman had given birth in the last day.

As he neared the end of the line, Cody wasn't sure the remaining citizens of Pharn would make it into the caer before mid-day. The capital's gates had been closed and secured; orders had been given to not let anyone enter or exit, and the wall-walks were more heavily manned than usual. Scouts were placed in the turrets and along the walks as messengers, prepared to bring any news to Jaes at a moment's notice.

A cry rang out in the street as an ominous crack of thunder rumbled overhead. Lightning forked through the sky, illuminating the city through the fog. Bodies surged forward, the masses frightened and on edge already from the uncertainty of it all. More cries rang out as people stumbled to the ground, their bodies being trampled by feet in the chaos. Children wailed, calling out for their mothers, as their parents and other nearby adults tried to shelter their tiny frames from the rush.

Shouts called out for order. Cody found himself racing over to the pile, yelling for order and peace to the stampeding citizens. To his surprise, his voice was clear and steady, sounding more authoritative than he felt. Heads turned as people heeded his instructions. Those pushing forward calmed, no longer rushing forward in a panic. The soldiers further up the queue managed to reach the pile of bodies and began disentangling everyone. Children sobbed, frightened, but were largely uninjured. Mothers cradled their loved ones, sending praise and thanks to the Siblings that their babies had not been hurt.

Another crack of lightning was followed by the peeling roar of thunder almost instantly, drawing forth cries from the already terrified children. Soldiers knelt over, trying to help parents soothe their children, and attempting to usher those in line towards the caer. Eventually, the group began moving once more.

Cody turned towards Caer Grey. The towers poked out from the blanket of fog, exposing the tiniest amounts of blackened sky. His stomach knotted as an ominous feeling of foreboding rolled over him. Just like in his dreams, he thought he saw a pair of eyes staring at him, through him, from the darkness. Ignoring all rational thought, Cody went to the end of the line and began hurrying the group as he shouted out orders to the soldiers higher up in the line from him. In as orderly a manner as possible, everyone marched towards the castle.

The young boy's eyes kept staring towards the small patch of darkness filtering through the fog. He would not allow anyone to remain in the city outside the caer by mid-day. The entire population would be brought in for safety, even if it meant that he scoured the capital all on his own.

XXXVI

The frantic beat of hooves on cobblestones echoed through the empty streets of Alocar. Glancing back towards his former home, Oldar thought he saw more and more of those shadowy monsters escaping through the windows. Aelthur's breath came out in ragged gasps, the steam pouring from his mouth and nostrils in the freezing temperatures, and sweat covered his neck and flank. Heavy gasps accompanied every hurried step. It took the king a moment to realize that they were his own.

Soon, the ringing of horseshoes against the stones increased as more horses raced through the streets. Oldar looked around and saw that, much to his relief, Ingmar and a small contingent of Madden soldiers followed behind him as the young king and his mount tore through the streets. The horses screamed in terror, foaming at the mouth, as they fled from Castle Strom.

Shrieks of the Faceless filled the capital, nearly drowning out King Storm and his soldiers' desperate retreat. Out of the corner of his eye, Oldar thought he saw shutters and curtains closing as the frightened inhabitants of Madden sought some small form of cover, but he wasn't sure if he had imagined it.

"Make for the outskirts of Madden!" Ingmar's voice rang out. "We'll draw them away from the capital and into the open fields of Alocar."

Acting on pure adrenaline, Oldar pulled on Aelthur's reins, guiding him away from Schaed's wine shop where he'd been unconsciously directing the dun stallion to go and instead towards the city gates. Muttering a prayer to any god he could think of, Oldar prayed that the gate was not closed or locked, allowing for a fast escape.

Despite his panicked escape, the wind generated by his flight did not seem to bother him. His numb fingers gripped the reins, his knuckles white from his exertions. Aelthur's breathing became heavier and heavier, and his speed began to lag, but Oldar encouraged the horse to continue forward. The horse's lungs worked like the bellows, but the beast continued to push itself further.

Shouts from behind him sounded strangely muted to the king, as though he were swimming underwater. The only sounds that rang loud and clear were the blood-curdling shrieks of the Faceless. To his relief, they didn't appear to be getting closer. Rather, they seemed to be maintaining the same distance they did when he first fled from Castle Storm. Having not been overrun by the hellish creatures yet gave him a small measure of hope.

"Gates ahead!" Ingmar's voice rang out.

Oldar didn't question why his voice cut through the bubble around his head. Instead, he pushed forward, lightly pressing his heels into Aelthur's sides in hopes of urging the horse faster. Ahead, the gates were being raised, and the few soldiers manning them hurried to aid the king in his escape. Shouts at the gates could be heard, but not understood as the winds howled in his ears and the strange muffling sensation continued.

By the time he reached the gates, they were only half open. Flattening his body as much as possible against Aelthur, Oldar continued through the gates, praying that he didn't get knocked off his horse as they raced out of the capital. The steel tips of the gates grazed his back as he made clearance. Behind him, the others copied his movements and made it through them as well. The king could hear the gears grinding once more as the gates began to close in hopes of trapping the beasts in the city. Oldar didn't know if his soldiers knew what they were locking within the capital, but he didn't spend long worrying about it. His mind screamed at him to make it to the grassy fields Ingmar mentioned, and that was all he could focus on.

Outside of the city walls, the wind ripped at his clothes, trying to leech what little heat he and the others managed to keep. His teeth chattered and his fingers ached, but he kept pushing. It wasn't long before Aelthur began slowing and ended up walking. The horse's flesh trembled as he struggled to breathe, thick clouds of smoke blowing from his nose and mouth as he chomped at the bit. Froth foamed around Aelthur's mouth, dripping to the ground as he tried to continue on. His ears were perked up and twitching, straining for any sign or sound of the nightmare creatures.

The soldiers behind him caught up and slowed their mounts to a walk to match the king's pace. They then took a defensive formation, with riders moving to his flanks to protect him from any unexpected attacks from the side. More than one tried to crack a joke about how their efforts probably wouldn't save any of them if one of the shadow creatures attacked. Oldar took advantage of their time together and explained what he'd learned from his uncle about the Faceless.

To his amusement, his soldiers tried to hide their dismay about the monsters. Instead, they attempted to build themselves up by downplaying the dangers of their foe. Ingmar remained quiet, his eyes downcast during the banter, and it didn't go unnoticed by the king. When there was a lull in the conversation, Oldar gently asked the veteran soldier what was on his mind.

"I don't know what happened to your aunt, but I managed to catch a glimpse inside the throne room. I'm sorry to say, but your uncle is dead. As the little light in the hallway lit up the room, I saw his body, and unfortunately, he met the same fate as your friend Schaed — torn to pieces. I'm sorry, your majesty."

The man's news left the king feeling conflicted. Oldar knew he should feel upset about his uncle's death, but he couldn't bring himself to feel pain or loss. Instead, he worried about his aunt. She fled from the room before anyone else could leave, her disheveled figure forever burned into his mind as she tore out of there panic-stricken. He hadn't always gotten along with Constance, but she'd never deliberately hurt Oldar. He hoped she managed to find safety inside or outside the castle. Perhaps she ran into a member of the staff and found her way into the kitchen, taking refuge with the rest.

"Thank you for the news, Ingmar," Oldar replied, his voice stoic. "We will need to plan a burial for him once we return. I hope Aunt Constance hasn't met the same fate."

"As do I," Ingmar said.

The group traveled in silence for a bit to honor the fallen man. Oldar wasn't sure if they did it out of respect for him or if they assumed that he would expect them to do it out of custom. Either way, the ride was surprisingly pleasant. The stifling quiet he'd experienced in Madden disappeared and was replaced with the natural peace that came with being out in nature. The horses, still exhausted, moved at a slow pace.

More than one of the guards slid off their mount, walking alongside the horse with the reins hanging loosely in their hands. The horses bent down to grab a quick bite of grass as they walked, their snack not disrupting the flow of travel. Following his men's lead, Oldar slipped off of Aelthur and gave his mount a well-deserved break. The dun stallion shook his head, the ends of his mane brushing against the king's arms, as he let out a grateful knicker.

Closing his eyes, Oldar took a deep breath and tried to still his racing heart. They walked along, the king remaining silent as he felt the adrenaline gradually melt away, leaving him heavy with exhaustion. The strength he'd felt from drawing Schaed's rune of protection had long disappeared. Now, all he wanted was to curl up somewhere and go to sleep.

A butterfly darted overhead, catching Oldar's attention. Its golden wings sparkled despite there being no sunlight. They almost appeared to be silken, such was their dazzling beauty. The king watched the butterfly flit about, always ahead of him but within his line of sight. After an indeterminate period of time, it struck Oldar that he hadn't seen anything other than the horses of Alocar since he arrived in Madden a few days prior. The bees didn't buzz, the cicadas didn't hum, and the birds didn't sing. It was almost as if the arrival of the Faceless had chased away all signs of life outside the citizens of Madden.

The butterfly followed the group, always keeping a short distance in front of them. Whenever Oldar and his party veered to one side whenever a fork presented itself in the road, the golden butterfly would take the lead, as if to guide them to their destination. All the while, Oldar took note of its behavior with keen interest. The others did not seem to notice the insect's actions and traveled onward, oblivious to the only animal to be seen for days. If the butterfly took a different road from the soldiers, it would fly over the king's head before fluttering off to the road it wanted them to take, causing Oldar to direct his troops at the whim of the butterfly.

As the day stretched on, both Oldar and the horses perked up, their steps becoming livelier. Aelthur nuzzled his head against Oldar's arm, hoping for a scratch, and the king happily obliged. Their surroundings became more field-like; groves of tall grasses grew to knee-length. The blades tickled them through their pants, bringing a little levity to their flight. Oldar could imagine the field's beauty on a normal day. The sun would shine down on the grass, warming his flesh as he waded through it, the blades waving gently in the light breeze that would be blowing through the area. Bees and butterflies would be floating around over the grass, and a symphony of birdsong would drift in the background. It was the perfect spot for a quiet afternoon sipping wine under the shade of a tree with a good book.

"Your majesty," a voice said softly.

Pulling himself from his daydream, Oldar turned to find Ingmar walking beside him. Unlike the rest of the soldiers, the veteran stood almost shoulder-to-shoulder with the king. Concern was evident on his face by the way he stared into Oldar's eyes. It immediately put him on guard.

"Yes?" Oldar dropped his voice so the others wouldn't hear.

"Have you considered that following a butterfly, the only animal around for possibly many leagues, may not be the best idea? I know we all want something to give us a bit of hope, and gods know you could use it more than most, but I am more than a little apprehensive, if I'm allowed to be honest."

It was a valid concern, one Oldar had asked himself many times as he followed it. He couldn't explain it, but there was something about the golden butterfly that filled him with a sense of security. He knew he very well could be taking them to their deaths, but some innate feeling told him to trust the butterfly.

"I can't explain it, Ingmar, but you'll just have to trust me. This butterfly means us no harm."

The veteran nodded, not wanting to disagree with his king. Oldar could see the exhaustion and pain in his eyes. The soldier had seen a lot, especially in the last few days. Words couldn't even describe the terrors that man faced, and yet he continued to act selflessly to help preserve the kingdom. When this was all over, Oldar vowed to award Ingmar with a plot of land for him to spend the rest of his days on, assuming they lived through it all.

"Your majesty!" another guard called out.

Both Ingmar and his king started, their hands flying to their weapons. Up ahead, Oldar could make out a small group of people in green tunics, gold insignias emblazoned on their chests, approaching. The men, he could now see, had their weapons raised in a defensive posture. Their tunics looked familiar to Oldar, but it was hard to tell from this distance.

"Zanir!" one of the lead soldiers called out, his hand moving from his hip to the air to show he was unarmed.

Squinting his eyes, Oldar realized that it was indeed a small band of soldiers from Pharn. He could now see the symbols of the quill and the sword adorning their green livery. Next to him, he could hear Ingmar mutter a prayer of relief at the sight of their allies. He wondered what brought them out here to the fields of Alocar when the world was going to hell.

"Greetings!" Oldar called out, his hands in the air to show that he, too, was unarmed.

The rest of his group followed suit, their hands reaching heavenward and the reins dangling loosely as they attempted to show they meant no harm. Oldar wished he was properly dressed to give the soldiers of Pharn some peace of mind, but he hoped that the blue livery of Alocar was reassurance enough.

"Men of Pharn, what brings you to my home. To Alocar?"

Oldar stepped out from the protection of his soldiers ringing him so the green-clad soldiers could see who spoke. He could feel more than see Ingmar sidling up behind him, his blue livery visible to the men of Zanir, while at the same time staying in range to protect his king should anything happen.

Bless that man, Oldar thought. *Always thinking one step ahead.*

The soldiers of Pharn lowered their weapons, their postures still defensive. One of the men ran back to their little camp. The groups stood at a standstill, the soldiers of Pharn not wanting to get too close and Alocar not wanting to risk an ambush from some archers. Time dragged by excruciatingly slowly, but Oldar waited, knowing he couldn't act rashly after his last interaction with his allies. After what felt like forever, a small group of three approached him and his soldiers. Like Oldar, the person in the middle held their hands up as well.

It didn't take long for Queen Hera to come into view. The queen's short chestnut hair was barely long enough to be tied back at the base of her neck. A green tunic and brown, skin-tight pants, similar to the livery of Zanir, clothed her, complementing her dark skin. No identifying symbol adorned her, leaving her to appear nondescript amongst her soldiers. The soldiers of Alocar snapped to attention once they recognized the queen, holding their position until she released them with a kind word and a wave of her hand.

Oldar sank into a deep bow, his gaze trained to the ground. The tips of the blades of grass tickled his nose, but he didn't dare lift his head too soon. Images of a distraught Cienna as her mother fought for her life after being poisoned by his only friend filled him with a heavy guilt. He didn't deserve to stand in front of the queen. Only when a hand delicately landed on his back did the king glance up. Hera stood in front of him, her eyes gentle as she beckoned him to rise.

"Please forgive me, your highness," Oldar stuttered. "I take full responsibility for the poisoning, but please know that it was not my doing. The offender has been dealt with most severely." A tear formed in the corner of Oldar's eye as he imagined Schaed's lifeless body laying somewhere in the streets of Madden in a pool of blood. "I would never want you harmed. Or your daughter."

Hera's eyes remained kind, but her tone came out constrained. "I forgive you, King Storm. Now rise. We have much to talk about."

Soldiers in blue and green accompanied their lords to the makeshift Zanirian camp. Oldar marveled at the close proximity of those in the camp. The queen had brought a sizeable number of soldiers with her, but they had crammed themselves into a small ring of smooth stones next to a crystal blue pond. A campfire weakly burned near one of the stones, the flames constantly tended so no black smoke drifted up to the heavens. Near the pond, a small golden flower stood alone. The silken butterfly Oldar had been following earlier landed on its delicate petals, rubbing its front legs together as it slowly opened and closed its wings.

"We've been here for two days now, and this is the first time the winds have not threatened to topple us once we left the safety of the ring of stones." She indicated to the larger smooth stones creating the outer circle. "I was called here by a dream, but unfortunately, we don't have enough manpower to figure out why we're supposed to be here. Whatever it is, Alocar is involved."

"I was afraid of that," the king said with a sigh. "Much has happened since we left for Xan, and it seems that it all originates with Alocar in some way."

"What do you mean?"

With a deep breath, Oldar struggled to find the right words to explain everything in a succinct manner. There was so much to say. He found himself beginning to tear up as the weight of everything that had fallen on his shoulders finally sank in. His exhausted mind just didn't want to think about it anymore; the very idea of calling up those emotions once more filled him with dread.

Blinded by the tears welling in his eyes, Oldar did not see the queen move forward until he felt her arms holding him tightly, pressing him to her body in a warm embrace. The delicate scent of her hair, some fragrant oil, possibly rose, having been rubbed into it before they left to follow her vision, reminded him of his mother. Though she wasn't someone who enjoyed hugs, Oldar remembered a time or two when he was younger where his mother had held him tightly, much like Hera did now. With a shuddering gasp, he fought back the tears as he rested his head against her shoulder.

The queen whispered soft words of affirmation to him, letting him know that it was going to be okay. The kindness she extended to him at that moment meant the world to him. After several long minutes where the soldiers occupied themselves with anything but facing their leaders, Oldar found the strength to break free of Hera's grip.

"Thank you," he said, wiping his eyes. "I — I'm sorry for that. I just haven't had a chance to process everything, and it's left me drained."

"Think nothing of it," Hera replied. Oldar found himself leaning into her motherly touch, savoring the contact. He wondered for a brief moment what life would have been like if his own mother had treated him similarly. The king knew that because of her gift, she struggled to show affection in a way other than by keeping a distance to make sure he remained safe. Gwyn had acted the only way she knew how, through practical means lacking the tenderness of emotion.

Clearing his throat, Oldar found the strength to provide a meticulous explanation of all that had happened since he'd left Pharn. Without sparing any detail, Oldar described the message he'd received from Schaed's hawk, his ride to Madden, and his hurried escape from the Myrani. At the mention of the mercenaries, more than one head swiveled in their direction, all pretense of not noticing the pair lost for a moment. With a deep breath, he then moved on to his confrontation with his uncle and his aunt's flight before finally moving on to the Faceless.

He didn't get much of a chance to describe the hellish creatures, however, before a familiar, blood-curdling scream rang through the meadow. A shiver ran down Oldar's spine, rooting him to the spot. Cries from the soldiers filled the air, only to be drowned out by more shrieks answering the initial call.

"What in the seven hells is that?" Hera gasped, her eyes wide with terror.

A strong gust of freezing wind raced towards the group, breaking through the protective barrier of Hera's little sanctuary and ripping at their clothes. Oldar immediately felt his body go numb with cold, his teeth beginning to chatter. The horses cried out in fear, bucking and stamping their feet as they sought to break free from their handlers.

To the side, Ingmar and the Alocaran soldiers could be heard muttering prayers and other fervent exclamations of terror. Seeing the veteran so frightened yet determined as he drew his sword from its sheath filled the king with mixed emotions. Following Ingmar's example, Oldar and the soldiers in the field drew their weapons as one. Even Hera pulled out a small dagger from her hip, her hands quivering as she held the tiny weapon out in front of her.

Ignoring the panic welling up inside him, Oldar took a step forward. He couldn't believe they'd managed to follow him without his noticing. He knew he couldn't dwell on that now. There was no room for running.

"Stand firm, everyone," Oldar called out. "These creatures are fast, but there has to be a way to defeat them. And we will be the ones to find it. Watch each other's back and stand strong. Do not give in to fear."

A roar erupted from the men as they waved their weapons in the air. The few archers who were amongst them tightened the strings of their bows as they prepared to unleash a hail of arrows into the Faceless. In response to the cry from the soldiers, the Faceless let out their own in kind. Oldar hoped that the unholy shrieks wouldn't scare the soldiers into paralysis. Sending out a prayer to the gods, Oldar took a moment to draw the rune of protection he'd discovered above Schaed's wine cellar door on his chest. A warmth filled him, lending the king strength. With a mighty battle cry, Oldar raised his sword high into the air and began sprinting towards the Faceless.

The Faceless returned the charge in kind.

XXXVII

WEAK RAYS OF SUNLIGHT struggled to break free from the darkness, staining the heavens red. Behind the clouds, Toron's moon fought to break free from his prison, the celestial orb ringed in a deep crimson. However, neither proved successful, as the blackened skies would not relent. Wind howled through Alocar, but after the initial gust announcing the Faceless' arrival, the grassy field remained still. The only signs of the mighty gusts were the shaking trees and the horrible noise.

Despite his bravado in leading the charge, Oldar couldn't begin to fathom what his next step would be. He was no warrior; he'd told himself that time and time again ever since he first went to Pharn to ask for Cienna's hand in marriage. And yet, he found himself once more heading into battle. The sword weighed heavily in his hands, and he feared tripping and impaling himself on the blade. Oldar couldn't imagine a more humiliating death than that by his own sword.

The blades of grass slapped at his legs, somehow managing to sting him with each strike through his riding pants. On each side, he saw soldiers in blue or green livery racing forward. Oldar became acutely aware of his lack of armor and felt a surge of panic course through him as he realized how exposed he truly was. He didn't have time to worry about that for long before one of the Faceless loomed in front of him.

Oldar managed to bring his blade in front of him in what he hoped was a defensive posture as he slowed to a stop. In the gloomy light, the king finally got a chance to see what he was up against. Taller than a man, the creature greeted him with outstretched arms. Thin claws formed at the ends of the hands where the fingers should be, and wisps of shadow curled around the body like smoke drifting away from a fire. The top of the Faceless' head ended in thick tendrils of shadow fading off where the hair should have been. Its face was slightly elongated, and razor-sharp teeth protruded as the monstrosity smiled down on him.

What scared Oldar the most were the eyes. White and catlike, there were no pupils or other colors inside. Only whiteness. The king could see that despite the lack of any semblance of a human eye, the creature watched him keenly, calculating. Knowing he couldn't read the Faceless' expression sent another wave of terror coursing through the king, paralyzing him.

Beside him, he could hear men calling out as they prepared to strike, the glint of their weapons in the gloom catching his attention. In front of him, the Faceless raised its claw and brought it down with blinding speed. Oldar could barely register the movement before he was yanked back and thrown off balance, landing on his backside. He felt the rush of air as the claws missed him by mere inches.

"Get back!" Ingmar's voice called out.

In his confusion, Oldar sat among the tall grasses as his trusted soldier stood between him and the Faceless, weapon drawn and jaw set. The creature let out a shriek of glee as it beheld its next prey. In the field, cries from the soldiers began to ring out as they suffered grievous wounds at the hands of the Faceless.

Shuffling back, Oldar put some distance between himself and the monster before scrambling to his feet. The cries around him intensified as more men in blue and green livery dropped to the ground, gaping slashes cutting through their leathers and ripping them open the way no blade could. Shrieks from the Faceless rang out as if announcing their victory over Oldar and his forces. In front of him, Ingmar and the Faceless circled each other, gauging their opponent for a weakness.

A mighty bellow tore from Ingmar's throat as he darted forward, sword poised to strike. With a quick slash, he brought the blade down where the arm should have been. The Faceless managed to slip back, evading the attack, so that Ingmar's blade only cut through the air. The creature narrowed its eyes, its teeth baring in rage at not being able to end the exchange in a few seconds. It dashed to the side, positioning itself on Ingmar's exposed side. With a slash, the creature swiped at the soldier.

The claws barely missed their target as Ingmar threw himself to the ground, his body disappearing in the tall grass for a moment. A shriek of rage escaped the Faceless as it rushed towards the veteran, who was finishing his dive and rolling onto his feet. Blade pointing at the Faceless, Ingmar succeeded in parrying several strikes from the creature, his sword landing several blows to the Faceless' hands, but not dealing any damage. A growl of frustration came from the soldier as he tried to figure out a way to wound the monster.

In a fit of rage, he launched himself into an offensive, his sword swinging wildly, startling the creature. His blade managed to hit the Faceless on the arm, drawing a scream of pain from it. So astounded was the veteran that he paused his barrage for half a second, throwing off his momentum as he had been pushing the creature back. Taking advantage of his temporary break, the Faceless brought its claws down in a swift strike, landing a blow to Ingmar's chest. The seasoned veteran cried out in pain as blood droplets sprayed in the air as the Faceless' claws pulled away from his chest.

Large gashes similar to what Oldar had seen on the Myrani were carved into Ingmar, blood blossoming on his blue tunic around the tattered cloth. The soldier dropped to the ground, his sword clattering against some small stones hidden in the tall grasses. The Faceless let out a cry of delight as it turned its attention back to the king.

His legs trembled as he tried to bring his sword up in a defensive posture like Ingmar had used only moments before. The blade wobbled in his hands in an almost comical fashion as panic coursed through the king once more.

Whatever strength he had been feeling after drawing the rune of protection on himself had long faded and now was replaced with sheer terror. Cries continued to ring out in the field as more bodies dropped to the ground, dotting the field with blue and green corpses.

Blood dripping off its claws, the Faceless turned its attention to Oldar once more. A smile twisted onto its face, its eyes flashing with delight. It shook off the blood on its claws and stalked towards the king.

"Oh, shit! Oh, shit!" Oldar muttered as the Faceless approached.

The creature moved in slow motion, each step bringing the king agony as he awaited his death. His heart pounded in his chest, and the pommel of the sword slipped in his hands as a thin sheen covered his palms. Each breath amplified around him, the sharp intake as he struggled to breathe roaring in his ears. The king's eyes zeroed in on his surroundings. Over the shoulder of the Faceless, tendrils of shadow wafting towards the heavens, Oldar noticed the golden butterfly fluttering about. He locked onto the dazzling insect, resigned to his fate and wanting to see something beautiful before he died. He was acutely aware of his legs shaking.

~~~

Hiding behind the line of battle, Hera watched as her men and the soldiers of Alocar were slaughtered. Neither brought a large group with them as they traveled, King Storm only having ten or so when she first encountered him, but as the numbers dwindled, so did the queen's hopes that they would escape the field alive. Blood pounded in her ears as she watched her men be cut down one-by-one. Sprays of crimson stained the coats of the men dressed in blue and green, just like in her vision.

"I've failed," she whispered, her voice sounding unnaturally loud despite the meadow being filled with the sounds of the dead and dying. "I've brought us all to our deaths."

Tears rolled down the queen's cheeks as she held her puny dagger in front of her. It would do no good against these monsters. Her lack of athletic
~~~

prowess didn't matter either. The monsters, the Faceless Oldar had called them, would overtake her in a matter of moments. She'd die a quick and painful death, unable to warn her daughter of what awaited her.

"Freyna protect us." Hera's voice came out in a strangled gasp.

In a vain attempt to find meaning in her dream, Hera's mind raced through all of her conversations with the dream reader a few days prior. Nothing they'd discussed mentioned a way to defeat the Faceless. It took her too long to reach the field. They didn't have enough time to explore. Cursing her luck, Hera wished she'd at least brought the dream reader or an academic to help guide her, even though she knew it most likely wouldn't have turned anything up.

Scanning the horizon, Hera then looked to see if she could find any hope of salvation. The air hung still, the temperature freezing since the arrival of the Faceless. Toron's moon faintly shone from behind the wall of darkness in the heavens, the crimson ring denoting the blood moon being the only part she could truly see.

Her mind raced once more as she tried to find meaning in the Faceless' arrival coinciding with the blood moon. For centuries, the blood moon had been thought of as a time of fertility and preparing for new life. Both farmers and midwives prayed that a blood moon would bring them a large bounty. Could they have been wrong all along? Was the blood moon a sign of death, not life? Nothing made sense anymore, and the queen found herself sinking deeper into despair as the death of each soldier brought her one step closer to her own.

With a resigned sigh, Hera slipped her dagger into the sheath on her hip and sat down on a rock. The queen rested her head in her hands, letting her emotions take over, and allowed herself to cry. Tears pooled in her palms as she let out shuddering sobs. She wished Jaste was there to wrap his arms around her one more time. Her husband always knew how to comfort her.

Several long minutes went by before Hera forced herself to look upon the carnage once more. Only a handful of soldiers remained, and those who did tried valiantly to hold off the creatures. Wiping her streaming eyes and nose, Hera stood up once more, pulling her dagger out of its sheath once more. If her soldiers were willing to give everything for a futile cause, she would at least do them the honor of facing the Faceless and dying after putting up some sort of resistance.

Her legs trembled as she contemplated leaving her sanctuary. Hera wasn't sure if the Faceless could enter the stone circle, but she didn't want to risk bloodshed in such a peaceful place. With each passing second, the shaking intensified. Startled, she looked around. It wasn't just her legs that were quivering.

XXXVIII

A SEA OF DEATH greeted Alverick and his group as they looked around the field of tall grasses. Surrounded by the white maples, men in blue and green livery fell at the hands of some sort of black shadow creatures. To his left, Swordbane let out a soft curse as Pram muttered a quiet prayer. The Avalanche heard both utter the word Faceless as they watched the shadow figures move deftly through the knee-tall grasses. Pruvencia's words about their foe's strength came back to Alverick. The matronly woman had no idea what hell-creature escaped into Corinth.

Without a thought, Alverick reached into his energy reserves and began pulling on the earth. The ground trembled as he built up his momentum. At the same time, Dez tapped into her energies and summoned the wind. It started as a breeze, but Alverick remembered how quickly it could become a windy funnel of black death.

Whimpers of panic could be heard as Cienna gazed down at the death in the field. Tears streamed down her face as she watched men get cut down by the Faceless without putting up much of a fight. Next to her, Caitlyn appeared frozen, her mouth hanging open as if she were about to ask a question. Even the barbarians stood in silence, the color draining from their pale faces. Only the gods appeared resolute.

"Apophos has finally shown himself," Hegvaldr's deep voice broke the hush. "After centuries of poisoning Man and the land, he has found a way."

Continuing to push the earth, Alverick felt a small glimmer of hope as the three northmen pulled their axes from their hips as one, ready to launch into battle. A low, rumbling hum could be heard as the trio began singing an ancient song of war, their bodies bouncing side-to-side as they prepared to strike. There were no words at first, but slowly they came, only to be drowned out by the wind and screams in the field.

The sudden appearance of heat in the frigid field caused Alverick's head to swivel back to his left. Both Swordbane and Pram had drawn their weapons, their battleaxes, warhammers, and swords spinning in slow arcs in the style only the Qu'ari elite could command as the weapons built up momentum. A scimitar danced hand-to-hand as Wyrd played with his weapon, bloodlust evident by the sparkle of his eye. Alverick wondered for a moment if the Faceless could even bleed.

"The only way to kill them is by stabbing them in the chest," Ghan addressed the group. "There is a triangular area where they are most vulnerable, starting right under their chin. It's an upside-down triangle, the tip pointing down to where the navel would be on a normal man, so do not go for the neck like you would for a normal enemy."

"They're devilishly fast too," Aria said. "As servants of Aphomet, their only goal is complete chaos and destruction. Watch," she said as she pointed to the closest Faceless as he struck at a soldier. "They slash at the chest primarily instead of anywhere else. They reveal their own weakness."

A spray of blood accompanied by a scream filled the air as the man in blue clutched at his chest. Red seeped through his tattered clothes, and he quickly dropped to the ground. Alverick couldn't tell, but it appeared that this Faceless also managed to slit the man's neck in the strike. Blood poured from the soldier's mouth before he fell face-first onto the ground. A shriek of excitement filled the field, sending chills down the Avalanche's spine that had nothing to do with the freezing weather. They celebrated their kills.

Throughout it all, the barbarians' song grew louder until it reached a crescendo. Finally, with only eight men standing, their song caught the attention of those fighting in the meadow. The Faceless turned at the sound of the singing, their white eyes narrowing in their elongated heads. Shrieks of rage rang out as they turned from their terrified and exhausted opponents to fully face Alverick and his group. Using their distraction to his advantage, Alverick gave a mighty tug on the earth, sending a wave rippling for many leagues and causing the Faceless to stumble. Men in blue and green cried out in surprise as they staggered to keep their balance while the Faceless screeched in confusion. The Avalanche found himself almost dropping to a knee as the familiar red haze blossomed in the periphery of his vision, quickly moving to cover the entirety of it.

At the same time, Dez threw her hands towards the group and unleashed a strong blast of wind in their direction, the silver lines on her arms glowing brightly in the darkened day. The Faceless stopped their advance, the tendrils of shadow on their bodies blowing wildly about. Though their faces were not human, their rage was evident. Their lips turned up in a snarl, exposing their thin, dagger-like teeth. The men behind them took the opportunity to scramble together, creating a united front and shoring up any holes in their defense.

Once the gust slammed into the Faceless, the northmen stopped singing. Their song hung in the air, echoing hauntingly for seconds after. A moment later, they let out a monstrous battle cry and tore through the tall grasses towards the Faceless. The Qu'ari and gods followed right behind them. Brody and Alverick shared a glance, the young man's face shimmering in the red haze of the Avalanche's vision, before Brody stepped in front of the remaining group, standing guard with his sword at the ready.

A twang snapped behind the Avalanche, followed immediately after by a shriek from one of the Faceless as an arrow bathed in electric energy lodged itself into the shoulder of one of the monsters. Alverick heard the redhead curse as she prepared another. The Faceless that she'd struck ripped the arrow out from its body and threw it to the ground. Ignoring those around it, the creature raced towards Alverick's small party.

It weaved in between the northmen and Qu'ari, swipes from its claws catching only the empty air as the humans ducked and dodged the blow. Just as suddenly as it had begun its charge, the Faceless came to an abrupt stop as Ghan stepped in front of it. A frustrated growl emanated from the creature as Ghan weighed his weapon in his hands.

"Your time is over." The deep, steady voice of the god filled the field, cutting through the shrieks and wind.

A toothy grin contorted the creature's face as its fellow Faceless let out a chorus of blood-curdling screeches. Cries from those rushing to monsters were met with more screams from their foe. The unsettling silence that followed left Alverick feeling disconcerted. Blade met claw as the two parties collided. The absence of the sound of steel meeting steel was foreign to the Avalanche.

Ghan and his opponent dashed forward. His battleaxe caught a strike from the Faceless as its claws raced towards his head. The two broke away and began circling each other, sizing each other up. The creature lunged forward once more, feigning a strike with its claws. Ghan, falling for the ruse, brought his axe up once more to parry. A gleeful shriek escaped the creature before it dipped its head and bit down on Ghan's arm. The god screamed in pain as the teeth sunk into his flesh. With a bellow, Ghan slammed the butt of his axe down on the creature's head repeatedly. Another arrow struck the creature's shoulder, this time with no electricity encircling the bolt, while the god continued to slam the monster until it released him.

As soon as the Faceless let go of Ghan, he sent another push into the earth, disorienting the creatures. A blast from Dez flew toward the battling parties right after. Cries of frustration filled the field as the Faceless, who had previously almost eliminated all life in the area, now struggled to maintain the upper hand. Ghan, seizing the opportunity, flew forward and buried his blade in the chest of the Faceless.

In a split second, the creature let out a death cry that froze all in the area. The other Faceless' heads shot up in time to see their comrade dissipate in a cloud of smoke. In its place, a human body dropped to the ground, naked and dead, the blade of Ghan's battleaxe embedded in the man's flesh.

⌐⌐⌐

Raging gusts of wind slammed into the wooden walls of the barn. The structure rattled, shaking bits of dust and debris off and onto those below. Eerie howls seemed to circle the barn as the winds tried to whip through the boards. Every blast drew forth screams from the people crammed inside. Ronan sat crammed in a corner, his hands clenched together in prayer as he listened to the older children cry. He could only imagine that the younger ones in the safety of the cottage were experiencing the same fear.

Calls to the gods beseeching their mercy rang out, cutting through the wailing children. Ronan found himself making similar requests in his own mind. Chilled air seeped through the cracks in the wood, bypassing the sections that had been resealed with clay, and filling the overcrowded building with a heat-leeching freeze. Bodies huddled together, trying to maintain some warmth, only to be denied. Out in the field, the cows lowed in fright, confined to the corral to keep them from running away.

A blast stronger than any of the previous ones threatened to tear down the roof. On the wind, a shriek unlike any other carried through the barn, drawing cries of fright from even the warriors. Closing his eyes, Ronan brought his clasped hands to his mouth and whispered a fervent prayer, begging the gods to let him get through this alive.

⌐⌐⌐

Dez struggled to keep herself from Snapping and losing herself to the curse of the Tempest. Her mind ached now that she was alone instead of sharing her mind with Aria. Every second that she used her blood magic was another second that tugged at her sanity. Her surroundings became blurry as she continued on.

When the first Faceless moved to attack her and the rest of the magi, she pulled her morning star from her hip, letting the weapon hang in her hand as she focused on growing the winds and trying to maintain her Anchor. Images of Vashe as a young girl filled her head, her mind having no idea what her parents looked like since she was only a babe when they were killed.

She also fought against the horror she felt when she saw the evil of the Faceless flee the body of the now fallen man in the middle of the field, his naked flesh barely visible in the tall grasses. The little party she'd traveled with stared in dismay at the turn of events. Dez wondered if they'd be able to continue the fight knowing that they would ultimately be killing humans. She didn't have to speculate for long as a whip of flame flew towards a nearby Faceless, wrapping around its arm and pulling it back far enough that it couldn't reach the dark-haired shieldmaiden.

An ear-splitting shriek sounded as a nearby monster darted towards her. Keeping the winds moving around her, Dez gripped her morning star tighter and widened her stance. The Faceless was quick, closing the distance between them in a matter of seconds. With a grunt, Dez swung her weapon towards the creature, while at the same time slamming a gust of wind against it. The spikes of the morning star cut into the Faceless, causing the monster to let out another scream as the winds sent it staggering back a few steps.

The death of one of their own didn't seem to faze the creature as it raced towards her. Alverick shook the earth around Dez while Caitlyn and the princess shot blasts of magical energy at the monster, but nothing seemed to bother it. Brody, having moved closer to Ghan to assist should he have needed more help, was now sprinting back to Dez. Raising her weapon, she began swinging it in tight arcs around her head.

Moving at a blinding speed, the Faceless dodged the morning star as she threw out a strike towards it, the shadowy smoke billowing behind it in long tendrils. Its claws raised up as it prepared to strike. At the same time, Dez and Alverick hit the Faceless with an attack. The creature dropped to the ground to avoid the gust of wind and negate the quaking effects of the earth at the same time. Dez's jaw dropped as the Faceless jumped back up and continued its rapid advance.

Preparing to summon the dark funnel like she did back in Fa'Tinh, Dez pushed herself as hard as she could. The funnel would hopefully suffocate the creatures and carry them away, possibly impaling them on a tree in the process. She pictured herself reaching up to the heavens and pulling down on the clouds. The darkness above resisted her pull, causing her mind to slam against whatever blocked her. A blinding flash filled her head as pain like she'd never felt before consumed her.

Wind exploded from her in all directions. Muffled cries rang out as her gale buffeted and pulled people and Faceless alike. Her group and other soldiers struggled to find something, anything, to hold on to as their bodies threatened to lift into the air like rag dolls. The Faceless shrieked in startled confusion, their bodies blowing everywhere.

With the turn of her head, Dez faced the field. Lifeless bodies in green and blue were tossed into the air, their corpses twisting about in grotesque directions no body should ever move as the winds played with them. A smile played on Dez's lips as she watched them flip about. Stilling the air, she let them drop to the ground with a sickening crunch.

Behind her, Dez heard a familiar sound. Turning towards the source, the Tempest saw a dimensional gate open and two dark figures step out into the field. Statuesque with alabaster skin and raven hair, Vashe exited the portal. Her hair was tied in a high tail, and she wore riding pants and a form-fitting blouse. Next to her stood a dark-skinned man with a gold band on his arm, his bottoms resembling a white skirt. Black sandals wound halfway up his calves, tied in an intricate knot. He had the same well-worn expression she usually wore; he'd seen many lifetimes.

The urge to toss the pair overwhelmed her, and Dez focused her attentions on the two. All around her, the winds swirled until they were ready. Dez's smile became hungry as she focused on the newcomers.

"*Naran?*" Vashe asked.

In an instant, the wind in the field died. Only Vashe's face, the concerned look of the child she once knew and loved, the girl she raised when Vashe had run away from her home, mattered in that moment. Dez's mind stilled as she gazed at the girl who stood out so clearly. A warmth she hadn't felt in many years filled her, and tears welled in the corners of her eyes. Her little girl had grown up.

A blinding pain tore through her back as the triumphant screech of a Faceless sounded right behind her. Eyes focused on Vashe, Dez dropped to the ground. The winds inside her finally stilled.

XXXIX

Pure anguish ripped through Vashe as she watched blood spray in the air behind the woman who raised her. The long, tapering claws at the end of the Faceless' hands dripped crimson beads. Making eye contact with Vashe, the creature grinned, licking the blood with a thin tongue. The Scrymmen woman's anguish disappeared as rage threatened to consume her. At the Faceless' feet, Dez's small frame lay face-first in the tall grasses.

Powerful gusts of wind that had previously blasted through the field were now replaced with an unsettling stillness. In the distance, a silver-haired woman let loose a keening wail, her face buried in her hands. Her cries went unheard by the Faceless around her, their eyes trained on the two newcomers. A few barred their teeth, anxious to greet the pair.

Vashe's body shook with emotion as she stared at the spot where her mentor once stood. Tears welled in the corners of her eyes, but she blinked furiously in an attempt to keep them from falling. Now was not the time to be consumed by grief. Dseti's hand rested on her back, the simple gesture pulling the Scrymmen woman back from the chaotic emotions that swirled around her.

"I'm sorry," he said softly. "But now is not the time. Don't give Apoph-met the satisfaction of knowing he hurt you. It will only lead to an eternity of heartache."

Pain flashed through the wanderer's face. He was only too familiar with the Ancient's tactics, and he didn't want anyone else to suffer the same fate he had.

The Faceless in front of them cocked its head as if inviting her to challenge it. Hardening her eyes, Vashe tapped into her Shadow abilities and reached out, hoping the creatures had something she could grab onto. The tall grasses made it difficult to locate any shadows, and the lack of sunshine made it even more difficult, but to her delight, Vashe managed to find a little spot in the grass that she could grab ahold of. A smile tugged on the corner of her mouth, her eyes staring daggers at the Faceless the whole time, as she seized the opportunity and locked onto it.

Shrieking in the field resumed as the other Faceless turned their attentions to the survivors once more. In the background, Vashe could see fyre bindings latching onto one of the creatures, holding it in place as a Qu'ari elite landed multiple strikes against the monster with his warhammer and battleaxe. The blows elicited a multitude of screams from the Faceless, but no sign of injury was visible. After playing with the creature, the Qu'ari went in for a killing blow, landing his axe squarely in the Faceless' chest.

Another death cry shook the field and froze all involved in the battle. The Faceless struggled to break free as its shadow essence leaked from the wound in its chest. In the course of its thrashing, one of the flame ropes was broken, and the creature managed to pull on the other fyre binding, throwing the Flame off-balance and roughly onto the ground.

Still fighting as its life leaked out from its wound, the Faceless wrenched itself free from the remaining flame rope and launched itself towards the Qu'ari. The man stood rooted to the spot, surprised at the creature's sudden aggression. He brought up his warhammer in a defensive posture, his axe still embedded in the creature's chest. As the Faceless closed the distance between the two, the blur of a second battleaxe flew toward the creature, sinking deeply into the Faceless' chest next to the other. A final death shriek ripped from the monster as the remainder of its shadow essence exploded from it, revealing the naked form of another man slumping to the ground.

Vashe couldn't believe what she saw. The two Qu'ari pulled their axes from the man's chest, shaking off the blood that now flowed freely from his wounds in the process. She found that she couldn't spend too much time focusing on the battle. In front of her, a black form lunged forward, hoping to get within striking distance. Vashe let out an involuntary gasp as Dez's murderer launched its attack. Her gasp was shared by the Faceless as the monster realized it could not actually move. Her Shadow magic proved successful, and she was able to restrain it.

Rage was clearly visible on its face as it let out a scream. Vashe found herself unfazed by its outburst, something that she was sure would normally leave her trembling as she faltered in her attack. The creature pulled and tugged at its leg, straining against her magic to break free, but Vashe held strong. Its eyes glowered at her, the whites seeming to stare into the depths of her very soul. Images of Dez, her smile dazzling in the bright sunlight, shifted to ones of her parents, their hands poised to strike her once more. Pain, despair, and love filled her in one instant as the memories flashed before her.

The Scrymmen woman found herself hesitating. In that moment, her grip on the Faceless weakened, and the creature charged at her in an effort to break free. In the back of her mind, Dseti called out to Vashe, his voice sounding muffled and far away as he called to her to focus. Her Shadow hold on the Faceless slackened as she was lost in her own emotions. The Faceless gave one final cry as it tugged against her, the strain on her magic catching her attention.

With a snap, Vashe redirected her attentions to her blood magic energy and clamped down on the Faceless, stopping its advance. The creature growled in anger as it tried to rip itself free from her grasp. Seeing that her resolve was unwavering, the growl turned into a roaring shriek of rage. The ground beneath them rumbled, their footing becoming tenuous as one of the Avalanche's quakes shook the earth. The Faceless was brought to its knees, unable to stand with its balance compromised.

In the background, another death cry from one of the Faceless reverberated in the clearing. With each death, the air became warmer as the effects of the Faceless lessened. Small spots of sun managed to peek through the darkness, the crimson ring of Toron's moon breaking through.

Dseti stepped in front of Vashe, the gold band on his arm glowing a brilliant white. The light illuminated the area, catching the eye of the Scrymmen woman and those around her. Its dazzling brilliance blinded the Faceless, its arm raised in an attempt to shield its eyes. A cry of fear tore from the creature as it struggled to get back to its feet and flee.

"I can only do this once," Dseti said, turning to face Vashe.

Focusing on the Ancient, Vashe studied his movements, reaching out to him with her own magic to touch his. The two connected, and Vashe was able to experience everything he did. Dseti reached into his own energy reserves and tapped into something the Scrymmen woman didn't fully understand. It was an Ancient magic that reminded her of the mystery surrounding Enlil. It was something that hadn't been seen in centuries. At the same time, it felt familiar, almost reminding her of the power that washed over her when she draughted the two vials of blood bathed in the holy water of Maeyu'dana's temple. Pure, raw, unbridled.

Subconsciously, Vashe found herself reaching into her own reserves and touching the same power she had within. Energy blazed within her, catching her off-guard and almost causing her to lose her grip on the Faceless. The two, now fueled with an energy that was unrivaled by anyone nearby, reached out to the Faceless.

Vashe penetrated the Faceless, gazing into its depths. Chaos swirled within the miasma of the creature. Hate, rage, pain — a multitude of emotions all competed with each other for dominance. Vashe sifted through everything until she found what she was looking for. Buried deep within the

Faceless, she found a small shred of human essence wrapped in layers of darkness.

With a small poke, Vashe reached out and touched the humanity. A shiver of silver shimmered on the surface. Its humanity hadn't been completely stripped and still survived. Following the Ancient's lead, Vashe and Dseti continued to reach out to the human essence, stroking it until the silver life force engulfed it. Warmth began to seep out from the essence, growing and illuminating the darkness that had once buried it. The two didn't let up.

Working together, the pair massaged the Faceless' humanity until, in a blinding burst of light, the creature was engulfed in white-hot brilliance. An ear-piercing scream pulled Vashe's mind's eye from inside the creature. Shadow essence burst from the monster, expelled in all directions as the creature's death knell shook the battlefield. Once the blackness had escaped, the naked form of a young woman, her curly hair falling to her mid-back, dropped to the ground. Vashe watched the spot in front of her where the woman fell with baited breath. Several long moments later, the woman sat up. She appeared dazed, but quickly noticed her immodesty and folded her arms across her chest to cover her breasts.

A burst of joy filled Vashe as she realized the true power of binding — the girl was still alive. She could free these people.

~~~

A pair of white eyes stared at Wyrd, its head tilted in mock amusement at the Qu'ari man who stood in front of it with just a scimitar in his hands. Bloodlust filled him as his adrenaline pounded in his veins. A desire to tear the creature into shreds filled him the same way his appetite for Fyre had consumed him. Let the thing underestimate him. His victory would taste all the sweeter when it lay bleeding on the ground.

Knowing that the Faceless was just a human cloaked in shadows only added to Wyrd's anticipation. His scimitar bounced from hand-to-hand, the
~~~

Qu'ari licking his lips as he waited for his opening. Somewhere behind him, he heard one of the creatures' death cries. Three down, if he was counting correctly. Wyrd didn't know how many were there at the beginning of the fight, but there hadn't been more than ten.

A low growl rumbled from the Faceless, the creature's mouth twisting up in a grotesque grin as it watched the Qu'ari. A moment later, something snapped, and the two dashed towards each other in one fluid motion. Wyrd's scimitar raised in preparation for a sweeping strike, only to be blocked by the claws of the Faceless. The two exchanged blows in rapid succession, the steel hitting claws as they rained silent blows upon each other.

Cursing as he could not land a clean hit, Wyrd put some distance between the two of them. He tried to reassess his opponent, but the creature kept pushing forward, throwing him off as he tried to formulate his next plan of attack. The Faceless moved through the tall grasses faster than he anticipated, closing the distance between the two of them. An arcing swipe from one of its claws caught Wyrd off-guard. He brought his scimitar up for a block, but the motion was sloppy.

The weight of the strike pushed Wyrd back, and he ended up stutter-stepping backwards as he tried to maintain his balance. Taking advantage of its forward momentum, the Faceless pushed down on the Qu'ari, causing him to drop to one knee. Gritting his teeth, Wyrd tried to push back, his muscles quivering at the exertion. Somewhere, he felt the ground beneath him shaking as the Avalanche sought to help those fighting the monsters.

"Damned Avalanche," he muttered as he strained to return to his feet.

A black mass shot out as the Faceless landed a powerful kick to Wyrd's chest. He felt his ribs crack as the blow landed. His body flew back, eliciting a gasp of surprise at the strength behind the kick. An excruciating pain exploded in his head as he hit a rock. Darkness engulfed him as the Faceless approached him with a toothy smile.

XL

WATCHING DEZ'S BODY FALL lifeless to the ground sent a wave of shock through Alverick's body. When Vashe turned her master's murderer into a young woman, dazed and confused as she sat naked in the tall grass, he couldn't believe his eyes. Despite knowing that these hellish creatures were actually humans transformed, seeing them return to their normal selves was nothing short of mind-boggling. The red haze steadily seeping into his line of sight stopped as he almost forgot to maintain his hold on the earth as he manipulated it with his Avalanche energies.

The arrival of the Scrymmen woman and her companion had been unexpected, but at this point, he wasn't sure if another god would join the battle, or whether he would have the energy in him to react. His body ached from the strain of pulling on the earth's plates, and the constant presence of the red haze in his vision was worrying, but he pushed aside his concerns. There were still Faceless fighting in the field, and he couldn't afford to be distracted.

In the distance, he heard men crying out as they were struck by the razor-sharp claws of the Faceless. Turning his attention to the tall grasses, he saw one of the creatures working its way through a group of soldiers dressed in blue and green livery. Their weapons seemed to have no effect on the monster as it decimated the small cluster with unnatural ease. Alverick grabbed the earth's plates and gave them a shake, causing it to rumble where the men stood and resulting in several of the men falling down, narrowly avoiding a death strike. The Faceless stopped its advance, unsure of how to best balance itself as the earth shook.

With each tug on the earth, Alverick's vision turned a deeper shade of red as more of it encroached on his normal sight. His body shook with fatigue at the prolonged expenditure of energy. Sweat beaded on his brow and arms, and his lungs burned like he'd just run a great distance. Alverick never realized that his Avalanche powers had the same physical drawbacks as a Tempest.

"Al!" Brody's voice called out. It sounded so far away.

Several others shouted to him as well, each one muffled and difficult to hear. Alverick watched as Vashe took off towards the field, hoping to release more of the people trapped in their Faceless bodies. Her companion, a dark-skinned man in strange clothing, trailed after her. The two headed to the nearest creature that was fighting against all three of the northmen. The shieldmaiden swung her battleaxe in a mighty arc, leaving herself deliberately open as her countrymen guarded her on both flanks. Each held their own axes in defensive postures, waiting to see how the Faceless would reply.

Movement caught his attention, drawing him away from the northmen's Faceless as it moved to attack. Alverick saw Wyrd face off against one of the creatures on his own with just a scimitar in his hand. He didn't even take advantage of the two-handed style of the Qu'ari elite. Alverick found himself wondering if the man even trained in the style of the elite, but the thought was pulled from his mind as a pair of hands roughly grabbed him.

"Al!" Brody screamed into his face.

Blinking, Alverick tried to push the redness away so he could focus on his friend. It didn't.

"Stop it!"

Brody pointed to his right, to Alverick's front. One of the Faceless raced towards their group, its claws raised in preparation to attack. Cienna and Caitlyn hurled bolts of electricity and waves of water at the monster in a vain attempt to slow it down. Neither seemed to have any effect on it. Cienna's voice could be heard speaking incoherently in a panicked, high-pitched voice as the Faceless quickly closed the distance between them.

Raising his sword with a curse, Brody stopped squeezing Alverick and turned to face the monster. With a mighty yell, Brody ran towards the creature, putting himself between the Faceless and the women.

"Al!"

The Avalanche's head snapped to the left, towards the sound. Bannen stood next to him, terror etched into his face as he watched his little brother approach the monster. His hand reached for the sword he usually kept on his back, but he realized he didn't have it anymore. As he watched his friend frantically reach for his blade, Averick came to the realization that he had left the sword back at Pharn after his return from the Abyss.

In a moment of clarity, Alverick shook away the red clouds fogging his mind and pulled his own sword. Charging towards his friend, Alverick sent a wave of tremors through the earth, disorienting the Faceless and halting its charge. Taking advantage of its confusion, Alverick let out a war cry and pointed his sword towards the triangular spot on the creature's chest.

Behind him, he could hear both Bannen and Brody shouting at him, their words lost to him. Brody let out a scream and charged the Faceless as well. Before Alverick reached the Faceless, an arrow embedded itself into the creature's chest, the electric energy wrapped around the shaft released upon contact, immobilizing the monster and drawing a pained scream from it.

Its body slumped from the dual impact of the arrow hit and the electrical attack. Barely standing, the Faceless' head drooped, its arms hanging slack at its sides. Using that moment, Alverick plunged his sword into the triangle almost to the hilt. At the same time, Brody thrust his blade into the sweet spot on the other side of the arrow. His hit went deeper.

The group was rewarded with a death shriek as the shadow essence was expelled from the Faceless. Blackness spilled from its body, shooting in all directions as it writhed in its pain during its final moments. Alverick and Brody watched as the shadows melted from the Faceless' body, revealing the soft, pink flesh underneath. As the chest was exposed, the swords and arrow remained stuck in the man's skin, blood pouring from the wounds in rivers. The entrance wound around the arrow was charred from the release of electric energy that accompanied the bolt.

Collapsing face-first onto the earth, the naked figure was quickly buried in the tall grasses. Alverick felt a hand on his shoulder and saw Bannen standing behind him. His friend stared down at the body, his eyes filled with pity as he looked upon the fallen man. Alverick's head pounded his vision so red that he could barely see anything else. Two death screams echoed back-to-back in the distance. They still sent shivers down his back despite the warming temperatures and the sun peeking through the dissipating darkness.

"I can't believe it," Bannen muttered, his voice cracking. "Who would've thought things would have come to this?"

"The attack on the mines kicked off an insane chain of events," Alverick agreed. "Are you glad you're gone?"

The question hurt Alverick to ask, but the thought of his friend living through such harrowing times caused him pain as well.

"Sometimes." The honest answer didn't surprise the Avalanche. "I wish Brody didn't have to go through this either."

"Aye."

"Thank you for protecting him," Bannen said after a prolonged period of silence. "I don't deserve how much you've done for me."

"I'd do anything for you."

The calm between the two stretched, the pressure of Bannen's hand on Alverick's shoulder fading with each passing second. Alverick felt a tear run down his cheek as another death scream shook the field.

"This is my last time seeing you, isn't it?"

A sigh.

"It's for the best," Bannen said softly. "I can't keep holding you back."

A sniffle escaped the Avalanche. He felt empty inside, in spite of the sharp pain in his head. Alverick tried to speak but found that he couldn't. All he could do was nod.

"Good-bye, old friend," Bannen whispered. "Until next time."

"May you find peace in the Halls of the Fallen," Alverick croaked. "Wait for me."

As the devastation continued in the field, blood spraying everywhere and staining the grass red, Hera could only watch in dismay. Somewhere out in the field, the deep, echoing song of the barbarians rang out, their voices sounding over the shrieks and death cries. Their rich, booming voices both terrified Hera and filled her with hope at the same time.

"Your majesty," one of her guards implored as he lightly tugged on her arm. "We need to get you to safety. It's too dangerous out here for you."

At that moment, the female barbarian let out a mighty cry as she dashed towards one of the hellish creatures. On either flank, her male companions charged as well, the three raising their battleaxes up high. The Faceless turned to meet the trio, its sharp teeth barred in a threatening grin as it lifted its arms to strike. The three never backed down or slowed their charge. Instead, the two men continued their song, their voices growing in strength despite their exertions as they raced towards the monster.

With a cry of shock, the creature staggered back a step as a ball of water exploded upon its chest. Turning its attention to the knoll where the attack came from, the monster let out a hiss that the queen could only describe as seething. Her eyes also followed the creature's, and she saw a mop of blonde hair and a ball of water appear in front of the person. A gasp escaped the queen's mouth as she recognized her daughter despite being so far away.

The distraction was enough for the female barbarian to close the distance between herself and the Faceless, giving her the opportunity to launch herself into the air and bury her axe into its chest. Almost simultaneously, a bear of a man with a mane of thick, blond hair approached from the side, thrusting his battleaxe into the creature's arm, stopping it from swiping at the woman. A moment later, a second barbarian, smaller than his enormous counterpart but large nonetheless, slammed his axe into the creature's other arm, immobilizing it and eliciting a scream of rage from the monster. Calling out to his god, the beast of a barbarian let out a mighty roar as he ripped his blade from the Faceless' arm, a dark spray of what appeared to be blood flying through the air from the wound, and slammed it into the monster's chest next to his female companion's.

As the creature let out its death cry, a tall figure seemed to approach the fight from the trees. The shadowy essence of the Faceless that exploded from it as it fell to the earth nearly obscured the man's arrival, but the queen saw him approach. Dressed in clothes similar to the dark-skinned man who arrived with the statuesque woman that Hera believed was Vashe, the newcomer entered the fray, a strange-looking sickle-shaped sword glinting in his hand.

No one else seemed to notice the man as the fighting continued. No one but the dark-skinned man. Pulling his own khopesh from his hip, the man made his way down the knoll towards the newcomer. Cries of the wounded and dying rang out, blending in with the occasional shriek announcing the demise of one of the Faceless, but it all sounded muted as the queen focused on the seemingly separate interaction between the two men.

Though she could not hear anything, Hera knew that a tense exchange was taking place. The dark-skinned man with a golden armband gestured to their surroundings, his brow knotted in consternation. The other man's eyes flashed dangerously, almost becoming a burnt orange color as he stood, unmoved by the other's words. There was something familiar about the second man with orange eyes.

Her mind floated away, and a vision came to her. Out on the field amidst the fallen bodies in red, green, and blue livery, a tall man stood in the shadows, his eyes flashing as he surveyed the carnage below. The picture came to her so suddenly and so vividly that she let out a gasp. In the background, she felt a firm yet gentle pressure on her arm, pulling her back, and a man's voice shouting to her incomprehensible words. A second vision popped into her mind — a young girl with periwinkle hair and a cream-colored dress stood next to her, her tiny hand clasping the queen's as they stared down at the death and destruction in front of them.

Everything faded away, and Hera watched the two men engage each other, their khopesh ringing out into the emptiness as the two blades struck each other. Dead bodies lay scattered on the ground, their eyes staring into the void. The shadow monsters that had been wreaking devastation only moments before faded away, leaving only the two men, the queen, the little girl that she now recognized as Freyna, and the circle of monolithic stones surrounding a golden flower.

As the strange man dashed at the man with the golden band, one of the stones in the circle surrounding the golden flower glowed a muted rust color for a brief moment. A second stone glowed with a pure yellow for an instance before it faded to the smooth luster of a dark grey river stone. Hera wondered what the importance of the glowing meant to their fate. On occasion, two of the other stones glowed silver and one a faint periwinkle as the fighting continued.

Why? The queen struggled to understand but gave up as the two men exchanged rapid khopesh strikes amongst the fallen bodies.

The two swung fast and hard, their blades a blur to the queen's eyes. The man with the armband danced back as he struggled to block his opponent's attacks. The orange-eyed man pressed his advantage, his strikes landing with deadly precision had they found home. Next to the queen, Hera felt the winds pick up as Freyna watched the battle with agitation on her face. Her periwinkle hair whipped around her and her eyes darkened, but the goddess did not dare interfere with the fighters.

"What's going on?" Hera asked, her words torn from her throat by the winds.

With the familiar hiss of the wind, the goddess replied, *"The Ancients must not be interfered with. Your fate is in their hands now."*

"Ancients?" the queen asked.

"Apophmet grew tired of Vahnyre's failures," Freyna explained. *"Dseti has struggled to keep him preoccupied while we aethren try to maintain the balance amongst ourselves. Re'niuhktet has been gone for too long; we don't know what happened to the Elder God, but if Dseti fails, Apophmet will be unstoppable."*

"By the gods," Hera cursed under her breath. "And there's nothing we can do? Damnation."

〜〜〜

Alverick watched as the two men engaged in combat, their blades ringing out in the air despite the cries of the dead, the dying, and the cries of the Faceless. His vision swam red as he pulled on the earth, shaking the ground as much as he dared to, but wondering if he should push both his powers and the quaking further. At the same time, his body was on the verge of collapse, the exhaustion and emptiness he felt at knowing he was alone. Without Bannen, the Avalanche found himself feeling vulnerable, exposed now that he didn't have anyone to watch his back.

Behind him, Brody's voice called out to him, the pressure of the young man's hand rubbing the Avalanche's back in an effort to snap Alverick back to the present. A rapid stream of curses escaped Brody's lips as he must have noticed the battling men dancing between the remaining Faceless. Glints of steel flashed in the light, the clanging ringing fast and furious as the two exchanged what would have been devastating blows with their khopesh. The fighters were impervious to the rumblings of Alverick's quakes, their feet moving deftly upon the trembling earth as the remaining soldiers in blue livery fell to the ground.

As the Avalanche's vision swam red, he felt himself slipping away from his surroundings once more. The sky grew dark, and the familiar, eerie feeling of being watched returned. With a shake, Alverick struggled to keep himself from slipping into Themba. The Land of the Dead continued to try to pull him back. As he hovered between the two realms, Alverick noted that the two men no longer looked like the strangers weaving their way through the battlefield. Their clothes changed, the styles reminiscent of some ancient civilization from long ago.

Wearing a gold armband, one man fought bare-chested, the thin sliver of a scar across his chest visible in the wavering darkness. The cream-colored wrap around his waist contrasted against the darkened flesh. A golden chain hung around his neck, bearing a key-like pendant that looped at the top, the chain fitting in between the hole of the loop on the top. Black sandals wrapped up to his knees flexed as his weight shifted with each movement. A thin line of kohl ringed his eyes, extending out to the side of each eye.

His opponent wore a similar garb, his wrap accentuated with orange thread and had bits of turquoise sewn in between the orange accents. No jewelry adorned his body otherwise. Upon his flesh, ancient symbols were inscribed along his side. His hair hung down his back in a low tail, the dark braids encircled with small circlets of gold.

The man with the bejeweled wrap darted forward, his head ducking as he slipped under a khopesh strike, and slammed his shoulder into his opponent's chest. With a gasp of pain, the other man stumbled back, his arm dropping as he fought to maintain his balance. Quicker than he could blink, Alverick watched as the man leapt upon his foe, taking him to the ground with a heavy thud.

～～～

Hera watched in horror as Vashe's companion, Dseti, fell to the ground, his opponent on top. A hungry grin spread across the orange-clad man's face as he repositioned himself. Beneath him, Dseti struggled to free his arms, but they were pinned to his side between Apophmet's thighs. Shrieks of the Faceless echoed around them, piercing the silence of the desolate land the queen stood upon now. Though she couldn't see them, Hera knew they were still wreaking havoc in the meadow she'd been in moments before.

At her side, the goddess Freyna hissed as Dseti's body fell. The aethren's body tensed as her petite frame shook. Though she came to Hera in the form of a young girl, the queen knew that an unknown power swirled within. A strong wind already encircled the two, tugging at their clothes and pulling at their hair. A steady stream of curses followed as the pair watched Dseti work to throw Apophmet off of him, the goddess' words coming out fast and incomprehensible to the queen. Despite his best efforts, Apophmet could not be dislodged.

"What can we do?" Hera asked, her voice coming out little more than a whisper. "Surely there's something to be done."

The ground beneath them roiled as if even the earth herself cried out in distress. Hera fought to maintain her footing, her arms flailing wildly as she repositioned her feet to stabilize herself.

No response came from the goddess, though the winds around them intensified.

XLI

Turning her attention away from the remaining Faceless, Vashe found herself slipping into some sort of trance. The scenery around her melted away, leaving her in the abandoned temples of Enlil. The stones crumbled beneath her feet as she made her way through the holy shrine. The eerie feeling of being watched, the same one she'd felt as she and Dseti fled the enchanted land, returned, sending a shiver down her spine. It felt like pure evil followed her.

Tendrils of ivy crept along the stone pillars, the tall grasses poking through the flooring. Sooner than she expected, Vashe found herself at the mosaic of Maeyu'dana. The Ancient stared back at the Scrymmen woman with a beautiful serenity, filling Vashe with peace. The blood in her veins warmed, and the new tattoos on her arms, the ones she'd achieved through the draughting, began to glow. Her heart pounded in her chest as she struggled to piece everything together.

The warmth in her arms didn't bother her as much as the deafening silence that continued to permeate her surroundings. Catching the gaze of the Ancient, Vashe felt a strong urge to return to the pool she'd visited once before. Each step she took filled her both with dread and confidence that she was making the right decision. Each step brought her closer to her destiny, one that she couldn't shake.

The waters of the pool were crystal clear, with lily pads floating on the surface. Beneath, the fish that had circled and blessed the vials of blood Vashe had washed in the waters only days before now darted about in agitated movements. Occasionally she saw a rune of protection, but more often than not, their direction was erratic, mimicking the chaos that befell Corinth.

Kneeling down, Vashe dipped her hands in the cool waters, tracing the ancient runes into the rippling pool as a means to calm herself. The repetitive act brought her a small measure of comfort, much like the mosaic of Maeyu'dana had earlier. Protection. Strength. Healing. Over and over, she traced the symbols. With each completed rune, the fish slowed, their motions returning to the lazy circles they'd drawn when she first beheld the pool. Soon, they joined her in creating the powerful symbols.

He must be awoken.

The words rang in her ears as smooth as honey, filling her entire being, while at the same time there was not a sound. Vashe paused her tracings for a moment, her body taut as she strained to find the source of the message. One of the fish bumped into her hand, still dipped into the water, as it continued its swimming.

Without the Elder Brother, Apophmet's desire for destruction will not stop here. The aethren dare not openly defy him, so it is up to you to summon Re'nukhtet.

"How?" Vashe's voice rang out in the emptiness.

Return to those you are meant to protect, and when Themba comes for you, do not fight the dead. The veil will reveal more than just what lies beyond.

Vashe suddenly became aware that the fish still touched her fingers. As it swam away, whatever she'd been communicating with disappeared, their connection broken. She found herself back on the knoll, overlooking the chaos in the meadow. However, the beautiful emerald grasses and the small patches of azure sky peeking out from the darkness that had prevailed the last few days were gone. In its stead, everything was dark. Barren. Dead.

Gnarled tree branches reached towards the heavens like the fingers of a mystic, exhausted after a lifetime of use. The earth was littered with stones and dirt, occasionally interrupted by a thistle or dry blades of grass.

A full moon, the blood moon, hung overhead, a ring of faded crimson encircling the brightly glowing orb. Gloomy clouds hid the stars, allowing only the light of the moon to peek through. The branches and sparse shrubbery that were surrounding her swayed gently, as if blown by a gentle breeze. No breath of wind disturbed the area. Goose flesh prickled on her skin as an electric current coursed through her as some unknown source observed her. Vashe couldn't discern its intent, so she kept her guard up. She almost reached out with her Shadow energies, but remembered Dseti's warning back in Enlil and restrained herself.

At her feet, Vashe felt a small rumble, causing the pebbles to dance across the ground. Taking a chance, the Scrymmen woman sent out tentative tendrils of Shadow energy. She kept her senses on high alert, ready to withdraw or drop the magic in an instance, but as she felt no resistance or unexpected energies in response, Vashe kept going. Her efforts were rewarded when she felt the familiar pulse of Alverick in the distance.

The clang of steel on steel startled Vashe, breaking her connection with the Avalanche as she tensed up, her senses straining as she tried to find the source of the noise. Following the sound, Vashe crept forward until she came upon the battling Ancients. Dseti and Apophmet, the latter glowing with a slight orange aura, moved with almost blinding speed, their khopesh flashing in a dizzying dance. With a blink, Vashe fought back a gasp as Dseti found himself on his back, Apophmet's blade closing in on the other's scar-marked chest.

Without a thought, Vashe reached out with her Shadow energies and pulled at Apophmet, freezing his arm mid-strike. At the same time, she found herself crying out with her mind for help. The stronger Ancient turned his head in her direction, a manic gleam in his eye and a hungry smile on his lips. Adrenaline coursed through the Scrymmen woman as she felt herself become paralyzed. Whether Apophmet had grabbed onto her or it was through fear, Vashe could not tell. All she knew was that her body would not respond to her commands.

Holy Aria, send help! she pleaded.

"You've saved me the trouble and come to me, I see," Apophmet's voice rang out.

Under Apophmet's weight, Dseti struggled, his muscles straining as he searched for a way to throw his opponent off. At the same time, Vashe fought to free herself as well. She noticed Alverick in the distance, but he did not appear to see her; his attentions were instead focused on something else, presumably preparing his next attack. Prayers to her patron goddess, Aria, raced through her mind, her voice caught in her throat as she felt the energy pulsating from Apophmet. Thoughts of how to awaken the final Ancient also darted through, but no answers could be found.

In a moment of despair, Vashe begged the Ancient, one she'd never explored or fully understood despite her endless hours of studies, for aid. Having abandoned her own goddess, Vashe hoped Re'nukhtet would both hear her and answer her call.

A wave of pain shot through her as Apophmet broke free of her Shadow hold, the strength of his primal energy leaving the Scrymmen woman feeling as though he ripped a piece of her apart the moment he freed himself. A cry broke from Vashe's lips, her body nearly crumpling but somehow managing to be held up by the Ancient's will. The tang of blood filled her mouth, causing Vashe to spit whatever was in there onto the ground. Sweat sheened on her brow, and her breath came out in ragged gasps.

Gods, spare me! Vashe implored.

Turning towards the Scrymmen woman once more, Apophmet met her gaze for the briefest of instances, a flash of victory twinkling in his eye, before returning his attentions to Dseti and plunging his khopesh into the other's already scarred flesh. As the blade fell, Vashe tried to reach out and grab the Ancient's hand, but her magic seemed to be blocked. Dseti let out a cry as the blade pierced his flesh, drawing blood as it sank deep into his chest. Apophmet also roared, his body going rigid as he relished his victory.

Mighty Re'nukhtet, have mercy on our souls, Vashe prayed.

〜〜〜

Bewildered at how the Ancient managed to see him, Alverick continued to tug at the earth in hopes of releasing Vashe's companion from his opponent. The powerful being's words terrified the Avalanche as they rang in his head long after he'd uttered them, unrelenting. Going in for the kill, the evil being suddenly froze mid-strike, as though something more powerful had grabbed his arm in an effort to stay his hand.

The pressure mounted in the ground below him as the Avalanche cajoled the earth, hoping to provide a big enough tremor to free the downed man. Using the momentary pause to his advantage, Alverick came up with an idea. His mind already nearly split and his vision swimming red, Alverick began stoking his Spark energies while still playing with the earth. He didn't think it was possible, but the red haze that distorted his vision became darker, almost burgundy. His mind stretched in multiple directions, his thoughts becoming chaotic and his memories muddled as his reality threatened to break.

Ignoring the danger, Alverick built up his energies. Currents of electricity licked around his fingers, the flow of his gift wrapping up his wrist and expanding into a shield of energy around his hand. His mind felt fuzzy as the Avalanche strengthened his strikes. Alverick struggled to find an Anchor to help keep his focus as the Spark energy around his hand flickered as he reached his limit. Fren's face flashed into his mind for a moment before fading to black, the smell of his famous stew filling his nose and disappearing just as quickly.

Alverick tried to call up images of others, but Brody, Ronan, Jaste, and anyone else from his time in the Guard only came up as shadows. Swallowing the lump that formed in his throat, Alverick had to accept that even Bannen would not come to him, leaving him feeling more alone than he was before arriving in Themba. Praying that he would find his Anchor, Alverick thought of Caitlyn. He'd hoped to use her as a last resort because the thought of not being able to think of her terrified him.

Seconds crept by as a darkened figure stood on the edge of his memory. A tear rolled down his cheek as he realized that he'd lost everything. His body slumped, and the electricity encircling his hand, having moved up to his forearm, flickered again as he almost dropped his concentration and lost it all. The Avalanche's head ached as his mind continued to pull itself apart. With a deep exhalation of resignation, Alverick focused what little he could on his god energies, preparing to strike. The bejeweled Ancient raised his khopesh and brought the blade down on his opponent.

A shout ripped from Alverick's throat as he slammed his hand to the ground, unleashing the full force of his quake and sending the electric current encircling his arm into the earth towards the Ancient. Unbidden, the image of Caitlyn and him kissing in the gorge blossomed in his mind. He could feel her soft lips against his, the tips of her fingers pressing against his jaw as he pulled her closer. In that instant, he was afforded a moment of clarity, and he watched in horror as the Ancient's blade struck home. At the same time, the Ancient let out a bellow as the full force of Alverick's Spark energy encompassed him.

<div align="center">~~~</div>

The battling Ancients carried on, much to Hera's horror. Dseti fought valiantly, but he was outmatched by Apophmet. The Ancient had an eternity's worth of experience to draw upon and countless lifetimes of studying the various fighting styles of the different civilizations. Try as he might, Dseti couldn't keep up, and as he landed on his back, Hera found herself uttering a small shriek. At her side, Freyna continued to hiss under her breath, the winds around the two growing stronger.

As Apophmet hovered over the fallen Dseti, his khopesh poised to strike, Freyna broke away from the queen's side and neared the two Ancients. Her periwinkle hair whipped around her as the goddess let her emotions get the better of her. The cream-colored dress billowed around her, and any bits of dead grass nearby flailed around. Apophmet's blade dropped, the tip pointed at Dseti's chest. Throwing her arms out in his direction, Freyna unleashed a blast of wind at the Ancient, slamming into his back moments before the blade pierced flesh.

A cry of rage escaped the Ancient as his body tensed from the onslaught of the attack.

XLII

A SHIVER RAN DOWN Aria's spine as a tingle tickled her mind. The goddess worked with her brother to slow down the advance of the Faceless. The northmen, strong sons and daughter of Re'nukhtet, and the brothers of Xan fought admirably, their attacks perfectly coordinated as they worked together to take down the servants of Apophmet. The northmen sang, their voices ringing in the meadow and breaking the haunting shrieks that lingered in the air after every cry. Aria noted how it filled the trembling men of Alocar with a shred of hope, their ranks tightening as best they could despite the rumblings from the Avalanche.

The tingle came once more, pulling her attention away from the field. The powerful song she'd been listening to moments before suddenly sounded distant. Scanning the area, Aria saw Alverick watching the battle intently. Checking the rest of the field, she saw Vashe staring off into the horizon, her eyes watching some unknown battle. Following her gaze, the goddess saw something that made her blood run cold: Apophmet had come down to Corinth. Realization struck her as she noted that there hadn't been any quakes from the Avalanche in quite some time. Neither he nor Vashe seemed to notice anything other than whatever they observed between the two battling Ancients.

Trepidation causing her heart to race, Aria looked to see if anyone else was pulled into the trance-like state that Vashe and Alverick were in. Arrows flew and water exploded upon and around the Faceless as the red-headed archer and princess of Zanir worked fervently to distract the Faceless. Their efforts were rewarded as the young Xanan leader slipped out from under the swiping strike from one of the monsters, avoiding a debilitating injury. His general took a swing and was rewarded with the blade of his battleaxe sinking into the Faceless' arm. The creature screamed in rage, wrenching its arm back and pulling the general along with him.

A blast of water caught the monster by surprise, followed shortly after by an arrow to its shoulder, giving the general enough time to free his blade and beat a hasty retreat. As the Faceless turned its attention to the women, the Xanan leader landed a slice to the monster's leg with his scimitar, drawing its attention back to him and the general. Their concerted efforts managed to distract the Faceless enough to slow down their progress. The group from Alocar and some of the Zanirian soldiers still fell, but not as quickly as they had before. However, there weren't many remaining despite the resistance from the small group of warriors.

Her attentions were drawn to the collection of Zanirian soldiers as they struggled to keep the Faceless away from a tall woman standing by the pond surrounded by smooth stones. Aria started as she recognized the queen standing a little ways off from Freyna, the young aethren's hair billowing around her as she focused her attentions on Apophmet. The dark Ancient lurched back and forth as he was hit with blasts from Freyna and the other two.

Glancing over at her brother, Aria felt confident that he would not miss her if she left. Ghan stalked through the field, drawing the remaining Faceless to him and away from the humans. His axe swung loosely in his hand, taunting the dark creatures and enraging them. Satisfied that he would not be in danger, Aria slipped off to the perimeter of the field and hid in the shadows. Allowing her mind to slip into herself, Aria focused on the two Ancients and let their energies pull her to them.

The vibrant colors of her surroundings melted away and were replaced by the dreariness of the Land of the Dead. An involuntary shiver, unrelated to the tingling in the back of her mind that brought her to Themba, ran down her spine. She hated visiting the realm, preferring to spend her time closer to the living, affording her the chance to help guide those in trouble down a brighter path. The last time she'd been there was before her little brother, Czand, had strayed from his duties and given himself to Vahnyre, becoming Alazi. A tear welled in the corner of the aethren's eye as she thought of her brother. She pushed the thought from her mind, knowing that that was an issue for another day. For now, she focused on Vashe's voice calling out to her.

In her mind, the song of praise and victory from the northmen echoed, giving her strength as she searched for Vashe and the others. It didn't take long, but she quickly located everyone thanks to the sound of the ringing khopesh. It almost felt muted, the volume of the northmen's song growing with each second.

The battle came into view, and Aria sucked in her breath as she beheld the true devastation of the scene. Dseti laid on the ground, the blade of Apophmet's khopesh sticking out of his chest. Blood flowed from the wound, and the Ancient's eyes were closed as he lay on the ground. Hovering above him, Apophmet let out a roar of rage as his body stiffened. He relinquished his grip on the khopesh's handle as he looked around.

Following his gaze, Aria quickly found Vashe and Alverick close by. A little further away, she was surprised to see Freyna standing near the queen of Zanir, the goddess' hair whipping around her as she braced herself for retaliation. Aria could see the anger and fear in the little aethren's eyes, her pale skin revealing deep scratches and bruises that were slowly healing. The trio were all staring at Apophmet, unaware of the others nearby.

Aria's attention returned to Vashe. The Scrymmen woman struggled to move, her muscles tensing as she fought against some invisible grip of Apophmet. Alverick and Freyna appeared to be untouched, but Aria knew it was only a moment before Apophmet would turn his fury to the others. Summoning the energies within, Aria took a deep breath and held it as she reached out for help. The aethren couldn't stop Apophmet on her own, but she knew someone who could. She prayed that he would heed her call.

The song of the northmen swelled within her. Using herself as a tether to channel the music, Aria broke the barrier between the land of Man and Themba, bringing the song for all to hear. Apophmet's head swiveled in her direction, having finally noticed her presence. Holding her ground, Aria continued her evocation.

"WHAT ARE YOU DOING, DAUGHTER?" Apophmet hissed, his gaze finally tearing away from Vashe and noticing Freyna and Alverick. **"AND YOU, TINY ONE?"**

Freyna barred her teeth, her hands balling into fists as her body tensed.

"Too long you have teased the realms, stirring up trouble and threatening to break the balance we have all worked so hard to maintain. You know that we should be keeping the harmony between the worlds, lest the evil that dwells in the other realms crosses over."

A smile filled the Ancient's face as he turned to Aria. Her heart stopped as she saw the unabashed glee twinkling in his eye. The Ancient made no effort to hide his elation as he stood over the bloody Dseti.

"YOU KNOW BETTER THAN MOST THAT IN ORDER FOR THERE TO BE BALANCE, THERE MUST BE CHAOS. THIS WORLD HAS SHOWN THAT THEY ARE NO LONGER WORTHY, AS DID THE PEOPLE OF ATUNARI. CORINTH WILL BECOME AS ENLIL, AND YOU AND MY BROTHER CAN START OVER ONCE MORE, WHERE I WILL WATCH THEM CLOSELY."

"You can't do this!" Aria cried.

Apophmet didn't respond. He merely stepped over Dseti's fallen body, pulling the khopesh out of Dseti's chest as he approached the silver-haired goddess. Aria suddenly found herself unable to move as he neared. She couldn't tell if it was fear, or if he held her the same way he held the Scrymmen woman. To her surprise, Vashe was finally moving, her slender hand rubbing her wrist before reaching up and touching her arm. Panic was evident on the Scrymmen woman's features as she watched the Ancient cautiously as he approached the now frozen Aria.

Bracing herself for his approach, Aria broke her concentration, stopped her entreaty for aid, and began tapping into her own energies. It had been a long time since Aria utilized her powers, but she could still feel them lying dormant deep within. She pulled on them, a burst of hope filling her as she felt them stir beneath her touch.

Before she could gather enough energy, Apophmet swung his khopesh, catching her off-guard as she rushed to dodge his strike. The blade passed next to her, the attack sloppy but strong, as she felt the wind from his swing barely miss her flesh. He missed on purpose. Just as the thought entered her mind, Aria fell to the ground as the Ancient landed a kick to her thigh, causing her leg to buckle. Catching herself with her hand, Aria scrambled to put some distance between herself and Apophmet.

In an act of panic, Aria threw her free hand in Apophmet's direction, sending a wave of ice towards the Ancient's chest. Using his khopesh, he blocked the attack with a lazy hand. The goddess gritted her teeth, frustration building as she chastised herself for acting in a rash manner. If she stood any chance, Aria knew she needed to focus. Gathering her strength once more, Aria pushed herself up and turned to face Apophmet. Concentrating on her attack, Aria raised both hands, forming a ball of ice surrounded by water in her hands. Once it was the size of a melon, which did not take long, she pushed both of her hands in the Ancient's direction.

Apophmet sliced through the swirling water and projectile, only to be struck with an arrow made of ice in his right shoulder. In the goddess' hands, a circlet of water flowed, ready to take shape at her command. The Ancient was suddenly thrust forward as a gust of wind slammed into his back. Aria watched as the tiny aethren prepared another blast, the winds around her pulling at her hair. Giving more of herself to her power, Aria allowed the water encircling her to grow, covering a wider section of her body.

Taking advantage of his distraction, Aria swung her arm over her head, the water that had been circling her spinning over her head like a whip, and released it in Apophmet's direction. With a thought, the stream wrapped around the Ancient and began squeezing him. Apophmet's eyes widened in surprise as Aria took control and commanded the water constricting the Ancient to also cover his mouth and nose. As his breathing was cut off, a scowl crossed Apophmet's face. He began wriggling his body, trying to break free from his bindings. As his arms managed to find some leverage, Aria closed her fists, tightening the water ropes holding him.

The Ancient's movements ceased. His body went limp, and he turned his attention to the goddess. Another blast of wind struck the Ancient, the gust engulfing him and squeezing the water bindings tighter against Apophmet. The Ancient's eyes never left Aria.

Using the moment to take a chance, Aria began her entreaty once more. The song of the northmen continued to resound, filling the battlefield with their strength and praise for the Ancients. With each rousing chorus, Aria could feel a small sliver of hope growing within her breast. Keeping her grip on the bindings around the Ancient, Aria resumed her efforts to summon the great Ancient. The winds around Apophmet continued to constrict him, but he gave no indication that they were a nuisance. The goddess found herself rushing through her invocation, a sense of dread growing within as the Ancient stood calmly before her despite the attacks from her and Freyna.

Without warning, a blast shook the entire area, reverberating against the trees and deep in the dead earth. Shards of ice from the arrow that had been embedded in Apophmet's arm flew back at Aria, cutting her with the jagged edges on her arms and face. A cry escaped her lips as she threw her arms up to shield her face. Aria heard Freyna scream before a powerful force slammed into her stomach. Blood filled her mouth as she doubled over, her breath knocked out of her. A second strike connected with her cheek, tossing her to the ground. Stars exploded in her vision as her crumpled body landed on the earth, the pebbles and coarse dirt scraping her soft flesh.

In the distance, Aria could hear other voices call out, but she couldn't make out what they said. Instead, she struggled with shaking limbs to push herself up onto her feet. Her arms could barely support her weight as she brought her knees up to right herself. A sharp tug on her hair yanked the goddess up to her feet. Vision still swimming, Aria blinked several times, slowly bringing Apophmet into focus as he held her by her hair. A feral gleam twinkled in his eye as he smiled down on her. With a sudden motion, the Ancient lifted her higher into the air before slamming her body once more with a blast of energy, sending her flying backwards.

Aria skidded along the ground, her body scraping and tearing until she finally stopped. Blood dripped down her face from a gash to her head and a cut on her lip, in addition to the numerous tiny cuts she'd acquired from the ice and debris. The goddess' breathing became labored as she tried once more to push herself up. A sharp pain shot through her arm, causing her to cry out. Her body trembled, but Aria pushed herself up, managing to find her feet.

As Apophmet approached, Aria threw out her arm, sending a wave of ice and water in the Ancient's direction, but he avoided the attack with ease. The goddess found herself near Vashe and Dseti, the fallen man's body now propped up in her arms as the Scrymmen woman worked to tend to his wounds. Aria continued circling, trying to keep the Ancient at bay while still trying to call out for aid. The song of the northmen continued to ring out, but sounded muffled in her head. To her horror, Apophmet crossed the distance between the two in what felt like an instant, the dead earth crunching beneath his feet. He ignored a ball of electricity as it slammed into him. Instead, he focused on Aria. Still unable to move, Aria found herself being lifted into the air as Apophmet grabbed her by the throat. His fingers squeezed her delicate neck, not applying enough pressure to cause her to fear losing consciousness but enough to let her know that she was in peril.

"Such a dainty neck," Apophmet mused. **"It's a shame I could snap it so easily."**

The Ancient began applying pressure as his grip tightened. Aria's heart raced as blood pounded in her ears. Her feet kicked in the air as she dug her nails into his hand and arm, frantically scratching at him in an effort to break free. Apophmet grinned at her futile efforts.

"Don't do that," the Ancient said with a small shake of his head. **"I'll kill you before you can even gather enough energy."**

A dead branch slammed into Apophmet's back, the wind ripping into him and causing his clothes to flutter around him. He turned to face Freyna, a scowl on his face. The little goddess had moved closer to him, putting more space between the Ancient and the queen. Her eyes narrowed in determination as a maelstrom surrounded her.

"You will receive no mercy from me this time, little one," Apophmet said to Freyna. **"I have no qualms tipping the balance further in my favor. With the two of you gone and Czand waiting to be reborn, it'll take centuries before the harmony will be restored."**

"You... can't... do... this," Aria grunted as she struggled for breath. Her vision began to swim, and her body felt weak from the lack of air. All her pleas earned her was a sneer from the Ancient.

"Good-bye again, Aria. Enjoy your time in the wandering the abyss."

Apophmet's hand began squeezing her throat tighter. Aria's body trembled, blood still coating her mouth and trickling down her face. A tear rolled down her cheek as darkness engulfed the goddess. As everything faded to blackness, Aria thought she saw surprise flicker across Apophmet's face as he stared at her body. Moments later, she felt herself go limp, and everything disappeared.

XLIII

W ITH A GROAN, Aria opened her eyes. Her head pounded, and the bitter taste of bile filled her mouth along with blood. Spitting out the contents of her mouth, the goddess pulled her elbow underneath her to see if it would support her weight. The limb shook, but she found she was able to push herself off the ground. Her vision still swam, but after several long minutes, Aria found herself standing on trembling legs. Her senses screamed at her to find Apophmet because she knew he wouldn't be far, but she didn't dare swivel her head lest she fall unconscious once more. In the distance, she could still hear the song of the northmen, always growing in intensity, never faltering.

The sound of steel against steel caught her attention. Without moving her head, Aria scanned the area for the source of the sound. An agonizing throbbing threatened to engulf her in blackness once more, but she managed to push the pain aside. Her knees buckled, but she managed to maintain her balance. The goddess dared to take a step, staggering forward but not falling. To her right, she heard the grunt of male voices and the clangs of blade striking blade. Aria's eyes focused on a large blur moving around to her right. Seconds passed before she could clearly see Apophmet engaged in ferocious combat with Re'nukhtet.

The two creators of all sentient life, the two who granted her life, exchanged blows with their khopesh flashing in the dim light despite the surrounding gloom. Grunts and curses in an ancient tongue broke the otherwise intense silence. Aria found herself mesmerized as she watched the two dance around, dodging blows and slipping behind trees and other dead overgrowth. Never stumbling, their deft footwork left the goddess breathless.

A hand grabbed at Aria's arm, causing her to gasp as she reached within herself for something to use as protection. Panic nearly consumed her as she felt herself tugging at the last bits of her energy. The emotion quickly faded as she saw that it was Dseti holding onto her slim arm. Face pale, the Ancient let out a ragged breath as he pulled himself closer to the goddess. Aria ignored the pain in her hand as he squeezed it tightly and helped pull him into a semi-seated position, letting the wanderer lean against her with his eyes closed as he struggled to breathe. Blood caked his chest from the khopesh wound. Aria examined the area and noted with relief that fresh blood no longer seeped from his body.

"I thought we lost you," the goddess breathed, giving Dseti's hand a squeeze.

"Hurts just as much as it did when I was mortal." The Ancient's face scrunched up in a pained grimace as he cracked his eyes open. "Damn near stabbed me in the heart like last time."

"We'll get you healed," Aria replied. "Zemé went into hiding after helping Freyna, but the little Windstrider can take us there."

The two fell silent as the battle between Re'nukhtet and Apophmet raged on. Aria tried to follow their movements, but the pain in her head made it difficult to concentrate. All the while, the song of the northmen grew.

With a blinding flash, the two khopesh clashed with such force that the ringing from the blades echoed in the still air. Re'nukhtet and his brother stood mere feet apart, their weapons raised in defensive postures. Sweat sheened off their bodies, their muscles quivering from the exertion. Apophmet's breathing was labored as he glared at his brother while Re'nukhtet stood tall. Aria could almost feel an aura surrounding the Ancient as her own energies tugged at her, pulling her towards the spirit of balance and harmony.

A steady stream of vitriol flowed fast and furious from Apophmet's mouth. Aria couldn't understand what was being said, but she could feel the power of the Ancient's elder tongue. At her side, Dseti murmured something that she couldn't hear and felt his body shift against her. Re'nukhtet's reply came out smooth as honey in his rich baritone. Whatever he said, Apophmet gnashed his teeth in response, his grip tightening on his khopesh.

"We have to leave," Dseti gasped, every syllable a struggle to speak.

"What?" Aria asked, ripping her gaze away from the two.

"This is more than just us and Man," Dseti explained. "This is an ancient battle from before my time. It will not end well."

Before she could respond, Apophmet let out a curse as he launched himself at Re'nukhtet. At the same time, the song of the northmen, still singing in the background, reached a resounding crescendo. At the height of the song, a call for Re'nukh, their name for the Ancient, to bring them victory or a glorious death, came ringing out. The sudden cessation of the song they had been singing for so long was jarring, even as the final cry echoed in the air like the khopesh strike had not moments before.

Apophmet swung his khopesh with renewed intensity, his blade a blur in the dim light at the speed of his strikes. Re'nukhtet countered, his khopesh matching the speed of his brother's. Each ringing clash brought a snarl from Apophmet as his frustration mounted. Seconds passed, and as emotion took control of Apophmet, Re'nukhtet used that to his advantage to move to the offensive. Parrying Apophmet's khopesh, Re'nukhtet began slipping in a few strikes of his own. At first, they did not faze the raging Ancient, but as they became more frequent, Apophmet switched to defense.

Despite the speed of their exertions, Apophmet continued to growl out curses as they moved closer to Aria and Dseti. It all happened so quickly that the goddess didn't even realize it until they were almost on top of the two.

With a groan, Aria wrapped her arms around the Ancient and rolled them over, the sharp pebbles in the dirt scratching her soft flesh. Pinpricks of blood emerged in droplets on her alabaster skin as she completed the movement moments before Re'nukhtet and his brother exchanged blows where the pair once sat.

The blades whipped around Aria, the wind from their strikes rustling her hair and missing her body by inches. A whimper escaped her lips as she pressed herself to the ground, grateful when Dseti pressed himself on top of her. The goddess squeezed her eyes closed in an effort to push away the fight that occurred above her; the music of the northmen was long gone, leaving the ringing of the khopesh to fill the air.

A sudden cry rang out, startling Aria and causing her eyes to fly open. A second later, she heard a sharp sucking sound as Apophmet let out a growl of pain. Turning her silver eyes to the dueling Ancients, Aria gasped as she saw Apophmet frozen nearby. Blood blossomed from a wound on his arm and stomach. Dseti's khopesh dripped with fresh blood. Re'nukhtet's still rested in the Ancient's flesh. With a tug, Re'nukhtet freed his blade, sending a spray of blood onto the dead earth. Apophmet gingerly touched his wounded stomach, ignoring the slash to his arm. When he raised his eyes, they were black with rage.

In a low voice, the Ancient spoke once more in his elder tongue. However, this time, Dseti whispered a translation:

"You chose the wrong side, priest."

Aria looked from Re'nukhtet to Dseti in confusion. They both were higher deities than her or any of the others. Dseti's voice caught in his throat as he relayed Apophmet's message.

"My brother will not be able to save you this time. This time, you die. And you, brother, will not be able to stop it. Maeyu'dana is gone, and soon her priest will join her."

"You will disturb the balance no longer," Re'nukhtet replied. ***"I am taking control, as I should have done ages ago."*** Turning to Dseti, still half-covering Aria on the ground, Re'nukhtet raised his hand over the Ancient. ***"Return to your home, my son. I bid you rest."***

A sigh escaped Dseti's lips as he began to fade from Themba. Relief washed over his face as his color returned and the wound on his chest slowly healed, his flesh knitting together and smoothing over once more. Apophmet let out a roar and moved to intercept his brother's actions, only to be stopped by Re'nukhtet as his khopesh struck home once more. Blood sprayed, several droplets landing on Aria's face as the blade landed near his shoulder.

Re'nukhtet's hand moved to Aria, and as Dseti had faded, so did Themba. The song of the northmen echoed in the air, drowning out the cries of rage from Apophmet. As Re'nukhtet and his brother disappeared, the world around her melted from the drab greys and gloomy blacks of Themba to vibrant greens. Aria found herself standing on a knoll overlooking a field. Ear-piercing shrieks rent the air amid the death cries of men, catching her attention. Her head swiveled towards the source of the sound, and she noticed that her vision didn't swim with the sudden movement. The aches in her body were gone, leaving her feeling invigorated once more. Quickly processing everything, Aria's attention snapped to her brother as he brought his axe down on the neck of one of the Faceless, its clawed arm raking against his chest.

The goddess found herself reaching within to create a rope of water to grab the Faceless' legs. To her surprise, she found a deep well of energy swirling inside her. Aria blinked back tears as the light from the sun above finally hit her, blinding her momentarily. It was as though she never left Alocar to fight against the Ancient.

As the liquid tether formed in her hand, the water flowing like a miniature river as it grew, she paused in confusion. Dseti, Apophmet, and Re'nukhtet were gone. Their disappearance wasn't even acknowledged by those on the battlefield. Her eyes traveled over the scene, trying to take in the chaos once more. Men from Alocar huddled together, shaking as they stood amongst their fallen comrades in the verdant grass. Zanir's soldiers held their ground, weapons raised, as they formed a barrier between themselves and their bewildered queen. Their queen twisted side to side in the ring of small, smooth stones, looking for the now invisible Freyna. Strong gusts slammed into the remaining Faceless, throwing them off balance, but no other trace of the goddess could be seen.

Looking further, she watched as the Xanans shook the black blood of the Faceless. The young leader stood over the lifeless body of one of his enemies, a satisfied smirk playing on his face. Nearby, the northmen worked in perfect coordination to take down their foe. Aria realized that, as she heard back in Themba, the trio no longer sang their praises to the mighty Re'nukh. Despite their song ending, a haunting echo of their exaltations hung in the air, resonating over the clang of steel and the cries of the dead.

On the outskirts of the field, Alverick gazed around, his face nonplussed as he blinked back the brilliance of the sun. Not too far off, Vashe rubbed her eyes, clearly disoriented as well. The limp body of Dez lay at the Scrymmen woman's feet. Her eyes welling with tears, Aria felt a lump form in her throat as she stared into the silver eyes of the woman she'd shared a body with for so long. There was a peace in the Tempest's face, a softness that the goddess didn't expect from the Snapped, that filled her with regret.

I should've saved her.

In the distance, she heard the growl of the Faceless. Forcing herself to look away, Aria said her good-byes to Dez and gripped the water rope in her hand. It didn't take long for her to find her brother on the battlefield. She had work to do.

~~~

A scream nearby startled Len. He shook off the blood from his battleaxe and looked around to find the threat. Pram stood not too far away, scanning
~~~

the field to find their next target and keeping a protective eye on Len's back. The group of huddled soldiers from Alocar and Zanir held their weapons out in front of them as one of the monsters charged towards them. Their battle cries wavered as it rapidly approached, claws raised and teeth barred.

A second scream caught his attention. Len spun around and saw one of the Faceless charging a lone man. The man did not back down. In fact, he lunged almost at the same time the Faceless did, his blade raised and ready to strike.

The young general watched in amusement to see who would be foolish enough to tackle these creatures on their own. A moment later, he realized that he recognized the man: Wyrd. His childhood friend matched the Faceless step-for-step without hesitation. Len couldn't help but feel impressed at the man's determination.

The two met together with a mighty clash, their strikes falling hard and fast. Behind him, Len noticed the Flame moving towards the gods, tendrils of fyre held in his hand, ready to grab one of the monsters. Returning his gaze to his childhood friend, Len followed the movement of Wyrd's scimitar. He never understood why Wyrd chose to only use one scimitar instead of learning the dual-handed style of the elite.

His musings were interrupted as another quake shook the earth. The young general was nearly thrown to the ground, somehow managing to maintain his balance during the rumblings. Len looked up to see Wyrd having dropped to a knee, the Faceless standing in front of him with a triumphant smile on its face as its clawed hand bore down on the Qu'ari's scimitar. Impervious to the pain from the blade, the Faceless appeared to be pressing its full weight on Wyrd.

Tightening his grip on the handle of his weapons, Len sprinted towards his childhood friend. Wyrd's body shook as he fought valiantly to push the Faceless back and regain his footing. However, he was no match for the strength of the creature. In an unexpected move, the Faceless kicked Wyrd squarely in the chest, sending him flying.

Pushing himself faster, Len let out a roar as he approached the creature. The Faceless hovered over Wyrd's body, a twisted grin on its face as he prepared to strike the fallen man. Len knew he couldn't cover the distance in time to swing a weapon, but he had to do something. With a mighty yell, he launched his warhammer at the Faceless. The creature screamed in pain as Len scored a solid hit where the sternum would be.

He continued running, hoping he could get to the Faceless before it attacked Wyrd in retaliation. Hoisting his battleaxe into his right hand, Len prepared to throw the weapon. Shrieks rang through the air as more Faceless fell. They were soon accompanied by one of rage as a flame whip wrapped itself around the creature's neck, pulling it off-balance and away from Wyrd's fallen body.

A battle cry sounded behind Len, followed by a Qu'ari prayer for victory. Pram's axe flew by Len's head, the blade spinning end-over-end as it sailed through the air. Striking home once more, the battleaxe embedded itself deep into the chest of the Faceless. A shriek spilled from the creature's mouth as blackness exploded from the wound. Stopping just short of the Faceless' claws, Len swung his own with all his might, landing a devastating blow next to Pram's.

The Faceless' body writhed in pain as it slowly died. The air echoed with its screams until it fell silent. With the death of this one, the entire field was engulfed in an eerie hush. Warm beams of sunlight broke through the remaining darkness, making the tall grasses shine like emeralds.

The last Faceless was dead.

XLIV

IT HAD BEEN THREE DAYS since the sun's rays shone on Corinth. With tentative heads popping out from their hiding places, birds soon filled the emptiness with their symphony of birdsong. Rabbits crept out from their burrows, their noses twitching as they checked on their surroundings. Bees came out of their hives, the gentle sound of their buzzing filling the air as they traveled from white flower to flower, pollinating the ones in the tall grasses.

Things returned to normal as those in the meadow searched for any survivors after the battle. Bodies littered the field, their blood staining the blades of grass that waved in the breeze. Oldar stood frozen in place, his hands still squeezing the hilt of his sword, as those around him moved to check on others. His knuckles were white, the palms of his hands slicked with sweat as they held onto the weapon, locked in place and unable to release. It took all of the king's focus before he finally managed to loosen his fingers and let the sword fall to the ground.

A nearby soldier in green livery, all those in blue having fallen in the battle, picked up the weapon and proffered it to the king with a gentle word. When Oldar didn't move to grab the sword, the man took the initiative and slipped it into the sheath strapped to the king's hip. Oldar didn't say anything; he was too numb from it all.

Voices floated around him, muted and incoherent, as he made his way through the field. The tall grasses rubbed against his legs and tickled his hands as they hung limp at his sides. He couldn't believe he was still alive.

After Ingmar died, he'd found himself paralyzed in fear as the Faceless bore down on him. His mind had screamed at him to swing the sword, but his body wouldn't react. Then the earth began to shake. At the time, he hadn't processed that it was the work of an Avalanche.

All he could remember was how grateful he was that a pair of strong hands had grabbed him by the arm and yanked him back from the hellish creature, bringing him to safety within the fold of the remaining soldiers of Alocar and Zanir. Not many remained, and those who did stood pale-faced as they stared out at the carnage the creatures had wrought.

Now, the king had to relive those moments as he made his way through the grass. Something pulled at Oldar, guiding him to the ring of stones he'd found Queen Hera in before this all happened. His chest tightened as he wondered if she had survived the chaos. It all passed in a blur, and his mind struggled to piece everything together. Everything came to him in snippets.

As his foot stepped into the stone ring, he found himself relaxing as some of the adrenaline he'd been feeling melted away. The numbness Oldar experienced as the last Faceless fell was replaced with sorrow. He would now need to document the dead and everything else that had happened once he returned home. Oldar wondered what he would find back home. The king found himself hoping that he would see his aunt once more, alive.

Further into the circle, the calming effects of the little sanctuary soothed him, easing his pain. The king marveled at the healing properties of the clearing. Its powers were extraordinary, and he found himself wondering if he was imagining it all. That thought was quickly pushed away. After all Oldar had lived through, he could afford to allow himself some room for faith.

A pair of arms engulfed the king, and a body slammed against him as Queen Hera held him tight. Her face buried itself into the base of his neck, and he could feel her tears as her hair tickled his chin. Her body shook as she sobbed into his shoulder. Relief washed over him as he held her, and he found himself thanking the gods that she escaped unscathed.

"Thank Freyna you survived," she breathed into his neck. "I thought for sure you perished with your people."

Oldar became acutely aware of how dirty he was. Blood, sweat, and tears streaked his body, soiling his clothes and, no doubt, rubbing off on the queen. The attack on the soldiers surrounding him by one of the Faceless nearly bathed him in their blood. However, she didn't so much as bat an eye at his state.

People trickled over to their clearing in ones and twos. Their ashen faces covered in grime couldn't mask their emotions. What they saw today would most likely haunt them for the rest of their days. Some returned empty-handed to grab a sip of water, while others returned with a body. The fallen were placed just outside the ring of stones, as if they were afraid of soiling the purity of the little sanctuary within.

The number of deceased in blue livery outweighed those in green, de-spite there being more than twice the number of soldiers from Zanir. Oldar couldn't help but feel guilty for leading his men to their deaths. Slowly, the naked bodies were also stacked among the clothed. The king found himself studying their faces, wondering if he knew them. So far, none were familiar.

A shout in the distance caught his attention. Looking up from the two nude men in the pile of dead, he saw two Zanirian soldiers supporting the limp body of a man in blue, while a third ran back towards the stone circle, calling for bandages and water to wash the wounds. Those within the circle began rummaging for supplies to give the runner, while another prepared a fire to boil some water.

"Clean one of the daggers," the runner called out. "We should heat it to seal the wounds. They're deep."

"Wouldn't a salve work better?" another asked.

"No time. He's bleeding bad," the first replied.

A ring formed around the man in blue as he hung unconscious between the arms of two Zanir soldiers. Hera gently touched Oldar's arm as they approached. The king found himself holding his breath in anticipation. It wasn't until they were nearly upon him that his breath broke free from him, only to be followed by a shuddering gasp. The grey-peppered hair belonged to one person in his group.

Ingmar.

"Make way!" a soldier shouted, motioning with his free hand for those around him to move. "Where's the damned wraps?"

In the chaos to treat the wounded Ingmar, Oldar decided to return to the field to see if others were still alive. The steady stream of green soldiers carrying lifeless corpses didn't inspire much hope, but if Ingmar survived, others may have too.

Outside of the calming effects of the stone circle, Oldar found himself becoming anxious. No additional blue bodies were being brought back, and the number of green ones was also dwindling the further he ventured into the field. Oldar could now make out the forms of several people not in blue or green livery. Two were very tall. The group appeared to be both men and women, filling Oldar with hope that it was Cienna and the others.

A little further away, he saw Swordbane and his general standing off to the side with their Flame. The trio knelt over something in the tall grass. He didn't have to wait for long before he saw Swordbane's general and the Flame bend over to pick something — or someone — up. A bloody gash at the base of the man's skull appeared to be the cause of death. Dressed in Qu'ari clothing, the king could only assume it was one of their own. He couldn't help but feel a bit of pity for Swordbane as they carried their dead towards the stone circle and pile of corpses.

Oldar found himself saying a prayer for the fallen man before he continued toward the group. The tall grasses made it difficult to maneuver around the few rocks that lay hidden. He found himself kicking one of them, the pain causing him to hop on one foot until the feeling subsided. His targets hadn't started moving from their initial spot, filling Oldar with a sense of dread. Why had they not come toward the others?

Weaving through the grass once more, Oldar tried to keep an eye on them as well as watch the field for any more rocks. The party began to come into view, and he breathed a sigh of relief as he saw Caitlyn's red hair and Cienna's wavy blonde hair tied back in a low, unmistakable tail.

"Hey!" Oldar called out as he broke into a run.

Heads turned his direction at the sound of his shout, but the group quickly disappeared as Oldar tripped and fell into the grass. For a few moments, he lay face-first on the ground, confused. He didn't kick another rock. Twisting to see what brought him down, the king felt his stomach clench as he saw the naked form of a man. His pulse quickened as he placed a hand on the man's shoulder. The body was cold. With a shaking hand, he pushed the prone form onto its back.

Cassius.

A strangled gasp escaped the king as he gazed upon his dead friend. Schaed's words in the Gilded Rose that night about how Cassius went missing shortly after becoming betrothed rang in his mind. It felt so long ago that both his friends were still there with him. Tears fell hard and fast on his friend's face as Oldar began hyperventilating. With a shaking hand, he moved one of Cassius' curly locks on his forehead. At least he looked peaceful, as though the king had stumbled upon his friend sleeping in the field.

He couldn't bring himself to look at the wound on his friend's chest, but he knew that he must. The king's body was wracked with emotion, barely able to remain conscious as everything raced through him at once. A single chest wound surrounded with dried blood. Probably a direct hit from the tall man. From Oldar's vantage point, that man had been the strongest.

Distant voices called out as the sound of bodies rushing through the tall grasses grew nearer. Oldar couldn't bring himself to look away from his friend. Cienna's voice could be heard above all others, but he couldn't understand anything he said — it was so muffled. The delicate pressure of a hand on his back alerted him to her presence. Like her mother, soft, soothing words were being spoken to him, but nothing made sense. All that mattered was that he was alone.

XLV

EVERYTHING WAS BLANKETED in a faint red haze. It was difficult to tell whether the darkness had truly subsided and sunlight touched the land once more or whether it was only the glow of the blood moon peeking through. Caitlyn's body felt heavy, her bow having dropped into the tall grasses only to be picked up by Brody. Her arm was slipped around the shoulder of a man with a golden armband, providing her with enough stability to remain standing. Alverick lay slumped on the ground, his head buried in his hands, as the man with the armband's companion, a woman with alabaster skin and raven hair, spoke to Swordbane, the barbarians, and the gods.

Cienna stood next to the redhead, rubbing her back and letting her know that everything was going to be all right. Caitlyn wasn't sure if she believed the princess, however. Her head throbbed, and the haze was not clearing.

A young woman stood amongst the group, her nude body covered by Brody's shirt. Her hands were clasped in front of her as she stood with her head down, her long, curly hair obscuring her face as she wept. The alabaster woman, who looked so familiar, held the young woman comfortingly in her arms, her hand stroking her hair.

"I can't believe that out of the eight monsters, only one survived," Brody's voice could be heard talking to the princess.

"Don't call them monsters," Cienna replied. "She's been through as much as we have. Let's give her some mercy."

"You're right," he replied. "Everything's just so unreal right now." His voice trailed off.

"You're right," Cienna said. "I'm sorry. I'm just as frazzled as you."

The two continued watching the group, ignoring Caitlyn for the most part. The redhead managed to turn her head to glance at Brody. Lines creased his brow as he watched his friend sitting in the grass. As Alverick began rocking back and forth, Brody started chewing on his lip. The young bodyguard seemed to age drastically.

A faraway voice shouted out, catching Brody and Cienna's attention. In her state, Caitlyn couldn't see who it was, but it sent Cienna and Brody running into the field. Her vision still blurry, Caitlyn closed her eyes and rested her head against the strange man's shoulder.

I'm so tired. We're not safe. I should kill the girl, and then I can rest. I just want to sleep.

Caitlyn's mind was a jumble of thoughts. Somewhere in the back of her mind, she knew they were not good, but her exhaustion led her to think irrationally.

Food. So hungry. Gods, I'm so tired.

Her attention fell on the girl once more. She felt herself reaching into her energy reserves as she grew a ball of electricity in her hand. The red haze obscuring her vision darkened, and her head began throbbing. Caitlyn's body drooped as she clung to the stranger's shoulder. Her legs trembled, barely able to support her weight.

"Quiet yourself," the man whispered. "You'll be all right. Release the energy and let yourself begin to heal."

"She's a monster," Caitlyn mumbled, barely able to lift her head. "She needs to die."

"My dear, she is no more guilty of her crimes than you or I. Please, release the energy. You cannot take much more of this."

Mumbling incoherently, Caitlyn found herself begrudgingly withdrawing from her energy reserves and letting the ball of electricity dissipate in her hands. Her body was drained, and she sagged lower, grateful that the man supported her.

"What about Al?" she managed to ask. "We need to help him."

When he didn't respond, Caitlyn slipped out from his grasp and immediately fell to the ground. She murmured something about being able to do it herself when he moved to help her. Pulling herself through the grass, Caitlyn managed to crawl over to a rocking Alverick.

"Al." Caitlyn was surprised to find her voice only able to come out in a whisper. "Al. Look at me."

When he didn't respond, his head remaining buried in his hands, Caitlyn rested her hands on his shoulders. The maneuver was partly to soothe him and partly to help her pull herself up so she could face him properly. He didn't acknowledge her presence.

"Al." More insistent. "Look at me. Let me help you."

Without waiting for an answer, she managed to gently cup his face in her hands. Lifting his head up, she heard herself gasp as he stared through her, his eyes unfocused just like they'd been when she found him in Aramaine. Alverick stared intently at Caitlyn, his mouth moving in silent speech. It felt like an eternity, but suddenly, his eyes slipped into focus.

"Cait?" he croaked.

Tears welled in her eyes as she nodded. "Yes, it's me."

"I'm broken," he whispered. "Bannen is gone. How can I go on?"

A sob got caught in her throat as the tears fell down her face. With a light squeeze, she forced his wandering eyes to lock onto hers again. Caitlyn could see that there was some piece of Alverick still inside there; she just hoped she could reach him in time.

"You still have me." Her voice was little more than a whisper as she rested her head against his. "Come home."

The two sat in silence for a long time, Caitlyn's tears dropping onto Alverick's dirty face and leaving streaks in the grime. Soft mutterings could be heard from the Avalanche as he let her hold him. She couldn't understand them, but at least they weren't as bad as when he'd returned from the Abyss. Caitlyn knew his mind was racing just like hers, and that thought allowed him to focus. Closing her eyes, she let his face fill her as she focused on him as her Anchor. Slowing her breathing, Caitlyn managed to find her Anchor and let a wave of peace wash over her.

When she opened her eyes, she found her vision had cleared a little, and she could see him better. Alverick's face rested against hers, his eyes closed. His lips stopped moving, and his body stopped rocking. He finally looked at peace.

"Al," she said once more. "Let's go home."

"Okay," he mumbled.

Locking eyes with the strange man as he watched their exchange with interest, she begged him to come over and help lift the Avalanche. Despair threatened to consume her when she found she could only mouth the request. It was enough, and he made his way over to the pair.

Caitlyn and Alverick could barely support their own weight, but with the help of the strange man, they managed to stand by themselves. Leaving Alverick with the man, Caitlyn went to find Styx. To her surprise, the horse remained tied to the tree where they left him with the other horses. She'd expected them all to break their leads and flee once the chaos started. The onyx warhorse stamped his foot as his tail swished, clearly agitated. Speaking soothing words to the beast, Caitlyn succeeded in calming him down as she rubbed his nose.

"We're going home," Caitlyn said softly to the horse. "Come on, boy."

Satisfied that the horse would no longer bolt, Caitlyn untied the lead and slipped the rope around her hand. When she returned to where Alverick was, the rest of the group had migrated over to where the pair stood. Silver-haired Aria stood in front of Alverick, her face inches from his as she caressed his cheek with her hand.

The goddess looked as bad as the redhead felt. Her clothing was stained with blood, a few splatters also marring her flesh. Though immortal, a heaviness pressed down on the woman's slight frame. Her brother, covered in blood, both red and silver with a red tinge, stood straight-backed. The handle of his battleaxe was slick with blood, and his clothing was torn. Long scratches left his clothes in tatters, and underneath, Caitlyn thought she could see wounds on the god's flesh, the silver-red blood leaking out and mixing with the human blood that covered him.

The redhead's approach caught Ghan's attention. His gaze focused entirely on her, reaching into the depths of her soul. A warm tingling sensation flowed through her, leaving the redhead with a sense of peace and tranquility. As the feeling moved through her, the god abruptly broke their connection to return to the conversation. However, tingling remained.

A light touch on her arm caught her off-guard but didn't dissipate the feeling. Aria stood to her right, holding Alverick's hand. Shadows creased on the goddess' face, signs of exhaustion spoiling her radiant beauty. As Aria helped lift Alverick into the saddle, she turned to face the redhead. Her hands moved deftly as she tied the Avalanche securely into his seat before motioning for Caitlyn to climb on behind him.

"We did what we can, but I don't know if it's enough." Aria's soothing voice tinkled like a bell as she spoke to the still-exhausted redhead. "I pray you two can live a peaceful life."

Handing the reins to Caitlyn, Aria cupped the redhead's face in her hands. A tired smile lit her face, filling Caitlyn with peace once more. Planting a kiss on the redhead's forehead, Aria stepped back to give Caitlyn room to leave.

"May you always be each other's Anchor," the goddess said.

Sparing one last look at everyone, Caitlyn found herself tearing up once more. All she could do was nod at the goddess, her voice failing her yet again. With a gentle tap of her heels into horseflesh, Caitlyn guided Styx away from the field and towards her home in Zanir.

~~~

Aria watched as Caitlyn and Alverick rode into the afternoon sun. Her heart brimmed with hope that the two would find happiness in the remainder of their days. No one deserved it more than those two. The goddess just prayed that her and her brother's efforts had been enough to save them. As the two disappeared around a bend, Aria went to stand by her brother.

Aches and fatigue weighed down the goddess' body. She hadn't felt this way since her fight with Vahnyre centuries before. Aria figured she should have expected it considering she'd just regained her physical form not even five days prior, but it still caught her by surprise. Unlike her brother, her flesh remained untouched by the Faceless. While on the battlefield, she discovered that she was able to pull on the Faceless' souls, distracting them long enough for her brother to kill.

Finding out they were human when the first one died came as a shock. Her duty was to guard Mankind alongside her brothers, and it pained her that they continued to kill the creatures. However, she knew that if they did not, Apophmet's army of Darkness would continue to grow in both number and strength. There had been no other option.

Dez's lifeless body, on the other hand, left the goddess feeling like a failure. She had been with the woman for over a century, sharing several lifetimes with the Tempest. The two had formed a close bond, and Aria considered herself the woman's mother ever since she joined with Dez when she
~~~

was a baby. The binding of the two came easier than Aria had expected, just as the unbinding did.

Even in death, Dez was a beautiful woman. An enigma. Aria knew her life would be incomplete without her. She knew the day would come eventually. Ever since their unbinding, she had to accept that Dez would someday die, but it was just too soon.

Ghan's arm snaked around his sister's shoulders, pulling her into him. Aria didn't realize how exhausted she was as her body melted into his. Sparing a glance at her brother, she saw that he felt as bad as her. The wounds on his chest and arms cut deeper than he would ever admit.

"Let's go and rest, brother," Aria said. "We have a lot of catching up to do before we go and search for Czand."

Leaving the humans to figure out the rest of their affairs, the two gods slipped away, disappearing into the trees.

XLVI

S TANDING IN THE MIDDLE of the stone circle, Cienna watched as her
mother's soldiers moved around in preparation to return home. The sun
moved past its mid-day spot and slowly began its descent. As the day
dragged on, birds continued singing, and insects joined the bees as they flew
about the flowers.

The men who rushed to treat the only surviving Alocaran soldier finally
slowed down as they managed to stop his bleeding. The soldier's screams as
they pressed a white-hot blade against his flesh to close up the wounds carried as loudly as the death knells of the Faceless, his agony almost tangible.
Every time she heard his voice, the princess found herself cringing.

A few of her soldiers left earlier in the day to bring a wagon back from
Alocar to help transport their dead. They now loaded the dead into the
wain, slipping the bodies of the Faceless in as well in hopes their families
could find them before they were burned. The bodies of the dead of Zanir
were already on their way back to Pharn, having left around the same time
as the riders left for Alocar. Now, all that remained in the field were her
mother, their soldiers, Oldar, his single living soldier, and the young woman.

It took a while, but the king of Alocar slowly returned to his normal self
the longer he spent in the little sanctuary her mother settled in. The death
of his friend had devastated him as much as when he thought his trusted
guard died; that was the least she could pull from him at the time.

Signs of the camp disbanding soon filled her with a sense of urgency. Cienna wanted an opportunity to speak with Oldar, but at the rate things were going, she wouldn't get the chance. While her mother was directing the final soldiers, Cienna decided to seize the opportunity.

"Oldar?" Her voice came out more timid than she expected it to. "Can we talk?"

A vacant stare attempting to mask his pain greeted her, followed by a nod. Smoothing her non-existent skirts, the princess sat down next to him. She squeezed his hand in an attempt to comfort him. The small gesture seemed to work. Oldar grabbed her hand and interlaced his fingers with her own. Cienna found her cheeks going hot as she blushed. Her voice caught in her throat.

The two held their gaze, neither speaking. As the silence stretched, Cienna found that it wasn't uncomfortable. In fact, she found that she was enjoying the moment, holding his hand. Time stretched on, the two lost in their own world. Oldar's expression gradually regained its clarity, and a small spark of light returned.

"Thank you for coming back to me."

Oldar breaking the silence first left Cienna feeling pleasantly surprised.

"I couldn't leave you," she whispered. "We have too much left to talk about."

The two continued sitting in silence in the middle of the stone circle sanctuary. A light breeze rustled their hair, the sound of the tall grasses waving in the background making the moment more peaceful. Cienna closed her eyes, savoring their time together. Oldar's hand holding hers filled her with a sense of security.

She felt conflicted. After her afternoon with Brody, Cienna didn't think she could ever feel the same tranquility with another. However, this time spent with Oldar showed her that maybe there were other options available to her. With each passing second, Cienna found herself embracing the possibility of the two of them forming a bond.

"I would like to visit you. When you are ready, of course." Cienna hoped she wasn't coming on too strong.

"I would like that," Oldar replied.

The king turned and stared into her eyes. Cienna never realized that long lashes framed his hazel eyes. She felt like she could get lost in them for hours. Time continued to pass at the speed of a snail, and Cienna couldn't be happier. She just hoped she could bring herself to say more. Without preamble, Oldar leaned in and kissed her. Heat blossomed in her chest as she returned the kiss. His hand reached and grabbed the back of her head, his fingers weaving themselves into her hair and pulling her closer. His lips were surprisingly soft, and she didn't want to pull away.

Oldar was the one to break the kiss. With a smile, he gave her hand a gentle squeeze. Cienna's voice caught in her throat as her face flushed a deep red. She was thankful that her tanned skin and freckles covered it a little.

In the distance, the queen's voice called out to the group, letting them know that it was time to leave. Cienna and Oldar shared one more glance before he slipped his fingers from hers with a shy smile. Smoothing her imaginary skirts once more, Cienna tucked a strand of her curly hair behind her ear before rejoining her mother with a little half-wave.

〜〜〜

The gates of Pharn opened to cheers from the men on the wall-walk. Swords and shields waved in the air as soldiers celebrated the arrival of their lords. Crossing the threshold, Cienna could hear the jubilation spreading throughout Pharn like a wave, rippling from the walls of the city and into the capital proper. People rushed out to the streets to see the good news for themselves. As the exhausted band rounded the corner, women dropped to their knees, shedding tears of happiness, while others shouted prayers of adulation to the gods. Cienna felt a sense of pride welling within her chest.

It had been a long journey, but she finally felt as though she was coming into her own as the future queen of Zanir.

Soldiers poured into the street as word of the queen and princess' arrival reached the ends of the capital. Flowers rained down on the returning party from the shopkeeps' upper windows. Small children brought daisies to the queen and princess as the older ones raced forward with snacks. A few musicians settled into place on the corners as the victorious party made its way slowly to the caer, their string instruments playing a lively tune as young women began dancing in the streets, waving their hair ribbons in the air behind them.

It didn't take long before word reached Jaes and his soldiers as they patrolled the exterior of the caer. When Hera saw her husband's brother, she broke down in tears as she raced towards him. The two shared a tight embrace, the duke planting a kiss on the queen's cheek and wiping away her tears. As the two broke apart, he made his way over to the princess. Pulling his niece into a hug, Cienna found herself crying into her uncle's shoulder.

〜〜〜

As the sun began to set, the heavens were painted in stunning shades of orange, purple, and pink. Stars dotted the sky like freckles as the moon came into view. Toron's moon, the crimson ring surrounding it having faded throughout the day, moved in the sky until he was barely visible. Festive music filled the streets as people danced, winding ribbons around a pole. A few of the city's singers joined the musicians, lending their voices to the music and sending it echoing throughout the capital. Flower petals lay strewn in the streets, covering the cobblestones with their fragrant beauty.

Despite the short notice, the bakers and other cooks of Pharn pulled together and created a fantastic feast. Tables were laden with succulent meats, buttery pastries, savory soups and stews, and sweet fruit. The Thurlish merchants who were unable to leave the city in time donated their meat buns and kebobs, the exotic spices lending their own aromatic aroma to the evening. Sweet creams, custards, and mini honey cakes were given their own table, separate from the main course.

Cienna danced with the other women her age, a yellow silk ribbon in her hand, as she wove between the others as she went around the pole. Her hair flew behind her, the sun's final rays making it glitter like gold. Occasionally, her eye caught Brody watching her as she celebrated. Her guard laughed with the other soldiers, but his twinkling eyes never left her for long. On their journey home, the princess worried that he would never regain his sparkle, so seeing them again filled her with joy.

Even Queen Hera celebrated with the others. Wearing a dress of light lavender with golden embroidery, the queen danced with her brother-in-law, Jaes' auburn hair cascading down the back of his peacock blue tunic. It had been too long since her mother smiled like she used to with Cienna's father. The two turned in time with the music, and for an instance, Cienna saw her father and his golden hair staring lovingly into her mother's eyes. The princess' breath caught in her throat for a moment, but as the pair completed their turn, Jaes let out a roar of laughter as he said something to the queen.

The merriment lasted into the late hours of the evening. Moonlight, pure and white, bathed the streets, happy to be back after being blocked by the darkness for so long. Twinkling stars blinked unfettered in the inky heavens, while Toron's moon faded away into the night until his next visit. In the streets, flames flickered in the iron lamps, extra candles having been brought to the windows of the buildings lining the side of the road for additional light.

Children snuggled against their mothers, heads lolling as they slept peacefully despite the music. Empty plates and mugs were being taken into the caer for cleaning, the ample food and drink on the tables having been mostly consumed earlier in the evening. Cienna sat on a stone step in the frame of a doorway, her back leaning against the door as she rested her eyes. She was just drifting off to sleep when a pair of voices caught her attention.

Perking up a little, she recognized Ronan as he spoke with someone. The soldier and remaining members of Pharn's armed forces ran into Hera's troops as they returned from the battle. The captain's face dropped as he saw the queen's small numbers, not knowing how many bodies had passed by earlier in the day for burial. Judging by the tone of the conversation with the other person, the people in Pharn didn't fare much better. They spoke in semi-hushed voices, the dying music providing cover but still making it impossible to truly mask their conversation.

"It was just as bad out at the farm," Ronan's voice explained. "The walls were nearly torn down by the wind, and it was unbelievably cold. What was the morale like here, Cody?"

The name sounded familiar, but Cienna couldn't put a face to it. He sounded young.

"Apart from the freeze, it didn't seem to bother the others as much as me." The disappointment dripped from his voice. "Her majesty put me in such an important position, but I couldn't keep my fears down."

"Take the next few days off," Ronan said. "Staying up for at least two days and showing your dedication to Zanir by giving your brothers extra breaks takes a lot of spirit. When you come back, we'll begin proper training with Thol and make you into the spearman you're meant to be. With a little training, I imagine you could hold a spot on the King's Guard for how well you've handled everything. I daresay Thol is getting a little old and might be looking into something a little less strenuous in the next couple years."

"Th-thank you, sir. I won't disappoint you."

Cienna could hear the quiver of shock in the youth's voice as she imagined him snapping to attention on the worn cobblestones. Her mother had mentioned that Cody had been one of her guards while she was battling the poison, and the princess couldn't be happier that the boy was being given what he deserved after going above the call of duty. Cienna wondered if she should talk to her mother about the matter to see if they could do something to expedite the process.

As the sound of retreating footsteps echoed over the festivities, Cienna noticed that they abruptly stopped. Hurried steps came her direction, causing the princess' breath to catch in her throat.

"Sir?" Cody's voice came out in as low a hush as he could to be heard over the music. "Do you know if anyone else ever mentioned anything strange going on during all of this?"

"What do you mean?" Ronan asked.

Cody hesitated before his voice dropped even more, causing Cienna to strain to hear the youth.

"When the queen was poisoned, I felt... something before she..." Cody faltered, his voice trailing off. "Never mind," he mumbled.

"Cody?" Ronan asked. Cienna could hear the fear in his voice.

"It's nothing," the youth replied quickly. "I must just be overtired. I'm sorry, sir."

Before the captain could reply, the sound of footsteps rushing away could be heard once more. Cienna remained seated, trying to piece together what she just heard and make sense of everything. Behind her, she could hear Ronan muttering to himself, doing the same. Just then, a hush fell on the streets as the music ceased. Cienna took the opportunity to open her eyes. Ronan's back was to her, affording the princess a chance to slip away from her resting spot and into the streets without question. Something told her that when she spoke with Brody after the festivities, it would be best if as few people knew about this as possible.

She made her way to the main throng, searching for her mother. Unfortunately, the queen was seated at the head of the main table, her uncle Jaes on her left and Vashe on her right. Cienna couldn't believe that Vashe finally joined the festivities. After returning from their fight, the headmistress sequestered herself in her room with the young woman they'd rescued. Now, the Scrymmen woman sat lightly in her chair, her face relaxed as she spoke softly to the queen.

The light tinkling of silverware against glass rang in the air. Any conversation that lingered instantly died away. Vashe stood up, her elegant form accentuated by her raven hair styled in a high bun and a simple indigo dress to bring out her alabaster skin and red-painted lips. The princess sucked in her breath, completely in awe of the grace and beauty her headmistress possessed.

"We have gathered here today to celebrate a victory unlike any ever seen in the last few centuries." Vashe's voice rang out loud and clear, reaching everyone still out in the streets or hanging out the nearby windows. "Though we suffered great losses, we could not have been able to succeed without our queen and the skill of our army."

A cheer rose into the night, echoing into the air and shaking the heavens.

"Now is a time for rest and reflection," the Scrymmen woman continued after the streets quieted. "Go home tonight and hold your loved ones close because we have received a reminder that nothing can be taken for granted.

"Our victory can be attributed to one primary factor: the gods walking among us."

An uneasy hush fell on the crowd.

"Thanks to our devotion, Her Holiness, Aria, and her eldest brother, Ghan, who joined us when we went to battle. And they weren't the only ones offering aid and protection. Without their help, Corinth would have fallen. I say this not to discourage and frighten, but to remind that there is still much out there that we cannot even begin to understand. Let us take this opportunity to learn, to grow, and to love. Every day we have is a gift, and we should treasure it. To our queen, our princess, and a brighter future."

Raising a glass, Vashe held the red wine high for all to see. In the light, it sparkled through the crystal-like blood. A thunderous roar erupted as everyone in Pharn followed suit. Cienna couldn't help but wonder what the future held as she stared at the blood-like liquid in the Scrymmen woman's cup.

⌒⌒⌒

Back in her room, a single flame flickered weakly in a lantern, providing the only source of illumination against the blackness of night. Navigating through her chambers, Vashe easily found her favorite, well-worn chair amongst the shelves, tables, and her scrying pool, despite it being barely lit. In the adjoining room, the young, curly-haired woman she'd freed during the battle with the Faceless slept. The poor girl spent most of their time in Pharn sleeping, overcome by exhaustion from the whole ordeal. Whenever she wasn't sleeping, she and the headmistress remained sequestered in the room, ignoring the visits from the other instructors of the Mageri, as Vashe documented the young woman's last few months.

More than once, Vashe found herself fighting back the bile that rose in the back of her throat as she listened to Alastaire's actions. After beating the poor girl to near death, he forced her back into consciousness to watch as her beloved Cassius lost his last shreds of humanity to his rage, stripping him of consciousness and transforming him into the Faceless with the help of a glowing, opalesque stone embedded in the pommel of a small ceremonial dagger. That same dagger had been used to filet her back in between beatings. Vashe couldn't quite figure out how, but the dagger clearly was integral to the creation of the Faceless and, if what the young woman said was true, also the only way to truly control them.

As she recounted the story, the young woman shivered as she remembered her ordeal. On more than one occasion, she would stop as emotion overwhelmed her. Vashe tried her best to soothe the distraught woman, but whenever the subject of her beloved, Cassius, came up, she would choke up and they would have to stop.

The narration was not yet complete, but the headmistress found herself wanting to leave the capital and ride across Corinth. Her story could wait, as could the girl's. Leaning back in her cushioned chair, Vashe closed her eyes, heaving a great sigh as tears rolled down her alabaster cheeks, creating small puddles as they dripped onto the top of her indigo dress. Nowhere felt like home anymore, now that Dez wasn't out there wandering the land.

Dez's silver eyes flashed in her mind as she remembered her mentor and mother figure. In her final moments, clarity had returned as the two women locked eyes. Vashe could see the fear and confusion she must have been feeling seconds before the Faceless slashed her back, cutting deep into her flesh and ripping through the muscle, exposing the ribcage. When Vashe finally managed to get to Dez, the woman was inches from death. The two gazed into each other's eyes, love evident as Dez beheld her adopted daughter one last time before drawing her final breath.

Vashe struggled with what to do with Dez's body. Her blood wasn't safe to draught; Dseti had warned her that any fallen god-blessed were to remain untouched, as he motioned to Dez's silver tattoos that were already fracturing on her body. All Vashe wanted to do was walk until exhaustion overtook her. In the back of her mind, Enlil called to her. Her skin crawled as the holy blood inside her tingled. The ancient magic that coursed through her pulled her towards the East.

As tears continued to run down her face, Vashe prayed that her gods would pull her into a dreamless sleep and give her a respite from her pain. The minutes ticked by, and still she waited, until at long last, the darkness took her and she finally slept; but even in her dreams, she couldn't find peace, and her tears still flowed.

XLVII

THE TREK BACK TO XAN went by quicker than expected. Wyrd's body lay wrapped in one of the wagons holding the supplies after having been cleaned and cleansed in preparation for burial. In the morning, the Honorable Mother would recite a prayer, beseeching the gods for favorable passage into the afterlife and invoking a holy ritual of protection. Len lay on his bed, Zaa'ni and Heru sleeping next to him, feeling like he was missing something.

Xan managed to escape from everything in relatively better shape than Alocar or Zanir. Yet, the balance of the clans shifted. Wyrd's murder of Vaarden and the narrow vote of victory by the council after the fight in Fa'Tinh left the Pshwani still struggling to recover. Viir surely would be challenged by someone to act as the clan's champion, and most likely would lose. With Yettan and the imbalance in Pshwan, his position as the Great Heart was in danger of being overthrown.

Len didn't fear battle. He knew that he would overcome adversity. No, his trepidation came from the insurrection that the two clans could build up as they chipped away at his legitimacy. He could solve this by having Yettan removed, but killing a champion was different from killing an insubordinate warrior. There would be questions, accusations, and if he wanted to maintain his rightful place as Great Heart, everything must be done with delicacy.

Freyna's absence ever since he left for the Bone Coast also troubled Len. Her comforting presence became a constant source of surety as he ascended to power. Knowing that the goddess watched over him and his daughter had filled him with confidence that he was following the will of the gods. Not that their approval ever mattered, but having her protection always felt like a step in the right direction. Once he'd returned home, Len sought out a seer and had them roll the bones. His heart sank as they revealed that his future was unsure.

So, he lay awake, grappling with his thoughts and unfamiliar emotions of inadequacy.

The rustling of Heru as he searched for his mother's breast caught his attention, pulling him from his contemplations. His mother was right — there was something about the babe that even Len couldn't quite place. An old soul, Intan had said.

Perhaps that was the answer to his problems.

~~~

Pink streaks tinged the early morning skies as the sun slowly pulled itself into the heavens. Len enjoyed the coolness of the day, the crispness of the air that could only be found before the sun had fully risen. The streets were empty as his people slept after their long journey. Fa'Tinh's main square still remained, the buildings acting as charred monoliths much like the ones found in the Bone Coast, a memorial to the destruction wrought on the capital.

Taking a seat by the fountain, Len savored the peace and quiet of the uninhabited streets. The tranquility was a welcome relief from the last couple months. Warm rays of the sun fell upon his face. Coupled with the cool air, Len smiled. It was truly a peaceful morning, and he intended to enjoy it to the fullest. It had been years since he'd been afforded the opportunity.

Some time passed with Len just sitting on the edge of the fountain, the water having spilled into the streets during the battle, leaving the structure still. A body slid onto the fountain, sitting quietly next to the Great Heart. Len did not bother to open his eyes, wanting to savor his few moments of
~~~

peace before diving into his problems once more. Whoever sat next to him didn't seem to be in a rush to speak either.

Time passed and the sun fully rose, bringing with it the beginning of the heat that would overpower the cool temperatures of the early morning. Even through his closed eyes, Len could now see the sun, and he decided it was time to leave.

"What is on your mind?"

A chuckle escaped Len as he recognized Pram's voice. The man was always there, anticipating his next steps. How his general knew he'd be up early baffled him, but Len found he didn't care. The almost fatherly concern Pram showed for him was actually comforting and much appreciated. He would never admit it, though. A Great Heart needed to be strong, composed, unlike Ras.

"Your timing is impeccable, as always," Len replied. "You're restless as well?"

A grunt of agreement was his only response.

"Pram, why is it that I feel so unfulfilled? I've brought Xan into a new age, protected us against demons, battled gods, and led the entire nation to safety against an unprecedented threat. How is it that I feel like my life is lacking?"

The general sat in silence for a bit as he formulated an answer. Len appreciated Pram and his analytical approach to every problem.

"The last year has been filled with constant movement, from your rise to power and acceptance of the title of Great Heart, planning and executing your attack on Pharn — including your dealings with the Myrani — summoning a demon, responding to an attempted coup, and now fighting creatures that were previously believed to be children's tales. Your life has not allowed for you to relax, so now you feel as though that is how your life should be.

"Family life and the quiet role of a leader have not had a chance to show you how rewarding they can be. You lead through action, through fighting. A normal life bores you and leaves you questioning your place."

"I might as well be like the pirates," Len mused. "Drifting around as I search for my purpose."

"That very well could be true," Pram said after a moment's thought. "Maybe their life suits you better."

"But I can't leave my family," Len countered. "And I'll be damned if Yet-tan or some Pshwani takes over as Great Heart."

"You know," Pram broached, "perhaps a compromise can be made."

Len perked up, intrigued by his general's proposition. He nodded his head for Pram to continue.

"You crave a life of action. I believe, and correct me if I'm wrong, you trust my judgement. Why don't you go and live the life you desire along the Bone Coast? I can watch over Zaa'ni, the kids, and Intan here. You could even take Hroth and Maen under the guise of acting as additional sources to establish a colony on the coast for Xan. A sixth one we could call the Blade, or something like that. If we explain your absence as such, there shouldn't be many questions. You've promised our brothers and sisters that you'll expand Xan's influence to the ends of Corinth, and this looks like a good way to make everyone happy."

The idea intrigued Len. A part of him hesitated to admit that he longed for the adventure Kayna and her crew had promised him. They would welcome him back, no question, and he could always come back to visit Zaa'ni and the children under the pretense of checking up on Xan.

~~~

With the sun to his back, Len made his way toward the Bone Coast. He felt guilty as Zaa'ni clung to him, tears streaming down her face as she begged him to take her with him, but he knew this new life wasn't safe for her. Bermet had taken the news rather well, her deep brown eyes taking him
~~~

in as she promised to watch out for her mom and little brother with the help of the blue-haired girl, shedding a few silent tears in the process.

Saying good-bye to Heru had been more difficult for some reason. As he held his son, the infant watched his every move with interest. A chubby hand reached out and grabbed Len's finger, and he felt a spark go between him and his son. The boy would make a fine leader for Xan when he was ready. Until then, Pram would bring the stability she needed.

When he broke the news to his general that he would be taking over as Great Heart, Pram became speechless. Len knew he would advocate for Xan in a way he never could. The two shared a tight embrace as Len snuck away from Fa'Tinh, hoping to avoid the detection of any of his people.

Hroth, Maen, and her children accompanied him, the children playing in the grass along the road as they made their leisurely journey. The Flame's presence afforded him a measure of comfort that Len didn't realize he needed as he left for Thallysis. Glancing over at the two, Hroth's usually stoic nature dissipated, and a wistful smile replaced it as he returned to his home. Perhaps Pram knew the Flame's true desires as well.

A smile played on Len's lips. The damned general was always right.

XLVIII

DAYLIGHT STREAMED into Oldar's room. Stretching to his fullest, the king enjoyed the comfort of his own bed. Pillows and silken sheets cocooning his flesh were luxuries he never thought he'd miss growing up. On his writing desk, his morning breakfast awaited him, a single daisy next to his plate. Ever since his return, Pru had gone above and beyond to ensure his comfort after smothering him in a tight embrace. The matronly woman's tears soaked his blood-stained clothes, but she didn't so much as flinch at his state.

Once he returned to Castle Storm, Constance awaited him, her head down in contrition before she prostrated herself at his feet, offering herself to her king for judgement. Surprising himself, Oldar threw his arms around his aunt as he whispered words of forgiveness into her ears. To his disappointment, she didn't stay long, instead leaving late in the afternoon to return to her home once more. Constance had left word with one of the soldiers that she would ensure that the tome containing the ritual to summon the Faceless would be burned, and she asked that the king come and throw it into the flame personally the following afternoon.

As the morning passed and his food cooled, Oldar didn't make an effort to get out of bed. He wanted to savor this quiet morning. A long day of ceremonies awaited him. He also wanted to make sure that his dedication to Ingmar for his unspeakable bravery went perfectly. The healers managed to properly treat his wounds and stave off infection, leaving Oldar feeling relieved. He wanted to keep the man comfortable for the rest of his life.

Reaching under his pillow, the king pulled out a piece of parchment he'd placed there the night before.

It was a letter from Cienna.

The princess' flowy script both thanked and apologized for her treatment of Oldar. She asked when it would be best to visit Madden to discuss the countries' futures. Oldar dared to hope that an engagement was coming, especially after their last encounter. Cienna didn't seem opposed to it any more. On his desk, his response was drafted. In his steady script, Oldar invited Cienna to come over before the next full moon and asked that she bring her mother. Next to his message to the princess, a request for a grand feast and minstrels to appear in the castle sat next to a sapphire necklace. If things went well, the king would present the gift to her as a token of his affection and begin the courting process.

A knock on his door followed by a soft voice calling out to him finally pulled the king out of bed. Pulling his robe tightly over his naked flesh, Oldar shuffled over to the door, opening it a crack. Outside, a member of the castle staff stood anxiously with a rolled, thick cloth held in his outstretched arms.

"Begging your pardon, your majesty, but this morning, when we were cleaning up the throne room for you, we found this. We weren't sure what to do with it and thought it best to bring it to your attention."

Lifting one of the flaps of cloth, Oldar gasped as he saw the dagger his uncle had been wearing right before his demise. The opalesque stone in the middle of the pommel glowed faintly in the morning light. Oldar took the bundle from the servant, thanking him for his efforts, and gently closed the door. The sound of hurried footsteps could be heard in the hallway as the man scurried away.

Placing the cloth on his writing desk, Oldar reached out with a tentative hand and brushed his fingers against the cold steel. When nothing happened, he did the same to the stone. Nothing. The dagger sat on his desk as the morning went by, Oldar checking up on it whenever he could. After a sufficient amount of time had passed, he felt comfortable that the weapon wouldn't do anything to him. Strapping it to his hip, Oldar headed out to his aunt's home outside the capital. Before burning the tome, he wanted to ram the blade through it cover-to-cover. After the book had been thoroughly studied, of course.

XLIX

A WARM BREEZE RUSTLED the leaves. In the days following the strange darkness that crept over Corinth, the weather had been unnaturally beautiful. It was as though the gods wanted to apologize for the chaos they had brought upon the land. Now, the sun beat merrily on the earth as flowers sparkled like jewels between grass of the truest green. Birds sang their melodic chorus, filling the air with birdsong as the planting season moved closer to harvest. Bees and hummingbirds flit from flower to flower, delighting in their sweet nectar with each sip.

The sudden appearance of a rabbit leaping across the dirt path was enough to startle any weary traveler from their dreams of a warm dinner. Its sleek greyish-brown pelt shone in the afternoon sun. With a twang, the hare dropped to the ground, an arrow having its mark — a wonderful addition to the night's dinner. Joining the collection of fowl and small wild game, the rabbit rested gently against the back, its body going cold as death sapped away its warmth.

Life was peaceful now in the quiet solitude away from the capital. Days were spent leisurely walking through the fields, the clover tickling bare flesh as toes curled in the loamy soil, digging little trenches in the rich earth. A nearby stream burbled happily, the crystal-clear water running over rocks smoothed long ago by the water's journey. Trout and salmon swam upstream, their scales catching the light with each stroke of their tails.

Hidden in the shadows, the family of deer that lived nearby watched warily, their ears straining to listen, their bodies tense, ready to flee at a moment's notice. The shadowed outline of the leaves mottled their golden fur, dulling the white spots on their back and tail. The youngest one had the most beautiful hint of red in their coat, having caught the creature by surprise in the sun one afternoon. The doe and her two fawns tracked the traveler intently, their heads following with each step until they could no longer see anyone.

A sheen of sweat built up on the brow as they neared home. The faint outline of smoke floating from the chimney brought a smile to their faces. Perhaps dinner would be ready before nightfall. A rumbling stomach seemed to share the sentiments. Quickening the pace, the once-tired feet managed to cross the distance to their home in what felt like record time. The prospects of taking a break in the verdant upholstered chair in front of the hearth, a real luxury that had been a spur-of-the-moment purchase a few years prior, overshadowed all thoughts of dinner at the moment.

The door opened without a sound, the worn maple wood feeling soft against the palm of the hand. The air inside smelled of simple vegetables as a pot simmered happily over the small fire in the hearth. Taking a taste of the pot's contents, the thick stew and hearty chunks of meat proved to be a happy surprise instead of the simple broth and vegetables that were expected. A mug sat on the table in the corner of the room — another pleasant shock to find it full of honey mead.

Back by the fire, the cushioned chair called out to be sat in. Tossing the day's spoils onto the floor to clean and prepare later, a sigh filled the room as the chair consumed the weary body. Feet throbbing, the fingers worked at taking off the boots, the thick leather dropping heavily onto the floor. Taking advantage of the moment of peace, they allowed themselves to fall into the contentment that swallowed them up as soon as they sat in their chair. The soft cushions consumed their sore bodies; down feathers packed into the pillows beckoned them to sink deeper into their comfort.

By the time they opened their eyes, the sun had moved closer to the horizon, threatening to set and teasing the household with tasks yet undone.

There was no sense of urgency, however. Nothing mattered anymore. Stew burbled in the pot, ready to be served, as the fire died down in the hearth, sending the room into darkness, the only source of light coming from the setting sun. Pushing against the armrest, a rumbling stomach demanded feeding, forcing a tired groan from exhausted lips.

Dinner ended in silence, the stew sitting comfortably in the now sated stomach, the cooled honey mead leaving a body sore from a day's strenuous work relaxed and on the brink of slumber. As sleep threatened to overtake them, the light brush of lips on flesh snapped the eyes open. In the darkened room, a shadowy figure loomed overhead.

"Did you get a chance to eat?" the voice echoed throughout the room despite coming out in a groggy croak.

The figure nodded.

Stretching in the kitchen chair, the pair walked back to the bedroom. Disrobing, the cool sheets against bare flesh invited slumber to consume the pair almost instantly.

"Did you have a good day?" Heavy with sleep, the voice sounded barely more than a whisper.

A non-committal grunt came from their partner. The disappointment hung heavily in the air. Rolling over, a sigh of contentment escaped their lips as they pulled the blanket tight around their shoulders. Tomorrow would be a better day.

"Good night, Alverick." Caitlyn let his name echo in the quiet room.

"Do you think they'll stop?" Alverick's question, the same one he'd asked every night since they returned to her home, was laced with concern. "Bannen hasn't come." Regret.

Images of the man she'd killed, his blood pooling around his limp body on the floor from the multiple wounds she'd inflicted, came rushing back to her. Lifeless eyes that had been pleading moments before stared at the ceiling. His plaintive cries for mercy were squashed in her anger. He was to have been married the next day, he explained as he begged. Her mind had almost been torn asunder from the experience. The visions never faded. They haunted her every night.

Alverick wasn't tainted, but she could see some of his tattoos fading on his arm. They were not completely gone, but they were not as distinct as they once had been. The screams as he thrashed awake every night would continue, especially since he no longer had Bannen as his other Anchor. Alverick would have to learn to live with his damaged mind, as only time could patch his wounds.

"Tomorrow will be better," she promised.

Rhythmic breathing greeted her in response. As her eyes drooped close and sleep wrapped her in its warm embrace, Caitlyn found herself mumbling once more:

"Tomorrow will be better."

<div align="center">~~~~</div>

Glossary

Anchor: A form of mental discipline that helps Sparks and Tempests prevent or delay Snapping. In order to Anchor properly, the mage must focus on a specific mental image or idea until their mind is clear once again.

Apophmet: One of the two Ancients. Is known as Apophos by those in the Northern realms.

Aramaine: An alternate realm inhabited by dragons, wyrms, and other evil creatures. Also known as the Abyss.

Avalanche: Practitioners of Earth magic. Their tattoos are thick and bulky, like the trunks of trees. Avalanches can trace the movement of others through the earth's vibrations. Strong Avalanches can cause earthquakes.

Draughting: The process of transferring the blood of one mage to another as a means to increase one's magical power and potentially acquire a new style.

Enlil: Ancient home of the gods. The land was believed to be deserted by all after the great collapse, but it was protected and preserved by the deep magic.

The Faceless: Thought to be old wives' tales, they are the demons of Enlil and part of Apophmet's army of darkness.

Flame: Practitioners of fire magic. Their tattoos twist into mesmerizing patterns and appear to dance on the mage's body like the flame of a candle.

Their personalities can be erratic, but they do not suffer from the mental instabilities like a Spark or Tempest would.

Flicker: A derogatory term for a Flame.

Ghost: Practitioners of night magic. Their tattoos are slim and a metallic black color. They can manipulate shadows. Night magi are used in Scrymme as assassins. They are found only in Scrymme.

Jyarl: A term for Ghosts in the land of Scrymme.

Halls of the Fallen: Thought to be the final resting ground for kings and great warriors. It is a neutral place where the gods meet to discuss the events regarding Corinth.

Konugrr: The title for the ruler of Grimmrheimr.

Liche: Practitioners of necro magic. Their tattoos are thick and sluggish-looking shadows. Liches can manipulate the dead either through animation of corpses or scrying through the dead. They are found only in Scrymme.

Naran: The title used in Scrymme for one's master.

Nannohav: A Scrymmen request for judgement by the king and Host of Scrymme.

Plague: Practitioners of biological magic. Their tattoos are a combination of fine lines and delicate swirls. They can use healing magics and bring about plagues.

Re'nukhtet: One of the original Ancients. Goes by Re'nukh by the Northern realms.

Shadow: Practitioners of shadow magic. Their tattoos are hazy. Strong Shadows can open dimensional gates and summon creatures to bring to their world.

Snap: The moment when a Tempest or Spark loses control of their mental faculties and succumbs to the erratic nature of their magic. Snapping usually occurs when a mage is fatigued or has recently draughted. In the case of Tempests, Snapping occurs when they lose their Anchor.

Spark: Practitioners of electrical magic. Their tattoos are sharp and jagged, like bolts of lightning. Those who use this style of magic are susceptible to mental destabilization but can control these side effects with great concentration and effort.

Stream: Practitioners of water magic. Their tattoos are graceful and flowing with rounded edges. Many practitioners of this style have calm demeanors and usually an interest in the healing arts.

Tainted: Those who tried to acquire blood magic, but failed. They are cursed with insanity.

Tempest: Practitioners of wind magic. Their tattoos are thin and branching with a hint of twisting or swirling. A practiced Tempest's mind is as fluid as the wind and constantly changing. This causes them to be highly mentally unstable.

Twinning: Taking two objects and linking them together with a mage's blood.

About the Author

K.N. NGUYEN is a fantasy author and founder of DragonScript. Growing up, she often found herself immersed in some imaginary world, conquering enemy nations, and saving the day. As time went on, her love for horrible puns and nerd culture pulled her out of these worlds and brought her back to reality.

It wasn't until she started working at her office job that she felt the itch to begin writing. Since 2015, she's been bringing her stories to life, one-by-one, and following her passion by delving into new mythologies.

A native of Sacramento, California, K.N. Nguyen spends her time singing karaoke, playing taiko, enjoying rhythm dancing games, and travelling with her friends and family when she isn't writing.

Other Works by K.N. Nguyen

The Fallen Series

King's Blood

Oath Blood

God's Blood

Other Books

A Song of Strength

Dragon Script

Anthologies K.N. Nguyen Has Appeared In:

New Beginnings by DragonScript

New Adventures by DragonScript

Coffins & Dragons by Dragon Soul Press

The Once and Future Kingdom by Irish Horse Productions

Towards the Sun by DragonScript

First Stain by Inked in Gray

Another World by SummerStorm Press

Wicked West by SummerStorm Press